HULA

HULA

A NOVEL

JASMIN ʻIOLANI HAKES

HarperVia

An Imprint of HarperCollins*Publishers*

Song on page 350 used with permission from Liko Martin.

HULA. Copyright © 2023 by Jasmin `Iolani Hakes. All rights reserved. Printed in the United States of America. No part of this book may be used or reproduced in any manner whatsoever without written permission except in the case of brief quotations embodied in critical articles and reviews. For information, address HarperCollins Publishers, 195 Broadway, New York, NY 10007.

HarperCollins books may be purchased for educational, business, or sales promotional use. For information, please email the Special Markets Department at SPsales@harpercollins.com.

FIRST EDITION

Designed by Janet Evans Scanlon

Library of Congress Cataloging-in-Publication Data has been applied for.

ISBN 978-0-06-327698-7

23 24 25 26 27 LBC 5 4 3 2 1

For Riana, Mila, Mom, and Katrina, and the dance we dance.
And for Hilo, where the heart beats loud and clear.

Hula is the language of the Heart.
Therefore the Heartbeat of the Hawaiian People.

King David Kalākaua

VERSE I

HOʻOMAKA

We are not what you think. To you who come on airplanes, who descend upon us, we are invisible as air. We are the ʻāina and the sum of its parts. Mauka and makai, past and present. Born of its waters, we are haumāna and kūpuna, ageless and ancient. The keepers of the stories, the watchers, the listeners. You think you've been here, you think you know us, you have the pictures to prove it. The pictures are wrong. You've seen nothing at all. We are not here for you. We were here before you came, and will be here when you leave. We are Hilo, one. We are we.

BACK IN THE OLD DAYS you introduced yourself by telling your moʻo kūʻauhau. Where you was from, who's your dad, your grandma, your relations. Your moʻo kūʻauhau told the story of where you fit, of your talent and ability, as well as your particular kuleana, the responsibilities and duty that contribute to the whole like a star in the sky. It said if you were of the mountain or of the ocean. It rooted you to your place.

The Naupaka Ohana was one of Hilo's first families, both creator and protector of Keaukaha, our land, our home.

Our jagged coastline was stamped into the veins of the Naupaka women. Laka, her mother, Hulali, her great-tutu Ulu—their collective mana ran through the crisp fresh water gurgling up out of the black lava rocks along the shore and in the whispers of the hala groves. Everybody knew the story of the Naupaka Ohana, of where they'd come from, of everything they'd done for Keaukaha and Hilo. Theirs was the hula of us, the telling of not only how they became they, but how we became we.

Like a moʻo kūʻauhau, star charts map ways both forward and backward. With them we find our way through the dark, we cross great oceans, we make our way home, to Hilo. With the Naupakas, we knew the canoe would stay on course. Like any ohana, there are many roots and branches to the Naupaka tree, many ripples in the water of each Naupaka spring, but this one, Hiʻi's story, was different. Her star chart was full of clouds. It muddied the waters of our history and left our future uncertain, our direction unknown.

HILO, BIG ISLAND'S HEART. Land of the kanilehua rain, the mists from which the red lehua flowers drink. Hilo, our curse and our blessing.

CHAPTER 1

1968

When Hi`i was a baby, we blamed her color on sunscreen. We are the color of curly koa, of burnt butter, of empty beer bottles forgotten on the porch from the night before. Our rainbow is made up of browns, greens, blues.

Our keiki roamed free. They tumbled naked on the same black sands of Richardson's that we'd tumbled free and naked on. Here, tucked away in our quiet, overlooked corner, the world made sense. But Hi`i's skin made her mother, Laka, do things only tourists do. That babe, so different from her mama, stayed parked under the shade of a palm tree, buried in hats and coveralls in Laka's arms, slathered from ear to toe in sunscreen so thick the ocean didn't know what to do with her. Ke kai bounced her on its vast blue glittering surface, a pink conch baby buoy. We itched to get our hands on that babe, the next in line of the great Naupakas, a true daughter of our neighborhood, finally returned to take her place. We wanted to strip off her clothes and wipe her free of all those chemicals, to hold her up to the sun and let her bake. But Laka stayed hunched over her baby, alert, anxious, like she was trying to keep a bubble from popping. She spread her towel on the sand on the other side of the beach as if we were contagious. We kept our questions tied to our tongues, dogs on chains.

The sky was bone-dry and the moon winked bright on the night the muddy gravel driveway off Kalanianaole Street filled with rusted cars toddling on spare tires and with cracked windows. We extracted ourselves from cluttered backseats along with the foil-covered pans full of noodles for long life, lomi salmon and poi brought up fresh from the valley, tako poke, rice still steaming hot in the pot, and all the other pupus expected of a party. Six-packs clinked their way into the coolers on the porch, waiting with open arms and melting ice. The fish, caught and cleaned that morning, were salted and laid out on the hibachi to hiss and sizzle and fill the air with a smell that made the tourists driving by wish they were invited. The warped plywood floor creaked and strained under the weight of what was becoming a very heavy party. On the porch, cigarette smoke exhaled in an upward tilt toward the current of breeze that had danced its way across Hilo Bay and into the yard; hands the kind accustomed to manual labor waved at the wispy tendrils if they dared linger. We wanted to welcome her home.

BUT LAKA WAS SKITTISH, a flight risk. We didn't want her to leave again. We got as close as we dared. We tiptoed, we teased. But into those waters, we never went deeper than our ankles. We whispered.

It's what happens when you move Maui and like be high maka maka. When you work in the hotels with all the haole.

THE LONG NARROW LENGTH OF DIRT that served as Puhi Bay's parking lot was already full. Laka fitted her car between two trucks, both with jerry-rigged lifted suspensions, their bodies towering a full foot above their oversized tires as if floating on air. She stared for a minute, puzzled. Had this existed before she left? How quickly things change.

"Eh, howzit stranger!" she heard someone call from a distance. She waved in the direction of the voice and then turned away, not quite ready.

She took her time rummaging in the backseat, gathering the accessories that were now her life: diaper bag, changing blanket, sunshade, and a squirming, fussy baby who was not happy about being stuffed in a hot car at what was usually her nap time. A passing car stopped in the middle of the road.

"Excuse me, hey," the driver called through the open window of the car. Laka turned, catching the small Hertz Rental sticker on a corner of the windshield.

"Is this some kind of event or something?"

Laka glanced toward the crowded grassy hill behind her and shook her head. No. This was very much a private party.

The driver was about to ask her something else, never mind the cars piled up on the road behind him all trying to be polite and not honk. She hurried away before he could say another word.

School had broken for summer only a week ago, but the tent city at Puhi Bay was already in full swing. Lines strung between trees were straining under heavy wet towels and freshly rinsed pareos. Sleeping bags spilled out from the doors of ransacked tents, the result of kids changing which tent they crashed in every night after pillaging leftovers off the long tables full of aluminum foil–covered trays in the main tent, swimming with the moon, and doing who knows what else. Laka remembered it well. Some things didn't change. She took a deep breath and followed the salty smell of roasting fish and chicken toward the fire. The uncles waved their stainless-steel tongs in greeting before returning to the cooking meat on the grill, her father among them. He offered her a sad, soft smile but did not approach her. After a moment he turned his back. Expecting as much did not lessen the sting. She wanted to run to him and bury herself in one of his bear hugs, wanted to tell him she understood why he was doing what he was doing, wanted to tell him that she understood and forgave him. Instead, she kept her distance. Her youngest sister popped into her periphery, running with a herd of kids toward someone handing out popsicles, but Laka no longer knew how to call for siblings or draw them close. She had walked away from that privilege and maybe there was no getting it back. She also did not bother looking for her mother. Laka had it on good authority that she wasn't there, which was the only reason she'd allowed the magnet of home to pull her in today.

In the kitchen tent where meals were prepared en masse, she lashed the baby to her chest using an old pareo and set to work slicing a head of cabbage. She earned a few nods and kissed a few cheeks. No one said anything, but she could feel the stares and stiffness, the uncomfortable politeness. When the baby fussed, a girl of about fourteen came and asked to take it. The girl pointed in the direction of the large group of keiki playing in the tide pools. Laka put a protective hand around the baby and pressed it closer to her body, shaking her head as nicely as she could. When it was time for the baby to nurse, she returned to the car instead of joining the semicircle of folding chairs full of women keeping an eye on the kids jumping off the rocks, cannonballs hitting the water below in loud splashes. On the way, she ran into her eldest brother. He introduced her to his girlfriend, who was so hapai her belly looked like an overblown balloon, but he did not go so far as to kiss Laka on the cheek, or hug her, or greet her as his sister returned.

She didn't feel ready for this, but did not know how to leave.

Later, when everyone's opus were full moons stuffed with that night's dinner, out came the ukuleles. This was it, Hawai`i at its best. A showcase of undiscovered master performers, a row of graying kūpuna telling stories, aunties playing cards, kids half naked running around free as birds, not a television or tear in sight. Tribe. Ohana. Where there was always enough for everyone, never an empty seat at the table but always an extra chair just in case. Laka closed her eyes and watched with her ears, this lullaby of her life. She wasn't sure if her father was still there but he felt near. That counted as progress.

The melody changed tune, calling to her, inviting her to join. There was no way she could listen to "Na Pana Kaulana o Keaukaha" by beloved Aunty Edith Kanaka`ole and not let the song flow through her body. The ukulele singing its rhythm swayed back and forth like hala in the wind. The lyrics gave love to their Keaukaha beaches, kissing each one in turn. The baby was sleeping, there was no excuse. She allowed herself to be drawn in, hundreds of invisible hands helping her up, pulling her toward the others who had long freed their feet of their slippers and were dancing barefoot in the grass. This was her place, where she'd lived nearly every summer of her life, surrounded by generations of the spiderweb of families that were as much a part of her as her limbs and fingers and toes. A space was made for her among the dancers, familiar faces whose smiles widened as they made room. Her body moved before she gave it permission, exhaling into this familiar rhythm, this particular beat. And then she was dancing, floating. Her hips synced with the ukuleles, in her throat the words of the song caught with a sudden fierceness, a painful pang of homesickness she was only now aware she had. A great weight lifted off her chest. She wanted to shout with joy. Her voice cracked with emotion as she sang along to the words of the song being sung by the musicians at the picnic tables. How much she'd missed this, the comfort and safety and knowing.

Headlights flashed across the grass yard of the beach, a blast of horns. The baby, startled awake, began to cry. The sound was a bell toll, a spell breaker. She sank back into herself. Things were different now. There were other considerations, other complications. The song was not over but Laka dropped her hands and withdrew from the circle, now broken and confused. She left without saying goodbye. It would have been too hard to explain why.

TWO ROTATIONS AROUND THE SUN BEFORE, there was no Hi`i, and Laka was our princess. Our hopes and dreams, our Miss Aloha Hula, her picture in the paper like newly crowned royalty—the white velvet gown making her skin glow, the silver gray hinahina flowers tucked in her mass of thick black curls, all of Hilo's pride filling the dark glint in her eyes. Laka and her father, Uncle George, taking up their usual table at Ken's for daddy-daughter waffles piled high with whipped cream, him fresh off the boat that had been out in the deep all night but was now resting in the small Wailoa harbor, he exhausted but caffeinated with pride, making sure everyone who walked in noticed her newly framed picture on the wall. Then poof. Disappeared without a trace like an eel down the crack of a rock. We were sweeping the last of the festival's flowers from the stadium floor and nursing Merrie Monarch hangovers when the news came that she'd gone to Maui. We peered at the sky, waiting for the blessings to rain down. But it had been dropless. Barren and silent. A sign.

She should have known better. By taking off she'd said none of it mattered—not the crown, not Miss Aloha Hula, not Keaukaha and her kuleana to it, bestowed upon her by her family's legacy.

All Laka left behind was silence. The next morning when Hulali realized Laka was gone, she stood on her porch and stared out across the ocean the way a mother does when your heart exits your body and enters the world without you. We turned to her for answers but got only a warning flash across her face and stony silence.

Hulali readjusted her pareo wrapped tight around her chest and walked barefoot to the coconut grove at Puhi Bay that she had planted years ago with her tutu. A tree for each Naupaka. She cleared the dead fronds from the palms, carefully and quietly, leaving the one planted for Laka untouched. An unspoken message that something was very very wrong. In the days that followed, Hulali went every morning to the grove, clearing leaves and knocking down nuts grown thick and husky so they didn't fall on stray keiki who might come to play. But she never again went near the tree she'd planted to honor the birth of her eldest daughter. The palm slouched and quickly took on the look of a dress left out on the line too long. Fronds bled out their green and went limp, dangling treacherously from sinews. Coconuts grew heavy and threatened to drop on our heads. We warned the keiki to stay away. The poi had gone sour.

If she had been ready to listen, we could have warned Laka about Maui, avoided all the hakakā that followed. She shouldn't have gone, shouldn't have taken that job, cleaning up after those haoles who walked around the resort with towels draped across their shoulders like capes, Laka waking at dawn to rake the sand on the beach to protect their fragile feet, smiling when they took her picture without asking. They turned her into a spectacle, a circus performer. She let them.

Laka wasn't the first to get hapai from the wrong guy. She wouldn't be the last. We only wondered why she'd kept it from us. We didn't judge. That might be how things work on the mainland, but this was Keaukaha. Things happen. What breaks you won't break us. We are made of glue. We hold things together.

ONCE UPON A KINGDOM, visitors wobbled their way down steamship gangplanks, trickling into Hilo one at a time, barely making an indent in our soil. Now airplanes vomit them out. Their planes smother the songs we sing in the backyard, jet engines extinguishing the strum of our ukuleles. Their shiny rental cars, their bumbling tour buses, they stop in the middle of the road for every mongoose in the bush or whale tail on the horizon, interrupting the flow like rocks dumped in a stream. The interrupters make us late for work. They cut into our periphery as we dance and pray, sneaking into the corners of the pictures we take to prove we are here too—that we are not landscape, not shadows in a postcard. Between their honeymoons and bucket list vacations we steal moments for ourselves. It is the only space where we are allowed to exist.

While we punch the clock and mend the pukas that show up in our clothes and roofs, we search for ways to end our poverty, our lack of jobs, the failure of our health. The airplanes idle on the tarmac, inviting us. Better jobs, better healthcare, better schools maybe some-where else? We consider it. We all have our What Ifs. Our imagined airplane ticket. Our destination.

Some of us took the bait, filled those seats, escaped our problems only to find someone else's problems somewhere else. Severed the umbilical cord connecting us to the ʻāina, ignoring the cry of our piko as we turned away from our life source.

The escapees all come home eventually. We watch them return, like Laka with her tail between her legs and a baby we didn't know what to do with.

We still had our What Ifs. Laka had a What Now. She'd gone, she'd come back, and what good had that done?

The year she left, the summer of '66, was the beginning. More than 600,000 interrupters interrupted—a record for Hawaii tourism. A war started in Vietnam.

By the time Laka came back, barely two years later, jumbo jets meant more than a million interrupters interrupting and Vietnam had already wiped out eighty-eight of our boys. McDonald's was getting ready to open its doors in Aina Haina. Duke Kahanamoku was dead. Rumors were that the University of Hawai`i was going to put a telescope on a sacred spot, Mauna Kea.

This was a war between Hawai`i our home and Hawaii the destination. We were losing ground—literally and spiritually. We needed all hands on deck. If we weren't diligent, if we didn't *all* stand together, our Hawai`i would slip through our fingers like dry sand. We would be scorched earth.

To protect a bay from a tidal wave, you build a breakwall. To protect a species, you put a kapu on killing it. But there is only one way to protect a place. You sit your `ōkole down and stay there. You stand guard. You learn from the kūpuna the old chants, the hulas from their memories, before those kūpuna are no more.

IN HILO, BABIES COME WITH dreams and rain. Hi`i came with neither. But these were the days we had so much to worry about that there was only so much worry to go around. If not for Laka's weirdness, we probably wouldn't have thought twice about it.

No one had the baby dream, so when we got word of her impending return, the coconut phone rang and rang, the gossip channel buzzing. We made ready. We calculated months and prepared for the sight of her watermelon belly stretching out her shirt. Laka's name hadn't passed her mother's lips since she disappeared off to Maui, but we had no doubt Laka would come home to give birth, with or without Hulali's blessing. Where else was she going to bury the baby's piko, where but under the ulu tree where her own piko was buried, to join the cord of life to the land that gave it?

Since Hulali refused to see her daughter, we made ready to clear a room for Laka somewhere other than the Naupaka hale. Whose house? Whose kids would we send to help with the baby? We pulled straws.

Instead of the watermelon we expected, Laka arrived with a mouth suctioned to her tit. She didn't want our room. We gave her a ride to the place she'd rented on the periphery of Keaukaha. We stole a peek at the babe, bundled like a laulau in banana leaf, caught a glimpse of a cheek. It was an odd color, we thought . . . maybe jaundice? As for Laka, motherhood had transformed her. It took us back to Hulali's baby-making days, when there was always one on her tit and one on her hip, with a few crawling around her feet. We kept that memory to ourselves. Laka was in no mood. We waited for her to come back to us, with nothing but history to say that she would. Without the Naupakas, there would be no Keaukaha. Without Keaukaha, we would have joined the ranks of the infinite and unknown, the languages and ways and tribes of the world who have faded into obscurity, who no longer make a ripple on the water. This fracture between mother and daughter, whatever had caused it, needed to mend.

Time, we thought. The medicine that would heal the wound.

As our mothers had to us and their mothers to them, we gathered our Keaukaha keiki and fed them in batches so we could run errands in town and clean the yard and hang the laundry and make dinner. But Laka didn't offer her tit to no baby except her laulau, and her laulau didn't want no tit except hers. We wasn't grumbling. If she wanted to stay home every day and never take her turn to freedom, we'd take it for her.

In the sand the babies crawled to her for the occasional suckle, precious bare buns tilted toward the blue sky. When Hiʻi learned to crawl, she stayed by her mother's side. After swimming all morning, the babies balled their forceful little fists and ground them into their drooping eyes. Laka led them back to the closest house for lunch. They followed her like ducklings. When the bowls of rice and poi were empty, she draped a towel over the futon in the living room and spread them on it, sardines in a can. Then she'd race through the chores and weave as much hala as she could before the gaggle stopped snoring, glancing at times at the pale limbs of her babe tangled among the others, as if she were worried the kid was going to fade away into thin air. Keaukaha kids, they're full of mana. Strong and powerful and resilient.

The baby didn't look too worried. Hiʻi slept on her back, arms splayed across the others, the posture of someone who knows deep in their naʻau that they are safe.

But Laka kept on, cautious and careful. Like she smelled something in the stillness, a hurricane on the horizon that we didn't see coming.

AS HIʻI LEARNED TO HOLD HER HEAD UP, sit on her own, and crawl, we thought maybe her eyes would darken. That the pink of her skin would eventually deepen—it had happened before. But months passed and her eyes brightened to the color of wet seaweed. Her skin shed its newborn chafe but the color went no deeper, skimming the surface from conch to coconut. The brown tufts of hair on the crown of her head turned a burnished red. We thought maybe it was her lava coming out, that maybe this was Hawai`i emerging from wherever it was buried deep inside her, that ehu color of Pele when she's molten. That maybe the sunburn her mother had worked so hard to protect her from had found her anyway.

When Hi`i grew old enough to suck poi from fingers and hold on to pulpy ripe banana with her fat baby hands, we took her. There was no excuse anymore—the girl could eat without her mother, and Laka got a job she needed to get to. By then Hi`i had turned `opihi, suctioned to her mother with the ferocity of that most stubborn of limpets who hold so tight to the cliffs of our islands even the strongest of waves can't budge them. Hi`i needed to bathe and eat and play at the beach with the other keiki. Hover over something and it becomes fragile, easily broken—Laka knew that as well as we did. We told her Hi`i needed to build up her immunities, her calluses. We had to make like the `opihi picker and pry them apart.

Laka stayed glued to the doorway of the kitchen full of toddlers and the smells of breakfast, watching the chaos of chubby confident arms grabbing for fistfuls of fish and rice. She stepped forward when her daughter reached for a sliver of papaya the color of a Kona sunset. We stopped her just in time. We ordered her out.

"You like her cry? No be selfish? Moe bettah you go when she not looking."

A boy wearing rubber slippers and not much else made a grab for

Hi`i's papaya. The girl curled protectively over her fruit and stuffed it into her mouth.

"See? She fine. She already forget you."

Laka drew an arm across her chest. We thought she might fight back, the old Laka would have, but now her eyes filled with tears. She retreated to her car. We listened as the rusted engine of her clunk of junk puttered to life. She threw her weight onto the manual lever of the car window and rolled it down. The glass moved sticky into its slot. She ignored us as we shooed her away, pausing as if to get one last listen to her daughter's voice, something to hold on to for the remainder of the day. But the surf across the street and the rustle of the palm fronds had already filled the distance between her and her daughter, the sounds of the `āina overriding any that might have come from inside. She threw the car into gear and drove off. We caught the relief on her face the minute she hit open road. We didn't blame her. We understood. Without the baby, Laka could be home. Without the baby, Laka could be who she'd been destined to be.

CHAPTER 2

1974

We didn't give Hi`i the idea, though she got it from us, from her tutu's legacy, from our ancestors. Hilo and Halau o Luahine, there was no one without the other.

Another summer of living together old-style at Puhi Bay. Hi`i now old enough to shrug off her mom always trying to put another layer of sunscreen on her or douse her with stinky citronella oil to keep away the mosquitoes, the other kids all laughing at the spectacle until Hi`i disentangled from her mom and went out swinging at anyone within hitting distance.

Haole Girl, mosquito food, the kids teased. Hi`i slugged one of the neighborhood boys, and dared anyone else to call her that. She was as brown as the rest of them, she said. On the inside. She'd lick anyone who said any different.

With that she earned some respect, at least from the boy she'd slugged, and in spite of the hard time the kids gave her, she never wanted to be anywhere else. Her friend Kainoa had an older brother who was training to race; after practice he'd bring one of the club's canoes from the other side of the bay and they'd swim out to greet him, hanging on to the outrigger as if they were mer-people catching a ride. She ran off when her mom said it was time to go (Laka no longer camped there with us and Hi`i could sense that half the fun happened long after the sun went down), jumping off the rocks with her cousins and swimming out to the deep where she could pretend not to hear her mom calling until Laka'd get fed up and wade out, Hi`i always coming in by the time the water reached her knees. But this year Laka brought her new man for us to sniff out and Hi`i was hot and cold about it, one minute clinging to her and staring death rays at the guy, sticking her tongue out (which earned a flick from her mom) and saying she didn't have a dad and that was how she liked it. Then the next minute acting like she didn't care, like it was no skin off her back. Laka offered her a consolation prize. Hi`i would be allowed to stay. Just that one night, but it was more rope than Hi`i had ever been given before. The girl was happy as a jumping bean. Laka piled on the instructions until a tall white woman wearing what looked like a brand-new visor and watershoes, the kind they sold at the tourist-fleecing store, appeared out of nowhere. Laka was in midsentence when the woman interrupted.

"Excuse me," she said in crisp American English. "Can you tell me how to get to the waterfalls?"

Laka turned from her daughter and looked the woman up and down. "Which one?"

"Oh, I didn't know there were more than one. Maybe the best one?"

Laka's back straightened.

"Da best one?" Her voice dripped venom. It was easy to see she was about to blow. We steered the woman quick back to her car and pointed in the direction leading out of Keaukaha while Laka fumed under her breath about the nerve of haoles, thinking they could just interrupt anything.

"We only hea fo' be of service? Pshhht."

But as soon as that lady skedaddled she didn't skip a beat and went right back to listing all the things Hiʻi needed to promise if Laka was going to leave her: to be polite and listen to the aunties and stay out of the way and help and be respectful and don't fall asleep in her bathing suit and wash her feet and make sure her hair was dry before bed or else she'd wake up with ukus. Hiʻi nodded and nodded.

Poor ting that one. Her tutu an invisible elephant in the room and no dad to speak of . . . the way her mom was acting, the kid was going to get the idea she was a guest in this hale. So when Laka finally left, her man waving out the window of the passenger seat looking relieved, we told her what she needed to know about her family.

She was seven, old enough to feel something was missing even if she couldn't know what. We didn't tell her that something was hula. She took that on herself.

WHAT HAD LAKA EXPECTED? When she'd returned to Keaukaha with Hiʻi bundled in her arms, she'd known what she was coming back to. They were a family of legends. Laka, our very own Miss Aloha Hula. And Hulali, granddaughter of Ulu, who'd saved our traditions and spent the last years of her life teaching Hulali everything about hula that she'd ever learned. Without her dedication to hula, without her carving a path forward for us, Hilo would still have a hand over its mouth. We'd still be shouting soundlessly into the waves with haoles telling us the only way to survive was by selling our culture to tourists.

Bloody feet and aching muscles paved the road to greatness. But at Halau o Luahine, half the battle was in the showing up, day after day, doing what Kumu asked, swallowing the pain, the embarrassment of forgetting a verse, of being called out for missing a step, of being willing and ready to learn whatever lesson Kumu decided they would learn at any given time.

Learning hula was studying a new language and a new way of moving, but it was also learning about the `āina, about the environment and the relationship of the elements, about how to treat the planet and how to appreciate the forces at work. It was the study of mythology and anthropology, of ecology and botany, astronomy and zoology. It was memorizing chants and getting to know the plants in the backyard that would be used to dye the fabric for the skirts. It was hand motions and facial movements, summoning fire from the belly and letting your heart beat through your feet. Hula was a way of seeing the world and accepting a role within it. Hula wasn't just something you did for a couple hours a week. You didn't just take lessons. You became it. To be a real hula dancer, your skirts were always on, in one way or another.

"EMBED DIS KNOWLEDGE INTO YOUR BLOOD," Ulu had told Hulali before every lesson, unearthing the hulas and chants Ulu had kept hidden from the missionaries crying idolatry and then from the hotels who wanted to put them on a stage. "So dat you can pass it on to da next generation, and dey can pass it on to da next. Dis is da most important thing you must do in your life, my mo`opuna. Today you are da last Naupaka. Make sure it doesn't stay dat way. Have babies, carry this mana`o, this `ike, forward. Knowledge will die if not passed on."

Hulali had promised her tutu she'd grow up and have a hundred babies. She'd teach them all the ways of their ancestors, she'd make sure the stories were never forgotten. She would start a halau and the students of that halau would go on to start halaus of their own, and in time hula would spill from Hilo's shores. At that, Ulu had laughed and hugged Hulali close.

"Good," she'd said.

WE'D SURVIVED EXTINCTION BEFORE. If we were going to survive what was coming, we were going to have to look to history to figure our way into the future. Star charts of the past.

THE DEAD KING HULA:

Hawaiian kings die faster than fruit flies.

King Kamehameha I united the islands in 1795, as a kingdom. He died twenty-four years later, survived by a host of wives and their children plus Ka`ahumanu, his relatively young, favorite wife who he'd made kuhina nui, basically a prime minister, a position he'd created specifically for her. His son, Liholiho, King Kamehameha II, ruled for only five years, dying of measles during a trip to London in 1824, with Ka`ahumanu calling the shots from behind the scenes.

Kamehameha III came next. In the middle of all that dying and handing over the kingdom like it was a baton in a relay race, ha-ole were coming in by the boatload (including some church folk that befriended Ka`ahumanu and got her listening to the Word of God, which she heard to say that heiau and ancient Hawaiian temples should all be destroyed and hula forbidden, so let it be written, so let it be done). The kingdom was (officially and internationally) recognized as a sovereign nation in 1843, but at the same time sugar plantations started popping up like pimples. With money just waiting to be made, haole started circling like flies to you know what. Plantation owners and missionaries put the Third's feet to the fire, pushing for a change in the way land ownership worked. But the question we had was how?

There had been no such thing as land ownership before, we are the `āina and the `āina is us and we're all just responsible to take care and maintain balance and pono. The king said we needed to catch up— owning the land the way the haole did was the only way to protect it from being taken away. (How we was supposed to come up with the money to do that? We was busy farming. Haole with their pockets full of gold beat us to the punch.)

Of all the kings, he lived the longest. But then, on December 15, 1854, his speech slurred, his eyes went dark, and just like that, Kamehameha III was no more.

IN 1863, ALEXANDER LIHOLIHO, King Kamehameha IV, died of asthma. He was twenty-nine. Now we have his older brother, Kakuāiwa, Kamehameha V, who says he's going to lift the ban on hula imposed by Ka`ahumanu (who'd herself died in 1832, surrounded by her clergied friends who'd come to see her off to their mansion in the sky). We dying off, he says when he gets pushback. The only way to protect our kingdom from foreign invasion is to keep living.

By 1870, he hadn't managed to get rid of the ban completely but the penalties and fines were less. Which was better than nothing. We needed the inspiration, the connection. We needed hula to preserve our history.

AS IF HEEDING THE call, in the Honolulu rose-gold of morning on July 17, 1869, Ulu Naupaka, Laka's great-grandmother, Hi`i's great-great, came barreling into the world. Surrounded by the Waikiki fishponds and loʻi the Naupaka Ohana had cared for since the beginning days of Wakea and Papa, Ulu took her first breath of life. She was the fourth child born of her parents, but the only one to live longer than a few months.

Before Ulu was old enough to think about things like hula and inspiring the kingdom to keep on living, the Naupakas were ordered off their land. A development called the Hawaiian Hotel was coming in, and they were in the way.

Ulu's mom told her husband that they needed to call the surveyor to make their claim. They needed a piece of paper to prove the land was theirs. Ulu's father said no need, it was family land. Who did these haole think they were? Besides, there was no money for the surveyor's fees. They would be safe.

They were not safe.

In a blink, Waikiki went from fishponds and loʻi to coconut groves and cottages. (The only thing more profitable than sugar was hotels. So they drained the entire district, those god-playing, disease-bringing haole, to erect their ka-ching factories.) The Hawaiian Hotel opened its doors in 1872. Ulu took her first steps in a one-room shanty in the middle of a sea of shanties built to temporarily house all the other Hawaiians, the ones who'd survived yellow fever, measles, pertussis, tuberculosis, leprosy, smallpox, syphilis, and gonorrhea only to lose their land and be tossed in the trash like bruised produce.

King Lunalino, grandnephew of King Kamehameha I and last of the Kamehameha bloodline, died of tuberculosis after ruling for a single year. Ulu was five.

* * *

THERE WAS NO HEIR. The Kamehameha patriarchy had hit a dead end. For the first time, the legislature (made up largely of haole land owners, the children of haole missionaries, and haole businessmen) would need to elect a new monarch. But who?

BIG DEEP BREATH.

This was it, the fork in the road of Hawaiian history that would determine the Naupaka legacy, that would hang over Hi`i's story like a cloud refusing to pass.

MEET CANDIDATE ONE: Queen Emma, King Kamehameha II's widow and distant relative of the Kamehameha line.

Strengths: of Kamehameha bloodline, a perpetuator and protector of that sacred ali`i lineage, and possibly the person best equipped to save Hawai`i. Staunchly anti-American.

Weaknesses: not pro-haole or friendly with foreign business owners. There was the question of how nice everybody could play if she was picked.

And then there was Candidate Two: David Kalākaua, ali`i, but of lower rank than Emma.

Strengths: Charismatic, smart. Liked to party. Insisted lineage was less important than culture. Hawai`i would survive if Hawaiian practices did. Friendly with haole businessmen, so he could maybe play their haole games with a bit more acumen and protect our kingdom from foreign takeover.

Weaknesses: friendly with haole businessmen.

Both insisted that they wanted to keep Hawai`i for Hawaiians, but there was room for only one of them at the top.

Blood versus culture. Tectonic plates crashing against each other.

On the day the legislature voted, Ulu's dad joined the crowd on the streets to await the decision. Haole with a few Hawaiians lined one side of the courthouse, crossing fingers for Kalākaua. Hawaiians with no haole stood on the other, praying for Emma. To the Naupakas, Emma represented tradition, Hawaiians deciding what was best for Hawai`i. So when the legislature came out of session and trickled down the steps, wallets lined with votes for Kalākaua, Ulu's dad rushed forward with everyone else to turn the bruises on their hearts into bruises on those legislators' faces.

God save the king.

NOT EVERYONE WANTS TO INHERIT a halau, to be passed a story, to carry a tradition with so much weight. Hulali, descended from the great Ulu, brought hula back to us, unlocked the iron handcuffs from its feet, and nursed it back to health. Brought back pride. In the case of Hi`i, hula was her birthright. Hawai`i is a story with dueling narrators, with multiple perspectives and paths. The girl had the right to choose one for herself, and she did.

Without roots, the tree falls over. Hi`i was going to dance hula.

"NO WAY," LAKA SAID when Hi`i stomped into the house demanding to begin her hula training immediately.

Laka clipped a clothespin to the unfinished fronds of the lauhala mat she had been weaving and set it beside her on the living room couch. There would be no getting that done today. Hiʻi had grown into a headstrong, stubborn little thing, but Laka had never seen her daughter so upset. Her baby-chub oval face was swollen with anger. She pulled at her own hair in frustration, desperate to express to her mother the urgency of her feelings. This girl who was barely forty pounds, who Laka could still carry with ease, had turned into a ball of uncontainable fury, but Laka faced it firmly.

"But why?"

"Cuz joining one halau not just 'bout dancing. You not ready."

"You danced," Hiʻi said between sobs, pointing to a picture on the wall behind the television console, Laka in costume.

A door on Laka's face slammed shut. That photo had been there when they moved in. All the pictures on the walls had. In fact, now that she thought about it, she hadn't changed much in the house. It still looked occupied by Hulali. Had she really thought Hiʻi wouldn't notice?

"Just because I wen dance no mean you gotta."

"But you was Miss Aloha Hula."

Hiʻi's voice dropped to a whisper.

"It's our kuleana . . ."

Laka held up a stiff hand.

"Stop right dea, little girl. Dat was a long time ago. Wat you t'ink you know 'bout kuleana?"

"How come we don't dance? Why don't we see tutu? How come you act so weird, how come you don't let us be part of da family? I hate you!"

Laka grabbed Hiʻi's arm and pulled the girl close, reaching around with her other hand. The whack left a raised imprint on her child's `ōkole. Red welts appeared on Hi`i's arm where Laka squeezed, as if squeezing would make this conversation go away. After a moment, Laka released her and stepped back, horrified. She'd done nothing more than any other parent would do, lickins to set her straight, but she wasn't any other parent. Hi`i was Laka's gift from the gods. What if akua took this as her disrespecting what she had been given? Would she be taken back?

Hi`i wrapped her arms around herself protectively as if she were afraid Laka might strike again, building up her walls. Laka tried to refocus the argument.

"We not going talk 'bout my maddah. Not'ing. Not one single word 'bout our family kuleana, or what you t'ink you know 'bout why she not around. Understan?"

Not waiting for an answer, Laka turned and left the room. She had always assumed raising children came with a certain amount of violence. Wooden spoons, brush paddles, bamboo switches, rubber slippers, and a father's belt were acceptable tools to raise a kid right. By Hilo standards, there was nothing brutal about what she'd done. But these were not normal circumstances.

Listening to Hi`i hiccuping in the other room, Laka wondered if coming back to Hilo and trying to raise Hi`i in Keaukaha had been the right thing to do. If she'd thought it all the way through. She slid off the couch and dropped to her knees, bringing her hands together at her chin. She prayed for the marks she'd made on her daughter to go away. She promised never to discipline her daughter like that again. Please let the marks show mercy, she prayed.

When Hi`i slid into her chair the next morning for breakfast, her arm was pale as the moon. Laka's prayers had been answered. She vowed to uphold her end of the bargain.

∗ ∗ ∗

WE WERE CONCERNED. A child needs to learn respect and discipline. How they going learn if the parent afraid? When our children outgrow us, when we gotta climb one ladder to slap their smart mouth, we do it. Respect is the most important thing.

She wasn't doing her kid any favors. We knew that Hiʻi, looking the way she did, was going to have enough to deal with. Hilo's no place for soft feet. Gotta build calluses. Then a girl can run on lava.

We waited. Without discipline, it was only a matter of time before she was going to start acting up and mouthing off, garenz. Stealing and drugs would be next, then a hapai belly and a GED if she was lucky. Laka would get upset and wonder out loud where she'd gone wrong and ask for help. But by then we'd all be worse for wear and Laka wouldn't be able to blame nobody but herself.

THE FULL MOON HULA:

He wasn't perfect, but Kalākaua did truly believe we'd all stop dying if he reinspired a great will to live. Our song had been silenced, he said. It was time to bring it back. The coconut phone buzzed all day, every day with wonderings, not *if* our country was going get scooped up, but by whom. Russia? The United Kingdom? The United States? The sharks were circling. His idea was simple: introduce the world to the Kingdom of Hawaiʻi. Its advanced understanding of science, human rights, art. He would issue royal coinage and open consulates across the globe. He would go on a majestic world tour, showcasing all the kingdom had to offer. He would build a kingdom of the kind the world respected, complete with a palace fit for a kingdom worth living for, a palace for the merriment that would stop the tide.

But all that was going to take money. Compared with kings past, Kalākaua didn't have much of it. As much as the sugar plantation owners were raking it in, they were also managing to keep the kingdom from getting a cut. So the new king took out a loan and did all he promised he would.

In the United States he left his hotel every night to give public concerts, offering our songs and dances to the crowds who came to see this Hawaiian king. In the United Kingdom he struck up a friendship with Queen Victoria, which earned him a royal welcome, a military escort, and a band when he and his sister and his wife returned to Britain for her Golden Jubilee. But for King Kalākaua's own jubilee, he waited.

`Iolani Palace was finished just in time to mark the king's fiftieth birthday and his silver jubilee. To celebrate, he issued a kingdom-wide invitation and ordered it printed in all the newspapers, complete with the planned program. It would be a luau, he said. With a full twenty-four hours of hula. Danced, wait for it, IN PUBLIC. Aiyah, even the fishing boats could hear the collective gasps of newly baptized Christians and all the descendants of missionaries who'd worked so hard to scrub Hawai`i clean of its sinning ways.

Ulu had no plans to go. She was fourteen, her mother dead from the fever and her dad long gone down a barrel of rum. She'd spent the last year as a boarder at the Kawaiaha`o Seminary School for Girls. On her first day, she was welcomed with an introduction that said, in summary: If you speak Hawaiian, you will not be successful. If you continue your Hawaiian ways, you will perish. Hawaiians are savages, but noble and well-meaning ones. Where she was stupid, the school would educate. Where she was wrong, the school would right. Where she was brown, the school would white.

Her days quickly filled with tending the school's garden and sweeping the grounds before the morning studies of household arts, sewing, and knitting. English and Bible study followed, then music and craft until dark. Every class began with a story of something Hawaiians used to do before the missionaries came, how bad and pagan and heathen. Some of the stories were so familiar to Ulu it was as though the teachers were speaking directly of her childhood, describing her parents and grandparents but with a sinister coat of paint. You are stupid, the teachers said over and over again, which she took to mean not only her but her ancestors as well. Fix how you talk, how you think, they said. Shame upon shame layered inside of her until she forgot what it was to live without it. She stopped talking, preferring to say nothing rather than risk the chance of saying the wrong thing.

Happiness was the gardens where the school grew its food. There she slipped off her shoes and buried her feet in the dirt, feeling like a plant with roots too long exposed. The sick she felt when she was indoors faded in the sunshine. She happily took on the majority of the farming work, although she was reminded all the time that they were there to turn themselves into New England ladies, good future wives, not farmers. It was as though there were ropes on her wrists, pulling her in opposite directions. When the headmistress saw the king's announcement on the front page of the newspaper, she covered her mouth and tossed it out.

But the night before the jubilee, a full moon shone through the window near Ulu's bed and stood between her and sleep. The ocean called. Moonlight turned waves into white fire. She snuck out of the seminary and tiptoed her way to the beach nearby to watch the flames.

After a moment, a tree stump bobbed silently through the surf toward her. The stump shifted into a honu, its glowing green shell glistening as the turtle found land and pushed its way across the sand in her direction. It dripped ocean on her toes. She leaned down to hear its whisper, nodding when it eventually went silent. When she finally stood to return to her room, her face was resolute. An ʻaumakua had come to deliver her a message, and she had heard it loud and clear.

Ulu never did say exactly what the honu told her that night, but bright and early the next morning there she was at the gates of the brand-new ʻIolani Palace with hula skirts on. She slipped past the guards, resplendent in their new dignified uniforms commissioned by the king, stiff black wool lined with kalo leaves of gold thread, into the staging area where we were getting ready. We was too excited to stop and wonder what she was doing, too jittery about hula finally coming back into the light, and in front of the very people who had tried so hard to bury it away.

The lineup parted as if it were the sea and she were Moses. She stepped barefoot from behind the bandstand and into the bright sunshine of the open lawn, the king and all the kingdom in front of her. This was a girl who'd been training to become a proper Victorian lady, not a dancer. None of the halaus recognized her. For all we knew, she'd never danced a hula in her life. Those next few minutes, what came out of her came from somewhere else.

We went silent. The king went still. The queen leaned forward in her seat. Her thick muslin skirt and starched white blouse with its long puffed sleeves and high neck, her lei poʻo at her crown, so similar to what we was wearing, but there was something else too, an energy that gripped even the air's attention.

Ulu placed her hands squarely on her hips and closed her eyes.

She extended a confident foot into forward position. She opened her mouth and began.

Her chant rippled through us, gaining steady momentum, a hurricane without a cloud in the sky, telling a story that was a spear straight to our hearts. Her hands brought her message to life.

In the time when the shark chief Kamohoali`i ruled Hana, the food supply became diminished. To save the people, the god Kuula-kai built a fishpond with walls twenty feet thick and ten feet high, and an inlet for fish to go in and out. Because of Kuula's power, the pond was always full of fish. Men came from far and wide to see its wonder.

On Moloka`i lived a handsome chief named Kekoona. Kekoona had the power to turn himself into an eel three hundred feet long. When he saw the fishpond swarming with fish, he slipped through the inlet and fed until he was too big to get out without breaking the wall. He hid in a deep hole. When Kuula and the chief found Kekoona's hiding place, they baited the Manaiakalani fishhook with roasted coconut meat and drew him to shore. Kuula killed the eel Kekoona with a stone.

The dead chief's favorite swore revenge upon Kuula. He ordered Kuula and his family be burned in their house. Kuula and his wife, Hina, ran into the sea; their son Aiai escaped the burning house when the smoke turned to the west. When three gourds popped in the fire, all believed it to be Kuula and his family.

The fish followed Kuula and Hina into the sea, leaving the pond empty. The new chief of Moloka`i threatened to kill the people if no fish were brought to him. Aiai gave his friend Pili-hawawa a kuula stone to drop into the pond, which brought the fish back swarming.

The chief grabbed a fish from the pond and slipped it into his mouth whole, then choked to death.

***

THE PHYSICALITY OF ANY HULA is stamped with the fingerprints of the kumu interpreting it. But Ulu's performance was not an act of choreography, not one given to her by any human kumu, at least. Her feet moved like the tides, her skirts the water. Her arms transformed into fishhooks. Her torso slithered as if possessed by Kekoona the Eel. She was the fire, the exploding gourds, the kuula stone that brought the fish back. An offshore breeze swept across the length of Waikiki. There, surrounded by missionaries and luna, landowners and haole lawmakers, Ulu's hula was a call to action only the truest of Hawaiians could understand. This was a message direct from the gods. *The pond that sustains the people will survive, therefore the people will survive. It is the greedy foreigner among us who will be killed by what he steals.*

The story came to its end. Her hands went home to her hips. Ulu became herself again, but somehow bigger, fuller. The king stood and nodded. She would drop out of school immediately and join his royal court. From that day forward, whoever came to see the king would be met by hula. The crowd cheered and happy-cried. We would not get swallowed up by the tide. In hula, our heart would live on.

Or so we thought.

AFTER WORD HAD SPREAD that she'd joined the halau, Hi`i would tell anyone who asked that her mother had caved and let her start dancing because she'd beaten her and felt bad about it. She began recalling the incident with such melodramatic flourish that Laka finally told her the entire memory was a product of her imagination, that Hi`i dancing hula was just something Laka had eventually come around to.

Hi`i countered. Accused her mother of trying to sneak into the room of her mind and rearrange the furniture.

Laka spiraled downward into the second-guessing maternal doubt that, once started, had not stopped. A midlife adolescence flared within her, the nagging need to point out inconsistencies between reality and Hi`i's memories whenever she could, to tease her daughter in the way tickling sometimes leaves bruises. It was a disorienting experience for her to be so unsure of what she was doing as a mother, slightly out of body, like tumbling down a rabbit hole.

CHAPTER 3

1975

Hi`i was barely eight years old, but that didn't mean she was too young to know what she wanted. Halau o Luahine was the halau Laka should have taken over, the one she'd sheepishly gone back to in the early days of her return from Maui, taking direction from someone else, only to quit for good because she wouldn't let us step in and help, like our mothers and their mothers before them. She wouldn't let Hi`i cry it out in the hall while one of us held her. Too attached, too protective she was in those earliest days. It was the halau that taught in the kahiko style, traditional, bent knees, with cosmic perspective, the halau that kept the teachings of Ulu Naupaka alive. To dance for Halau o Luahine was to become the fire of the volcano, Pele herself. By then there were plenty of other halau in Hilo, but only one for Hi`i, no matter what her mother felt about it.

NEW HAUMĀNA NEEDED TO LEARN all the basic steps and the protocol. They needed to be walked through the makings of their skirts and implements. Taking on new dancers was a big commitment for any halau, but especially for one as steeped in tradition as Halau o

Luahine. Because of this, its heavy wooden doors cracked open only once a year, in the fall when Puhi Bay camping was pau and the keiki were back in school. Laka hoped this alone would dissuade Hi`i, but the more Laka tried to keep her away with stories of her early hula days, the tears, the missteps, the bleeding feet, the aching arms, the more determined Hi`i was to follow in her mother's footsteps. The halau might not yet be open to her, but she was willing to wait.

Eventually the open enrollment announcement was posted. The sign was simple: classes were divided by age and years of training. Open slots were limited. Previous knowledge of dance was unnecessary. A commitment to put the halau before all else was nonnegotiable.

As the day neared when Hi`i would stand in the clustered hallway of nervous hopefuls, Laka was overcome by the sense that she was dumping her child into the ocean deep without having taught her how to swim. She'd shared stories only as deterrent. Giving Hi`i advice and preparation would have been acknowledging something she wasn't ready for. On the first day of open enrollment, Laka delayed as long as she dared, offering Hi`i a feast of after-school snacks and circling the parking lot twice before finally settling into a space as far from the door as possible. Outside, parents were already returning to their vehicles. Hi`i jumped out of the car before Laka could turn off the engine. Laka scrambled after her, pulling her back toward the car. She knelt to meet Hi`i at eye level. She fussed, untying and retying the knotted cords of Hi`i's skirt as if it were a parachute that would keep her from falling.

"Too tight, Mama!"

Laka squeezed her hand. "You sure?"

Hi`i nodded. Laka let her go.

***

THE HALAU WAS HOUSED in a large open studio above the drugstore downtown, so most of the people in the parking lot were there to pick up their blood pressure pills or the six-pack of Budweiser that was on sale until Saturday. Hi`i wove around the shoppers and climbed the rickety wood stairs by the ice machines at the far end of the store. She listened for the sounds of hula, a ukulele or a pau drum.

Hi`i took smaller and smaller breaths as she ascended. The air was too hot, too thick to inhale. When she got to the top, her stomach sank. She'd hoped to be the first one there, front and center. Instead, a mountain of rubber slippers and jelly sandals flanked the entrance. She recognized half the faces, from the beach or Puhi Bay mostly. Some in the hall did a double take when they caught sight of her, like her cousin Leilani, daughter of Butch, the eldest of Laka's brothers. Hi`i fiddled with the cord holding her skirt in place and ignored her. She removed her slippers under a black-and-white photo of Hulali, a dried maile lei draped over it.

A reverent silence fell over the studio when Kumu entered the room. She was barefoot, regal with an invisible crown on her head. The woman was barely half the size of her mother but Hi`i's legs wobbled at the sight of her. She couldn't have weighed more than a nene bird. As one of Hulali's students, Kumu was known to be able to ask rain to stop, for wind to cease, and for animals to help her when she needed it. During Kilauea's last eruption, the lava covered an entire portion of lower Puna, but went around the place where she'd been born. So Hi`i was surprised. For a woman who had Pele's ear, a woman who had helped Hulali with all the classes as the halau continued to grow and expand, a woman who had stepped in when

Laka stepped out, Kumu was surprisingly compact. Hi`i tried to picture how things might be different if her mom had chosen to become kumu of the halau instead, but Kumu's energy was so powerful and encompassing that it was impossible to imagine the halau as anything other than what it was.

All eyes watched as Kumu reached a hand to her hair and extracted a worn pencil from its thick black coil. She bit into the nub with her front teeth and held it there as she readjusted her bun, giving the hair a twist and a firm tug before digging the pencil back into the fold. Her eyes moved from one face to another, assessing. She swished on her heel toward the mat centered along the mirrored wall at the front of the room and sat. She looped the rope attached to the neck of her double-gourd ipu heke expertly around her wrist and slapped its bottom on the floor. The sound was like a throat clearing. She opened her mouth to begin, then paused and frowned. She motioned for the class to stay where it was, then padded over to the open doorway of the halau and closed the doors in the faces of all the parents trying to sneak a peek of their child's first step as a hula dancer. Kumu had established who was boss without saying a word.

She belted out her first instructions to the three rows of hopefuls. Their lines were as crooked as shark teeth. She rearranged them by height and general age, directing most of the boys and the taller of the girls toward the back rows, evening the spaces between them.

"After this practice," she said, "you will all be required to wear kupe`e anytime you are dancing."

She held up two long strips of ti leaf and demonstrated how to twist them into a band that they would tie to their ankles.

"Like your skirts bound with hau cord, your kupe`e bind your feet to the earth and to your hands telling the story. When you are standing at the door of the halau, asking permission to enter, it is like knocking on the door when you go to someone's house. Your chant announces your intentions. By putting on your kupeʻe, you give yourself over, leave everything else outside. You are no longer a dancer. You are the dance. Bound to our history and to the elements of our islands. Understand?"

The group—mismatched heights, untucked shirts, messy ponytails, some wearing goofy, nervous smiles, others so terrified they looked to be on the brink of tears—nodded. Satisfied, Kumu resumed her place on her mat and hit her ipu on the floor. They could finally begin.

For the rest of practice, Kumu introduced the children to the basic mechanics of the four main steps of hula, the foundation. She demonstrated how to bend at the knees and disconnect the hips from the lower back. How to keep head and shoulders locked and solid. How to turn their hands into words, images, pictures.

(THEY LEARNED THE BEGINNING VERSE of a hula too, and though we know you're waiting for that verse, the mechanics that gave it life, you're not going to get it. Our story is a hula, to honor and preserve in our ancestral fingerprint this place we love, not a hula how-to masquerading as a story. Besides, we couldn't walk you through it step by step even if we wanted to. The choreography of any hula is sacred, interpreted and composed with cultivated care. Like the degree needed to teach a college course, you have to be qualified. Ordained. Allowed. What Kumu taught Hiʻi on that first day and every day after belongs to Kumu and the halau, not to outsiders, not even to others in the neighborhood. It's not ours to give away.)

* * *

HI`I KEPT HER EYES ON KUMU, never letting them stray to the mirrored wall they faced. Too distracting, seeing the way she stood out from most of the group. Every so often she felt Leilani look her way. She refused to meet her gaze, didn't want to give her estranged cousin the satisfaction of being bothered by her presence. She'd been dreaming about this day for as long as she could remember. But now that she was in the room, her body taking its first steps into its destiny, the reality of it gave her jitters. Watching surfing and coming from a line of surfers was entirely different from getting on that board and trying to catch a wave. She was going to have to concentrate and focus as much as she could if she were to become as good a dancer as she expected herself to be. During those initial steps she floundered, her body gawky and uncoordinated. The next few weren't much better. It was only a few minutes in and her arms were already burning.

"Elbows stay up!" Kumu yelled. "Now go again."

Hi`i's cheeks flushed. She prayed Kumu's comments hadn't been directed at her even though she was pretty sure them having to repeat the exercise was her fault. Kumu belted out another set of movements to copy but Hi`i forgot them as soon as Kumu was done demonstrating. She tried following the movements of the girl in front of her, but when the girl misstepped it was all Hi`i could do not to trip over her. This was going to be harder than she thought.

The hour passed in a blink and an eternity both. When Kumu finally released them, the kids poured into the hall, gasping and sweaty. Hi`i pushed her way through the crowd toward her bag, thighs and calves wobbling.

"Hey, that's mine," she said to a small haole girl bent over her things.

The girl jumped. "Oh, oops. Ha. Look at that." She giggled, reaching for the one right next to it and holding it up for Hi`i to see. "We have the same one."

"White girls t'ink alike," someone said. A few snickers.

"It's a haole takeover," someone else whispered. More snickers. Hi`i suspected it was Leilani who'd commented. She hurried to get her things.

The girl, an inch or two shorter than Hi`i, had hair yellow as a banana and eyes big and round like buckets of chocolate milk. She held out a freckled hand. Hi`i stared, not understanding. She was eager to put distance between them. The girl giggled again. "My dad says you're supposed to shake hands when you meet someone, but I guess that's stupid. I'm Jane," she said, dropping her hand and rubbing it against her hip. "We moved from Colorado. Where are you from? I always wanted to dance hula, but that was kinda hard. Not like in the movies."

Hi`i sniffed. "I'm from here. My mom was Miss Aloha Hula. You probably no even know what dat is. And my grandma is a famous kumu." Hi`i tossed her skirt over her shoulders and dug through the piles for her slippers. The sooner she got away from this girl, the better.

"Wow," Jane said. "I thought you were, um, new, like me. You must know everything about hula."

Other cousins from Keaukaha gathered around Leilani. They nodded at Hi`i, listening. Hi`i pretended not to see and cocked her head. "Pretty much."

Jane grabbed the banded end of her braided banana hair and gnawed at it as if trying to think of a way to prolong their conversation. Hi`i wished she'd go away. This girl with her mouth full of hair had no business being there, no business trying to be Hawaiian. Why was she just standing there, taking it? Hiʻi went in for the kill. "Kumu not going say not'ing, but haole not supposed to dance hula. Only Hawaiians."

Hiʻi waited for someone to correct her, but no one did. Her tutu was Hulali Naupaka. Hula, this halau, was her blood. Jane looked toward the door. A tear sank down her cheek. The moment she disappeared down the stairs, a cousin laughed and chucked Hiʻi on the shoulder.

"More bettah she learn now," Hiʻi said, slinging her bag over her arm, following them out the door.

WE HAD OUR DOUBTS, but in the four years that Ulu danced for the royal court, King Kalākaua was making good on his promise to lift our chins. We were prouder than peacocks when the U.S. president, Ulysses Grant, and his wife opened their doors for the White House's first state dinner, receiving our king as their guest of honor. After decades of missionaries and other foreigners tsk-tsking us as if we were children getting everything wrong, coming here to guide us to the light, we thought maybe this would show them that our kingdom had things handled.

But warmer summers mean colder winters. With rainbows come rain.

We were getting the squeeze, even if we didn't know it at the time. Sugar plantations, Pearl Harbor, trade, cash. The haole buddies of the king were raking in the dough more than ever, and they didn't like the thought of us banding together and putting a stop to it.

Ulu met Lorrin Thurston only once, but she never forgot his face. He was a card-carrying believer of Manifest Destiny and acted liked it. Walked around the palace as if he owned the place, chest puffed like a peacock, shifty unflinching eyes and a handlebar mustache adorning a tight angry mouth. She'd just finished performing for a visiting dignitary when she felt a shift among the royal household, everyone putting on invisible armor and holding themselves stiffly until there he was. She wondered if this was how fish felt when a shark was nearby. He strode down the hall without bothering to announce himself, glancing briefly in her direction but looking right past her. His rudeness and the casual way he treated the king was unforgivable, but what could any of the household do? Thurston was a son of missionaries turned prominent lawyer turned powerful member of the legislature of the Hawaiian kingdom. Ulu would for years return to those minutes where he was in her proximity, tormenting herself with what she might have done or said if only she'd known then what he was up to, if she'd only known what was about to happen.

Less than a month later, the truth came to light: he and twelve other men of prominence had joined forces, pooling their resources and power to form the Annexation Club, dedicated to making Hawai`i a U.S. territory. Eleven days before Ulu's eighteenth birthday, July 6, 1887, Thurston came again to the palace, this time to hand-deliver a new constitution he'd taken the liberty to write. (Earlier that week, he wrote to friends in America, bragging: *Busy drafting a new constitution. Will be bringing the Honolulu Rifles should the king need encouragement to sign, haha.*) Hence, the Bayonet Constitution.

The Bayonet Constitution annointed Thurston Hawai`i's interior minister *and* stripped Kalākaua of his power *and* allowed foreigners to vote (foreigners meaning Americans and Europeans. Asians absolutely not. Does any other nation in the world allow noncitizens to vote in its elections? Asking for a friend). We was allowed to vote, but only if we made the kind of money you make if you own a sugar plantation. Or a pineapple one. (Dole, we looking at you.)

That's one way to move in and make yourself at home.

Ulu lost her job, lost everything. Kalākaua died like the fruit fly, as quick and suddenly as the Hawaiian kings before him. He was replaced by his sister, Liliʻuokalani. She promised to undo the Bayonet Constitution and give us back what had been lost. But Thurston wasn't having it. On January 17, 1893, backed by the U.S. military, the Annexation Club declared a provisional government with themselves as the new rulers. They turned ʻIolani Palace into a prison, locking the queen away in an upstairs bedroom. Took the kingdom right out from under her.

Whoosh went the tide.

One of their first acts? To declare themselves the new owners of 1.8 million acres of ʻāina belonging to the crown.

IN EACH PASSING YEAR after the takeover, after the theft of Hawaiian lands, we lost something we didn't know could be lost. The new "government" passed a law that all schools would teach in English. English was the language of status and opportunity, while Hawaiian was sentimental and not in our interest to use, they said. Because they had our best interests at heart.

Eventually, pro-annexationists figured out how to get their cake and eat it too. They needed the entire support of the U.S. Congress to pass a treaty, but they needed only a simple majority vote to pass a resolution that insisted they had somehow already annexed Hawaiʻi. And voila. Just like that, we went from a sovereign, Christian nation to a republic to a United States territory by sleight of hand. Smoke and mirrors.

Were we happy? Hell, no. But who was more powerful than the United States? Who could we turn to for help? Auwe. Our voice grew weak.

We used to grow taro, bananas, sweet potato. Now we grew headstones. The only remaining place where Hawaiians were still a majority was in the cemetery. We were a species on the brink of extinction.

To Ulu, it was like watching a great body of water evaporate.

Numb, she spent the next two decades working among the sharp thorny bougainvillea rambles of the Hawaiian Hotel gardens, offering rudimentary hula lessons to drunk tourists. Time sludged by, marked with the pain of being on what had once been her family's land, working in a capacity that would have brought her ancestors shame. Places got renamed by foreigners to names that were familiar to them, names they could pronounce but meant nothing. She'd grown up hearing the chant of "Hawai`i is for Hawaiians" but she wondered if ultimately Thurston and his men now in charge of her islands were right. The newspapers, all now white-owned and printed in English, insisted these men should be hailed as saviors, that the kingdom had been squandered away by kings who drank too much and knew too little, her people dying in droves because of their heathen ways. Hawaiians formed the Ahahui Kalai`aina only three short months after that shameful, horrible day of overthrow, lobbying and organizing in the manner of American politics, collecting tens of thousands of signatures in protest of what they say was inevitable, annexation to the United States, but their efforts only attracted scorn and public ridicule from the white business sector. Something inside her was collapsing, withering, retreating. She'd seen for herself things that countered how Hawai`i was being portrayed—how smart King Kalākaua had been, how extensive he and his sister's knowledge of astronomy and geography and so much else—but she was tired of being told she was wrong, tired of being told her ways were antiquated, tired of being told that it was time for her to catch up with the rest of the world. The messages she'd been plied with in boarding school now echoed everywhere. The newspapers and teachers and clergy were all saying the same things, so they must be right. This was God's plan. The true righteous path of survival was to erase what remained of the old and embrace the world as it was now. Besides, there was rent to pay, and money needed to purchase the food she no longer had the ability to grow.

Her spirit waved a white flag. She married a decent, hardworking man, one who wanted a large family of the kind they both remembered, but who was also adapting to the times. After the birth of their first child she told him there could be no more. If she missed any more work, the hotel would find someone else, and she needed the job.

WHEN HI`I LEFT PRACTICE THAT FIRST DAY of her hula career, Laka was waiting in the parking lot, her smoldering cigarette dangling out the driver's window. Another red glint from the passenger window. Tony.

Tony was now officially Laka's Puerto Rican boyfriend. He lived in Mountain View, or had before attaching himself to Laka. Now all he did was hang out at their house, quietly brooding on the porch, untangling fishing nets or smoking pakalolo in the yard with the rest of his crew, all beer bellies and sagging surf shorts.

Tony's one redeeming quality was that he ignored Hi`i with a religious faithfulness, as if he might catch fire or turn to stone if he touched, looked at, or acknowledged her. This was fine with Hi`i. She wished only that she was as good as he was at pretending someone out of existence. The noises that came from her mother's room since he'd entered the picture were unsettling. He'd stolen the silence of their life and replaced it with rhythmic creaking and little cat meows. That, and a closed door that used to always be open.

Hi`i had been about to turn four when Tony came along, although for the first few years Laka had kept her relationship separate from their life in Keaukaha. Hi`i hadn't paid much attention when he was brought to Puhi Bay and introduced around, and then when he started spending time at their house. She'd thought he'd eventually fade away. But months later, the nightly noises had only gotten louder. That's when menehune started sneaking into her room and waking her up, sending her crying out for her mother. They'd never bothered her before, but obviously those troublemaking little people didn't think any higher of Tony than Hi`i did. They liked making Laka come running from her room and down the hall. But more than that, Tony put too much shoyu in scrambled eggs and no brown sugar at all on the Spam before he fried it. He made breakfast taste nothing the way it was supposed to, and in all the wrong colors.

Hi`i dragged her feet across the parking lot and yanked at the rusted handle of the rear door, squeezing in among the damp beach towels and empty plastic containers cluttering the backseat. Laka took a final drag of her smoke and flicked it onto the asphalt before throwing the car in gear.

"So . . . how was it?" Laka asked cautiously once they were on the road. She glanced in the rearview at the backseat, where Hi`i was busy staring out the window, trying to disappear.

"Hey," she said when there was no answer. "I t'ink we should go out, mark da occasion." She smiled at Tony, her tone artificially bright. She did that when Tony was around, fill the silence, as if she could create something that wasn't there. She prattled on as if it had been her idea for Hiʻi to dance, as if this hadn't been a fight that she'd lost.

"You only get one first day of hula. Life so different once you dancing. Not'ing da same aftah. You part of one whole oddah ohana. My baby, so grown up! Where you like go? Orange Julius? Anyt'ing you like. Man, I 'member when da plaza was not'ing but one grass field. Dis da kine stuff I talking about." She slapped Tony on the thigh and snorted. "All da Hawaiians when get dey panties in a bunch when DHHL give land for build da mall, but den who no need go fly Honolulu now for buy school clothes? Who go line up for work inside?"

When they parked, Tony said he'd wait in the car. He mumbled that it was stupid for Laka to reward her daughter for doing something she hadn't wanted her to do in the first place.

After Orange Julius (Laka said Hiʻi could get whatever she wanted, but Hiʻi was overwhelmed by the possibilities and choked. At home, she was expected to eat what was on her plate. There was no choice. Plus, they never went out, so she had to take full advantage and pick the right, best thing. But then she was holding up the line. She chose a small regular orange-flavored Julius, the first thing on the menu), Laka stopped by Aloha Spirit, where she'd been working ever since Hiʻi was a baby, to talk to her boss, Old Lady Tanaka. Hiʻi stayed outside and threw good-luck pennies into the volcano-shaped fountain. Old Lady Tanaka had stink breath and was always getting into arguments with her mom about the merchandise. Aloha Spirit sold cheap shell leis imported from the Philippines and shirts that said "I ♥ Hawaii," plus soaps and perfumes with cloying, fake gardenia and jasmine scents that made Hiʻi's eyes sting. Shops in Hilo were like a Monopoly board, only one of everything, so some said Old Lady Tanaka was providing a service. It was only after months of Laka insisting they should carry more things from Hawai`i that she cleared a single shelf for Laka to prove her idea a good one.

Laka filled her small section with the braided lauhala creations she spent hours making at home—bracelets and hats, fans and mats, baskets woven tight enough to hold water, strips as thin and fine as hair—but had to raise the prices when everyone chopped down their hala bushes to grow coffee. Given how much time hala took to gather, clean, and strip, Hi`i wondered at her mother's business sense. Tourists seemed happy enough throwing money away on things like coconuts with their name painted on the side.

Hi`i slurped up the last of her Julius with her straw and stared into the bottom of the cup. She wished she hadn't taken off her practice skirt. It was probably against the rules to wear it outside the halau, but she wanted everyone to see. In her skirts, no one would wonder if she was visiting from somewhere else. Her cousins might finally stop teasing her that she was an alien from outer space. She was a hula dancer from Keaukaha. A Naupaka. Deep down, though, she dreaded the next practice. Hula was a thousand times scarier than she ever thought it would be.

Laka came out of the store, sitting heavy next to Hi`i along the pōhaku wall that circled the volcano fountain. "Dat guy who was all excited about da bracelet for his wife and made a huge deal about keeping it on da side until today so he could buy wen he get paid nevah even show. So rude, some people." She stared into the fountain for a minute and shook her head. She offered Hi`i a weak smile. "Eh, my hula dancer, let's get you a souvenir."

They went to the Sanrio Hello Kitty store. Hi`i focused her attention on the Under $5 bin. They left with two lead pencils and an eraser shaped like a strawberry. Back at the car, Hi`i was so happy with her new things that she shoved them in Tony's face from the backseat to show him. He smiled. It was something.

That night they went to Ken's House of Pancakes for dinner. They were seated in a booth with no cracks in the vinyl. After much pondering, Hi`i got a loco moco with extra gravy. The bowl was as big as her face. Tony got fries and gave her some.

That night the menehunes let them be.

Hula was already doing what she knew it would.

THEN, TWO PRACTICES LATER, Hi`i wobbled into the car with screaming red welts the shape of pu`ili running the length of her skinny calves. Laka didn't glance in the rearview mirror any more than she usually did. She turned up the radio to drown out her daughter's sobs. She'd warned her.

They waited through the three stoplights and drove the entire length of Keaukaha's beachfront without saying a word. When they got home, Laka put her hands on her hips as Hi`i stepped gingerly out of the car. Be grateful, she told the girl. Kumu wouldn't waste time correcting a dancer if the dancer wasn't worth correcting. Every welt was Kumu showing favor.

"She see somet'ing in you" was how Laka left it. It was something her mother used to say after Laka's feet would bleed, or bruises popped up on her legs. She could still hear Hulali's voice.

If need wood to build a house, you don't go to a rotten tree.

Laka dragged Hi`i to the spiky aloe bush in the backyard. Snipping off the ear of a branch with her fingers, she filleted it with her fingernail as if she were gutting a fish and rubbed the slime along Hi`i's knock-knees and stick calves. Hi`i gasped. Laka snorted.

"Stop. No hurt. Going heal faster wid dis."

Hi`i pawed her nose and shook her head, face red and mottled. "It does hurt," she insisted.

Laka flicked a welt, her patience gone. Hi`i winced.

"You like 'em hurt, I make 'em hurt," she said. "No one said hula easy."

Hi`i wouldn't stop crying. Laka threw up her hands and went into the kitchen to start dinner, but Hi`i's sobs seeped through the window screen. Laka pulled pots from the cupboards and made her own noise. By the time the rice in the cooker started to bubble, the sobs had subsided into gulping sniffles. When Laka went to the porch and scanned the yard, Hi`i was exactly where she'd left her. She straightened her shoulders and marched outside. "How many times I tole you? No need dance. I said: going be hard. Going ask for more den you get. You say no, you tough, you can handle. You say you like learn. Now you no can handle, you like quit? Quit. Plenty oddah t'ings to learn, plenty oddah fights to fight. Bigger fish to fry. A kingdom to get back." She pinched her thumb and forefinger together, held them up to her eye as if peering through. "Hula only one tiny sliver to see t'rough."

Hi`i shook her head. Not dancing was not an option. "I wanna be like her. Like you."

Hi`i didn't say what she didn't know how to say but they both knew. She wanted to dance hula to show the kids down the beach that she was a part of their family. That she was Hawaiian. To prove she belonged.

Laka looked over Hi`i's head toward the wild gardenia bushes lining the border of their property. She pressed her forehead to Hi`i's and smashed their noses together. "You too young for have dese kine thoughts. You don't know wat you asking for. Hula not going change not'ing . . . it not going do what you t'ink." She paused, uncertain how much to say. "It's just not, Baby Girl." Laka shook her head as if she had water in her ears. She tilted Hiʻi's chin and kissed her tenderly on the cheek. Hiʻi pulled her face away from her mother's reach. Laka sighed.

"You not too young to start learning wat really going on hea. Mom going teach you, 'kay? First lesson: no evah drop your head. Hold it up high. Be proud. You one Naupaka. And dat kuleana is more den hula. Dancing not going give us our islands back or protect us. Dancing not going make you same like e'rybody else. You no like be same like e'rybody else. More bettah you quit now, when only your toes in the watah."

CHAPTER 4

1975

Those early days in Hi`i's dancing life, over the weeks of open enrollment, the mountain of slippers dwindled into a hill. Inside the halau, the rows sprouted gaps. Fourteen of the original thirty-eight remained. Jane was a no-show. Hi`i didn't feel bad. If her words were enough to scare the girl away from hula, she had no business dancing anyway.

Hi`i's body hurt in places she hadn't known were there. Her upper arms were as heavy as lead but she ignored their burning weight, refusing them permission to droop. Her thighs felt like overused punching bags. Still, despite how hard she pushed herself, she left every practice feeling like she'd somehow failed a test. When Kumu gathered them around her on the final day of the enrollment period, Hi`i prepared herself for the possibility of being asked to leave, for the idea that maybe Kumu didn't see enough of the Naupaka in her. Instead, Kumu asked them all to sit. They did as they'd been taught, sitting on their shins with the bottoms of their feet respectfully hidden, using their skirts to cover.

"Look around," Kumu instructed the group, speaking formal, classroom English, somehow making eye contact with each of them all at the same time.

"Each of you made a choice to be here. Halau is not just learning hula. You want to shake your `ōkole, there's plenty other places to go. Here you will learn the hulas that will connect you not just to the gods and stories of the past but as they exist today. Here you will not become a dancer. You will become a keeper of tradition, connected to the essence of Hawai`i. You will become a mirror that reflects the world around us. This will demand your time, focus, and energy. If you are not learning anything, maybe we will ask if you are better doing something else. Here you will learn protocol. What is protocol? It is the behavior. It is knowing how much to take, how much to give. Knowing how much to leave behind, but also knowing how to go somewhere and leave nothing of yourself there, not even a single footprint. It is intention and respect. Awareness. It is asking permission and understanding your relationship to this `āina. This is why the language of our ancestors is directional, rooted." She paused and looked around the semicircle as if waiting for one of them to object to the level of commitment she expected. When no one did, she continued. "What you will learn here is an honor, a torch. Here you will malama honua, learn the ways, the language of our blood. You will be the caretakers of our land, our ocean, our culture and community. This knowledge, this `ike, is already inside you. It is your na`au. Here you will ask it to speak louder, and you will learn to listen. One day we will look to you to keep this knowledge alive, to pass it down. To be here is to accept that responsibility."

Kumu gestured toward the stone altar in the corner facing east.

"This is the kuahu. Upon it we place the forest plants, the shells of the ocean, the pōhaku of the earth. Everything has mana, energy. We bring to the kuahu the energies of the chants and stories we are invoking. In this room, we are disciplining ourselves to understand. If every drop of water wanted to be its own, there would be no rain, no ocean. No life. If every star demanded its own sky, where would we be? We would have no map to lead us home. Ua maopopo iāʻoe? Understand? From now on you are bound together, one."

The students glanced sideways at one another. Understanding settled upon them like Hilo's morning mist. They were Kumu's new class. Hiʻi was one big step closer to claiming her place in the legacy of her family. Even if she wasn't quite sure what that history would mean, she was going to be a dancer.

HILO'S SUCH A RAINY OLD TOWN. Listen to the rain come down. Wash away the interrupters.

Springtime, Easter, the time of year we expand. We fill to bursting. The Hilo Hawaiian and every room in old Uncle Billy's plus all the bed-and-breakfasts, booked a year in advance. The FedEx airplane bounces down the Hilo Airport tarmac three times a day, bloated with the weight of boxes of costumes and lei, of dresses and dark Tahitian pearls. We make ready, cleaning our spare bedrooms, washing the sheets on the puneʻe in the living room. At the school, we sweep out the gym and cafeteria and roll in the cots for the halaus that booked rooms late.

Merrie Monarch tickets sell out before they go on sale.

The festival was named after him, conceived in his honor. King Kalākaua. By the 1960s, all the dead kings had names, and that was how we called him. The Merrie Monarch, because he dredged hula out from where the missionaries had buried it. Now it's a week of partying as if statehood hadn't happened even though it's been twenty years. People come from all over. From Oʻahu, Kauaʻi,

Maui, and Lanaʻi, from Molokaʻi, but also from Tokyo, California, New Zealand and Tahiti, Texas and Alaska. We starch our best ho‑lokū and muʻumuʻu, we shine our black pearls. We dress as though the flag of our ancestors is still snapping in the wind above ʻIolani Palace.

Under the light of the burning midnight oil we bow to our sewing machines, piecing together the quilts and skirts and hand towels to sell at the craft fair. For weeks we show up for work in the morning with burns from the hot glue gun we use to make fabric flowers stick to finicky hair clips. Every year could be the last it will be this way, so we smoke and eat and drink, we dance and sing and be Hawaiian. We'll do this until we can't anymore.

Kingdoms fall, but they never really go away.

PENCIL SCRATCH HULA:

On a night in mid-April 1920, the dazzling light of a new moon poured once again through Ulu's window to stand between her and sleep. She got up dutifully, a bit slower now, fifty-one-year-old knees creaking in protest. She covered her moʻopuna with a quilt she'd made out of an old muʻumuʻu, saying a prayer of protection and making sure the girl was still snoring before slipping out the door. Her husband long gone, her daughter taken by pneumonia not six weeks after giving birth herself, Ulu and her granddaughter, Hulali, were all that remained of the Naupaka Ohana. Her family so marred by death, rippling endlessly outward. Her kingdom has died as has her ability to hear the ground under her feet. The plants and trees and winds and moons have long fallen silent, or she has lost the ability to hear them. She exists now in a vacuum, the place of numbness. The call of this moon is distantly familar, more like a dream she once had rather than a memory.

She glanced at her mo`opuna a final time and then closed the door softly, tiptoeing down the creaking hall of their tenement, following the sounds of the lapping water's edge. Flames danced across the waves. She was not surprised when the bobbing tree trunk came into view. It turned again into the honu—the very same `aumakua who had brought her the mo`olelo of Kekoona the Eel all those years ago. Ulu waited patiently as it made its way to shore. This time, the honu's flippers did not dig into the sand. It did not crawl to her feet. Its shell did not glisten. Its message did not come in the form of a whisper, soft and sweet as the offshore breeze.

The honu was dead. A picked-over corpse. A silent scream. Belly up, empty black holes where its eyes had been.

Ulu's skin started to tingle. The tingling turned into a burning that spread across her body and drove fire into her heart until she was consumed by a flame as hot as Pele's belly. The honu had chosen her to deliver a message. Thinking herself powerless, she had allowed herself to be broken, allowed her voice to be silenced. The honu had rotted in wait of her. She had failed.

Back in her apartment, she went to her mo`opuna and put a hand on the sleeping girl's back. The thump of her heart echoed into Ulu's palm. All was not yet lost. If the culture survived, so would the people. Time for Ulu to get to work, for real this time.

After her encounter with the honu, something important had changed. Before, Ulu had ignored the invitations to join our talk story sessions, our two-heads-are-better-than-one efforts to figure out how to untangle the net we were caught in. No sense, she'd said. The life had already been sucked out of the soil of Waikiki and Honolulu, the old family farms were long gone. Beating a dead horse, she'd said. But at the next community meeting, Ulu was the first one there. She banged her fist on the table as if it were a gavel and she was calling us to order. Hawaiians needed to perpetuate to perpetuate, she said, and there was only one way to do that. We needed to make things pono again, bring the people back to their land and the land back to its people.

Maybe it was that her eyes lit up like Pele erupting when she cried foul at what was happening to Hawai`i, or the way her voice cracked when she talked about her family's lost land, how that vacuum had sucked all sense of purpose from her parents, or maybe it was simply that her added voice made us loud enough for someone to finally hear, but pretty soon newspaper reporters were showing up at those meetings, pencils and notepads in hand. She told them: Return us to our `āina. Return our `āina to us.

BY THE END OF THAT YEAR the call was answered.

The Hawaiian Homes Commission Act of 1920 put 200,000 acres of scattered scraps of undeveloped (crown) lands into a trust. The American government would lease it to Hawaiians in need who met the requirements of being eighteen or older and a blood quantum of at least fifty percent Hawaiian, a notion inspired by what Uncle Sam had written into Native American land deferment programs. It took some time to figure things out, because they were worried that they might accidentally "give away" valuable land. Any land that had so much as proven itself useful enough to grow a weed was exempt. Any land already under use was exempt. Any land with fresh water was exempt. Basically, we could go back to the `āina, but only if the powers that be were sure we weren't going to be able to do anything with it.

Ulu Naupaka was the first to apply. More than fifty years after the Naupakas lost their land, she was going to get it back.

In 1924, fifty-two families were selected from a lottery and awarded land on an undeveloped homestead in Hilo on the Big Island of Hawai`i. Ulu was on the list. A few weeks later, she arrived by steamship to claim her two-acre plot. She brought only three-year-old Hulali, her mo`opuna, the only child of her only child, and a large honu shell.

Auwe.

The promised homestead was nothing more than pahoehoe and pits of dirt. A joke. A stray cat would have turned up its nose before calling it home. But when the other families made to return to the ship and back to the slums of Honolulu, she held them steady. If this was where we could be Hawaiian, she said, then we would make it be what we needed it to be. Malama the `āina, and the `āina would malama us. She squeezed Hulali's hand and held up the knot of their combined fingers for all to see. With the sky and Mauna Kea as witness, she said, her family would never again lose their land to the haole who came from the other side of the ocean.

Turning toward the water, she chanted out the first lines of the Mo`olelo no Kuula, the message of the honu she'd danced for the king all those years ago.

Okay, then. We were staying.

Once upon a time, there was a kingdom. In Keaukaha, it would be again.

CHAPTER 5

This is what we told Hi`i: It wasn't that hula died. Only that, by the time Hulali and Ulu moved from Waikiki to Keaukaha, hula was so battered and bruised by history that there was no recognizing it. Before the waves brought Captain Cook and the disease and death that followed, hula was the keeper of our origin stories. It was our generational memory, our celestial genealogy. Hula told the story of who we were. There was Chief Lohi`au dancing for Pele on the Napali Coast in Kaua`i, there was Hopoe the dancing stone, teaching Hi`iaka how to dance like the current as it moved up a pebbled coast, like the wind blowing through pandanus trees. There was hula's divine patron Kapo`ulakina`u, one of Pele's sisters, dancing one of the earliest hula, a hula ki`i, on Ni`ihau. There was us.

When the waves brought the men with Bibles to save us from ourselves, these men pinned a scarlet letter on hula and called it immoral. Sinful. To appease them we cloaked our hula in heavy clothes, covered its skin, and erased mention of gods and goddesses. We tucked the ancient stories away where the Church couldn't frown on them or cast them out.

Tides, they turn.

By the time Laka was born, hula had been kidnapped by the entertainment industry, dressed in a cellophane skirt and shackled by its adorned ankles to a well-lit stage decorated with plastic shells and overly bright flowers. Hulali started her closed-door, performance-free halau in 1961, focusing its mission on the learning of ancient protocol and the perpetuation of hula as it had been once upon a time.

When a group of Hilo business owners put their heads together to think up ways to bring money into town, Hulali remembered her tutu's words to carry the Naupaka mana`o forward and proposed a festival. A hula festival, different from what was being offered at the hotel luaus in O`ahu. It would display both ancient kahiko and the modern `auana styles. To attract locals instead of tourists, it would focus on authenticity and tradition. They would name it Merrie Monarch, after the merry monarch King Kalākaua, in honor of his desire to bring honor and dignity back to the Hawaiian people. They would have a contest to see who best could embody the Hawaiian spirit, body and soul. It would be almost like having a queen again.

And so it was.

It was Hulali who did all this, who unburied hula from its grave and resuscitated its breathless corpse. Hulali who set hula free. How could Laka think she could bring her daughter home and then keep her from it? (We kept that part to ourselves; the girl's eyes were wide as it was, history turning like a wheel in her mind.)

IN 1971 EVICTION NOTICES started raining down on Kalama Valley in O`ahu.

Twelve whole years we been a state, and we had the scars to prove it. History was working in circles. The American navy was also bombing the island of Kahoʻolawe, which was a little like killing a termite with a bazooka. They'd gotten their grubby hands on it when we were buckled down under martial law during the war. It had once been Celestial Classroom Island, where we'd learn how to read the stars. Now it was Target Practice Island, where the trigger-happy had gone from torpedo testing to TNT bombings to missile droppings, and they was starting to get sloppy. They bombed Maui. An accident, they said. Oops.

Gotta make them stop. If not us, who? A group formed, we called it PKO, the Protect Kahoʻolawe Ohana.

At the same time, with the state warning the Kalama farmers that they better heed the eviction orders, Hulali sounded the pū, blowing the conch to raise the alarm. She came from Keaukaha to fight with us. We heard the cry, began to gather. And then her beloved husband, Uncle George, died. In the last years of his life, Uncle George lived the way he always had, getting up before dawn to go holoholo, strolling to get his styrofoam cup of coffee at Suisan and watching what the boats brought in, tending the backyard in the afternoons, and most of all, never contradicting his wife regarding their children, particularly when it came to laying down the law. Laka had been his darling, but when she returned to Hilo, there'd been no contact, no attempt to see his daughter or her baby. If she and Hulali were on the outs, he could have no part in it.

It broke his heart. Stretched between a daughter who refused to take that final step home and a wife too stubborn to open the door, his heart cracked right in half. In death, he found the only way to bring them back together.

Hulali had been in O`ahu for only a few months when word came that Uncle George had passed. Hulali flew back to Hilo on the first plane out to put him to rest. But how did she expect to put anything to rest without seeing her daughter? It was the hakakā between her and Laka (and Laka's coconut-colored `opihi) that had killed him in the first place. If anything, Uncle George dying was the match that lit the flame that threatened to burn everything down.

CHAPTER 6

1979

After the first full moon of the year and only three weeks before Hi`i was supposed to leave on a class trip to Waipi`o Valley, two mounds mysteriously erupted on her chest. Which was enormously unfair. She'd been looking forward to this for as long as she could remember. Plus, she'd been thirteen for nearly an entire year and counting, and only now, after months of boys pulling the straps and snapping the backs of the bras that all the girls in school were suddenly wearing, they decided to show up. Mauna Loa and Mauna Kea. She tamped them down with duct tape. She would have rather poked out her left eye than go on one of those mother-daughter bra shopping trips her friends had gotten dragged into. Not that it was likely her mom would take her. Laka didn't seem to know really what to do with her now. It was as though she had never been a teenage girl. Laka certainly never offered Hi`i a glimpse of what her life had been like when she was Hi`i's age. As much as Hi`i poked around for clues, it was as if Laka had always been a woman with a moat around her. As far as her parenting style went, she ran hot and cold. As long as Hi`i's grades were fine (which they were—Kumu didn't tolerate slacking in any area, including school) and her chores were done, Laka didn't press her. She disciplined in hesitant spurts, losing her temper and then apologizing, promising she'd never do it again. She acted as if Hiʻi were a guest, their connection fragile and something that could be dropped and shattered, someone she loved but didn't a thousand percent know.

Hiʻi examined her taped chest in her bedroom mirror. There'd be no way to tape them in the valley. She'd have to bury them in layers. She ducked across the hall and stole one of Tony's shirts.

As if her new mounds weren't bad enough, she had black coarse hair sprouting in all kinds of places. She felt like she was turning into a kamapuaʻa—half human, half bristle-covered pig beast. If this trip was to anywhere else, she would have found an excuse to miss it, fake a cold or something—but this was Waipiʻo. It meant everything to go. A week of being in the loʻi instead of stuck inside a classroom, but also a week of being with Kainoa day and night. She sighed.

Kainoa wasn't her boyfriend, and she wasn't sure she wanted him to be. He'd been around for as long as she could remember; there were pictures of a group of them during early Puhi Bay summers, he and she a couple heads apart, all of them naked as the day they were born. When they were in elementary school all the Keaukaha homestead kids hung out together by default (now that they were middle school kids everyone still seemed grouped by neighborhood and race, the Waiakea haole and Japanese, the Keaau Filipinos, and so on, but Hiʻi had always considered these clusters more a fact of life than a deliberate act: you were where you were from), so being with him didn't mean anything. They'd go on bait runs for the uncles together, catching fish in the cracks between the rocks on Coconut

Island and opai in Lili`uokalani Ponds. He'd carry her bucket and she never gave him another thought. He was just Kainoa. And then came the day a few months ago when a group of their friends were together at the beach. There'd been a winter swell and the waves were crowded with surfers. Some guys from off island started acting up, dropping in on the locals and whistling at the girls. Two started in on Hi`i, calling her a haole, teasing about where she might have come from. She'd done her best to ignore them, pretending it didn't bother her, pressing her fingernails into her fisted palms to keep from flying into a rage, her temper rising like a fever. Without saying a word, Kainoa came up next to her and put his arm around her shoulder, pulling her tight against him and staring the bullies down until they moved on. After that, he was no longer *just* Kainoa. Now he was Kainoa who made everyone laugh, Kainoa who pointed out star constellations, Kainoa who found bits of sea glass or heart-shaped rocks that he'd give to her when no one was looking. Up until now she hadn't noticed how sweet he was, giving kids at the beach piggyback rides, and, unlike a lot of other boys in their grade, was completely unconcerned with being macho. When she was around him, her stomach knotted like an eel around a hook. She didn't need that in her life. If she was going to be the next Miss Aloha Hula, she couldn't have a boyfriend. It was one of Kumu's unspoken rules. Boyfriends made girls skip practice. They listened to loud music in the parking lot and smoked cigarettes. If Hi`i was going to do her family proud, she had to show Kumu that she was dedicated. And yet, the more she tried to avoid Kainoa the more present he was. Whenever she tried to tell him she couldn't hang out, he'd say something funny and pretty soon she'd be laughing so hard she'd forget all about telling him to go away. Her body and mind were working against each other, drawing lines in the sand that kept getting erased. She would pass him in the hall at school and pretend not to see him, resolved to keep away and stay focused. He jogged over and asked if she wanted to hang out, maybe grab a shave ice after school. Her mind screamed no. But when she opened her mouth, out came yes.

Over the past couple of years, she'd done almost nothing outside of hula. Her mother had slowly resigned herself to it. Laka never asked how it was going or what Hi`i was learning, but sometimes Hi`i caught Laka staring with a strange look on her face at her hula bag full of the implements she had made with the halau, her pu`ili and ipu, her `ūli`ūli and kāla`au. When it came time to dye and stamp and sew her costumes, Laka helped her iron her seams crisp and straight. Kumu had instructed them to always show respect to the role their garments and implements played by storing and treating them with care, for they were tools that connected them to the story they were telling and allowed them to reaffirm and re-create their connection to the `āina, but Hi`i thanked them also for giving her the hope that maybe the careful attention coming from her mom was because Laka was proud of her, she just didn't know how to say it. Which made her that much more determined to stay focused. But the universe wasn't helping. The halau had moved to a strip mall, which meant better bathrooms and a larger practice space, which everyone except Hi`i was happy about—the halau now shared a wall with the dojo where Kainoa did judo. Like some cruel joke, they had practice on the same days. Avoiding him only made her late. But at least on a day like today, one where they both had practice, she didn't have to worry about trying to decline one of his invitations.

* * *

"HI`I!"

Kumu's voice boomed.

"Where you stay, girl? Get your head outta da clouds and pay attention. And fix your pa`u."

Hi`i looked down as she went inside. Sure enough, she'd skipped a cord. Done right, the three tiered ropes sewn into the waist of a hula skirt were stacked from the small of the waist to the widest point of the hip, sloping smoothly in a clean wedding cake A-frame. Her torso looked as warped as a balloon animal a day after the party. Face burning, she shuffled through the rows to the back of the room and retied her skirt. When she returned to her place in line, she caught Leilani rolling her eyes. A little flame of anger deep in her belly flared to life.

They might have technically been related, but it had been a long time since Hi`i had thought of Leilani as her cousin. They'd spent nearly every day at the beach together up until a handful of years ago, pooling their allowance to buy crack seed, keeping each other awake all night with ghost stories, jumping off the rocks at Leleiwi. And then one day Leilani had wanted to borrow one of Hi`i's favorite books, which Hi`i just knew she would never get back or if she did the pages would be all dog-eared and ruined. When Hi`i said no, Leilani told her she was acting like a haole. In return, Hi`i had pushed her. Just a little, Leilani hadn't even fallen over. But the next time Hi`i rode her bike to the beach, Leilani pretended not to see her, running off to the fishponds with their other cousins. The sleepovers stopped immediately. Now they were strangers, and Hi`i was fine with that.

Leilani acted like she was hot kaka. Everyone treated her like a princess. Hi`i knew it was because she looked like a cross between a tanning oil ad and an airline stewardess. Leilani knew it, too. She danced as though waves crashed from her hips and flowers grew out of her fingernails, but inside she was ugly as a goatfish. Not that anyone other than Hi`i saw through her. When Leilani danced, everybody bought the act hook, line, and sinker. Hi`i knew better. Last year, Leilani had floated a rumor that the only reason Kumu paid Hi`i any attention at all was because her mom had been Miss Aloha Hula. Worse, that she sometimes forgot her chants or messed up the choreography or was off time in her steps because she wasn't trying as hard as everyone else, which couldn't have been farther from the truth. In her four years of studying hula, she'd clung to Kumu's every word, every instruction. Her body was still gawky and stiff, but in her mind there was a clarity to the story she was trying to make her body tell. It wasn't her fault that her brain and body weren't in sync. It wasn't her fault that the more Hi`i practiced at home, the more she tried to prove Leilani wrong and show everyone the effort and dedication she'd committed to the halau, the worse she seemed to get. Like today. She couldn't even tie her skirts correctly. Leilani threw her a smug stink eye. The cords of her skirt were always perfect.

THAT DAY HI`I'S SKIRTS weren't the only thing crooked. Her timing was off, she mouthed the second half of the opening chant because her mind blanked on the words, and her thighs kept cramping during an extra-long series of back bends, leaving her sitting lame on her knees while everyone else did the work. She blamed Leilani. The girl's bad vibes had stiffened her joints and cursed her. Kumu kept

68

her mouth closed, venting her irritation through the beat of her pahu. Sweat dripped from Hi`i's elbows, decorating the wood floor with snowflake-shaped splatters. Hi`i's rhythm remained one step behind.

A dancer should never stand out or be noticed, not like this. A dancer emulsified, melted, molded, merged into the group and became one with it. Kumu stopped mid-slap on her ipu and held up her hand for everyone to stop. When she spoke, her voice was thick with frustration.

"Limp noodles! What kine dis? You guys going through the motions, but your head somewhere else. No can, this kine. You no like be here, go! No waste my time! I want to see the fire in your eyes. I want to see those skirts snap. Pull that mana from the ground up through your feet. Now, again from the beginning."

Kumu's stick continued having plenty to say, and Hi`i knew it was speaking directly to her. Thwack against Hi`i's legs when she didn't bend enough, thwack against her spine when she leaned too far forward during their duckwalks—Kumu corrected her so much that the sound of the stick against Hi`i's body became part of the melody. The more Kumu scrutinized, the more Hi`i's frustration grew and the worse her dancing got.

They eventually moved on to the dance they had been learning for months. Rain hammered through the thick soupy air, pounding on the roof. Kumu closed the windows. Browbeaten, the ceiling fan lost motivation. Its circles slowed. Red blotches appeared on Hi`i's neck and spread to her cheeks, climbing to her ears like vines. Her shirt clung to her chest. Mauna Kea and Mauna Loa rose. Self conscious, Hi`i pulled at her shirt to loosen it from her skin. The small act threw off her time. She tried to ignore her reflection in the mirror but it was impossible. At every turn she caught sight of herself and couldn't help but think about Leilani's accusation that she was riding on the coattails of her mother's hula fame. How much she wanted to prove her wrong. She longed for grace and the ability to give people chicken skin, to leave them spellbound and breathless—all the many things people had told her about her mother's dancing. She wasn't ever going to look like her mother, but she'd thought that with enough training she would at least dance like her. So far that wasn't happening, and it was killing her. The group pushed on, again and again, unable to get through the dance a single time without a misstep, a misplaced hand, or a failure in formation. At every fumble, Kumu made them start from the beginning.

There was no room for mistakes. This was a story of Pele and her sister Hi`iaka, of Pele's journey from her distant homeland across the ocean to Hawai`i, of bringing Hi`iaka as her companion, of Pele falling in love with the handsome young chief of Kaua`i and sending Hi`iaka to bring him to her, of Hi`iaka's betrayal and failure to do so. The choreography was full of violence and passion, anger and emotion, of volcanoes erupting and the chaos leading to the birth of the Hawaiian island chain. Pele, stunning in her beauty, with a back as straight as a cliff and breasts round like the moon, passionately digging a hole within the earth that would be home for a lover who would never arrive, passion replaced by fury when she learned why.

Hi`i knew the steps, knew the story. But it was coming out all wrong, muffled, as if someone were putting a hand over her mouth. Her body jerked and sputtered. The group distanced itself. They were a murmuration, she a broken-winged pigeon. The thirteenth piglet, the lame-legged foal. The flowers that were supposed to rise from her hands failed to bloom; the rain in her fingers came down dry.

Fast-forward rewind pause repeat. Kumu's stick, exhausted, went limp. She dismissed them with a toss of her hand and an exasperated sigh. Water break. Everyone made a beeline for the door and flooded into the hall.

"Hi`i, stay."

Hi`i remained in her place, alone on the dance floor.

"Do it again," Kumu said.

Hi`i ignored Leilani watching from the hall and focused on her reflection in the mirror, acutely aware now of the un-Hawaiian green of her eyes, the un-ehu red of her hair. There were bigger problems than Leilani right now. She braced herself for what was coming, whatever punishment she had been held back to receive. Kumu wanted her to know the dance, to place the knowledge of the story firmly into her body. This was why she was standing there, alone. She knew this, but it was impossible to get rid of the nagging suspicion that maybe things would be different if only she looked more like Leilani, or like her mom. That she'd blend in more and be less awkward if only she actually looked like the Naupaka she was. She thought of the girl Jane from the early days, the girl she'd chased off. If she was still here in the halau, Hi`i might not be the different one, might not be the one standing out. Kumu pounded her ipu into the mat and began to chant.

Hi`i knew the timing, she'd practiced at home countless times. She heard the beat that marked when she needed to point her toe, then lift her heel and snap her thigh, then spin to the side and cut the air with the wedge of her arm. But the motions fell flat. Her body had gone on strike. Instead of Hawai`i's origin story, Hi`i was dancing the hula of ice and death, of something struggling to live. She stood, hands fixed to her hips, as Kumu, no longer restarting and stopping to correct, made her way through the verses. By the final movements, even Leilani had turned away.

When it was over there was no yelling, no whack of the stick. The silence was worse than anything. Kumu slid her things into her bags. The rest of the class, still lingering in the hall in case Kumu had decided to call them back in, went quietly home.

1971

When one life ends, another begins.

The closest Laka ever got to reestablishing a relationship with her father after she ran away to Maui was the hint of a smile he'd offered her that first time she'd brought Hi`i to Puhi Bay. That smile had sustained her over time, giving her patience, allowing her a hope that one day the past would finally be the past and, when that happened, she and her father could go back to the way they had been. But the tide waits for no one.

Uncle George died unexpectedly, leaving Laka with a hole in her heart that would never fill. But what it did for Hi`i, well . . . let's just say that the death of the grandfather she had never met was a concrete piling dropped smack across the length of the road that her story had been traveling down. With the concrete mass in the way, the story stopped short and changed direction.

After the funeral, Laka stood in the overgrown grass of the front yard with little Hi`i clinging to her calf. It was the first time she'd been to the Naupaka hale since returning from Maui. When the screen door opened, she gave Hi`i a gentle nudge toward the gardenias at the far end of the yard and told her to go play. Then she faced her mother.

"Ma," she said in greeting. The syllable hung in the air, cold. Hulali's large frame filled the doorway. She looked pointedly at the young child skampering across the grass.

"We going spread his ashes up mauka," Hulali said. "You know da spot."

Laka nodded.

"Yeah, I figured. I like go, but . . ."

"We can manage wid'out you. As we have been. Not dat you would know."

Laka sighed. Hi`i ran toward her, a large white gardenia blossom in her hand. Laka smiled. She accepted the gift, tucking the flower behind her ear before pulling Hi`i close.

"She getting big," Hulali had said eventually.

Laka nodded.

"Bring her inside, out of the sun. We have t'ings to discuss."

"We're fine out here."

"Your choice."

Not bothering with her slippers, Hulali settled her callused bare feet on the top porch step and gathered the folds of her frayed pareo, swirls of fern green against cream that brought out the deep gold in her skin. She tucked the ends of the fabric between her legs and negotiated her body down, leaning over her knees for leverage.

"You get her birt' certificate?"

She flicked her chin toward Hi`i, who had caught sight of a cat sleeping under the shade of a plumeria tree and was slowly army-crawling toward it.

Laka bristled, angry tears threatening her eyes. "After all dis time, dat's what you have to say? You accusing me of somet'ing? She's mine," she said, letting out the words one by one as calm as she could.

Hulali thumped a palm against the splintered wood deck. "I not trying start one fight. It's da girl dat mattah now. You say she's family, she's a Naupaka, okay. Dis land, Keaukaha . . . you know how hard we fought for dis, how hard we still fighting. I gotta know you can prove dis keiki is who you say she is."

"Why, why dat matter? You hea, your precious land is safe."

Hulali's spine lengthened. She had a way of expanding, of changing shape without actually changing. She was a moʻo, a shape-shifter. When Laka was little, Hulali insisted on taking the guts of their dinner down to the sharks, calling to them as she stood in the bloody water, silver fins flashing at her hips. Once, Laka had followed her down to see how it was her mother was never eaten by the sharks. In the dark shadows of the evening, just as Laka was crossing the street, Hulali melted into a long narrow lizard, fourteen feet tall. When Laka ran to get closer to shore, the figure that had been her mother disappeared into the darkness of the water. Laka had raced home, buried herself in the blankets on her bed, and never followed her mother again.

A tremor rippled through Laka's body as if she was shaking off the memory, steeling herself from the familiar shiver she'd lived with her entire childhood. She wasn't a child anymore. Her mother's magic couldn't scare her. Besides, this conversation had been building silently between them for years. She was done running away from it. She forced herself to look directly at Hulali when her mother answered.

"I gotta spell it out? Because you saying she da eldest daughter of my eldest daughter, da hiapo. You know what dat means. Dis yours," Hulali gestured toward the house, the plumeria trees, the rusting van in the driveway, the slightly wild grass in the yard, the pōhaku wall along the road.

(GOOD OLE BLOOD QUANTUMS. Laka could prove her fifty percent, but her child's ability to inherit the family's land depended on having a father that contributed the right amount of Hawaiian blood to the mathematical equation. Laka knew that as well as we did. But she was stubborn, like her ma.)

"EVERY PERSON BORN WID ONE DUTY. A responsibility unique to dem. Dea kuleana. You know dat. Dis one—taking care dis land, making sure Keaukaha homeland stay intact, keeping da Naupaka mission alive—is yours."

"No talk to me about kuleana anymore, Ma. You drilled dat shit inside my head all my life, but you like know wat I t'ink? You talking 'bout *your* kuleana, not mine. My kuleana belong now to my daughter."

Laka stopped Hulali before she could open her mouth to respond.

"Why we even talking 'bout dis right now? Dad just died. Can't we be sad for a minute? No need rush, we get plenty time for deal wit dis."

The porch creaked. Hulali rose, gliding down the steps and across the yard until she was nose to nose with Laka in the wild grass.

"Girl, you haven't been paying attention to wat I been trying fo' teach you all dese years. If dea is one t'ing we Hawaiians don't have, it's time," Hulali said.

The words rose slow and low from her throat, as though she were chanting.

"I going back Oʻahu, I gotta help in Kalama Valley. Dey kicking Hawaiians off land to make room for high-rises and hotels . . . same old story. Dey saying we get no chance of fighting da evictions and getting everybody dat was living in da valley back on da farms, but you t'ink dey going stop with da Kalama development? No. Tomorrow going be somet'ing else. Dey not going stop unless we stop 'em. Not enough to stay on homestead land now. We gotta get serious, orga-nize, push back. Dis going take time. PKO need help too. Dis about protecting a way of life."

"Ma, what da hell you talking about? Since when you involved wit da PKO?"

Hulali's eyes narrowed at her daughter's question.

"What you mean, when did I get involved? We always been in-volved, girl. Me, *you*"—she jabbed a finger into her own chest, then toward Laka's, her words sharpening in anger—"we *are* da PKO. Kahoʻolawe is sacred. Once dey destroy it, who's to say dey not going take another island, and another?"

The cat in the bushes that Hiʻi had been after flicked its tail and darted under the house. Hiʻi scrambled to her feet and tried to fol-low it. Hulali watched the girl search for a way in. Her voice soft-ened. "With your dad gone, I gotta help, gotta kōkua. You know I no can leave dis place empty. Da state would take it back like dat." She snapped her fingers. "Our family home, all we fought for, would all be for not'ing."

Laka pulled her gaze away from her daughter and stared at her mother, her aging mirrored image. (How can two people so physically similar be so different? They were two sides of a coin.) If her mother wanted a fight, she'd give her a fight. She tossed a length of her thick black hair behind a shoulder.

"You t'ink da state cares what a group of Hawaiians wit empty bank accounts have to say? You was always so ready to fight fo' Hawai-ians, but wat about dis family, wat about us? Go Honolulu, I not going judge. But no talk to me 'bout my daughter's birt' certificate, no tell me wat you doing is fo' da family. You care more 'bout blood quantum, 'bout getting approval from America. Am I Hawaiian because dey say so? Ma, if you believe dat den sorry, you fighting one losing battle. Pretty soon not going have any Hawaiians left if kanaka like you keep giving America da power for say we is who we say we is. Dis house belongs to our family. How many times we gotta prove dat?"

The words hung in the air and all of Keaukaha fell still. Turtles paused eating their limu on the rocks to lift their heads. Uncles checked the horizon, aunties sniffed the air. A neighbor sitting on his porch across the street flicked his cigarette into the gravel of his driveway. It sizzled a death rattle when it hit a puddle. The crickets in the yard waited to see who would strike next. The silence might have lasted forever if at that moment Hiʻi hadn't tripped over a rock and released a curdling shriek as she fell, shattering the glass in the air. Her cries echoed up the street. Dropping her shoulders for a temporary truce, Laka raced across the yard to gather her daughter, clearing the dirt from her knees with a firm hand before slinging the sobbing girl into her arms. She made for her car. Hulali called out.

"So you no want da house."

Laka turned. Met her mother in the eye. "I want da house. But no foʻget: Hiʻi is mine. If da house mine, it's hers too."

ON MAY 11, 1971, a few days after Hulali returned to Oʻahu and in spite of all their efforts, seventy policemen arrived in Kalama Valley to battle the pig farmers and car mechanics. Ordered there by the governor and dressed in full riot gear, they dragged thirty-two women, children, and elders, all wailing and pleading, out of their yards and into vans with doors that locked from the outside. Hulali was handcuffed, arrested, and bundled in like the rest of them. *This isn't over*, she called out in Hawaiian. It was both a threat and a promise.

Bulldozers descended as soon as the vans disappeared around the bend. It was a full moon tide.

The beginning of another end.

AFTER PRACTICE, LEILANI FOUND Hi`i at Back Pond, washing away her humiliation. In Keaukaha, where everyone knew everyone, underwater was the closest thing to privacy. The pond was embedded in the jagged volcanic cliff, the walls high enough to keep out the salt water. The fresh water coming from the springs was icy, biting.

When Hi`i came up for air the sun was hitting Leilani from behind. She was the only girl Hi`i knew who stood that way, poised as if she were in the middle of a photo shoot. She hopped across a break in the lava rock and climbed down closer to the edge of the pond, sitting at its lip.

"Watchu like?" Hi`i asked, treading water in the deep middle.

The wind played with Leilani's long silky black hair. She tucked a wisp behind her ear. "Remember dat turtle who used to come at high tide and den get stuck when the tide went out?"

Hi`i cupped the water and let it drain through her fingers. How was she supposed to answer that? Of course she remembered.

When it became obvious she wasn't going to respond, Leilani asked another question.

"Hi`i, why you dance?"

Hi`i swam toward a ledge and lifted herself onto it. "Why shouldn't I?"

Leilani pulled her knees to her chest and wrapped her arms around them, tilting her face so her cheek rested on her knee. She watched the horizon. The sun was sinking. "My dad says Aunty Laka used to be so different. Dat dey was all super close. Wanna guess when t'ings changed?"

Hi`i stared into the water. The blue in the pond was different than the blue in the bay. She was starting to get cold. Goose bumps ran up her arms. She forced herself not to shiver and tried to pretend that she wasn't bothered by what Leilani was saying.

Finally Leilani got up to leave. Hi`i shouted at her back.

"Not my fault da way I look. I nevah do not'ing to you."

Leilani took a step and then stopped. She wheeled back around toward Hi`i.

"If look haole and act haole, must be haole, yah? You know, wen I tole my dad I nevah like hang out wit chu he got all sad. Dat was wen I heard him later talking to e'rybody, dey was all saying how Aunty Laka was always taking care of dem wen dey was small, how aftah you it was like she wasn't even part of da family anymore."

"Whatevah. None of dat my fault. Maybe my mom no like hang out wit all you because you're all jerks!" She climbed out of the pond and grabbed her towel, wrapping it around her waist before sliding her feet into her slippers. This time it was Leilani who called out as Hi`i walked away. She turned. They locked eyes. Now that they were acknowledging the tension that had been building between them, there was no stanching the flow. Even if what Leilani said was true, that she was the reason Laka was no longer close with the family, that she was the cause of the divide, that Hi`i had created the polite distance that Laka and her siblings—established after she returned from Maui with Hi`i—had never been able to transcend, she was unprepared for what Leilani said next. What it looked like Leilani had been waiting to say for a very long time.

"Got everyt'ing to do wit chu. Your mom wen find you in one

Dumpster. Dey say she brought chu back from Maui and told e'ry-body you was her kid and stayed away from da family because nobody wen believe her. You only t'ink you one Naupaka. No one else goin' tell you cuz dey feel sorry, but you should know so you can stop making one clown out of yo'self, trying fo' be some hula star. Why you t'ink Tutu Hulali nevah come watch us dance? Cuz she shame. You made da whole family shame. Go back where you came from already, Haole Girl. Back where you belong."

Hi`i kept walking.

CHAPTER 7

1979

elong. What does this even mean? Our dictionary was created long ago, passed down through the generations, imported by the outsiders, the interlopers, the conquerors who keep changing the rules. Their words are like an invasive species, squeezing the necks of our flora and fauna, snuffing them out.

We watched Hi`i struggle. Instead of growing into the kind of Naupaka we recognized, Hi`i grew more foreign. Gawky, all limbs and elbows, whiter than a haole Christmas, sticking out from her sea of cousins like the eye of a storm. Her hula skills were grim, made more apparent as the halau buckled down to prepare for their upcoming Merrie Monarch performance. With the family she had, the reality of that was salt on a wound and suddenly all Hi`i wanted to talk to anyone about was being a Naupaka. She ignored any conversation that wasn't about hula or being Hawaiian. She yelled at the haoles moving to Hilo from places like Wisconsin and Wyoming. She flipped them the bird and told them to go back to where they came from. She even made up stories about reunions with Hulali, though we all knew where Hulali was and what she was doing.

***

THE SLIPPERY-SLOPE HULA:

Once upon a time, we looked to the missionaries, the men who crossed oceans who told us everything we did was wrong, our gods and ways, our prayers and language and life. We trusted them, these preachers who came to teach us how to be right. To teach us from a book of rules they said explained how they were surviving while we were not.

Before them, belong meant we belonged to the earth, all that we could touch and feel and see, what came from above and below, we are one and the same, the heat of lā and falling grace of us, the grit of the ʻāina and splash of kai. And yet their book said no, the sun and rain, the earth and ocean, it was separate, apart, it belonged to God. We understood, our world, too, was ruled and created by those to whom we paid tribute, our many gods and deities, our ʻaumakua and ancestors.

Lowercase *g* versus uppercase *G*.

In those twenty-nine years and one hundred ninety-two days of King Kamehameha III's reign, half our population died.

The land reform known as the Great Mahele that had been insti-tuted under King Kamehemeha III disrupted the way we had passed our land down from generation to generation. Private ownership. What did these words mean? How to claim ownership of what was grown by the earth and the sun? We'd never considered such a thing. Chiefs had ruled the lands, yes, but like shareholders of a publicly owned company, as long as we worked our portion and shared what it produced, the land was our kuleana, to care for, to manage, to pass down, to inherit. Haole plantation owners convinced the king that dividing up Hawaiian land and bowing to the gods of paperwork and land titles was a great idea. So he split the land in three—a third for the crown, a third for the chiefs, and a third for the public. What was he thinking? Probably that this was the way he was going to protect Hawaiians, that this was a way for them to get those haole holy pieces of paper that would keep plantation owners from buying up all the farms and ponds. Haole eyes saw only land deeds. Without them, everything was up for grabs.

Today those haole, the all-powerful holders of the dictionary, say all that had once belonged to their God now belongs to the person holding the papers claiming ownership. This paper they created, they wrote.

At the king's stipulation, royal lands would not be threatened by the Great Mahele's land reforms—he would place them in a trust that would protect them from foreign purchase. A trust, he said, for the native Hawaiian people, the native people of Hawaii. Are those two things the same?

Native. Being the place or environment in which a person was born or a thing came into being; inherent. Big *N*, little *n*. Of the blood; of the soil.

Trust. An arrangement whereby a person holds property as its nominal owner for the good of one or more beneficiaries. We memorized the precise verbiage. Clung to it, our lifeboat for when the tide rose above our heads.

Beneficiary. The person or persons who receive benefit from a trust.

Hawaiian. Citizen of the United States is the first requirement.

Trust in the trust. Hawaiian lands, land for home, Homelands. Reserved for the Hawaiian people to live as they always had.

The trustees do not have the power to change the will's intent, they say. They don't, until they do. Trustees appointed by the state, the fox guarding the chicken coop.

The royal lands added up to nearly two million acres. The Hawaiian Homes Commission Act of 1920 put 200,000 acres of scrap land into a trust. We were supposed to ignore that math? And those 200,000 scraps, how and when were we going to start benefiting from them?

Good ole America. They have all the colonial answers. Slave trade taught them so much. One percent African American might make a guy Black, but if they used the same ruler to measure American Indian, they'd be writing checks until their fingers bled.

They argued that "part-white Hawaiians were so much more adept and industrious." Legislators said those Hawaiians didn't need a hand up the way the rest did. That shot of white blood gave them what they needed to survive and thrive. It was the more-than-half ones, the "lazy" ones, who needed the help. So it was decided that only those with no less than fifty-one percent Hawaiian blood (proven with American documents) would qualify for the waiting list. It was brilliant, eliminating the worry that there might not be enough land to go around. Hawaiians were a finite population (fish in a barrel). Wait out enough generations, there wouldn't be a single one of us left who'd qualify. One percent Black, you Black. One percent Hawaiian, nah, you nothing. When the U.S. government is making the rules, there is only one guaranteed winner.

By the year 2044, it's said, there won't be a single full-blooded Hawaiian left. That's a lot of blood lost. Not lost, gone. If we were a seal or a whale, there'd be a worldwide effort to save our species. They wouldn't be able to touch us. If we swam up to the beach they'd put cones around to protect us.

Where did the king say a Hawaiian with fifty percent blood should be valued over one with forty-five, or twenty? Where did these numbers come from? Still. We dug up our birth certificates, we played by those American rules. They call it Hawaiian Home "Awards," as if we won something. One of the first drawings saw 2,905 people apply for 261 lots.

That was 1920. It was now 1979. In the entirety of that fifty-nine years, only eight thousand homeland leases were granted. Twenty thousand were still waiting. Blood quantum march going nowhere. We were living and dying on the waiting list.

Bloodless coup, they called it. Bloodless, like a corpse, the walking dead. Haole. Meaning without breath.

Land of aloha. Alo, to share. Ha, breath. Aloha, to share breath. How to share breath with those without breath?

America to the rescue, it says. Cue the superhero symphony music. Special government-created programs. Not for all Hawaiians, but certainly for full Hawaiians, half Hawaiians, according to the definition in the dictionary they wrote. Pretty soon none of us will qualify to be ourselves. They'll say there's none left, and yet we're all still here.

In the time of our kings (and queen), we replaced the food we'd grown in our fields with sugar to feed America's sweet tooth, sold it to them tax free. To thank us, they bound our mouths, our minds, then our hands and feet. Now we wait at the docks for the barges to fill the shelves of our supermarkets, to fill the needles fixed to our veins.

They promised we could keep our sacred places. Now we go to Richardson's Beach to swim, and when the sky goes orange the mosquitoes rise in droves and rain down upon the interrupters who slap their skin and race across the blazing sand, dripping towels and foam coolers, snorkels and cheap soggy boogie boards. The mosquitoes herd them to the hot innards of their rental cars, their rented rooms. The lifeguard pulls the wooden panels over the windows of his stand and pretends not to see us as we pull in the nets laid out across the channel, same like he'd pretended not to see earlier, when we'd come to throw them. The state says it's illegal to drop nets across the channel.

Why are they they, and we we? Who drew the lines?

Who belongs to what, and what now belongs to who?

AFTER HULALI MOVED TO O`AHU during the Kalama Valley protests and got released from jail, she focused her energy on volunteering with PKO (we'd had to gather, to pule, and eventually paddle over—some of us even gave their lives. But we'd made progress. We'd gotten the courts to consider that Kaho`olawe might have cultural and religious significance to us, and put it on the American navy to conduct an environmental impact study, because haoles need experts to tell them that bombing an island with the full force of the American military does have an environmental impact). Hulali's involvement with PKO led her to push for the state to call for a constitutional convention (the last one we'd had was ten years before, in 1968). Most of us who went had never held political office, but that didn't stop us. Maybe we caught America by surprise. We weren't done organizing. In Hawai`i lots of things had been going on too long, and some things not going on long enough. So many broken parts needed paying attention to at once (when the body dies, the lungs, the heart, the brain, the liver, the kidneys—they shut down one by one but all at the same time), and because of this, we went to the convention with an agenda and stuck to it. We wanted to make sure Hawaiian rights of access to land, water, and religious sites stayed protected.

With all the gatherings leading up to it, Hulali had noticed that fewer and fewer keiki knew Hawaiian, so she sent out a group ahead of time to travel through the islands to see if she was just imagining things, but when the group came back she cried at what they said. Of all the keiki in all the `āina, fewer than fifty were `ōlelo. *Fifty* kids, speaking Hawaiian fluently. In total. We'd died, and now our language was dying too. Auwe. We bled tears into the dirt, drip, drip. Hulali picked up the mud, rubbed it between her fingers, and took that to the convention, too. Hawaiian needed to be the state's official language alongside English. The keiki needed the language of the `āina. We needed education programs, health programs, employment programs, vocational training, children's services, substance counseling, conservation programs, indigenous wildlife protection, agriculture programs, and language immersion programs. Basically, we needed to be in charge of ourselves before we went extinct. Who better to know how to fix this? Who better to care about us than us?

Out of the convention emerged the Office of Hawaiian Affairs. A official office dedicated to representing Hawaiian rights. Accepting OHA as representation meant also accepting our islands were forever lost to the overthrow of the kingdom, which didn't sit well with us. Hulali pointed out that it was impractical to think the United States would withdraw from Hawai`i, and that we should focus on reparations instead. Some decided Hulali was right. The ones who didn't formed their own group, which didn't have the blessing of the United States. (That was sort of the point.) Needless to say, Hulali was busy, and not doing all the things Hi`i claimed they were doing together.

We didn't want to make the girl feel bad, or make it clear we knew she was blowing smoke about her reunions with her tutu. Hi`i had enough on her plate. The rift between Hi`i and Leilani was kid stuff, but we considered getting involved. There wasn't enough time in the day to play referee in every teenage catfight, and yet . . . in every joke there's a thorn of truth, and the same goes for insults. When it came to the kaka Leilani was slinging in Hi`i's direction, all the talk about Hi`i not being Laka's blood child, Leilani might have been dead wrong. She might also have been right, which would leave Laka with no one to take over their homestead lease, and mean it was only a matter of time before the Naupakas lost their home. And if the Naupakas could lose their little bit of Keaukaha, any of us could. So, if Leilani was standing on the solid ground of fact, we didn't know how to feel about it. Hi`i didn't look like a Naupaka, but we weren't ready to try to figure out what that actually meant.

CHAPTER 8

1979

Less than two weeks until the school trip to Waipi`o and Hi`i's nipples were splotchy from all the tape she'd used to hide them. She needed a better solution, but with Leilani's words ringing in her ears, Kainoa noticing her growing boobs didn't feel like as much of a concern. Hi`i searched the house and found Laka in bed, balled up like a baby in her red pareo.

"You need a bag of ice?" Hi`i asked.

The walls were thin. The first time Tony had beat on her mom she'd run into the room and tried to put herself between them, an act of solidarity that earned her a mind-your-own-business from Laka. Since then, she usually put a pillow over her head and tried to go back to sleep. If they were loud enough to shake the windows she went to the beach to wait them out.

A blackish green bruise ran the length of Laka's cheek, distorting its shape. She could have been sucking a jawbreaker. She scooted over and patted the mattress.

"Come sit for a sec."

"Where's Tony?"

"Not here."

Hi`i pushed the bundled sheet aside and sat at the edge near her mom's calves. "He coming back?"

"No. Dis time I promise going be diff'rent. But nevah mine dat. Honey, I goin' need your help."

Laka reached out to pull Hi`i closer and stared out the window for a time. Hi`i stayed where she was, sensing her mother had more to say.

"Hi`i, I'm hapai. You goin' be a big sister."

Hi`i was glad she was sitting. "Wow."

"Yeah. And it's knocking me on my `ōkole. You t'ink you can handle t'ings around here?"

"Sure. But just wow." People were having babies in Hilo all the time, families expanding faster than bellies at Thanksgiving, but Hi`i had never considered the possibility their family would ever consist of more than she and her mom.

Laka watched Hi`i absorb the information and then patted her on the thigh, putting on one of her big plastic smiles before trying to change the subject.

"Eh, how's hula going?"

Hi`i waved the question away. "It's fine, Ma. You need somet'ing, juice? I gotta do homework."

Laka patted her on the arm and put her head back on the pillow, closing her eyes and groaning. "Ew. Don't say any words wit food inside. I going puke. No juice. I need moe moe. So tired."

Instead of going into her room to do homework, Hi`i went outside where it was cooler. She hadn't told her mom what Leilani had said, though it didn't matter. Leilani was full of it. She crossed the porch and noticed Tony's fishing nets were gone. Good riddance. They didn't need him. Even if her mom *was* hapai.

The night was murky. A pueo stared its big yellow eyes at her from a telephone wire, watching as she made her way to the main road before it flew off. Laka had always said pueo were protector `aumakua, guardians. The moon ducked in and out of clouds. The bay was washed out. Smelled like a storm was coming. Hi`i walked on.

When the rains came, they came all at once, clattering pots and pans and buckets. Hi`i ran toward the tarp overhang at Puhi Bay and huddled on the picnic table to wait it out. As a kid, she'd loved summers at Puhi Bay, living old-style, feeling like they were sticking it to somebody. It was the last holdout, the only beach in Keaukaha still technically part of Homelands and not swallowed up by the county, the last place she and her cousins could still roam day or night, to swim naked and run around barefoot as their parents had (or, in Hi`i's case, parent singular. She'd never bothered trying to imagine her father among the Puhi Bay uncles—to the entire community, he did not exist, not even in story form. There was no mystery to solve, only a fact to accept, like how no one knew where Kamehameha the Great was buried. There were no stories the grown-ups recounted when drunk, no one ever told her she looked like him or acted like him or attributed her dislike of certain foods to him. She was just Laka's daughter, as though she'd spontaneously come into the world, fatherless).

The benches under the big tarp were generally reserved for the uncles to play music and talk story, smoke cigarettes, and drink beers. Was it possible that every summer the uncles had been seeing her the way Leilani did, thinking that it was her who had driven a wedge between Laka and everyone else, whispering and wondering if she was really Hawaiian? Her life had been plagued by an anxiety that she'd tried to convince herself would go away the moment she proved herself a hula master and therefore a Naupaka. She had considered her looks some kind of joke the universe had played on her, but had never considered the possibility that she wasn't a Naupaka at all. She'd convinced herself that her cousins teased her but in fun, like they would if she'd had an extra-large gap between her teeth. But now . . .

Now she was going to be a sister. Tony was Puerto Rican, with lighter skin than her mom. Would Hi`i and her sister look alike? With the new baby she would have proof for everyone to see that Hi`i was indeed a Naupaka, this was just how they came out. She stared at the unsettled skies, wondering what they were trying to tell her.

When the rain eased, she walked home. To the few cars that passed, she sent a silent question. Did they see a Hilo girl walking home? If not, what did they see?

THE STORM WAS STILL HOWLING the next day at practice. Hi`i waited as the class of older, more experienced dancers finished up, wiping the sweat off the floor and extracting their slippers from the pile in the hall, chattering about their plans to meet up that weekend to go up mauka to gather new plants for the kuahu. Getting to that stage, being given that responsibility and entrusted with the knowledge of their gathering spots, was a rite of passage Hi`i anticipated with excited impatience. She stared at them without bothering to hide her fascination until the last of the older class had gone the way of the stairs. The halau began to fill with her group. Hi`i raised an eyebrow at Leilani, daring her to say something when she took her place on the floor. Being caught at Puhi Bay the night before with the stormclouds raging over her head had left her feeling resolved and confident.She was a Naupaka. And soon enough there would be a baby to prove it. She threw a smug look at Leilani.

Dey found you undah a rock, Hi`i mouthed.

Leilani raised an eyebrow back and gave her one of her shark smiles, all teeth. Kumu's ipu could barely be heard over the roaring rain pounding like marbles on the tin roof. Merrie Monarch was coming up, and while their halau wasn't competing, it was performing for the Wednesday Opening Night Exhibition, when the doors of the civic center were opened for all of Hilo to come. Kumu pushed them, calling out to them over the pounding of the storm.

In that moment, Hi`i experienced a feeling she had never felt before in all her years of dancing. Her mind got out of the way and something else took over. She chanted her oli from so deep within her that she felt the vibration in her chest. Lightning and thunder clapped back as if responding. The building trembled. Hi`i felt it in her feet, then her calves. It took over her entire body. Before she knew it they were moving, the entirety of them, a sea across the floor, knees flaring in perfect unison. The shape of them shifted, a cloud moving across the sky, an `io, beak sharp, cutting through the winds. An `ohia, clawing its way through layers of hardened black lava. A lehua, bursting red feathered blossoms. The life that followed Pele's fire.

In the spell there was no time, no space.

It ended in a great seismic shudder, pulsing as the story left them. The ipu fell silent. When Hi`i came back into her body she became aware she was panting. The entire room was. Her toes and fingers tingled. Leilani was to her left, a tear down her cheek. They'd all felt it.

"Maika`i," Kumu said, voice cracking with emotion. "So good."

Hi`i had wondered what the skies were saying. Now she knew. They were calling for her attention. What she had always wanted, to truly dance hula, could not come through choreography or perfect timing.

There could be no mimicking the elements of Hawai`i. There was only becoming a part of them.

WITH TONY BANISHED FROM THE HOUSE and Laka stuck with her face in the toilet half the day, Hi`i offered to stay home from the Waipi`o school trip to help her mother weave and prepare everything for Merrie Monarch. By now her mom usually had entire boxes of hats and fans, purses and bracelets already done. But this year most of the lauhala was still out in the back, dusty and flat, waiting to be stripped and rolled. Hi`i knew Laka counted on that money to fill in the gaps of the manini paycheck she earned from working at Aloha Spirit. The class trip was four days long, nearly an entire week. That would mean a lot of nothing getting done with her mom as sick as the pregnancy was making her. Still, Laka wouldn't hear of it. She even stayed up late the night before the trip baking, all so Hi`i could bring Laka's coveted sour poi bread to the potluck dinner their school had planned with the Waipi`o farmers, an offering of thanks for welcoming the students into their lo`i and teaching them how to plant and harvest taro. When Hi`i woke before dawn the next morning, the house was full of that distinct sweet yeasty smell. It made her smile as she grabbed her backpack and sleeping bag.

Hi`i imagined how it would go down. They'd arrive in Waipi`o Valley. With the bread in her hands, she would follow the traditional protocols and give ho`okupu by leading her classmates, her teacher Miss Kapua, and the valley farmers through a prayer ceremony that would culminate in the slow eating of the offering. She'd present it in a gourd, laying it at the door of the farmer's house facing outward. They'd say a prayer for the ancient chiefs and the Hawaiian people of the past, then pray for those present before putting the bread on their tongues and letting its prayers melt into their bodies, binding them to one another. They would spend the remainder of the trip in the valley of the ancients, pono.

She believed in the otherworldly now, in the possibility of transcendence. Or at least that was what she was telling herself. She needed to believe this. What she'd felt during hula practice the day of the storm—the little tweaks in her feet, the vibrating hum in her fingers, the gravitational current of the dancers moving as one—was the proof she needed that the ancient mana of the `āina was calling to her, that she knew now how to heed that call. Maybe this was how Kumu had started, maybe instead of being born knowing how to speak to the winds and the rains, the earth had one day risen up and begun speaking to her.

Hi`i was relieved that Laka was forcing her to go. In class they'd studied the Kumulipo, the Hawaiian creation chant, for months, their teacher drilling into their heads the sacred connection between taro and the Hawaiian people.

The Kumulipo was a two-thousand-verse poem both cosmogonic and genealogical, memorized and passed down for hundreds of years, her teacher explained. When Captain Cook landed in Kealakekua in 1779, everyone thought he was the god Lono returning. The priests came out and chanted the Kumulipo to receive him and to introduce themselves. Cook and his men let them all think he was Lono. It didn't end well.

The Kumulipo laid it all out like an epic family tree. Everything connected, born one from the other, the seaweed and rats, the flowers and fish, the Kumulipo left no one out. Wakea, the sky father from which sunshine and rain fertilized Papa, his wife, the warm upper layer of Earth Mother, who then had a baby with his daughter Hoʻohokukalani. The baby Haloa was stillborn. They buried him outside. From him all taro was born, and from their next child came everyone else. When taro is harvested, the leaves and root are eaten and the stalk is replanted to grow again. Taro and Hawaiians, brothers, one and the same (although, Hiʻi noticed in hindsight, when she'd first started studying the Kumulipo she'd processed it as a Hawaiian girl from Keaukaha. After her fight with Leilani, she couldn't help but wonder if somewhere in the Kumulipo might reside an explanation for her white skin, her green eyes, her red hair).

Preparing for the trip, Hiʻi and her class had spent a day in the school cafeteria, taking turns with a big wooden spoon, stirring pots deep enough to bathe in, the whole seven hours for the taro to cook. They'd turned out the cooled taro onto a heavy stone poi pounder, mashing it with a pestle until it turned into thick purple paʻiʻai paste. Half was diluted with water for poi and half was mixed with coconut milk to make kulolo, delicious, sticky sweet pudding.

The welcome potluck was more than just the field trip kickoff or an auspicious starting point that would have them sinking their feet into the mud of their ancestors. No. The potluck was Hiʻi's chance to take her mother's sour poi bread and show her people how much she understood. It would be the beginning of everything.

AT THE TOP OF THE STAIRS she caught a whiff of sweat and fish. Tony's jeep was in the driveway. Her stomach sank. She hoped he wasn't there for more drama. If he started fighting with her mom again, tearing the house apart or trying to break down the door to get in, she'd miss the bus.

They met in the stairwell, he on his way up and she on her way down. Mouth full and chewing, he grunted out an acknowledgment and pushed past her. Sick with premonition, she leaped the last of the stairs into the open room that served as both kitchen and eating area. Sure enough, the three tin loaf pans that her mother had set out on the long wooden table the night before to cool had been demolished. Two were nothing but crumbs, a battalion of ants already moving in. The third had a two-inch gap. A fork stood crooked in the loaf like the shovel of a sloppy and audacious grave robber, tines buried in the remains. She stomped up the stairs and burst through the closed door of her mother's room.

The bedroom was full of quiet morning light, books stacked in corners, the ironing board buried under a pile of wrinkled clothes. Laka and Tony stood in the middle of the room wound around each other as if dancing to a slow song only they could hear. Laka lifted her head from Tony's chest when Hi`i came in.

"Who eats two *entire* loaves? Who said you can? Why you here? Go away! We don't need you."

Laka untangled herself and looked from one to the other in shock. "What da hell you going on about, girl?"

"Ma, he ate da bread."

Tony held up his hands as if in surrender. "Wasn't all me. Da boys was hea wid me earlier. We was hunting all night. Starvation nation. Eh," he said, chuckling and tilting his chin toward Laka, "was ono."

"Aiyah. It was for Hi`i take down da valley," Laka explained.

Tony shrugged. "Sorry eh. Nevah have one sign."

Hi`i huffed.

"Hi`i, no be disrespectful."

"Me disrespectful? Did I go his house and inside his fridge and eat his food wit'out asking?"

Laka recoiled. "Girl, you like one slap? Show some respec'. I wen raise you bettah den for talk to one adult like dat. And anyt'ing we get is for e'rybody share. Dat's da Hawaiian way, you know dat. Go grab one bag potato chips from da pantry. Hele mai, we gotta go."

Hi`i went downstairs and stared at the chips on the shelf, barely able to breathe. Her chest was tight. Offered as ho`okupu, that bread would have been her ticket to an earned respect—a finger to Leilani and anyone else who questioned her belonging. To offer a bag of potato chips to the valley of Waipi`o as a ceremonial gift would be an insult. She considered not going. But with Tony there, that meant four days of listening to him and her mom scrap or make up or both. And now Hi`i was crying. She stuffed the chips in a grocery bag and went to wash her face. The door of the downstairs bathroom didn't shut all the way, so she shoved a bucket behind it to keep it closed tight.

In the bathroom, she splashed water on her face and rubbed her chest. Mauna Loa and Mauna Kea felt bruised. She loosened the straps of the bikini top she'd planned to wear for the trip in place of tape. She felt a sudden urge to pee. She pulled down her shorts. Her panties were wet with dark brown blood.

She knew what a ma`i was, she'd been forced to watch the sex ed video in school since her mom hadn't signed the waiver to get her out of it. (Laka said only Americans were scared of sex, and they weren't Americans, so . . .) They'd all laughed at the condom scene, but the menstruation part had only been a brief flash of a girl in a two-second cartoon with a bunch of tubes drawn across her stomach.

Laka called for her to hurry up. Hi`i heard the car start. She yanked on the toilet paper roll and doused a handful in water, scrubbing away the blood the best she could. She thought about telling her mom. But then there'd be some kind of big deal, her mom would send her down to the valley with pads and who knew what else. Maybe it wasn't really her ma`i. Maybe it was just a warning it was coming soon, a flare. There hadn't been that much. And it had been more brown than red, whatever that meant. She had nothing to worry about. She'd tell her mom and deal with it when she came back from the valley.

WAIPI`O. VALLEY OF THE THREE KINGS, Land of the Curving Water. Where Maui got his gourd. The valley that fed us when famine came. One of the last outposts in Hawai`i where there were no resorts or hotel developments, only farmers living the way they'd been living since before Captain Cook. This trip, sponsored by OHA, would teach Hi`i and her class the ways of the lo`i. It would bring them back to Hawai`i, back to us.

It took over an hour for the buses to wind their way across the Hamākua Coast and through the trenches of Honoka`a. The road into the valley was steep enough to be declared forbidden territory by rental car agencies. Our final frontier, with an entrance too narrow and treacherous for school buses. The students unloaded their things at the lookout point at the top. A truck took their sleeping bags and gear down. From where they stood, below seemed very far away and small, a postcard. The cliffs were coated in thick lush greenery, spreading open to a coarse black sand beach that dropped into a sapphire sweep. They moved toward the edge of the two-thousand-foot cliffs that stood as guardians of the valley and began their descent.

Leilani, Kainoa, everyone was there and then some. Hi`i was

surprised to see Jane. Since she'd dropped out of hula, their paths hadn't crossed much. She knew Jane went to a different school across town (their paths might not have crossed, but this was Hilo, it was easy to keep tabs). Miss Kapua had mentioned there would be multiple schools on this trip together, but it hadn't occurred to Hi`i that that might mean spending a week working alongside a girl she'd elbowed out of her halau.

HI`I PRETENDED NOT TO see Jane.

Kainoa asked if they could walk together. She shrugged. The morning had beaten her spirit down. She had no energy to do the mental cartwheels Kainoa usually inspired. He drifted off with his friends halfway down when she didn't try to make conversation. Her mind was too occupied with the lost sour poi bread and the inadequate bag of potato chips in her backpack.

Since some kids were faster hikers than others, they were instructed to wait at the valley bottom for everyone else before heading inland, away from the beach and toward the area where Hawaiians kept homesteads and farms.

Leilani and three other girls reached the bottom first, shouldering their bulging backpacks down the steep road as if they were full of pillows. They stood with either hands on hips or arms crossed over chests, watching as the rest of the class slowly clambered toward them, one student in particular. Jane. Who'd made a fatal decision that morning when getting dressed. An unforgivable choice, in this crowd. Of all the things she could have worn on her feet, she'd gone with sandals. T-strap raffia-colored macrame with a paper-thin sole that looked made of canvas.

Jane was trying to compensate for her footwear by hugging the edge of the road, using the cliff face as a railing, taking slow measured steps. Leilani was shaking her head, making gestures with her hands as if she couldn't believe what she was seeing, as if she were personally offended by the footwear.

"Where does she t'ink she is? Where did she t'ink she was going, vacation?"

The other girls murmured their agreement, their words echoing upward.

Jane either didn't hear them or was pretending not to. Hi`i felt pity at first, but that feeling quickly turned into relief. Better the group focus on Jane than her and her lame potato chips. Besides, no one had forced Jane to wear those ridiculously inadequate, silly shoes. And she was, after all, haole. A visit to Waipi`o couldn't mean anything to her, not really. She had no history or place there. But that was beside the point. As much as Hi`i was relieved the spotlight wasn't on her, she still wanted to punch Leilani in her beautiful Polynesian face. She'd been back and forth about wanting to come on this trip for so long, and now that they were there with the valley opening up in front of them, Hi`i didn't want Leilani's presence reminding her of all the seeds of doubt she'd planted. Being in the valley was like traveling back in time a hundred years. Without Leilani there, Hi`i could have imagined herself simply a Hawaiian being home.

CHAPTER 9

Waipi`o rose up around Hi`i and her classmates. Time was swallowing them, cutting them off from the outside. They passed wild chestnut horses drinking from the river and waterfalls cascading down the ripe valley walls. By the time they reached the farm, the sun had burned itself bloody. It was so removed from anything Hi`i had experienced before—no paved roads, no electricity, no fish markets or restaurants, no tourist traps—that she felt sure everything was going to be okay. Sour poi or potato chips, none of it mattered here.

The farm was a wood house on stilts tattooed with termite holes. The wood beams were rough, unvarnished, and varied in shape, as if they had been scavenged, perhaps washed in from a storm. The structure seemed crooked, like the person who had built it had simply eyed the measurements. To Hi`i, it was alive with an inviting weathered warmth.

The property stretched toward the outer reaches of the valley. Acres and acres of rectangular lo`i plots, some flat and dark, others filled with neat lines of taro, green bursting from the mud. It was brilliant even in the fading light.

They were welcomed by Uncle Harvey, the owner of the farm.

The students, still recovering from the hike down, introduced themselves wearily. Uncle Harvey led them to the faucet for a drink. Hi`i slid her feet out of her shoes while she waited in line and dug her toes into the ground. The dirt was complicated, layered, soil mixed with coarse black sand and twigs and leaves from the forest.

Uncle Harvey told them he'd lived there all his life, inheriting the farm from his father, who had inherited it from his father. Life in the lo`i patch was all he knew, he said. It was where things made the most sense to him. Hi`i liked him instantly. He was tall and thin, with the compact body of a much younger man. From his tank top emerged deeply tanned muscular shoulders and a thick strong neck. His salt-and-pepper hair hung down to his chest. His feet and ankles were encased in rubber Japanese fishing tabi, the thick sponge-bottomed socks giving him the leverage he needed to leap from rock to rock across the streams and rivers and through the mud of his valley.

As Uncle Harvey led them around his land, Jane paused at a thin burbling stream and asked if there was somewhere else to cross, which earned another round of groans from Leilani and her friends. Jane's skin shone pale against the rich earth. Hi`i was embarrassed for her and thankful Uncle Harvey was too far ahead to hear. She moved swiftly around Jane toward the deepest, muddiest section and crossed there. As Jane hesitated, Hi`i's feet squished their way through the wet earth toward the other side of the stream.

Uncle Harvey led them to wide wooden platforms where they set up their tents, boys on one and girls on the other. For their meals, they would meet at the tables in the middle. For those four days, this would be their village, he said. They would start and end their days together at the table and spend the rest of their time learning about life working a lo`i. Exhausted from the long day of travel, their faces drooped at the sight of all the unrolled sleeping bags and unhung blue tarps, the unassembled tents. Uncle Harvey laughed, a great booming sound that echoed into the valley behind him.

"First we kau kau!" he cried.

Everyone but Hi`i cheered. The group of roughly seventy stampeded to their belongings, excited to reveal their contributions to the potluck. From backpacks and coolers came a parade of foil-covered trays and bulky plastic containers filled with Chinese noodles, rice, mac salad, teriyaki chicken, pastel-colored mochi, kalua pig and cabbage, beef broccoli. Not a single person had something store-bought. Hi`i let the paper bag containing her chips dangle from a finger, reluctant to claim it as her own. There was enough food to feed twice the amount of people there. It was possible no one would notice. Kainoa, always the one to know when someone was alone or unhappy, appeared at her side. He held up a freezer bag full of fat red lychees and smiled, nudging her shoulder with his until she laughed.

"Come on, take some. Not plenty, but da best of da best from my backyard. My braddah helped me pick um. You get first dibs before I put on da table fo' everybody else."

She shifted the bag in her arms cautiously to the other side of her lap and plucked out a lychee. Kainoa noticed. He raised an eyebrow jokingly.

"Watchu when bring, I no get first dibs?"

"Oh, dis, uh, oh, don't," she stuttered as Nalu, one of Kainoa's friends, ran up to join them and grabbed the paper bag out of her hands.

"What, Kainoa, you giving her all your lychee? What so good she hiding and no like share?"

Nalu opened the bag and pulled out the chips, confusion replacing his teasing tone. "Huh?"

Hi`i snatched the bag of chips and tossed them on the table.

"Who brings potato chips to a potluck? No more even kamaboko dip. Hi`i, your faddah hunt, yeah? Where da smoke meat?"

"Tony's not my dad."

Others began turning their way, but thankfully most of the group's attention stayed on the tables quickly filling with food. Surrounded by greenery and flanked by steep mountainsides, it didn't feel as muggy as Hilo usually did, but the students fanned themselves with their paper plates as they stood in line, peering over shoulders to the dishes they hoped would still be there when their turn came up. As if she could smell something was going on, Leilani gave up her spot in line and edged closer to Nalu.

"The two haole should be in a tent by demselves. I'm sure they like find one bettah place, where they can be all high maka maka togedah, all fancy feet and potato chips. Hi`i, she too good for stay wid us."

Nalu (who Hi`i suspected had a crush on her cousin) nodded eagerly at Leilani as she needled her way into the conversation. From the corner of her eye Hi`i noticed Jane drop her eyes to her feet. For the second time that day, Hi`i felt sorry for her. She crossed her arms over her chest as if pulling her entire body inward.

"Shut up," Hi`i ordered, and then bit her tongue from saying more. Leilani would just turn anything she said into ammunition to keep the fight going. All she wanted was for all of it to stop. She turned her back on the group and walked away as quickly as she could without breaking out in a run.

THIS WAS NOT HOW THE TRIP was supposed to go. None of this would have happened if she had brought the sour poi bread—her mom's bread would have been the hit of the meal. Everyone would have been lining up for a piece. She forked a pile of cold noodles onto her paper plate and skirted the edge of the wood deck until she found a corner that looked out over the loʻi. Evenly planted rows of taro shot out from neat rectangular plots of mud field that stretched toward the edges of the valley. Hovering above the deep brown underbelly, the taro shoots glowed with a vibrant green phosphorescence that held in the twilight. The heart-shaped leaves of the plants were healthy and thick, flat and big as elephant ears. Hiʻi had only ever thought of those leaves in relationship to laulau pulled fresh from the imu, juicy pork and chunks of salt fish surrounded by a thick layer of those very leaves.

Her stomach now sour, the noodles on her plate tasted rubbery and flavorless. Even so, she shoved them in her mouth and forced them down her throat. Only haole wasted food. She was a Naupaka. She knew everything about how life in Hilo was supposed to be. Somehow, she'd find a way to prove it.

THE BOYS WHISTLED THROUGH the night to poke the spirits in the valley because local boys have death wishes inherited from their fathers.

The teachers mapped out who was sleeping where. Hiʻi was assigned to share a tent with Jane. They smiled politely at each other while laying out their sleeping bags. Hiʻi was tempted to apologize for the things she'd said all those years ago on that first day of hula, but Jane either didn't remember or wanted to seem like she didn't, so Hiʻi played along, acting like this was the first time they'd really met. At first Jane didn't understand that they needed to keep the zipper of the tent closed as tight as possible, that they couldn't go out into the night to use the outhouse, that the whistling wasn't funny. Whistling woke up the huaka`ipo, the night marchers.

"Ancient Hawaiian warriors," Hi`i explained when Jane admitted she'd never heard of the night marchers. "Whistling invites them. If you listen at night sometimes you can hear their drums and chanting, warning you they're close. If you have to go outside tonight and you see them, lie on your stomach and put your head down. Don't look them in the eye."

She told Jane about the time she'd gone camping with the uncles at King's Landing and had spent nearly the entire night staring at the moon and listening to the huaka`ipo march in circles around them. Jane closed the zipper and told her about the time she and her parents had gone camping in Yellowstone, back when her mom was still alive. Which made Hi`i wonder if they had more in common than she was ready to admit, one parent each. But no. Jane had her mom, at least the memory of her. Hi`i had no father, not even the ghost of him. She changed the subject, asked Jane what other parks she'd been to, what the mainland was like. The best part of traveling, Jane told her, was boarding the airplane. Lifting off, the rush of air pressing against your chest making your heart beat faster, floating above the clouds, entire cities reduced to tiny specks you could barely see. Hi`i tried to imagine it. As far as she knew, she'd never been on a plane. She'd never considered the endless possibilities they promised, she'd been too busy trying to fit into where she was to think of anywhere beyond the Big Island. The girls eventually fell asleep while compiling a list of destinations around the world that they were going to one day see, Jane naming cities and countries that were like seeds in Hi`i's imagination, places she had not heard of until just then but that turned instantly into dreamscapes offering all she could never fully get where they were. She fell asleep under a blanket of hopes and wishes.

AS THE FIRST HINT OF SUNLIGHT was hitting the tips of the valley walls the next morning, the students burst from their tents. They'd all counted down the days to this trip for months. Now that the time was finally here, they were simmering and spitting, oil in a hot pan, ready to fry. Uncle Harvey laughed.

"What, no one like one long breakfast? I was going make scrambled eggs and Spam."

They struggled to wipe the disappointment from their faces, not wanting to be disrespectful. Uncle Harvey laughed again, pulling on a wide-brimmed, cone-shaped hat that made Hi`i think of rice farmers.

"Okay, okay, you guys like get in there. Good. Grab one granola bar and we go."

The group tore through the box of granola bars on the community table. Amid the cloud of fluttering green wrappers Miss Kapua circled the tables, touching each girl on the shoulder and asking her to come with her for a moment, which they did without question. She wore her long brown hair in a tight knot at the base of her neck the same way she did every day at school and still carried the same air of authority, but there in the valley, she looked younger. More human. Her khaki shorts hugged thick muscular thighs that looked the way legs do after a lifetime of dancing hula. Which made Hi`i wonder who Miss Kapua was outside the classroom. What did she do in her free time? What was her family like? Was she a hula dancer too? She noticed Uncle Harvey giving her teacher a thumbs-up. He held up a hand to the boys and said he wanted to tell them a story. When the group's collective attention turned his way, Miss Kapua led the girls to the far side of the camp and sat them down. She pressed her hands together in prayer position.

"E kala mai. Forgive me for not doing this earlier."

She spoke in that low, quiet way she did when she wanted everyone to work to hear her, to make sure they were all paying attention.

"I want to first say how proud I am of all of you. You've had to earn your way here, and Uncle Harvey welcoming us to his fields is a great honor. When you work the lo`i you learn your connection to your heritage. Those plants are your family, they need you to care for them so they can sustain us through the generations. I know how much you have all looked forward to this part. But . . ." She paused, taking a moment to make eye contact with each girl. "As young women, you must learn a different kind of kuleana. When a plant is young it needs protecting so it can grow strong. Time is needed before it becomes something to harvest, something we can take from and plant new. You are all of the age of crossing over, if you haven't already. No longer children. To be a woman is a sacred thing. Your moon time connects you to the oceans and mahina."

She held up a hand to quiet the groans. Ignoring the crinkled noses, she continued.

"This is the part of valley life we did not discuss in class. A woman's ma`i is a sacred time, a time to spend in quiet, in rest. In ancient Hawai`i, it was treated with reverence. It was seen as how women cleaned out their insides, ensuring future generations. Because of this, women with their ma`i did not work in the fields. To do so was kapu. In this valley, the tradition is respected to this day. Uncle Harvey has asked if anyone is on their ma`i to please refrain from coming into the lo`i. We don't have to make a big deal, it won't be embarrassing. I will be staying behind, and anyone who needs to will stay to help me with work here at camp."

The girls looked from one to the other. Leilani leaned against a rail and rolled her eyes. She did not step forward. No one did. Hi`i thought about the soiled wad of toilet paper she'd dropped in the outhouse that morning. A brown little speck, nothing huge. She wasn't even sure if it qualified as blood. The taro field stretched out before them, the perfect blocks surrounded by jungle, protected and hidden within the towering valley walls. She thought about what they might do that day, what Uncle Harvey might teach them. How the mud would feel between her toes. Of working alongside her classmates who had studied so hard and long for this, of all the weekends they'd spent washing cars and selling shortbread cookies to raise the money to pay for their buses to get here. It wasn't her ma`i. Her body was just in preparation. Besides, this wasn't the time of `aumakua and ali`i. Who would know the difference?

Miss Kapua nodded and led them back to the main camp, where the boys were busy dragging large metal trash cans to the edges of the lo`i to catch the weeds they'd pull. As she'd promised, Miss Kapua announced to the group she'd be staying behind. Giving the girls a knowing glance, she asked if anyone would like to stay behind to help her with the preparations for that evening's dinner. A Japanese girl who always sat in the front row and raised her hand to answer any question the teacher asked stepped forward. The others raised their eyebrows at one another. The girl looked barely old enough to wear a two-piece bathing suit. Hi`i looked away and took a step closer to Uncle Harvey. Just as Miss Kapua was motioning for the girl to follow her to allow the rest of the group to get to work, Jane separated from the group and moved toward the Japanese girl and Miss Kapua. The disappointment on her face was as clear as the waters of a secret lagoon. The girl next to her pulled on her elbow and whispered furiously in her ear, but Jane shook her off.

"It wouldn't be right," she whispered.

Some people were so high maka maka, Hi`i thought.

The boys were done stalling. They entered the mud with the unbridled glee of surfers on the North Shore during a clean winter swell. Hi`i and the girls followed. She hesitated for only a second before she sank her feet into the mud of the lo`i. It was colder than she'd expected and the shiver that moved through her caught her by surprise.

The mud warmed as the sun rose. They worked in three groups, Uncle Harvey rotating among them to deliver instruction and demonstrate technique. One group pulled weeds while one planted seedlings. The third group was put in an older field of mature plants and charged with identifying kalo ready to harvest, reaching under the flapping elephant ear leaves and gently tugging the tuberous roots from their necks, releasing them from the ground only after Uncle Harvey approved. After a time, the groups rotated. Eventually everyone had had a turn working every section.

The weeds offered instant gratification. Thigh-deep in mud, Hi`i could see how much she was needed, could feel it with each suctioned pop of celebration the mud released when she pulled one out. Her hands grew angry and chapped as the morning wore on but that, too, was reward. The glowing cheeks of her classmates told her they were experiencing the same thrill. This was the halau on the day of the hurricane, the sync that she'd experienced, the tribe taking over.

Mid-morning, Hi`i's group was moved to the nursery. She handled a stalk with as gentle a touch as she could manage. Uncle Harvey demonstrated how to drive it like a stake into the flooded field. Again and again she did as generations of her people had done before her, perpetuating the cycle of life, ensuring their continuance, actively participating in her heritage. Mud clung to her rubber boots and her jeans. The boys started getting silly, squirting one another with mud. Kainoa squealed, acting like something below was holding on to his foot and dragging him under. Hi`i turned her back and tried not to laugh. She didn't want to encourage him. Kainoa lit any room he walked into with a happy glimmer; making people laugh was as easy for him as breathing. It was one of the things she liked most about him, but here in the valley, she wished that he'd take something seriously for once.

When the shadows disappeared, Uncle Harvey took his hat from his head and waved it in the air. He flipped it upside down and pretended it was a bowl, scooping from it with his free hand as if holding a spoon. He waited at the edge of the field with a hose.

By the time it was Hi`i's turn to rinse, Nalu and Kainoa were standing in a huddle with a group of kids a few feet away. Leilani had her lips pressed to Nalu's ear. They watched her come forward and bend to wash her hands at the hose. She took her time. She wouldn't give them the satisfaction of rushing.

Then Nalu pointed.

Before Hi`i could finish washing the mud from her hands, Uncle Harvey turned it off and asked her to follow him. Nalu, Leilani, and Kainoa watched silently as she followed him away toward camp. Her ears were on fire as her mind raced. She couldn't figure out what she'd possibly done wrong. She traced her steps backward in her mind.

When they found Miss Kapua, Uncle Harvey asked Hi`i to wait on the bench. They spoke quietly under the leafy canopy of a breadfruit tree, Miss Kapua glancing her way every so often. Finally, Miss Kapua came forward.

"Hi`i, can you come with me?"

Hi`i nodded. The laughing on the other side of camp stopped only when Uncle Harvey returned.

Hi`i and Miss Kapua walked along the outer edge of camp.

"I . . . I don't understand," Hi`i stammered. "Did I do something wrong?"

Miss Kapua sighed and looked at the sky as if searching for answers. She put a hand on Hi`i's shoulder and gave her a soft pat.

"You have your ma`i."

"What, how did you . . ."

Miss Kapua glanced around before gesturing for Hi`i to look behind her. She twisted her neck until she could see her backside. A bright red splotch bloomed from her inseam. She squeezed her eyes shut, dread like an avalanche in her stomach. This was a bad dream.

"Miss Kapua, I didn't know. I swear. I'm sorry, I didn't mean to."

Miss Kapua looked at her sadly. "Okay. But I think you should apologize to Uncle Harvey, and you'll stay back with me for the rest of the trip. No need to cry, Hi`i, but this is serious. I tried to explain this morning. You have to think of the traditions farmers like Uncle Harvey are trying to uphold here in the valley."

"I want to go home."

Miss Kapua asked her if she was sure. She was.

She didn't bother rolling up her sleeping bag. After offering Uncle Harvey the best apology she could muster, cheeks on fire, knowing her sorry was inadequate but having nothing else, she turned away from his face so full of what looked like sorrow for her and stuffed her things into a garbage bag as quickly as she could. She would have preferred him angry. She pulled the messy bag of her things onto her lap as the jeep that had brought down their supplies took her away.

Halfway up, she allowed herself a look back while forcing herself not to think about the satisfaction Leilani was no doubt feeling. Having Kainoa know about her ma`i was mortifying enough. She tried to picture how things would have been different if she'd stayed behind with Miss Kapua and Jane. It wasn't fair. She'd needed to be in the lo`i for reasons Miss Kapua and Uncle Harvey wouldn't have understood. Missing out wasn't as big a deal for Jane as it was for her. She was Hawaiian. Jane wasn't. Jane probably saw this as a nothing field trip, the kind haole take on the mainland, meaningless and forgettable. Maybe she was even glad to have gotten out of getting muddy.

The jeep continued climbing. In the distance she could see a corner of a lo`i patch, the small blurry brown bodies of her classmates among the shimmering green kalo. It was like trying to see through a waterfall.

THE FOLLOWING MONDAY when everyone was due back, Hi`i braced herself. She wasn't thinking of any kapu-breaking repercussions, of any ancient wrath she might be bound to suffer, she was just being practical. Four days in high school land was equal to four years. Field trips, especially overnighters, *especially* multi-nighters, warped both time and allegiances, rattled friendships, and upended hallway hierarchies. They turned popular girls into groupies, reduced the football quarterback into a boy afraid of the dark, and transformed anyone who hadn't been there into an irrelevant pariah. Worse than a cockroach. She didn't know what to expect, but she knew it was going to be bad.

Sure enough, the halls buzzed with inside jokes and secret double meanings, but there wasn't a single stink eye thrown her way. At recess when she saw Kainoa and Nalu coming around a corner, she dipped into the bathroom and stayed put until the tardy bell. She needn't have bothered. They hadn't noticed her, nor had anyone else. She was invisible. She spent the rest of the day stumbling from one corner of campus to another, a weak swimmer doggy-paddling in uncharted water.

The silence hit her harder than she would have imagined. The days she had forfeited had done the worst possible thing. They had erased her from her own world.

CHAPTER 10

That Saturday morning after Hi`i returned, a tragedy. The waves had been mellow, no reason to be on alert; the three who had paddled out didn't seem to be in any danger. No more than usual.

For the hours and hours that the Coast Guard helicopters chopped back and forth later in the day, and the search-and-rescue divers widened their radius, the two still there held on to their half-truth version of the events leading up to the moment they saw the boy go under. They didn't do it to hide anything—a drowning was a drowning. Boys was just being boys. The bulai was automatic, knee jerk.

But they had been buss-up drunk Friday night down at the party at Old Airport. They probably should have slept in. They were just having a good time, being boys. `A`ole pilikia. No trouble. They were good boys. Das why hard, we said.

They'd come at dawn, straight from the party. The sets had rolled in slow. The nose of the boy's board had pearled, his body was an inch too forward. But it happens. He was good, better than average. Both of the other boys insisted they thought at the time, watching from their own surfboards, that he was going to make it. Garenz. He could handle anything.

The wave had launched him up and over. Classic wipeout. There'd been a riptide, a murky ripple, but they'd seen it, they knew that water better than their own `ōkoles. He was a blue-ribbon swimmer. They stared down into the sets waiting for his head to pop to the surface, snorting hune kai from his nose.

The ocean spat the surfboard out in bits and chunks, fiberglass that cut our hopes, diced it to pieces.

A diver surfaced with his hand up.

The water was beautiful, so mālie that day. The surface glittered, brilliant and timeless. How could something that evokes such calm be so treacherous? Why are the most beautiful things in the natural world also the most lethal?

The ocean gave us no reasons, no anger, no apology. It answered to no one. We belong to the `āina, the `āina does not belong to us. There are no answers, just facts. It gives, it takes.

Aiyah. Water, the bringer of life, the taker of breath. No can, this kine. It rained, it poured. Clouds huli maka flipped a bucket of tears on our heads as we wailed.

WE CARVED THE BOY'S NAME into the cross we placed at the lookout. Sadness like a blanket. Too often, this kine. Our mourning clothes still in the hamper from the funerals of the weekend before and the weekend before that. We emptied the fridge and lit the stove because there was going to be a memorial. Gotta eat. We picked the flowers with no smell. The birds, they chirped and sang and we forgave them.

The boy shouldn't have died. He was one of the good ones, kalohe, always making trouble that made his mama laugh. Had a shelf in his room sagging with baseball trophies. He stayed away from the batu and put up his fists only when some dummy who didn't know what was what made him. He liked the beer, but no more than anybody else did. He worked sometimes with his pop laying concrete. No GED for him. He was going to get his high school diploma, graduate with cap and gown and everything. He was buying his own tools, he was going to manage a crew himself that summer after graduation if he didn't go pro. He was maybe going to be the next Doug Capilla and play for the White Sox, or John Matias for the Cardinals. None of that possible anymore.

The calendar didn't pay attention. Merrie Monarch marched forward. It was time to sing until the hurt went away.

No one except Hi`i put two and two together. The blood of her spirit had seeped into the land and infected it. Her decision to violate kapu in Waipi`o was a violation against the `āina. A desecration that consequently impacted everyone connected to it. The dead boy's sister was in Hi`i's class. They'd been down in the lo`i together. His sister had brought Hi`i's curse home with her.

THE GUILT FOLLOWED HER EVERYWHERE, relentless, punishing. Hi`i searched for a way to redeem herself, or at the very least do something to make things right. Enough blood had been shed.

It was her mom's shop, Aloha Spirit, that finally gave her the idea. Hi`i typed MADE IN HAWAII into the label maker and glued it to the bottom of one of Laka's lauhala creations. Then she did it to everything else in the room. Laka's work had never brought in a whole lot, little bonus sales here and there that helped when her Aloha Spirit paycheck fell short, but after all that had happened and with Merrie Monarch on the horizon, Hi`i was going to turn her mom into a bestseller. It wouldn't bring the boy back or erase what she'd done in Waipiʻo, but she had to do something to make her feel like she was making amends, one way or another.

IT HAD BEEN TONY who had picked her up from the Waipiʻo lookout point when she left the school trip early. She spent the entire drive home staring out the window trying not to cry while Tony chain-smoked cigarettes and steered with his knee. For once, she was grateful Tony and his shoulder-shrugging ambivalence toward her was back. Even though her mom hadn't hit her in years, Hiʻi used their time in the car to steel herself for the beatdown of a lifetime that her mom was sure to give her, but what was waiting for her at home was so much worse. Instead of a beatdown, there was a formal politeness similar to the way her mom treated the people who shopped at Aloha Spirit, impersonal and stiff. Like her invisibility cloak at school, it was a gulf that appeared out of nowhere, a distance that was so much worse than any lickins would have been. Laka was buried in unfinished projects she needed to sell at the Merrie Monarch craft fair and distracted with her pregnancy. She made room at the table and pushed a pair of scissors toward Hiʻi. They had worked silently side by side all the days that she'd been scheduled to be working the loʻi. If her mom noticed the MADE IN HAWAII labels, she didn't say so.

When they took a break from the crafts, Hiʻi dyed her skirts for her halau's performance and Laka weaved her lauhala until it was time for bed. Then they retreated to their separate rooms with hardly a word. It was the farthest Hiʻi had ever felt from her mom.

The next few days after the drowned boy's memorial passed in a blur as she searched for a way to explain her side of the story, beginning with Tony and the bread, to explain exactly how and why things in Waipi`o had gone so horribly wrong. Laka knew about Hi`i getting her ma`i while down there, but Hi`i wasn't sure if her mother fully comprehended the extent of her crime. She had not just gotten her ma`i and asked to come home early. She had knowingly and willingly gone into the lo`i. Knowingly and willingly violated kapu. She felt compelled to confess that she'd been the reason the boy died, but one minute passed into another and another and the time never came. When they were done with one craft they moved on to the next, Laka pushing a box of metal clips in her direction and handing her a glue gun. They weren't big moneymakers, hair clips for a few bucks apiece, but Hi`i glued those tiny lauhala flowers onto those clips as if her life depended on it, as if they were going to make any sort of difference. She fell asleep at the table with the gun in her hand.

SOON THE HALAU'S MERRIE MONARCH performance preparation squeezed out everything else and Hi`i became almost busy enough to forget what had happened. There was no time for school, no time for anything except dying the fabrics, sewing the seams, collecting the shells, drying them, cleaning them, stamping, carving, weaving. There was barely even time to practice their dance. She knew it, though. She wouldn't blank, hadn't since that time Kumu called her out for it. In all her years of dancing, she'd never actually performed at Merrie Monarch, but she wasn't nervous. This was her destiny. She wanted to fast-forward through this, to not have this be her first year but rather her hundredth, to already know all the pits and grooves of that famous stage.

In the week leading up, she got to the halau early and stayed late.

She cleaned the dead leaves and flowers from the kuahu. When they practiced their oli, she made sure her voice was heard. After Merrie Monarch, she would ask for Kumu's blessing and assistance to study to be the next Miss Aloha Hula. She was ready to dance out there on her own, to win the flower crown that had been worn by her mother. But first things first.

MERRIE MONARCH ALWAYS BEGAN the day after Easter, Hawai`i's very own day of resurrection. That Monday, every hotel lobby in town became a stage, music bursting onto the street, vendors lining the sidewalks. We hummed our way to work, bright pink hibiscus pinned behind our ears. We locked up early, the smell of hulihuli chicken too tempting and the bosses all looking the other way. We headed to the airport, leis in hand, to pick up all the aunties and cousins coming from off island. Instead of school, kids woke up early to report to their kumus for one last practice or an early morning solo in a hotel lobby. We brought our coin purses and hauled our savings to the stadium because the weeklong Merrie Monarch Craft Fair had begun and we needed one of everything.

Hi`i worried about her mom lugging the boxes to their booth. Laka was now doing laps across Hilo Bay every morning, church she called it, but even with that exercise, her opu was starting to look like a bubble about to pop. She'd kicked Tony out again, this time for selling pakalolo, but Hi`i suspected he hadn't gone far, probably sulking out in the bush somewhere with his friends, hunting pigs and getting stoned, but where he was wasn't the point. He wasn't around to help, and Laka was too hapai to do everything herself. Hi`i would have helped except she was scheduled to go up mauka with the halau to pick the palapalai and lehua they needed for their leis. Kumu only invited performing dancers to accompany her up the mountain to pick the flowers and ferns and learn the protocol. Hi`i had been waiting years for her turn. It was a rite of passage. Laka encouraged her to go.

Kumu liked to describe hula as the memory of a winter flood. Of a tree bending in a hurricane. Of the eruption of Kilauea. Of the seaweed rocking in a tide. When a hula invokes the mana of an element, the rains of Hamākua or the white cold of Poliahu, that element is then incorporated into the costumes. Since their halau was performing choreography that told of a story between Pele and her sister Hi`iaka, the ferns and greenery Hi`i and the others would wear around their necks, ankles, and on their heads would come from the groves of Pele's home on Kilauea near Halema`uma`u Crater. As a former Miss Aloha Hula crown-holder, Laka knew even better than her daughter what it took to prepare, as well as the significance of going with the halau to gather what they needed. She waved off Hi`i's offers to stay, insisting she would be fine. Still, guilt followed Hi`i to the Keaukaha Gym parking lot, where the white cargo vans waited to take the dancers up to Volcano. She was one of the last to arrive. Kumu waved her over.

"Your mom doing da craft fair by herself?"

Hi`i nodded.

"She almost due. She need your help?"

"No, she's good."

Kumu's face said it all. Hi`i knew that look. She put her hands together and begged. "Please, Kumu. I need to go. My mom said I should. I going help her when we get back. Most everything is already done. I'll help her break down when we get back. Please."

Kumu's mind was made up. She turned toward the van and got in.

"There will be another year to see the groves. We will get enough for everyone to use," she said through the window.

"But I've waited so long." The whine in her voice was embarrassing. But Hi`i *had* waited. Every year she'd hovered on the periphery while the older, performing group of their halau returned from weekends together, their car trunks full of plastic tubs and damp newspapers loaded with ferns and flowers, leaves and shells they'd collected. The dancers had seemed so bonded to one another, even more connected to the process of their dance. All these years she'd wondered about the gathering places where the ceremonial flora grew, kept secret to protect them from being overpicked. She'd counted the days until she could be one of those dancers.

Leilani smiled and waved through the tinted back window as the van pulled away. Hi`i flipped her off but only for a second, in case Kumu was watching.

Hi`i spent the rest of the day tucking flower pins into buns of hair and minding the cash box while Laka went back and forth to the lua, grumbling every time that the baby was making her shishi so much she might as well stay in the bathroom the rest of her pregnancy.

Hi`i tried to want to be there. Tried to care. But the more she tried, the more she wished she'd forced her way onto the van. There were plenty of aunties who could have helped her mom, and Laka barely noticed Hi`i was there. Everything sold. People ran their fingers over Hi`i's MADE IN HAWAII label and handed over their money. If Laka noticed, she didn't say so.

Tony showed up with lunch, chicken katsu with rice and potato mac salad and a kimchee burger with fries, acting like he'd been around all day, as if everything was fine, holding out the foil-covered plates of food like peace offerings. Hi`i said she wasn't hungry. Laka slapped her arm and told her no be rude. Hi`i slid toward the other side of the table, straightening what was left of the tray of lauhala bracelets and ignoring Laka and Tony.

Hi`i was tired of the back-and-forth of her mother and Tony fighting. She watched from a distance as Tony put a hand on Laka's stomach and held it there. Hi`i mumbled that she was going to eat her burger outside. She grabbed the food that Tony had brought for her but stuffed it into the nearest garbage can as soon as she was out of their sight.

She did two laps around the building, trying to shake off her gloom. When she got back to their booth, Tony was rubbing Laka's back. Hi`i cleared her throat.

Tony and Laka glanced at each other. Then Tony stood and asked Hi`i if they could talk. Laka looked ready to punch her in the face if she said no.

He dropped to his knees in the parking lot. "I tole your maddah I sorry for what I did to her, but I sorry to you, too." He held a hand to his heart as though he were pledging allegiance. "I goin' do right. No more drinking, and no pakololo at da house. I goin' take care dis family. Be a good man, a good faddah. I promise."

Hi`i was hit by a wave of curiosity laced with sadness. She'd always only seen Laka in the context of being her mom. Of course she was a person outside of that, but what was that person like? What had she dreamed and hoped for? Had Laka imagined her life would turn out this way, struggling to make ends meet and a boyfriend who was good when he wanted to be, and not when he didn't? Laka had been famous, a star. The glowing offshoot of the esteemed Hulali Naupaka. Miss Aloha Hula. Although Hulali remained a complete mystery to Hi`i as a grandmother, her presence and influence in Hilo was palpable enough to exist even in her absence. Hulali's strength, singular focus, and dedication to Hawaiian culture were legendary. Laka was different. She could have been anything she wanted. Was this the life she had chosen, or a life she'd been reduced to?

Hi`i was frustrated and tired of seeing her mom cry herself to sleep and doing everything on her own while pregnant. Tony wasn't the reason Hulali continued to stay away or why their family was seemingly so different from everybody else's, but he wasn't exactly a catch. Although, if Hi`i had been asked to come up with a picture of how life might be with enough money, without the occasional slap in the face, without the frantic search when the rolling papers went missing or when the beer ran low, the only examples she had of parents and how they operated were from movies or TV, but those were all about haole and haole problems. Hilo was not the mainland. When she tried to imagine the kind of guy she'd prefer her mom to be with, she drew a blank.

Tony got to his feet and waved to a group of aunties on their way into the fair. Instead of replying to him or trying to make sense of all the thoughts exploding in her mind, Hi`i closed her eyes and thought about hula. In all the stories and legends she'd danced, never once had she questioned Pele's fiery flashes of anger, her bursts of jealousy, the violence of her passion. If her mother and Tony were gods, she would have told their story without thinking twice. Pele fell in love repeatedly with beings who hadn't necessarily brought her roses on Valentine's Day.

She imagined how a hula about Tony and her mother might look. Legends offered background, where so-and-so had come from, the origin story. She wondered who Tony had been in high school, if he'd been a Kainoa or a Nalu. She wondered who her mother had been, if it was anything like the way she was now. Her mother had had Hulali Naupaka for a mother. A woman who the entire community exalted as a leader, role model, and trailblazer. What kind of pressure and expectation had come with Laka being her firstborn, her hiapo? How much of that had shaped Laka into the person she was now?

Hi`i tried to imagine what a hula about herself might look like. She had always believed hula could explain nearly everything in her life. But if she were a hula, there was no clear story to tell. Her beauty queen cousin Leilani belonged to Hilo and Hilo belonged to her. Even Jane had a clear place—she was haole, forever outside with all the others who had moved here from somewhere else, and that was the end of it. Hi`i, on the other hand, was stuck in a freak body that did not look like it belonged to her family. Neither outside nor in, stuck in the doorway between two worlds.

Hilo was a tangled happy mass of family, all connected in one way or another. But Hi`i felt like a stray piece of string dangling out the side. She closed her eyes and prayed. If the universe and all the gods and goddesses of the world had any compassion whatsoever, the baby in Laka's opu would come out looking like Hi`i. Not Tony or Laka or anyone else. The baby would be who she could share her stuck-in-a-doorway life with.

Not that Pele and Hi`iaka were the ones to be looking to for an example of sisters without issues. After Pele carried the younger Hi`iaka in her armpit to cross the seas to live in the lava womb of Kilauea, Hi`iaka was tasked with going to Kaua`i to find Lohi`au, Pele's lover, and bringing him back to her sister. Before she leaves, Hi`iaka asks Pele to watch over her ohi`a forest. Hi`iaka is gone a long time, and Pele begins to fear her sister has fallen in love with Lohi`au. She burns Hi`iaka's groves to ash in a jealous rage. Hi`iaka finds out, and goes to seek the only thing that could possibly keep Pele away: water.

Pele is the land, and Hiʻiaka is everything that grows upon that land.

There is no fire without the forest, no forest without the fire. They are intricately connected. Neither sister can destroy the other without also destroying herself.

For Hiʻi, this meant the baby might be her salvation, but there was also the chance it would be something quite the opposite.

CHAPTER 11

On the morning of Hiʻi's first Merrie Monarch performance, she woke to the sudden realization that somewhere in the audience later that day, her tutu would be watching her perform. If she'd ever met her, she didn't remember. Would the legend be at all the way she imagined her to be? Given that Hulali was one of the festival's founders and the organizing committee put much effort into dedicating a portion of the opening ceremonies to her contributions to the hula community, Kumu Hulali never missed a Merrie Monarch. But up until now Hiʻi had never been part of the performing group and Laka had always said she preferred staying home to watch the performances on TV, though she never skipped the parade on Saturday. Which meant they'd never bumped into each other. Or at least that was what Hiʻi had always assumed. Now she thought it more likely that Laka had made sure they didn't.

Over the years, she had compiled a collection of snapshots, borrowed memories cut from other people's moments, observed from a distance, a cousin getting chewed out by a grandma who thought him overdue a lesson on respect, a grandma showing up after practice with arare and mochiko chicken just because, a flock of grandmas batting woven frond fans in unison while chaperoning a class field trip to Nani Mau Gardens. She imagined being smothered by a musty mothball sweater hug and wondered if Leilani got a different version of Tutu Hulali than she did. While she couldn't believe there was any truth to what Leilani had said about her being the reason their grandma was so absent, she didn't have any evidence to contradict it. But today she was feeling giddy with hope. Her mother couldn't stand between them anymore. Hi`i imagined Hulali coming toward her first with a keen side eye, critical but ultimately approving after seeing her dance. She conjured scenario after scenario of exactly how their first meeting would go, her coming off stage fresh from her hula and being swept up into her tutu's arms, or maybe her tutu standing proud and tall in the front row, giving her a standing ovation. She gave it more thought than she did her performance. But it wasn't nerves. She was excited. Whatever shape her grandma would come in, it would be the shape of the hole living inside her. They'd be a normal Keaukaha family, she a normal Keaukaha kid, once Hulali was back. She was the missing puzzle piece.

Hi`i allowed herself a minute to stare into the silver-gray sky threatening rain clouds through her bedroom window before pulling herself out of bed to face the list (as long as a river) of things she had to do before she could step foot onto that stage. She threw on a wrinkled cotton shirt and rummaged through her laundry basket for a pair of shorts before helping her mom squeeze her expanding body into a mu`umu`u. Since his great plate lunch apology, Tony had moved back into the house, but that didn't mean he'd become useful.

Laka helped spread Hi`i's hula skirts flat in the backseat of the car so they wouldn't get wrinkled. Together they made sure her leis stayed happily encased in their moist paper towel nests as they moved the big plastic container from the fridge to the trunk. Hi`i made sure her kupe`e were in her bag. Then they headed to the Edith Kanaka`ole Stadium. Hi`i said nothing about Hulali, and neither did Laka.

Following her mother through the double doors at the rear of the open-air stadium, Hi`i felt as though they were passing through a portal that existed only for the chosen ones, the anointed, those who dedicated their lives to hula. A symphony of greenery and bright bursting color coming from leis around necks, oversized headpieces, lei po`o, and the fronds plastered over seats and walls had transformed the space into a moving, living garden. Halaus moved like schools of fish, their dancers uniform in shirts proudly displaying their halau name. Frazzled parents and assistant kumu swam in and out and around the groupings. The heavy perfume of ferns and flowers that filled the stadium was tinged with hair spray and ironing starch. A handful of spectators had begun milling up and down the tiered stands, searching for the best place to sit.

Hi`i was, oddly, still not nervous about performing. She waited for the jitters, expected them, but they never arrived. Like the dancers around her, she was too busy checking the knots of her skirts, her kupe`e, and trying to tie her lei po`o to her head tight enough so it wouldn't drop over her eyes while they were performing, but not so tight as to cut off circulation. She did keep one eye open for Hulali. She'd studied every picture of her tutu she'd ever seen. She'd know if the woman was nearby.

It wasn't easy keeping track of all the faces coming in and out. The backstage dressing area was a Category 4 hurricane, two hundred plus hula moms and stagehands in a bouquet of aloha wear running around to complete the finishing touches on stage decorations and dancing costumes, shouting for bobby pins or a sewing needle, for extension cords to curling irons. The cacophony ricocheted off the empty bleachers, bouncing against the sloped rain cover. She had been going to the stadium since her hanabata days, she knew every corner and crevice of it, but now towers of cardboard flower boxes, mountains of crumbled damp newspapers, and foam coolers had turned the normally familiar concrete space into new territory. Hi`i felt a gap between herself and the scene, as if she were peeping into a window or staring at a television screen, observing without being a part of what was happening. She imagined she was her mom taking her first step on stage before her winning Miss Aloha Hula performance.

The feeling of being on the outside looking in did not disappear once she located her halau and changed into her costume. Even wearing skirts and lei po`o identical to her hula sisters, there was an ominous gap dividing her from everyone else. Taking her place in line as they got ready to mount the stage, she placed her fists on her hips but could not imagine going a step farther. They would just have to perform without her. Her mouth watered as if she were about to vomit. She felt light-headed, tingly. She began rehearsing the apology she would no doubt have to give Kumu later that night. The first chance she'd ever had to dance for her tutu, and she was going to wimp out.

The stands were now nearly full. People waved down those they'd been saving seats for. Others shouted their hellos across aisles. The lights on the stage went on. The entire stadium went silent almost instantly.

When Hi`i heard the slap of Kumu's ipu and swept across the stage to her position, muscle memory and the months of practice took over. There was no thinking, no scanning the audience. The story took over. She raised her arms above her head and became Kahalao-puna, daughter of Kahaukani. She was the Mānoa winds that turned seamlessly into Kauakuahine, the falling Mānoa rains, explaining the union of the winds and rains of Mānoa Valley. Hiʻi's body became the glowing light of Kahalaopuna's happiness and beauty, her back-and-forth tug of the winds and the rains moving throughout the valley. The group swayed from one end of the stage to the other. The stadium melted away. There was no audience, only the dancer in front of her and on either side. There was the switch in formation and the chant as the winds whipped the rains across the valley's peaks. There were the marks she had to hit. Her heart beat in her ears so loud she could barely hear the others. When they moved to their knees, the rain of their hands sinking into the earth, Hiʻi tried to sneak a peek of the audience, at the space with the seats reserved for the Importants, where her tutu would be sitting. She wanted to glimpse Hulali, to catch her eye for only a second, just long enough to see a hint of recognition, of any pride she might have in seeing her grand-daughter dancing in the halau she had founded all those years ago. But as soon as she did so she found herself a half second out of step. She could either scan the audience or perform; be a part of her halau or be a Naupaka. At that moment, there was no way to do both. She readjusted her focus back to her group, forced herself back inside the story she was helping tell.

It was over before it began. The crowd cheered as they chanted their oli back the way they had come, reversing down the gangplank until they were out of sight. Breathless and full of adrenaline, they lingered at the foot of the stage, hugging one another. They had done it. After they peeled off their costumes and climbed the bleachers to watch the other performances, Hiʻi was finally able to devote herself to catching

Hulali's attention. But by that time the seat reserved for her tutu in the middle of the Importants was empty, if it had been occupied at all. A reporter caught Hulali outside the stadium. The audience hushed as the interview played live on the large television monitors near the stage. Hulali looked directly at the camera when she spoke.

"This continued legacy is as important to my family as it is to the people of Hilo. To protect this tradition is a great honor and duty."

The reporter asked if Hulali had any more potential Miss Aloha Hulas up her sleeve. From her seat, Hi`i held her breath. Hulali smiled and shrugged. "My daughter is hapai, who knows? Dea so many young ones throughout Hawai`i dedicated to hula now, so much heart and talent . . ."

Hulali kept on but Hi`i stopped listening. If Hulali had seen her perform, it had made no difference. Hi`i did not exist to her.

IN THE END, THERE HAD been no need to seek her tutu out. Hulali came to them. Pulled right up to the house in Keaukaha that night in her rental car and ascended the front steps as if she'd never left. Hi`i didn't need to be told it was Hulali. Her energy was a force like a wind. A moment before she reached the front door, Laka went rigid and silently made a motion with her hand for Hi`i to go upstairs. From her room above, she pressed her ear to a crack in the wood floor to try to hear into the kitchen, but it wasn't until their rumbling spilled into the driveway and she was able to press her ear against the window screen that she caught any decipherable word. What she overheard didn't give her any insight into who her tutu was, but it did reveal something she'd never considered. The divisions within the Naupaka Ohana ran deeper than Hi`i would have ever guessed.

***

MOTHER AND DAUGHTER HAD PICKED UP where they'd left off, a fight that had been going on since the time the first navigators were in their canoes charting the stars to find the islands. Hulali accused Laka of losing sight of their mission, of rejecting her role in the family and saddling their name with gossip and speculation. Of forgetting all the suffering and sacrifice that had been required for the deed to their land, of the blood spilled. Laka scoffed. "I well aware of all da blood, Ma. Truss me, I take dis as serious as anybody."

"Den why you going put dis house in Hiʻi's name? Why you playing dis game?"

"How anyt'ing going change if we no force dem fo' change?" Laka's voice lowered, Hiʻi couldn't make out the rest of her answer. When their voices finally rose enough to be heard again, the argument had moved on to what made a Hawaiian a Hawaiian, or rather, what Hawaiians were supposed to do about being Hawaiian. Hiʻi didn't understand it all, but eventually Hulali belted out a long defense of OHA and her work there, hitting the rail of the porch with her palm as if to punctuate her point before turning to go.

Laka followed Hulali down the driveway saying OHA was corrupt, just a puppet organization that ultimately bent to the will of the Big Five, the handful of companies started by missionaries and foreigners. The answer wasn't in wasting time pushing papers for an organization with no ultimate power to fight the corruption still rampant in Hawaiʻi politics. Hulali and her colleagues were deluding themselves, focusing on all the wrong things.

Laka's voice cracked in anger. "Watchu doing is part of da problem. Sovereignty da only answer, da only solution. You no ask one occupying government for permission to reinstate, or ask dem nicely to treat us better. Ridiculous. People getting pushed out of Keaukaha now too. Only a matter of time befo' we all lose. You still trust da state goin do da right t'ing?"

Laka said she'd heard rumors that OHA was mishandling the money coming from trust lands. That it was one thing for haole to come to Hawai`i and pillage but quite another for Hawaiians to take food out of each other's mouths.

At that, Hulali got back in her car, slamming the door. She rolled down her window and leaned out, pointing at Laka's opu and then the house, the yard, the stretch of road, the beach on the other side.

"I fighting to make sure all dis land stays ours. For dat baby, and dat baby's baby, and dat baby's baby," she said.

Laka rubbed her belly protectively. "So am I," she shot back. "Being here, raising my girl, tryin fo' figure out a way to get out from undah da foot of America—dat's me fighting. You not doing not'in but exactly wat captive people do—following da rules of da captors t'inkin' somehow dat going set you free. Only going dig your hole deepah."

Listening to them, Hi`i had a hard time sorting who was for what. Their land, their house, she had pictured living there always, her own kids running around the front yard one day. Why did Hulali consider that a bad thing? Did she think Hi`i wasn't going to care for it properly, or lose it somehow? The only thing that was loud and clear was that the fight between her mother and her tutu was a storm that wasn't going to pass anytime soon. Her performance that day hadn't been enough, hula hadn't healed anything. From what Hi`i could see, everyone agreed there was plenty wrong. Problem was that no one agreed on what would make things right.

PLENTY WRONG INDEED, we knew.

For one thing, in the months leading up to Hi`i's performance at Merrie Monarch, it stopped raining. Instead of our usual soggy Hilo morning blanket of clouds, there was blue sky that wouldn't go away. The towels on the line held their shape when we took them down— they was so stiff they could have been surfboards. Keaukaha Market's permanent parking lot puddle of mud dried up for the first time any of us could remember. Up mauka, the rain catchment tanks went dry. We started hauling water from town. We stopped flushing. The cloudless blue kept on. Sticky turned to static. We didn't want to bachi; we acted like we didn't see when the ants circled around a drop of water that escaped the hose.

No can buy water *and* pay rent *and* buy food. They promised us land. They promised us water. We'd done what they told us to, we took our birth certificates and paperwork to DHHL to get on that list. We waited and waited and paid for rented land with the last pennies in our pockets.

Maybe it was the dry skies sending sound through a crackling amplifier, making the airplanes coming into Hilo Airport louder. Our kitchen windows rattled every time a plane dove down onto the tarmac. The water in the pot rippled. The airport was built in Territory days, a strip barely bigger than a paddleboard that ran the length of Keaukaha's back like a spinal column.

We went to the back porch, pulled the laundry drying outside on the line. They were there with their measuring sticks, tromping along our side of the chain-link fence that marked the boundary of where we were allowed to live our lives.

With knowledge comes the burden of responsibility. We were never revolutionaries. Only accidental activists. Once you know something, you can't unknow it. Once you see the crime, closing your eyes to it makes it yours.

THE SNIP SNIP SLICE HULA:

Keaukaha wasn't always full of tour buses coming in on the regular and the county telling us what we could do along our shores and in our backyards. Count backward from this almost–Merrie Monarch faceoff between the Naupaka wahine what, twenty maybe thirty years ago? The fifties, the forties. We went where we wanted, did what we wanted. In Keaukaha it was safe to live Hawaiian, to run through the yards, climb the trees, pick the fruit, dive, throw net. We left our broken car in the yard just in case we could fix it. People called us poor, but they didn't know. We always had plenty food, plenty everything that mattered. When it came time for pa`ina, we dug the imu in the backyard no problem. Everything was everybody's. They called us Communists. Bah. Commu-nothing. We Hawaiian.

Hilo was easy to figure in those days. There was an unspoken agreement among its sections. The high maka maka lived on Banyan Drive. We didn't bother them, they didn't bother us. The bridge over the harbor and Suisan, that was where the Japanese put down before the tidal wave swept them inland. The business district, the theater, the bowling alley, owned by haole we'd never seen. The argument between Laka and Hulali after Hi`i's Merrie Monarch performance?

Never would have happened. We trusted the Hawaiian Homelands Act to do what it said—keep the royal lands held in trust for the native Hawaiian people, for those of us who could hold on to them, to be used by the native Hawaiian people, to fish, to plant, to live. To allow the perpetuation of our way of life. It wasn't a great deal, and it didn't help all of us, but something was better than nothing.

We weren't throwing up our hands in joy about living under America's foot, but what could we do? We had Keaukaha. Where we could hold our heads up high. Go barefoot, dress how we like, talk how we like, live how we like. We gathered at Puhi Bay. As long as we didn't break that unspoken rule of crossing the bridge, as long as we kept to our neighborhood and didn't give anybody a hard time about what was happening outside of it, we would be okay. We wasn't going to make a stink.

Time was an aʻama crab, scrabbling sideways, always moving but never going anywhere.

As Hiʻi got ready for her Merrie Monarch performance with high hopes of impressing her tutu, the notices came that some of us would have to move. That's when we started to think maybe we wasn't going to be okay, that Keaukaha wasn't as safe as we thought. That's when we had to turn back the pages of time and read:

> The Act of May 31, 1944, c. 216, § 2, 58 Stat. 260, repealed so much of the above section as designates the lands hereinafter described as "available lands," and restored such lands to their previous status under the control of the Territory of Hawaii . . .

(Wait. By "restoring their status under control of the Territory," did the writers of this mean restoring those lands to status of STOLEN?)

. . . comprising several parcels of land as follows:

portions of lots 96, 97, 182, 183, 184, 185, Desha Avenue, and twenty-five-foot alley . . .

the true azimuth and distance . . .

. . . and the coordinates of said point being two thousand five hundred and twenty and thirty-one one-hundredths feet north and fifteen thousand five hundred and fifty-three one-hundredths feet east . . .

(Snip snip slice, no one will notice.)

. . . thence running by azimuths measured clockwise . . .

And on and on it went. By now your eyes have glazed and you skipping through, yeah? You think that's by accident?

Think about it: How do you cover your ʻōkole and create public documents that you don't want anyone to read? Same way you answer a question you don't want to answer. Say too much, talk in circles, point in multiple directions, turn right and then left and then spin them around until they're so dizzy they drop to the ground and forget what they were asking.

Pay attention.

WE TOOK OUT OUR RULERS, read line by line.

The airport wanted to expand. No can. Those designated Homestead lands. Protected.

Ah, but can.

Take whatever they need.

If no can, no can. If can, can.

Can.

THEY HAD STOLEN A FINGER, then a hand. Then an arm, a shoulder, a hip, a leg, and soon the entire body. Now they wanted our breath, our soul.

We finished reading. They had land for those of us getting booted out of Keaukaha, and land for us still waiting for any land at all. On the award letter, relieved tears left water marks like the rain that used to fall.

Try wait.

The award said in order to get the land, we had to build a house on it. How we was supposed to turn five dollars an hour into something with a roof and four walls? DHHL said the subdivision process meant they had to divide the land parcels, had to bring in water since the area didn't have a groundwater well, and had to build roads. But that took money they didn't have, they said.

How long until the money comes? Shoulder shrugs. Seven years, give or take.

We'd already waited that long for land. What was another seven years?

We trundled back to Hilo and called Hulali in Oʻahu. She was planning to come to Hilo for Merrie Monarch anyway, but when she saw the papers she booked an earlier flight. Everything would be okay, she said. Trust, she said. As in: rely on the truthfulness or accuracy of; hope or expect confidently. The law was on our side.

Hulali studied the maps and did the math. Twenty-eight thousand acres of ʻāina (of the two hundred thousand acres initially set aside to give back to Hawaiians, cut from the original two million acres of crown land stolen from the kingdom) had been awarded so far.

That math, though!

Hulali kept digging. Twenty thousand acres were unaccounted for. She put a magnifying glass on the maps of Waiakea, the `āina surrounding the Prince Kuhio Plaza. As Hi`i was laying out her Merrie Monarch skirts, her tutu was taking her findings to DHHL.

Ahhh, no can, DHHL said. The Waiakea lands weren't agriculture, not zoned for residential. They saw her to the exit. They were doing some restructuring, they said.

She paused in the doorway. Hadn't they rezoned a portion of Waiakea land before, to build Prince Kuhio Plaza? Oh, but that was different, they said. That was to help Hilo. The mall brought jobs, which got people off welfare and food stamps. See?

Hmmm. But you said you don't have funds to develop and that's why no one ever leaves the wait list?

While Hi`i was stepping out onto that stage and scanning the audience for the only person she hoped would be there, DHHL was looking at the clock and seeing Hulali to the door. She got in her car and headed to the stadium where we gathered, Merrie Monarch wrapped around our shoulders like a blanket, our last remaining possession.

CHAPTER 12

Wednesday, Exhibition Night, might have been the end of Hi`i's official involvement with Merrie Monarch, but Merrie Monarch itself had only just begun. On Friday the halaus would perform their hula `auana and Saturday their hula kahiko, but Thursday was Miss Aloha Hula night. Hi`i snuck into the Merrie Monarch stadium by hanging out in the parking lot, watching delivery trucks come and go, until she saw someone unloading flowers from the back of a truck and got the gumption to act. She offered to help carry a box and then floated through the backstage cyclone, careful not to stand too long in any one place until she was sure security wasn't onto her. Miss Aloha Hula night was ticketed entry only.

It was clear even before they dressed who the competitors were. Of all the fluttering, they were the calm ones, the ones with their foreheads pressed to the foreheads of their kumus saying pule. Two Hi`i recognized. One, Kanani, was a year ahead of her in school. The other had graduated the year before, but Hi`i couldn't remember her name. Even in their understated pareos, hair and makeup in unfinished states of application, they stood taller than everyone else. The proud tilt of their necks and taut bodies were full of promises. Hi`i wished she could travel back in time, back to the night her mother won the title. She'd stared at the pictures of Laka on stage enough times to be able to perfectly reconstruct the image in her mind and place it within that stadium, but it was static. Her mother did not talk about the hula she'd danced, or why it had been chosen. She changed the subject whenever Hi`i had tried to ask.

The excited crowd simmered to a low buzz when the announcer called the first dancer. On the large screen behind the stage, a short video introduced the girl, her kumu, the story behind the dance she would be performing, and why it was chosen. All eyes went to the stage.

Every Miss Aloha Hula contestant's performance required three things: an oli, a chant with no music or dance accompaniment; an `auana, or modern hula; and a kahiko, or traditional hula. The dancers would be judged on their authenticity, interpretation, and embodiment of Hawaiian culture. Each dancer represented her family, her halau, and her lineage, and would be judged as such.

Hi`i flattened herself against a wall near the ramp at the far back of the stage where the dancers entered and exited. Nine dancers in total competed that year. One after another she watched the girls transform into the legends held sacred in Hawai`i. Kanani stepped on stage wearing a jacaranda lei and danced like the moon lighting the cliffs of Moloka`i. The girl who'd graduated from her school strode onto the stage with the proud bearing of Pele, a crown of yellow lehua set on top of her black hair that swayed like the licks of a forest fire. From her diaphragm came ancient tales of `aumakua, animal guardians, sharks and geckos and hawks. One by one the dancers shifted into the shape of the wind rattling the branches, the rain pattering upon the grasses, the dew dripping from the leaves. Stethoscopes pressed to Hawaiʻi's heart. Through them Hiʻi could hear it beating.

SHE DIDN'T CARE THAT SHE WAS CRYING. When she saw Kumu walking toward the back gates, she grabbed hold of her fate and let her dream spill out. She described the synergy and power she had felt with her hula sisters dancing on stage the day before. Kumu nodded and smiled, gave her a little hug, and said she did good. But when Hiʻi got to the part where she said what she wanted to do next, how much she knew she was ready to be the next Miss Aloha Hula, Kumu was quiet. She looked Hiʻi over with an unreadable face.

"Hiʻi," she said after all the stars in the sky had faded. "You know to compete for Miss Aloha Hula is a very big thing, yes? It is a decision that can't be made by one person. It is made by a haumāna, yes, but also her kumu and ohana. When the time is right, when the dancer is ready. Not just in her head or her heart."

Hiʻi nodded eagerly. This was it, the bigger thing, the only thing possibly big enough to make her tutu realize that she could be trusted with their family legacy.

"Yeah. I get it. I do! And Kumu, I not going let you down. Dis not just cuz my tutu is Hulali Naupaka or cuz my ma was Miss Aloha Hula. I feel it. I ready."

There was sadness in Kumu's eyes. Hiʻi thought later it might have been pity.

"I've already chosen my haumāna for next year's Miss Aloha Hula, Hiʻi."

Hiʻi didn't have to ask who it was. The pit in her stomach told her.

The girl who everyone saw as the perfect embodiment of dedication to her family, her home, and her culture.

Leilani.

LAKA HAD TO DRAG HI`I to the parade on Saturday. Of all the annual Merrie Monarch festivities, the parade had always been Hi`i's favorite part. This year, she didn't want to go.

"Not one single ounce of aloha in Leilani, Ma. She no get heart or soul. All she get is pretty."

"Bah. No act like dat, make you sound jealous. Be happy fo' her. Your cousin is a good one. And you gotta give Kumu more credit den dat. She not going fall fo' pretty. Why you care, anyway?"

Hi`i looked at her pointedly.

"You? Miss Aloha?"

Hi`i said nothing. Laka floundered. "Aiyah. Babe. Competing one enormous commitment. All da time and responsibilities you get for da halau? Double 'em."

Hi`i rubbed her eyes and looked at her feet. "Hula is my everyt'ing, Ma."

"Just because I was Miss Aloha no mean da t'ing meant for you. Hele mai. Da parade starting."

Hi`i and Laka opened their folding chairs where they always did, on the sidewalk outside the Wailoa Art Center under the pointing arm of Kamehameha's statue. It was the first year of her life that the parade failed to move her. The pomp and circumstance, the horses so proud and dignified, the Merrie Monarch royal court, local couples from all the islands chosen every year to represent their respective one, the women in their velvet holokū, the flowers in their hair.

In the end, after the fanfare, all that remained were overlooked piles of horse kaka and bruised flower petals drifting like tumbleweeds through a once-upon-a-time town.

HI`I QUIT HULA. Without telling anyone, without a big announcement, she just stopped showing up. She'd tried to think of something to offer Kumu as a reason, but how to explain the crushing realization that dancing hula would do nothing to bring her family together? She had held on to that idea for so long that in her mind it had solidifed into an inevitable fact. A fact that now seemed silly. She had performed at Merrie Monarch, where she was sure Hulali had been watching. But there had been no acknowledgment, no celebrating, no grand reunion. Yes, she loved the way she felt when she danced, the fierceness and physicality of it, the way all the worries of life stopped at the door of the halau, inside a sanctuary of ritual and focus. But the halau was also a constant reminder of what wasn't, Hulali's framed picture still in the hallway, the Naupaka legacy seeping from its walls. She had failed to be chosen to represent their halau in the next Miss Aloha Hula competition. Another Naupaka had been chosen instead.

She told herself Laka didn't know. She had enough to worry about. The baby was on the way.

The tricky part was where to go when she was supposed to be at practice. Most times she just walked around. Hilo was full of places good for feeling lost.

On the sixth consecutive practice she'd missed, the toe wedge of one of her rubber slippers broke as she was running across an intersection. She flapped down the side of the road until she reached Ken's House of Pancakes. The restaurant was full of people fitting their faces into pot-sized bowls of saimin and fried rice, the best comfort food in the world. She threw her slippers into the bushes lining the diner's parking lot and headed into Keaukaha barefoot.

She was about half a mile from home when she heard the shouting. From the looks of it, Tony and Laka had been fighting in the yard for a while. The dogs were resting their heads on their paws looking bored. Hi`i made a detour toward Puhi Bay. She took a seat near the kuahu of the fishermen, where it was far enough to not have to hear them, or at least not as loudly.

Puhi Bay had always been an extension of home. The inlet of water, the grass lawn, the lava outcropping where they jumped when the tide was up, the glinting ocean beyond, behind her the row of coconut trees and palms, the road leading into Keaukaha Homelands, Puhi Bay's contours were as familiar to her as her own face. There was talk about building something there, a place for Hawaiians to congregate without having to turn to Jesus. Her mom said that talk had been around since the beginning of time, but Hi`i could picture it. It was a Very Important Building, invisible yet impenetrable, where Hawaiians would be free to be Hawaiian, whatever that meant on any given day. It was going to happen.

Hi`i stopped tuning out the yelling coming from her house and tried to piece together the details instead. From what it sounded like, Laka had let Tony back in and he promised not to drink. But Tony's best friend was out of jail, and the friend needed the guys to rally. He'd walked out of his cell into the sunshine of freedom, but when he'd hitchhiked over to Reuben's, where the mother of his three children was supposedly working, she was found pounding down a plate of wet enchiladas and a pitcher of margaritas, spilling out of a pair of jeans, rhinestones bejeweling her ass, which was being rubbed by a bronzed Australian surfer with a Crocodile Dundee accent.

Braddah needed his boys. You only get out of prison once (unless you get busted again). Why was she being so hard head?

> LAKA: Hard head? They had a baby on the way. She was having contractions. Small ones, but still. The baby could come any second. He needed to start getting his act together, worrying about his family instead of everybody else's pilikia.
>
> TONY: Wasn't that what he'd been doing? Why was she being such an ungrateful bitch?
>
> LAKA: Ungrateful? What did she have to be grateful to him for? It was her house; she took care of everything. He was just another Hilo deadbeat acting like a primo. What had he done, except get her pregnant?

Tony had spent most of Laka's pregnancy in the doghouse. But he didn't drink or smoke any more than any of the other uncles. He disappeared into the bush when it was hunting season and dropped everything whenever the waves were up, but who didn't?

At some point the yelling stopped. The shivering palms settled into quiet. She held her breath to make sure. As she gathered her things, she heard Tony's truck roar to life and squeal down the road. She looked up the stairs toward the house.

Backlit from the porch light her mom was the shape of a question mark, all top. Her swelling belly had changed the way she held herself, made her look like she was about to fall over. She was bending down trying to throw gravel at the ghost of Tony's truck, but the baby kept getting in the way. After a few handfuls, she gave up and slammed back into the house. Hi`i wasn't sure Laka had seen her. She counted to sixty and went around back to rinse off in the outside shower. From the open window of her mother's room came thuds and the scraping sounds of furniture being moved around. It was a good sign. Some people cut their hair when they want a fresh start. Laka moved furniture, rearranged rooms when she was ready for big changes, as if everything wrong could be fixed if the couch faced in a different direction.

THE NEXT MORNING LAKA'S DOOR was closed. Hi`i almost knocked but stopped when she heard her on the phone, talking too low to make out words through the wall. When she finally came out her eyes were swollen and puffy, the crying kind, not the kind that fists make. She forced a watery smile for Hi`i when she noticed her eating breakfast on the porch.

"I goin' do my laps," she said, grabbing her fins and board. "But we gotta talk when I pau."

Hi`i said okay and took another bite. When she was done, she went down the road to sit on the rock wall that separated the ponds from the bay so she could watch. Her mom kicked through the water from one end of the bay to the other. The morning was crisp, the drought had been going on so long that the muggy humidity of rainy Hilo mornings was close to being forgotten.

Laka kept an even pace. From this distance, she looked the way she always had when she did during her daily workout, a black head of hair knotted in a bun and two brown arms hanging on to a board, a trail of whitewash following the churn of her fins below the surface. It could have been any other day, but it didn't feel that way. Hi`i felt antsy, unnerved. She blamed it on the fact that Tony's stuff was still on the front lawn, left over from the fallout the night before.

A familiar old yellow Toyota Corolla rolled to a stop on the road at her back.

"Eh, Hi`i, your maddah home?"

"Aloha, Uncle," Hi`i said lightly. She shook her head and pointed toward the bay. "Laps," she said by way of explanation.

Uncle left the car idling as he got out and stared at the surf. He frowned.

"We need to go get her," he said, pulling off his shirt and tossing it to the ground. He jumped the rocks and dove into the water.

THE JUDGE REFUSED TO DELAY the trial. There was no Get Out of Jail Free card. After Tony and Laka finally stopped fighting in the front yard, Tony had gotten in his truck, run a red light, and hit someone. Laka was about to give birth, but that didn't change what happened. A boy was dead. A life for a life.

Tony was not present for the birth of his daughter.

It was Hi`i who held Laka's hand and adjusted the pillows behind her head as she writhed on the futon in the back room of their house. When the midwife pushed Laka's pareo aside and caught the babe that came from within, it was Hi`i who first welcomed Malia into the world.

WE BROUGHT THE SOUP that would let down the milk.

THE MIDWIFE RUBBED THE BABE with a towel and placed it naked on Laka's chest. Labor had lasted through the changing of the tide, time enough to mold the babe's head. From the egg-shaped cone came a dark swollen face with two slanted eyes and a shock of black hair that stuck straight up to the sky, part doll, part pruned old man the color of burnt butter. The infant rooted like a piglet toward her mother's engorged nipple. This cut through the grief, gave everyone a much-needed reason to smile.

The trial began a week later. Laka lashed baby Malia to her chest and snuck her past the flashing cameras and news vans into the courtroom. When Tony turned around in his chair, she lifted the fabric so he could see. The judge flattened his lips when from Laka's chest a mewling sound grew. This is not a circus, he said. The forensics expert paused in his testimony when Laka and Hi`i slipped out of the room. There would be no mercy for Tony. Even Laka understood that.

Hi`i and Laka bounced the baby back and forth across the long parking lot lined with banyan trees that fringed the county building. The baby bawled and bawled. The cameras never stopped rolling.

THERE WAS ONLY ONE TELEVISION around that worked; we didn't watch the way we used to, the catastrophes always rolling in like a winter swell that doesn't stop. So the next day the working TV was dragged to the Naupaka House and put on the porch so we could watch and Laka could listen from the room when she put the baby down for her nap.

THE SOLE THING THE JUDGE HAD to sort was not the if or the when or the how but rather the why. Between Tony and the popo, here's what they agreed:

Tony was behind the wheel of the truck. The truck ran a red light (whether it was yellow when he crossed the line into the intersection or not, Tony's lawyer said was still in question). The kid behind the wheel of the other car was dead.

TONY'S VERSION WENT:

Tony met a group of buddies at Aunty Kim's Korean Bar to celebrate his friend's release from prison. He'd had one too many. Close to midnight, he left the bar alone. He needed to go home, his old lady was going to give birth any minute, he'd told everyone within earshot. (Supported by testimony and obvious evidence.)

Somewhere near the intersection, he'd reached for a cigarette, taking his eyes off the road for no more than a second or two. The light may have turned from green to yellow, but he was sure he was already past the white line and continued through. He may have been going a few miles over the speed limit. No, he wasn't sure exactly how many.

The tiny Civic hatchback had come out of nowhere. Tony slammed on his brakes. Too late. The nearest pay phone was a block away. It would be faster to drive than to run. That's where he'd been going. For help.

HIS LAWYER INSISTED:

In no way did Tony set out to hurt anyone. It was a horrible accident. It could have happened to anyone.

THE PROSECUTOR'S VERSION WENT:

Defendant Anthony Acosta, forty-two, left the bar with a .22 BAC, a blood alcohol concentration egregiously above the legal limit.

A waitress noted Acosta stumbling across the parking lot. He struggled to unlock his door. He "burned rubber" as he left the bar.

The light turned red. Kalani Bridges, twenty, currently training day and night to prepare for his first Moloka`i Hoe, the men's world outrigger canoe racing championship that would take him just shy of forty miles of open ocean through the Ka`iwi Channel from Moloka`i to Waikiki, left the Keaukaha Canoe Club along the shore of Hilo Bay and proceeded into the intersection when his light turned green. Acosta pressed the gas and increased his speed.

The defendant's truck slammed directly into the driver's door and its immediate vicinity. Kalani Bridges was killed instantly.

Defendant fled the scene. Clearly a case of gross negligence.

HI`I'S VERSION:

Kalani Bridges is Kainoa's brother.

Was.

Kalani was Kainoa's brother.

The curse of the ma`i.

WHEN THE COURTHOUSE PARKING lot emptied, we turned off the television. Guilty. Gross vehicular manslaughter. The baby wouldn't have a daddy until she was ten, at the very soonest.

The coconut phone, it rang and rang. They were flying Tony to Oahu to begin serving his time immediately. If we hadn't told Laka, maybe she wouldn't have known. They weren't married, weren't family by American standards, so the courts weren't going to bother letting her know. The braddahs in Honolulu were watching out for us. They knew what was what.

Hana hou. We said goodbye to Kalani the way we do. His mother picked out the photo we used to make the posters for the grocery store collection jars. We carved his name into the wood. At his surf spots, we piled the rocks. Big Island Candies hosted a chocolate sale to raise funds for the funeral. We bought the chocolate. We picked the flowers and made the lei. When the sun was a pinprick on the horizon, we caravanned to Honoli`i to dance the hula of weeping flowers in water. Laka wasn't there, but only because the baby was barely a week old. We didn't blame her. Didn't blame Tony either. We was just sad for him. Ke akua, to forgive was the only way we could kōkua this. The boy Kainoa, the younger brother, led the thirty-four men, the father and grandfather, the cousins and closest friends. We moved in silence down the cliff steps to the beach. Our boards made a teepee under the shadow of the lifeguard tower, waiting until every kūpuna had their feet in the sand before we began.

The day had no color. Everything—surf shorts, normally fluorescent bright bursts, the leis dangling from necks, their tropical pinks and purples—was gray. Sunrise, gray. The waves breaking as we entered the water, gray. The can of ashes the mother hands off to Kainoa, her only living son, silent tears streaming down her face, gray.

He kissed her on the cheek and went to the water. We drew close, making a loose border around him. We set out.

We paddled beyond the breakers where the water went still and deep. We reached out our hands and held on. The ocean rolled back and forth under our unbroken circle. We bowed our heads and began to pray. The waves lifted the pule and sent it to the clouds; we heard it as it went. Kainoa opened the can. We set our lei free. The flowers bobbed along the surface of the water. The waves came and ate them.

The second pule, Kalani's father did not move toward the incoming swell with the others. He sat on his long board, arms hanging limp. The wave broke high and sharp, glassy. We caught the wave for Kalani.

The hall of the Hongwanji echoed with the beat of the bon dance. The temple ran out of chairs. Our cars spilled from the parking lot out into the dirt gullies up and down the street. We came burdened with aluminum trays of noodles.

Kainoa held tight to his red solo cup. We did not shoo him from the keg. There are times to be treated as a man. Burying your brother is one of them.

When the lights of the Hongwanji went dark, we accepted the paper plates heavy with haupia and sweet potato, the little plastic cups stuffed with lomi salmon, the bowls of stew and chicken long rice. We would not leave Kalani's mom to face the leftovers. We would eat for Kalani, eat so she would have nothing to throw away.

CHAPTER 13

Hi`i went to the memorial to tell Kainoa she was sorry. She left without going in because sorry wouldn't change a thing. She wanted penance, not forgiveness. Kalani was dead, and it was her fault, she was sure of it. She had gone into the lo`i with her ma`i and in doing so had upset the balance between the `āina and the people of it. Forgiveness was something she didn't deserve.

On her way through the parking lot, she caught sight of Jane and Kainoa sitting on a bench in the garden. Hi`i ducked behind a car. They were deep in conversation. Kainoa had his back facing in Hi`i's direction. His body usually bounced with an energy that matched the jokes rolling out of his mouth, but now his head and shoulders drooped. Hi`i remembered the wish she'd made in the lo`i, the wish that Kainoa would not laugh at everything. Her stomach turned, although not in the way it had when her crush on him was beating strong. Now it was territorial. Kainoa had been her friend since their hanabata days. He was basically family. Jane was an outsider.

As if she could feel herself being watched, Jane lifted her eyes. Hi`i froze. But instead of judgment, Jane offered her a soft, sad smile. Jane wore her grief naked, not trying at all to mask it as anything else. In her smile, she told Hi`i that they were in this together, that they were

all a part of something—a shared, mutual pain. Hiʻi lifted the corners
of her mouth, offering Jane the best attempt of a smile she could muster before getting out of there as fast as she could.

At home, the new baby was crying all the cries.

Dark shadows pooled under Laka's eyes. There was no sleep. No
matter how much Hiʻi rocked held pat burped walked Malia, it was
never enough. Even during her lightning-quick naps, the baby demanded constant attention. She was beautiful, though, that squalling,
demanding thing. She was like a feather in Hiʻi's arms, yet the first
time her finger got caught in the grip of one of Malia's tiny fists she
thought she'd never felt anything more weighted with pleasure. She
was the most beautiful baby she had ever seen. Whorls of silky black
threads of hair, skin like cocoa butter. Dainty yet strong. Hiʻi was so
proud (and exhausted). Even if Malia looked nothing like her.

The baby was also a vacuum of energy. Hiʻi was glad for the dis-
traction and helped as much as she could. She couldn't remember
the last time her mother had gotten out of bed or left her bedroom.
Laka didn't ask Hiʻi why she stopped going to school. Everything was
wrong; it was simply one more not-right thing.

The truck came late one afternoon while Hiʻi was standing over
the stove making a pot of Top Ramen for herself. She ignored the first
honk, but when it didn't let up, she sighed and gave the soup one last
stir before turning off the stove.

The truck was from the port. She signed the papers with the de-
livery instructions, explaining that her mom was sick in bed. She
showed them where to unload the boxes that had been sent over on
the barge. She was too exhausted to be surprised or upset, although
she hadn't expected so much stuff. A suitcase or two, maybe. Enough
for a few weeks. But from the looks of it, Hulali Naupaka had booked

a one-way flight. By the time the men were done, it was clear whose house it really was. Hulali was not just coming to help with the baby. She was taking back her home.

She arrived two days later, swishing up the stone walkway in a crisp white holokū as if she were Queen Lili`uokalani walking through the gilded entryway of `Iolani Palace.

She entered without knocking. Hi`i took in her grandmother's full visage for the first time. The delicate green fern print shimmering over the white fabric of her dress. The giant alabaster clip holding up a thick mass of salt-and-pepper hair. The pattern stitched into the lace of a high collar tight around her neck. Hi`i stood. The woman leaned forward, awkward, stiff. Hi`i kissed her on the cheek as was expected.

"Where is she?" Tutu Hulali asked.

"Mom? Sleeping."

The collar of Hulali's dress was so tight to her neck that her entire skirt rustled with the impatient shake of her head.

"No. My mo`opuna. I need to see her."

Right here, Hi`i was tempted to say, Your granddaughter is standing right in front of you. Two mo`opuna.

But Hulali looked down at Hi`i, looked right through her. She lowered her eyes to the floor and stepped aside so her grandmother could continue on to the bedroom. Her steps were quiet and slow as she followed.

Hulali gathered the sweeping skirt of her dress. Laka's eyelids fluttered when Hulali fitted her body around her and the newborn on the futon. Her legs were thick and strong and brown as tree trunks. Laka had her hand on Malia's back. She let it be pushed aside. Hulali leaned in, pressing her face into the crook of the baby's neck. Her chest doubled in size as she breathed the baby in. The sound was the tide being sucked back into itself, of water over sand. Malia squeaked. Hi`i jumped to tend to her out of habit, but there was no need. After months of being the only one to care for her sister and her mother, Hi`i watched as the need for her services vanished in an instant. Her brain took in details and tried to piece them together to make sense of what was happening. She watched as Malia curled, a cat in the sun of a window, tucking her legs under her. Hulali scooped the baby up with a quick practiced hand and pulled her into her body, cradling her in one arm while using her free hand to graze. She went over every finger, every toe, pressing as if trying to imprint their shapes into her memory. Malia squeaked again, and this time the squeak spurred Laka into action. She shifted her body to bear her breast. Hulali conceded, loosened her hold. Sucking filled the room. Hulali bent her head, fixing her lips to the delicate slope of Malia's forehead. A peculiar dread rose up within Hi`i as the figures on the bed transformed into a circle of the same person, snapshots of a woman in a spectrum of the stages of her life, maiden, mother, and crone. Leilani's words returned like ghosts through the window.

You only t'ink you one Naupaka.

The figures on the bed were one and the same. Between them a magnetic pulse, mirrored noses and jawlines and brows. This was what family was. Reflection and endowment. Blood. The truth came to her then, as pure and clear as a glass of water. There was nothing of Hi`i in them, and nothing of them in her.

VERSE II

CHAPTER 1

1962

Laka never questioned the reverance that Grandpa dedicated to the honu shell hanging on his wall. It had as much history and significance as the Naha Stone had for Kamehameha the Great. That stone—bigger than a double-hulled canoe and heavier than a monster truck—currently lived in front of the Hilo Library, but in Kamehameha's day, the stone was unmoveable. It was said that the person who could overturn it would be given the power to unite the islands of Hawai`i. Kamehameha tried many times to flip the stone. When he was fourteen, he succeeded.

As for the shell, it didn't have the power to crown the new king of the islands, but any Hawaiian worth his salt would have bowed their head and cried to have it. Not that there was ever a doubt about who would inherit it. Laka was hiapo, the eldest daughter of the eldest daughter. The only thing Laka ever questioned was how her father's parents had come to be the keepers of the shell—the honu had come to her great-grandma Ulu on her mother's side, bringing with it the hula that had led Ulu to Kalākaua's royal court. Ultimately, it was the honu that had made the Naupaka family what it was, but that was her mother's side.

Hulali waved Laka's question away, saying vaguely that the shell was too sacred to keep in a house crawling with babies. Laka could only assume Hulali had given it to her in-laws for safekeeping.

The shell hung from a series of thumbtacks shoved into the thin plywood paneling in the living room of Laka's grandparents' small three-bedroom house. The house sat on a red-gravel plot lined with purple and blue puffs of hydrangea, up mauka in Volcano Village, where it was too cold for mosquitoes and centipedes, where Grandpa had lived since retiring from the factory. Laka did not think of it as Grandpa's house, it was Grandma's through and through, but the living room was definitely his domain. For as long as she could remember the room had revolved around the crystal decanter holding his whiskey, the silver tray with the glass waiting for his highball, and the rocking chair poised to catch him when he sank into that first sip. An entire room dedicated to a single hour every afternoon. Minus the storage shed where he went to pretend he'd quit smoking cigarettes all those years ago when the doctor ordered, the living room was where Grandma left him for the most part alone, and where Grandpa was his happiest.

Grandma ruled the kitchen (the house was her kingdom, the kitchen her throne). The kitchen was where the woman not only lived but worshipped, a zealot of the religion of Improvisation. Pantry cupboards and drawers of quarter-full unlabeled jars and bottles stood at attention, ready for her gospel.

When Laka and her siblings would visit, they'd make a day of it. They'd pile in the back of the van while her parents sat up front, George driving and Hulali telling him how to drive from the passenger seat. George would throw a wink over his shoulder at Laka and grin, turning up the radio and singing over Hulali's instructions. Grandpa would be rocking in his chair on the porch waiting for them, and when they pulled up he always kissed all the kids on the head. They'd disappear off into the garage to play cards or shoot darts and wait for Grandpa's buddies to come kanikapila. Laka peeked from the door as they'd bust out their ukuleles; some had hands with only three or four fingers. They were factory men, Grandpa's friends, who'd come from all over to work the sugarcane and then the pineapple and then the nothing when that was all there was left. George would shoo Laka inside and tell her to go help her mom. Grandma and Hulali could always be found in the kitchen, Grandma making food, Hulali trying to help, Grandma fussing about Hulali needing to sit and rest her feet.

Those were the days Hulali was always hapai, spitting out keiki one after another.

When the uncles came inside to wash their hands for supper, they removed their hats and paused in front of the honu shell. Heart's desire.

The shell was a greenish brown, the layered colors of ocean. Across its length lay a thick braid of Ni`ihau shell lei, a cluster of delicate white shells dancing across a dark floor. Legend had it that right before the traitors put Queen Lili`uokalani in her prison, the queen got word of the coup and quickly distributed her most valuable feather capes and artifacts to her trusted staff for safekeeping—including a Ni`ihau shell necklace that she placed into the hands of a former dancer of her brother's court. Laka knew how precious this lei was to their family. It was one of the few things they owned worth money, although that had little to do with its value. Laka pictured hunched figures in ancient grass huts on the shores of Ni`ihau, sifting through sandy beaches, drilling microscopic holes in the tiny coral nubs, stringing them together, merging the strings, twisting prodding joining merging. The queen, wearing the final product for an official party, surrounded by dignitaries and royalty. The lei, Laka knew, had a worth you could write on a sticker. The honu did not, yet somehow it was more valuable.

Of the growing string of Hulali's children, five and counting, all no more than a year or two apart, only Laka, the eldest at thirteen, was nudged by Grandpa's encouraging hand to touch the honu, to feel its smooth lacquered slope, its surprisingly sharp edge and rough underside. She kept it to herself that there had been nothing mystical about the experience. The novelty of being singled out faded as she got older, and Laka began avoiding Grandpa's room with its whiskey highballs and precious shells, preferring the yard, where her cousins punched one another in the arms and legs or threw balls over the fence in order to climb over and go tromping in the forest of hapu'u fern and orchids behind the house, where they terrorized the chickens and sent them clucking in droves. Grandpa didn't hide his disappointment in her failure to produce the reverence for the honu that he'd expected, but Laka by then was so used to receiving disapproving, critical sighs from her mother that his dismay was to be expected. No one envied Laka or asked her about her inheritance; it was a fact of life, same as the fact that Hulali didn't think her daughter amounted to all she should. As far as her cousins and siblings were concerned, Laka was the eldest and therefore not to be envied, regardless of the crown jewels in her name. To be the eldest was to take the brunt of the storm that was Hulali.

Grandma passed a year before Grandpa. She'd never complained about her heart; it broke when no one was looking. In those next twelve months, Grandpa smoked all the cigarettes and drank all the whiskey he wanted, but his heart ticked on no matter how many times he took himself to the hospital and told the nurses he was dying.

The day before Grandpa fell into his forever sleep he'd told Laka he was ready to go, that he'd spent most of his life with Grandma bossing him around, that drinking and smoking without having to sneak took all the flavor away, and he was ready to get up to heaven already so Grandma could start telling him what he can't do again. Laka didn't cry at his funeral. How could she be sad about a man getting what he wanted? Her dad didn't cry either, but that was different. George was old-school.

The Volcano house was cleaned out, the hydrangea clipped one last time, and Grandma's jewelry divided throughout the family. Hulali removed the honu shell and its Ni`ihau adornment from its throne upon the wall and locked it away where no one would find it. It was only in the vacuum of its absence that Laka understood its value. The tears finally came. She begged for the shell's return and wailed for a week when Hulali refused. Given all the babies, there was too much crying as it was, so Hulali finally took out the belt. Laka went back to silence.

(WE MINDED OUR OWN KULEANA. Hulali was both the eldest and the mother of the eldest. She was the only one with any say in the matter, and the only thing Hulali was willing to talk about was hula.)

BEFORE HE'D DIED, Grandpa insisted to anyone who'd listen that Laka was the most beautiful hula dancer in the world. Whenever he saw her dance, he whispered like a prayer in church. She was only thirteen, but her hands could make worlds appear.

When it came to hula, Hulali pushed Laka until her feet bled and the tears ran. In her grandfather's eyes, Laka could do no wrong. In her mother's, she could do no right.

SOMETHING WENT QUIET in George once both his parents were gone. Three times a week he'd disappear on his boat to fish and wouldn't return until late the next morning, when he'd slip into bed and sleep clear until the next day. Though that didn't mean there was silence in their house. There was no halau back then, no fight about who would carry on its legacy. There was only their dirt driveway and her mother's hawk eye and body that dripped babies. Hulali's promise to her grandmother Ulu—that their family would never again lose their land to the white men who came from the other side of the tides, that she would have Hawaiian babies and dance hula and dedicate her life to the perpetuation of the Hawaiian people—lived like a cross on the wall. When Laka was fifteen she started complaining about wanting to take a break from hula. This made Hulali launch into the entire Naupaka saga, beginning with the arrival of Captain Cook and their farm in Waikiki, and ending with Ulu and Hulali taking their first steps into what would become their treasured Keaukaha. She'd grab Laka by the chin and ask her if she wanted it all to disappear. Because that's what would happen if Laka didn't dance.

Hulali never complained about the hours of hula. Even birthing didn't cause her to miss a day. As soon as she popped one out she'd set it aside and grab her ipu. If the baby didn't fall asleep to the boom of the pahu it would be carted away and left to cry in a room well out of earshot. We all said that if there was ever a woman who got pregnant every time she drank a glass of water, Hulali was it, but Laka knew it wasn't something in the water. It was the ghost of Ulu in the walls.

After Hulali gave birth to her seventh child, she birthed her halau, and there were no more babies, only haumāna. The first students were extended family, cousins sent by their mothers to learn what their generation had not had the chance to, then others.

We are only responsible for the brothers and sisters who are younger. But for Laka, that meant wiping hanabata from the noses of an entire crew. Between taking care of her six younger siblings and hula she barely registered when her father was home. Hulali always threatened to "tell your faddah," but most of his time at home was spent snoring.

AFTER A YEAR WITHOUT IT, the Miss Aloha Hula competition was added to the Merrie Monarch Festival to spice things up. With the sugar industry going kaput and all the businesses in Hilo feeling the slump, the town needed a boost. When Hulali decided Laka would be competing, she chose her daughter's oli, kahiko, and ʻauana with careful consideration. She did not bother to explain or justify them, and Laka dared not ask for reason. She did not question why her mother had chosen that particular ʻauana, a tribute to the sacred shells of Niʻihau. They never spoke of the necklace, her inheritance. She practiced the hula as a stranger might, blank-eyed and robotic, emotionally detached. Laka wasn't even sure Hulali trusted her to wear their family heirloom when it came time for the actual competition. But Hulali's decision for Laka's traditional dance, her kahiko, earned a very different reaction. Laka put her foot down. What good had the Moʻolelo no Kuula ever done? The legend of how Kuula had bested the evil eel Kekoona and ultimately saved the Hawaiian people from famine had not saved the king. It had not helped the Naupakas.

Besides, it was her great-grandmother Ulu's hula, not hers. She told her mother she would dance anything else, anything but that. When Hulali tried to force the matter, Laka resisted so much that to have her dance it would have served not as homage but as insult. In the early years of Laka's training, Hulali had learned that as much as Laka grumbled and protested before hula practice, once she got dancing, the hula took hold of Laka's body and spoke through it, which encouraged Hulali to continue pushing. If Laka's destiny wasn't obvious to Laka, it was nakedly apparent to Hulali. But in this fight, no matter how many times Hulali insisted Laka practice the Mo`olelo no Kuula, the dance remained an uninvited stranger to Laka's body, and eventually Hulali grimly conceded.

CHAPTER 2

1966

Two months before Laka competed for the Miss Aloha Hula crown a slipper caught her on the ear. She made like a pill bug under her blanket.

"Don't make me t'row da oddah one, girl. Time fo' get up."

With that, Hulali padded back to bed. A moment later, a baby stopped crying. Other than inside the halau, where Hulali was her kumu first and her mother second, the brief interaction summed up Laka's relationship with Hulali. To give her credit, she wasn't the kind of mother who was soft to any of her keiki. She didn't have it in her to be one of those women who covered her babies with hugs and honis, who kissed booboos and tucked in the blankets at bedtime. Hulali was of the mind that her children would be worse off for any of those things, spoiled and weak. She showed her love the way she knew how—through biting attention and critique. But for Laka the bite had always had more fang than necessary. Growing up, she'd learned that silent acquiescence was key to her survival. Better to starve a fire than give it oxygen. Over the years they'd come to a sort of under-standing. The fewer words spoken between them, the better, which had ultimately amounted to this: Hulali issuing orders concerning housework, chores, and taking care of the younger Naupakas, and

Laka finding ways to live her own life within whatever space between those things allowed.

Laka stretched and untangled her feet from the sheet sticky with her sweat. Outside, the sky was dumping. The room she shared with two of her sisters was humid as a boiling pot with the lid on.

She pulled a pareo around her body, knotting it between her breasts before padding into the kitchen to race through breakfast. When she had time, she made waffles or pancakes with guava syrup. For Christmas one year she'd gotten fancy, filling muffin tins with ham and eggs that she called ham muffins. Huffins. There was no time for huffins or pancakes now. Didn't matter. The kids in the house responded to those meals the same way they did to milk and a box of cereal or sweet bread and butter. Always starving, voracious bottomless pits.

Just as she was putting out what was left of last night's rice pot and a can of tuna on the table, her eldest brother, Butch, came through the door wearing his trademark scowl. Pua and Lilinoe, the two youngest besides Moku, the baby, followed closely behind. The girls were singing a nursery rhyme on repeat, gleeful of the effect it was having on their brother, who had his fingers stuffed firmly in his ears. Laka quickly finished what she was doing, caught Lilinoe for a quick kiss on her head, and headed upstairs to finish getting ready. If they didn't like what she served they could make their own food. She reminded Butch that they were in charge of washing their dishes, pretty sure he could hear well enough. Anyone who left even a spoon in the sink would get it, she told the girls, who continued with their song.

She gave her outfit for school little thought, grabbing the first item on the top of the pile on her "dresser," two milk crates with a plank of plywood between them. Her backpack was zipped and waiting by her door. She slung it on her shoulder and paused in the hall to listen. The clinking sounds of spoons against bowls drifted in from the kitchen. They were fine. She shut the door on her way out.

She walked toward the front street a few steps but then hung a sharp right toward Back Road, the evacuation route for whenever there was a tsunami, going in the opposite direction from Hilo High School. Windows flickered with the glow of televisions—those were the days we all had to have a TV, and the things never went off.

(THERE WAS SO MUCH HAPPENING that we thought maybe if we turned the TV off the world would end and we'd be the last to know. U.S. President Johnson was coming to Hawaii—how he could come to Hawaii when his country was up in flames with Freedom Riders and angry haoles blowing up buses, we had no idea—we got our own professional baseball team, and Russia shot a person into space.)

LEAVING BEHIND THE LAST of the streetlights, Laka followed the chain-link fence that divided Keaukaha from the Hilo Airport property until her house was completely out of sight. She rummaged through her backpack until she found the pair of fishnets she'd buried underneath her books. The first time she'd changed her clothes in the bushes she'd been terrified, stomach clenched tight enough to cut off circulation. The earthquake in her legs had nearly ripped the stockings in two. Now she wiggled and crouched like an old pro, sucked in, doubled over. She was stuffed like sausage in casing in no time at all. The jean skirt and crop top took less than a minute. She combed her fingers through her hair and swiped red lip gloss across her mouth. Then she tossed the backpack behind a tree and waited.

Laka and David had discussed the possibility they were getting sloppy. When they'd first started sneaking around, Laka had forced them through layers of precautions, mapping out stories, stirring up the silt, muddying the waters for safe passage. But no one had seemed to notice, and after a while, she'd wondered if she was expending all that energy on nothing. Her legs stopped trembling. She got bold, daring the world to find out. She'd kissed him in the wet grass near the plumeria bushes under her window. She'd snuck him into the shed where the uncles stashed their stash, where they hung their pakalolo from the ceiling to dry.

There was nothing wrong with David. She wasn't ashamed to be with him. That wasn't it.

A rancher with a horse's work ethic, he was as honest as he was clean. He'd never done a drug a day in his life, drank only at parties, and even then, only a beer or two. Nothing like any of the other boys she knew. When they'd first met, she'd thought him standoffish and shy, an oddball who didn't care if the surf was up. He never went to the beach. She didn't even know if he could swim. But she quickly learned of the joy that filled his face when surrounded by animals, stomping around the mud in his boots and cowboy jeans. It was there he'd opened up, and she'd felt as if she'd stepped into an unknown world, a private one made just for them. His dream was to someday own his own ranch, riding horses and raising cattle. His family, from what he'd told her of them, were loving and supportive of their only son. They were divorced, but both lived in Vegas. David lived with an uncle, but now that he'd turned eighteen, he was going to start looking for his own place. Then they could stop sneaking around.

One day, he promised, he was going to fly her to Vegas to meet his mother. Laka never mentioned the possibility of introducing him to her parents. It was impossible.

For one thing, he rolled his eyes at night marchers and menehune. He didn't believe in ghost stories, he said. (Laka kept the Naupaka historic encounters with the honu ʻaumakua to herself. If he didn't believe in night marchers, she didn't want to know how he'd feel about a message-bearing turtle.) And the only thing he liked about hula was that she danced it. When his friends grumbled about saluting the American flag, he said to stop moaning and get over it—the United States government wasn't giving anyone any kingdoms back, least of all Hawaiians. On one of their first dates he'd refused to tell her where they were going, saying only that she should wear jeans and covered shoes. They drove and drove until they reached the cool, misty town of Waimea. He turned down a long gravel road and parked the car in front of a locked gate that they then climbed over. Through a trail of craggy trees and overgrown grass she followed his muddy footsteps. He stopped at the crest of a small hill, pointing with shining eyes at the vista on the other side—fog-shrouded fields as far as the eye could see, marshy pond, a thicket in the distance. When he turned to her his eyes were shining with joy. He held a finger to his mouth to signal for her to be quiet and led them to a gathering of grazing cows. One day, he whispered in her ear. One day he was going to have enough money to buy this land. It would be his, a full working ranch where he would be the boss. Bought and paid for with his blood, sweat, and tears. For shame, he said, Hawaiians waiting around for years for America to throw them a scrap of "Hawaiian Land" and then tell them where and what and how. Never mind DHHL with its leases and rules. That wasn't how reparations were supposed to go.

Laka did not try to change his opinions about Homestead lands. She had no desire to argue. Instead, she'd thrown her arms around him and nibbled his ear until he forgot what he was talking about. What could she have done? She was a Naupaka, and the eldest.

When she eventually told him about how her grandpa had been guarding a special honu shell for her and a void had buried itself in her heart when her mother took the shell away, David accused her of tribalism. It was a sliver of an infraction compared with the way it felt to have his hand grasp for hers in the car or the movie theater. No one she knew had ever been able to put her at ease the way David did. He didn't have to do anything more than put his arms around her and all of life's enormous problems shrank to the size of a grain of sand.

When it came to their different perspectives on being Hawaiian, she left well enough alone. She knew the real reason David said those things. It was the same reason her parents would never approve of him. David had only a sliver of Hawaiian blood. Which meant nothing except that George had been a sugarcane mix—Hawaiian but only in part. This meant Laka had enough Hawaiian blood to keep the Naupaka land safe, but any children she might have were a different story. If she had David's child, their baby might not qualify. The thought of having a baby with David made her blush—they were nearly babies themselves—but she knew her mother.

In spirit, David was as Hawaiian as they came, a cowboy from Moloka`i who for the most part understood the rules of Hilo and the tangled ties of Keaukaha even if he rejected the myths and legends that came with them. None of that would have mattered to Hulali. To Hulali, being Hawaiian meant blood. David and Hulali were like Keaukaha itself: homelands, non-homelands, county land, non-county land, sovereign territory, non. We were the whole damn lot of it. No matter how anyone cut it up into sections, Keaukaha could never be clearly defined by any of those individual bits. We, and it, were bigger than the sum of our parts.

Laka was not without hope. Her mother had often argued that "the most important thing a Hawaiian could do was be Hawaiian," telling anyone who'd listen that their culture, after being abolished and buried so long, needed to rebuild itself, that they were all duty bound to dedicate their lives to the arts and humanities of their islands. Which sounded a lot to Laka like a dog chasing its tail, but it also meant perhaps there was wiggle room, that one day her mother might see David the way she did—as Hawaiian as they were.

David flashed his headlights when he rounded the corner. She waved from the shadows.

He was the only person Laka had ever met who told her she was perfect. In his eyes, there was not a single disappointing thing about her. In the early days of sneaking down to Puhi Bay to meet him behind the coconut trees on the three days a week she didn't have hula, she'd stress that her brothers and sisters were taking too long to fall asleep, that he'd give up and leave before she was able to escape, but no matter how long it took, he was always there, waiting. She was his queen, he said, and she'd never been worshipped before.

Behind the coconut trees he'd bring her gifts, wooden hair picks he whittled himself, songs he made up to sing into the soft place behind her ear. The first time he told her he loved her, tears welled in his eyes. She'd shivered with his words, body reacting to every syllable.

When the rains came and didn't stop, Laka felt sure it was her mother at work, drawing her out in the open. The uncles got tired of drinking in the wet and got it in their heads to build something at Puhi Bay, a community center so Hawaiians could congregate, as the missionaries had done for so many years. Which meant Laka and David had to move their meeting spot to Back Road. She knew it was only a matter of time before they lost that, too.

In the car, he rubbed his hand appreciatively over the portion of stocking covering her thigh, teasing her skirt up another inch.

"Hmmm. New pair?"

She slapped his hand away and laughed. Keeping one hand on the wheel, he pulled a paper bag from the backseat and tossed it into her lap.

"Coconut anpan for breakfast. And fresh gardenia from my yard for your ear."

She strained against her seat belt to kiss him on the cheek. He would take care of her always. They would be happy. She rolled down the window and shook out the gardenia to get rid of the tiny black bugs hiding within its pillowy petals. She tucked the flower behind her ear and took a bite of anpan. The soft steamed bread was still warm. She leaned back into her seat and let its sweet salt melt on her tongue.

The sun followed them as they made their way across the island. He slowed as they passed the rodeo grounds, straining his neck to catch a glimpse of the horses being unloaded from their trailers. She tapped the large silver belt buckle he was wearing, just one of many trophy buckles he'd won over years of rodeo competitions. He laughed and returned his foot to the gas pedal.

By the time they pulled into the parking lot of Hapuna Beach on the other side of the island, nearly two hours had passed and she was hungry again. Hapuna was notoriously popular with the tourists, but David had his secret spot. He unpacked the trunk, tucking a large blanket under his arm and pulling out a cooler that he sat on while she went to the bathroom to change into the bikini she kept in his car for emergencies. She hid her remorse at having to change out of her new stockings so quickly—he loved to surprise her and she loved that he loved to, but it meant she was often left wearing slippers for hikes through the `ohia at Bird Park or a simple beach pareo for playing tourist in Waikoloa Village. She consoled herself with the rare yet enjoyable image of David changing into surf shorts, so different from his thick jeans and scuffed leather boots.

She followed him across the sand past the haole kids building castles and the college girls waging war on their tan lines. At the rock outcrop where it looked like the beach ended, they glanced around. When they were sure no one was paying attention, they hopped the rocks toward the hidden white sand beach on the other side. Other than the occasional shout carried over on the water, they had the entire place to themselves.

The picnic was left to sweat and melt in the growing sun. Fine white grains of sand clung to their exposed flesh. The abrasiveness heightened the slow heat taking over Laka's body, bursting in tingling sensation from somewhere deep inside. If she'd felt the satisfying click of the puzzle piece when he'd told her he loved her, now she felt almost painfully incomplete, full of an emptiness only he could fill. She pressed him closer as she closed her eyes to memorize the rippled strength of his shoulders, the hard swell of his everything else. It was only when she felt him shudder slightly that she realized he might be as inexperienced as she was. The thought increased her sense of the moment's intimacy, its rightness, rather than make her nervous. They were both feeling their way, letting their bodies intuit what happened next. His narrow hips fitted perfectly within her wide ones. Suddenly he pushed himself up, and there was a tight inhalation when their bodies came apart, but as soon as he was on his feet he knelt down and picked her up, carrying her as she might have carried one of her younger brothers or sisters. She attached herself gladly to him, arms to neck and legs to waist. They moved toward the ocean. In and out the water along the shore moved, drawing them deeper, farther and farther until only David was tall enough to touch the bottom. The blue encased them in the continuous rocking of the gentle waves, in and out, in and out. Hypnotized, Laka felt one with David, with Pele of the earth, with the mana of the ocean, one with Hawai`i itself. David's hands moved from her waist to her breasts, bikini top dripping with seawater. She moaned involuntarily as he pressed his legs against hers, the ocean helping her fit tighter around him, inviting him to continue. He nudged her bikini bottom aside. She moved toward him and closed her eyes as he entered her. She dug her fingernails into the soft skin of his shoulder blades and tried to process the fact of his body inside hers. It was impossible to know where they ended and the water began. The waves set their rhythm.

Later, drops of water turned into specks of salt on their skin. They stretched out on the blanket and fought off the ants trying to steal the slices of watermelon David had brought. A contented, perfect sleep came soon after.

LAKA WOKE WITH A SHIVER. Clouds had taken hold of the sun. She shook David awake. The last school bell had rung more than an hour before. It was way past time to go.

No words were needed for the long drive back. The silence was satisfying, comfortable. So different from her loud, chaotic life at home. Her physical body felt different too, as if a part of him was still inside her. Laka wished that moment with David could last forever.

When they crossed the Singing Bridge into Hilo, David squeezed her hand and pressed it to his lips.

"We should go Maui. Haleakala Ranch hiring. I can work and make enough money to buy us one ranch. Eh, no laugh. Seriously. I going take care you da way you deserve. Dis could be our life every day."

She smiled. He was always saying things like that. She responded the way she always did.

"After Merrie Monarch," she said.

Two months. She would give that to her mother, this contribution to their family legacy. She would compete in the Merrie Monarch's first Miss Aloha Hula contest, and then she would owe her mother nothing. She would be free.

He left her under the canopy of trees on Back Road. She changed into the clothes stuffed in her backpack, Hapuna white sand and the smell of happiness lingering on her skin. Then she walked the block home.

CHAPTER 3

A pillar of black smoke rose from the Naupaka backyard. Gasoline fumes like sulfur clouds. The stink was laced with something more sinister, acrid and vague. No sirens came, we knew not to call. This was Hawaiian business.

THE SMOKE STUNG LAKA'S EYES and burned her nose. She pinched her nostrils with her fingers and took shallow breaths through the corner of her mouth.

Her brothers and sisters were scattered around distant corners of the backyard in varied degrees of naked. Moku's diaper drooped low and heavy. Pua and some of the older ones shirtless, in panties with tired elastic bands, hand-me-down bathing suits stretched unrecognizable, generations of use. Without being conscious of it, Laka ticked them off in her mind, a running tally of who was accounted for, a habit developed over years of being in charge. Her net came up short. She expanded her search to include the rear porch, locating Butch and Kekoa, the final two, fighting over the last jar of pickled mango. She pressed on toward the smoke.

The imu pit jumped wild with an unnatural blue flame. She fanned the air in front of her, trying to see. Blind, she rubbed her burning eyes with her fists. Through the haze she made out the faded silhouette of her mother. Hulali poked the fire with a long stick, staring into the flame with red vacant eyes, pupils dilated to needlepoints.

"Ma?"

The word was a thermometer, a toe in the water. Hulali's head turned with slow, possessed precision. After a long silent look, eyes black and impenetrable, she opened her mouth and spat at Laka's feet.

"Pilau," she hissed.

"Ma?"

This time the word was a plea, a cry. Hulali turned her attention back to the fire, poking again with her stick, jabbing its sharp point into the flame. A tortured, haunting shadow flickered across her face, distorting her features until she was nearly unrecognizable.

"You pilau. Dirty. You drag our family, our ancestors, into the mud of pigs."

She spoke quietly, but with the force of an earthquake. Laka wrapped her arms around her chest protectively. Her eyes, still trying to process the scene before her, moved from her mother to the pit. Even warped and peeling and doused in an unnatural blue flame, the shape of her honu shell, majestic and proud, was clear.

"No!"

She lunged forward. Smoke flushed through her lungs and choked out her scream. She tried to pull Hulali away from the fire, but nothing could stop her stick, prodding, poking, stabbing. Hulali's body contracted as if in pain, but she pressed through it as if forcing herself to do this thing, wincing with the effort. Laka watched, helpless, as the fire ate her birthright, her roots.

She'd run her fingers over the entirety of that polyurethane coating only once, but the pads of her fingers recalled its bumpy surface, the dips and grooves of the shell, the shape of her `aumakua. Being reunited with the shell had been an inevitable fact that she'd taken for granted, both honored and burdened by the weight of its inheritance. The iridescent octagons contorted and yielded to the flame. The honu hissed, its spirit crying out in pain. She could not watch, but when she turned her face away, Hulali was on her quick as a snake. She clawed a hand into Laka's hair and twisted her head, pulling it toward the imu pit.

"No. You no get fo' hide your face. You t'ink dis punishment just fo' you? No. Dis fo' me, too, for my failure to raise you right, da failure dat live inside you. Too late for looking away. You watch."

Laka had not noticed her siblings drawing closer. They made a tight circle around their mother and sister, observing in silence. She swallowed a cry when Hulali twisted her grip on her ear. She felt the blood draw.

"Why? What for?"

Hulali hissed in her ear.

"Honu our `aumakua. You bring shame to our name, to our ohana. Whore!"

The shell curled into a black ball. Hulali pushed Laka to the ground and tore the backpack from her shoulder. She ripped it open. Into the fire went the stockings, the skirt. The flame reached up and ate them.

Hulali's face transformed yet again, a hurricane of fury and sadness, tears dripping down her cheeks as she watched the flames, but she made no move to put them out.

"I used to t'ink dis honu would see generations of Naupakas being strong, staying focused, dedicating dea lives to da perpetuation of our people. I tried to keep dat promise, I raised you to know da responsibility dis honu was entrusting to us. But you nevah saw da honor in being da one who get to carry da honu's mana forward. And now you act like some common rubbish—I would rather da honu turn to dust and join da stars den it fall into your hands, you and dat boy. You would t'row away our land, all our family worked so hard for? Dis honu not'ing but one souvenir to you. A trinket."

Her voice cracked. She went still. Laka was too stunned to think of a way to respond, a way to tell her mother how wrong she was.

Laka's brothers and sisters broke open their circle. Hulali dragged Laka into the house. They did not dare follow into the room where their father was sleeping.

Fists full of her daughter, Hulali aimed a kick at her husband's limp body. "Wake up! I don't have time for dis. I gotta go to da halau, time fo' class and I gotta teach. Your turn take care dis girl. I no can. She no good. I give up already."

Laka's father lifted his head groggily but said nothing as Hulali left the room. Balling her fists, Laka crumpled to the floor and screamed at her mother's retreating back. "You no even get time for dis? Why you wen have kids at all? Why, if all you care about is hula?"

Hulali hesitated at the door but kept her back to Laka.

"Why do you hate me," Laka sobbed.

Hulali turned. Cold dread gripped Laka's stomach. Her mother returned to the room, slow and deadly. On her face, that shark smile. "You." Hulali spoke with marked intention, every word delivered with a crisp formality, as if she feared her daughter didn't speak her language. "You are my biggest failure. And now we all must pay." She pulled her daughter up from the floor. "Wash your face. You coming with me. Still get Merrie Monarch. You going learn your kuleana if it's the last thing I do."

By the time they returned from hula practice, the smoldering honu was no more.

USUALLY, GEORGE SAID HIS JOB was to stand by his wife, especially when it came to her decisions regarding the children. But that night while Hulali was taking a shower he found Laka in her room. He held her hand and told her about how sugarcane farmers burned the crops to harvest the sugarcane. In Hawai`i, he said, fire brought life. It created. In Hawai`i, fire was the beginning, not the end. Then he kissed her hand and slipped quietly out of the room. Laka watched him go, not sure she had it in her to believe him.

CHAPTER 4

For the next six weeks, hula dragged the sun across the sky and carved itself into the moon. There was no time to see David, no time to explain why she couldn't meet him, no chance to fill in the blanks of whatever he had heard through the coconut phone that kept him from contacting her. Her mother watched her every move, and she couldn't afford the risk. She needed to get through Merrie Monarch, and then they could be together. Not that she would have known what to say if she'd found a way to him. How to explain to him the significance of what Hulali had done when even telling him about the honu had set him off muttering about tribalism and nonsense superstitions?

Soon enough she had other things to worry about. She was starting to get tired in a way that a good night's sleep did not relieve. Her breasts now hurt if she did so much as lie on her stomach. Everything smelled stronger than usual. When she didn't get her period, she didn't need to go to the doctor to know what that meant.

By then the silence between her and David had gone on too long for her to just reach out and tell him, and she was too exhausted trying to keep up with her Miss Aloha Hula training to figure out exactly what needed to happen next. She needed time to think. Instead, she ate soda crackers.

She ate soda crackers to keep from gagging at every passing smell. Her belly wouldn't be flat for much longer, but the ropes of her hula skirts cinched her waist enough to evade her mother's daily scrutiny. Merrie Monarch would come just in time. She would compete for Miss Aloha Hula, but it would be the last thing she ever did for her mother. After that, she would disappear.

There was no question she would keep the baby. She'd realized that the moment she'd climbed down into the pit, raking through the cold ashes that remained in the backyard, her fingers searching for even the smallest remnant of shell to salvage.

Her mother was wrong. Laka had never thought of inheriting the honu as a small, inconsequential thing. She and her mother just had a different idea of what the honu had called for them to do—Hulali saw only the responsibility to perpetuate bloodlines, and while Laka felt a deep responsibility toward her culture, her ʻāina, and her people, she wasn't sure if she and Hulali agreed on exactly what the definition of those things were. Burning the honu had not disconnected her from what she was beginning to feel was her kuleana, or from any other part of her heritage. You could take a lighter to a root, but that didn't make it any less part of the tree. If anything, burning the shell had made the honu become more a part of her, as the smoke had entered her lungs, she'd breathed in the shell's particles and absorbed them into her body.

She would love her child in a way her mother was not capable of. She would do whatever needed to be done to make sure her child inherited their land, even if it meant spending the rest of her life fighting the laws that made that impossible.

* * *

IT WAS NOT DIFFICULT TO HIDE the pregnancy. At practice, her mother watched only her arms, her feet, the snap of her skirts. Laka swallowed her nausea, blamed her fatigue on the exertion of her training. She knew little about prenatal care, but with discretion took the precautions she'd seen countless aunties take, removing the gold necklace she'd always worn and being careful not to cross her legs whenever she sat down—both to prevent the baby from being strangled by its umbilical cord. She refrained from putting chili pepper water on her food and, in response to the sudden swell of her breasts and their new extreme tenderness, started to hunch. Ever since the burning of the honu, Laka and Hulali took deliberate caution never to be caught in the same room at home (they had to be with each other at the halau, but they treated that as business, both just showing up for work). Her father gave her a funny look as he passed through the hall and found her eating soda crackers in the middle of the night, but he was fishing so much that he was too tired to say or do anything beyond getting himself a beer and going to bed.

Her brothers and sisters were more difficult to avoid. Now that she knew she would be leaving them soon, tears gathered in her eyes when they left their dirty clothes on the floor or spilled their juice or picked their nose at the dinner table. She found herself studying them, memorizing the shapes of their toes, the smell of their skin, the rumble of their laughter. She found secret ways to say goodbye that she hoped they would remember. She hugged Lilinoe extra tight until the girl squirmed her way free. She picked Moku up and rubbed his back whenever he pulled at her hand. She answered Pua's unending questions with newfound patience. She even went out of her way to make plates of food for Butch whenever he skipped meals to go surfing, covering them with a kitchen towel and putting it where the ants couldn't reach. She blamed her sentimentality on the hormones, but it was more than that. There was no way to leave Hulali without leaving them, too. She knew they would not understand. Leaving wasn't in their dictionary. In Hilo, Keaukaha especially, you stayed with the tribe. It was the only home, where you belonged.

Eventually, she wrote David a letter and sent it before she lost her nerve. In it she explained nothing, asking only that he not come to the stadium to watch the competition. There was no telling what Hulali would do or say to him if she saw him there, and Laka didn't think she could handle a confrontation. She knew she was taking a chance by not telling him in the letter; David needed to know she was pregnant before Hulali got to him, but when it came time to write it down, she couldn't. Telling someone they were going to have a baby was something that should be done face-to-face. So in the letter she included only a postscript of how much she missed and loved him, words she'd never really told him in person, imagining him reading them as she danced.

MERRIE MONARCH FLASHED BY like a scene through the window of a moving car. The stadium was standing room only. President Johnson was fresh out of a conference he'd called in O`ahu in an attempt to pump people up about the war in Vietnam, but more soldiers were dying every day and the war was already ten years old with no end in sight. Everyone was ready and eager to turn their attentions back to happier things. For a year like this, hula was medicine. Prep was a flurry backstage. There were two contestants before her. Laka chewed her crackers while people pinned flowers to her hair and fussed with her makeup.

By now, Laka's relationship with both of her parents had become stiff and strained. George was always either sleeping or out fishing and Hulali became agitated anytime Laka came near. So they escorted her down the ramp to the Merrie Monarch stage during the first Miss Aloha Hula competition not because they were particularly close but because it would have been scandalous not to. Laka was still thinking she could fly under Hilo's radar. But once she'd forced herself to thread her arms through their offered elbows, she experienced a great sense of relief that they were there to prevent her from running out the back door of the stadium if she lost her nerve.

(IT DID NOT MEAN what we thought it meant at the time. That everything was okay. That there was love and unity within that family.

We found out later about the fissures. The night before the competition, Uncle George came home with a wooden chest the size of a small cooler that he laid at Hulali's feet. When he opened it to reveal the Naupaka Niʻihau shell lei, Hulali stared at him and didn't move. He nudged it closer. Laka was in the kitchen dishing out food to her brothers and sisters. They fell silent and didn't dare breathe. He nudged it again. Hulali sent the kids to their rooms.)

WHEN HER NAME WAS announced over the loudspeaker, Laka approached the steps of the stage with a parent attached to each elbow.

At the foot of the stairs, her father kissed her on the cheek and presented her with a velvet purse. Laka hesitated and shook her head. Uncle George assumed his daughter was just nervous. He smiled and gave her a nod of encouragement, dipping his hand ceremoniously into the purse. The crowd leaned in and cheered as he lifted the thick shell necklace and clasped it around her neck. Laka bit her lip to stop herself from protesting; surely wearing something around her neck just this once wouldn't hurt the baby. The only thing that kept Laka from yanking it off was the hand squeeze given by her mother, sharp enough to leave little half-moon indents the shape of her fingernails across Laka's knuckles. She tried to ignore the new weight on her chest. Acknowledging the lei somehow felt more harmful to the baby. George stepped out of the spotlight. Hulali and Laka climbed the stairs. Since Hulali was Laka's kumu, she would join her on stage, as musical accompaniment and narrator of the story being presented, as much a part of the performance as the dancer. Laka faced the audience, waiting for her cue. Hulali took her position at the microphone and began.

ALL THE MONTHS OF TRAINING, and the only feeling that prevailed once Laka began executing her motions was the slight strain of her growing belly against the fabric of her holokū as she danced her ʻauana, reenacting the lei's passage from the queen to her great-grandmother. She'd never been accused of being skinny, she was big-boned and broad long before puberty, but in pregnancy it was like everything about her body was recouping itself, leaving her feeling like someone else was behind the wheel. Afraid of crying (since lately her tears were always waiting somewhere nearby), she tried not to think of the child growing inside her and its inherent connection to the woman of her dance, focusing instead on not losing her balance. She glanced toward the back of the stage where Hulali was singing. It was all she needed to erase any feelings of nostalgia for the life of hula and expectation she was about to leave behind. Even there on that stage, surrounded by cameras and applause, Hulali represented the past. She was carrying the future.

The kahiko they'd ultimately settled on was a tribute to the `o`o, the small Kaua`i forest bird whose striking yellow and black feathers had been used for the robes and capes of ali`i, a native on the brink of extinction. When it was almost time for Laka to return to the stage to dance her kahiko, her hula sisters removed her makeup and the flowers in her hair, letting her thick black curls tumble freely down her back. They helped her into the feathered costume that just barely hid her body's new curves. The cords of her skirts made it hard to breathe. The story had been decided upon by Hulali with uncharacteristic arbitrariness, but Laka said a small thank-you that it wasn't a performance that required anything more strenuous than a backbend or two—no volcanic explosions, no crouching crawling squatting duckwalks or pounding heels into the ground to make it shake with thunder. Instead, she pulled a nose flute from the cords of her skirt and filled the stadium with the `o`o's haunting call. She fluttered from the green blanket of a canyon, valiantly defending herself from introduced species, the rat, the pig, mosquitoes. She struggled to catch her breath as the audience cheered. She held her mark at center stage until Hulali chanted her out.

Backstage, their halau was exuberant, hugging her and one another. Laka barely heard them. Now that it was over, she wanted only to be reunited with David, to tell him they were going to be a family, that they could begin their life. She squinted past the glaring stage lights to scan the rows of seats. It wasn't until she stood with her parents, waiting for the judges to compile their scores, that she caught a glimpse of what she thought was David's face in the crowd. Her stomach did an involuntary flip. She glanced sideways to see if her mother had noticed, but both her parents had eyes only for the judges. He was too far away and there were too many people and too much noise between them for her to catch his attention. She talked herself down. David was there. That could only mean he'd gotten her letter and ignored its plea. But instead of being irritated or angry, her heart melted at the sight of him. He was there to support her the only way he could, from a distance. He would understand everything the moment she told him about the baby. She stared at the enormous crowd now shifting toward the exits, trying again to find his face. He was gone, if he had ever been there at all.

WHEN LAKA'S NAME WAS ANNOUNCED, Hulali accepted the grand prize and the maile lei with a generous smile and a thank-you to the judges. Back at home, she would remark that luck had been with Laka that night. She could have sworn she'd seen Laka's elbow dip once or twice, and her timing had been a blink off.

If Hulali was right about Laka's performance being flawed, she was the only one who'd noticed.

SHE HADN'T CONSIDERED the possibility she might win. Laka had thought only of fulfilling her family obligation. But with the crown digging into her temples, everything felt different. Winning was a wave that swept her away, a rising tide that filled the space between her and everything else. In the days and weeks after, she forgot what life was without being besieged by newspapers wanting her picture, without the steady stream of leis that always found their way around her neck and flower arrangements that filled every spare inch of their house, without the constant trill of the phone. As kumu, Hulali got much of the praise and attention, and they both obliged when people asked for their photo together, but other than that, their interactions went from terse to nonexistent. Now that training for the competition was over, there was nothing more to say.

She was busy, but not too busy to keep from wondering why David hadn't reached out. She'd asked him in the letter to lie low while she prepared but had said nothing about staying away after it was over. Now that she thought about it, he was the only person on the entire island who hadn't congratulated her.

WE THREW A LUAU down Puhi Bay to celebrate Laka's win. We'd never been prouder. It rained in the morning while we was making the food, but by the time the chow mein and rice was pau cook and it was time to fire up the grill, the clouds had burned off and the sky was bright blue like a gemstone. We brought the poles, the tarp, a tent, just in case. We set it up so the babies could moe moe in the shade when they pau swim.

The first hour or two we had the place to ourselves. The way it used to be. The keiki jumping in the cold pond, the boys surfing the break and jumping off the rock, huli chicken and salted menpachi on the grill. Ukuleles out.

Then the buses came, the interrupters. The Keaukaha tours used to come once, maybe twice a week. Now they was coming three, four times a day. Usually they went to Richardson's Beach. Maybe this bus thought this was a public party, a festival. Maybe haoles need signs that say PRIVATE: KEEP OUT. Maybe even then it wouldn't have mattered. Maybe they didn't even see us.

Either way, the bus idled on the side of the road with its tinted windows. Its innards poured out, all sneakers and sun hats. We ignored them as they skirted us. They spread like fog. And then the downpour came. Raindrops big as buckets, as if the gods were bombing water balloons from a window in the sky. The tourists yelped and ran, but the bus was too far. They headed for the shelter of our tarp, trampling us like a herd with their careless white feet on the blankets laid out on the ground where the babies were sleeping. We put down our ukuleles and asked them to go, to respect the blankets. They called us rude, unwelcoming. They called the cops. They called us threatening, menacing. Inhospitable and unwelcoming. The police, local boys, came, they kissed us on the cheeks and blushed, embarrassed. They was just doing their job.

If we had had a community center, we could have closed the doors. We could have had our luau without invasion from the tourists who come without respect, without understanding. From those who come to take from this land rather than come to love it.

County rules said no permanent structures on the beach. But this wasn't the county. This was Keaukaha, this was Hilo. Where the flag of Hawai`i flies high, flapping in the makani. We left that tarp up, shelter from the storm.

We dared anyone to try take it down.

* * *

TWO WEEKS AFTER THE FESTIVAL, Laka could not put it off any longer. She left a message with David's uncle, asking him to meet her that following Saturday.

On the night they were to be reunited, the world was tinted in silver. The sharp tips of the crescent moon matched the waves as they crested and crashed along the channel beyond the tide pools. At Puhi Bay, Laka made her way through the rushes to their spot under the coconut trees. After a time, her legs grew stiff, but she refused to consider the possibility he would not come. She cleared a seat in the sand and leaned against a tree, crossing then uncrossing her arms. The tenderness in her breasts had continued to increase as they grew. She pulled her hands under her shirt and cupped them gently, marveling in their new shape while wondering if the pain was normal. So far, pregnancy was nothing like what she'd imagined. It was too early for belly kicks and waddling—she hadn't yet gone to a doctor, given that there was no doctor she could go to in Hilo not connected in some way to their family—but already a presence was making itself known to her, a life force that was both hers and distinctly its own. Every new ache and pain was a reminder her body was doing what it was made to do. But it took so much energy. The tree was stiff against her back, the ground hard and uncomfortable. Still, she felt she could sleep anywhere. She closed her eyes.

The moon had settled among the coconut fronds above her head when she jerked awake. She didn't see him at first. Only the quick flash of moonlight against his rodeo belt buckle gave him away. He was leaning in the shadow of a nearby tree, his back to her. She wondered how long he'd been there, and why he'd let her continue sleeping. He didn't move away when she padded over and leaned into his back, although closing the physical space between them did not make her feel closer to him. In some ways, pressed against him, he felt farther away than ever. She waved the unnerving feeling away and mumbled a hello into the folds of his shirt. Inhaled deep as she could. She'd missed his scent, salt and sunshine and grass. His heart thumped against her hand.

"I missed you."

He did not respond. When he finally turned to face her, his face was stone, his body rigid. Hard and angry. He couldn't have gotten her note and been this angry. Was it simply this moon, its light playing tricks? He took a step back, out of her reach. She launched into the explanations she'd practiced, the apologies. He held up his hand, did not let her finish. Shook his head as if shaking himself of her words. She was too shocked to try to continue. The way he looked at her, his face under shadow, he had not come for answers. Something had changed. Glad for the dark to hide the tears now rolling free down her face, she reached for him again, to use her body heat to hopefully melt the ice he had become. This time she could feel him soften, his internal resolve to stay separate from her start to crumble. She parted her lips as if she would try again to speak, to say the right thing to convince him. This time he silenced her with his mouth, pressing, sealing them shut, kissing her almost involuntarily. His arms wound themselves around her and squeezed so tight it was hard to inhale. She wound her arms around his neck and pulled him even closer, returning the urgency of the kiss. Too soon, he pulled back and spoke into her mouth.

"I signed up."

Three words, barely four syllables. They ping ponged in her head, loose and disconnected. This conversation was all over the place, but now it felt like it had left her behind completely.

"Signed up? For what?"

"Marines. I going Vietnam."

Everything stopped. The waves no longer crashed against the rocks. The crickets in the grass went quiet. She shook her head. No. This was a bad dream. Maybe all of it. Miss Aloha Hula, the honu, the pregnancy. But his words. They rattled in the hollow silence. "I no understand. To fight for da country dat stole us? Why would you? How could you?"

He placed his hands on either side of her head and forced her still. "Stop. Open yo eyes, yeah? America nevah going give up Hawai`i. Nevah. We stuck wit 'em, mo' bettah you accep dat already. Understan? You wen disappear, just drop off da planet, now you Miss Aloha Hula. I seen you and yo maddah up dea on stage, I t'ought, no way dat lady going let me be wit her daughtta. I was just somebody you was messin' around wit. Cuz you was bored or wanted to make yo maddah mad or somet'ing. I dunno. But no mattah, yeah? I wen sign up. Show you bot' I not one nobody. I going be somebody. Fight fo' dis country den come back and buy my ranch and show e'rybody."

Laka let his neck loose and let her arms dangle at her sides. She stepped back and tried to meet his eye. Could feel the gathering anger at his accusations. He didn't understand a thing. If he really thought she was capable of sneaking around and even sleeping with him out of boredom or a desire to rebel against her mother, he didn't know her at all.

"I wrote, I tried to explain. I t'ought you would understand."

David huffed and turned away. "Understan wat? You tell me no come watch you dance. You love me but shame to be wit me. So okay. I head to training next week, leave you alone like you want."

Laka tried to swallow her frustration with him. She had another little person to think about now. She clung to his arm. "Dat's not what any of wat I said meant at all! No. You can't. Please. Tell 'em you changed your mind. I . . . I need you."

She wanted to tell him. But not like this. Not with this anger and darkness between them.

His laugh was not his. It was serrated, cynical. "You need me? You get everyt'ing you need, right here in Keaukaha. Wen you was up on dat stage, oh my god, Laka, my heart almost exploded. You was so beautiful, so strong. Gave me chicken skin. Den I t'ought, eh, no wondah she stop talking to me. Wat one girl like her going do wit a guy like me? Wat kine life I can offah? I holding you back. You get your land, your family. Trust me, your maddah going be happy. I doing what she want, getting out of your hair. You bettah off."

I'm pregnant I'm pregnant I'm pregnant. She tried to force the words out. But this baby, their baby, deserved a celebration. Tears of happiness. Its existence should not come to light in the middle of a fight. He was so closed, so angry. She let out a sob.

He growled in frustration, pressing his nose to hers roughly and locking eyes the way they used to. "Wait fo' me. I going make you proud. Wen I come back, I going be somebody."

He wasn't leaving until next week. She begged him to meet her the next night under the coconut trees of Puhi Bay, to be with her every night until he left. That was more than enough time to tell him. Once he knew, she was sure he would change his mind. He nodded a promise. But by the next morning, he was gone. It would have been too hard to say goodbye. So he didn't.

CHAPTER 5

The strange girl was all knobs and knees, bony and delicate as an `elepaio bird, but she barreled into Laka's room like a boar. Granted, the door to the termite-infested room was hardly secure—the thing looked ready to part ways with its rusted hinges at any moment. The walls were thin as rice paper too, but for what the old boardinghouse in Hana lacked in luxury it made up for in affordability. When she'd decided to go to Maui to have the baby and wait for David to return from Vietnam, Laka had grabbed all the money she'd been given as high school graduation gifts and used it to bluff her way into the rented room, assuring the woman with the keys that she was a good girl with a job that just hadn't started yet. And then she'd locked herself inside her room, curled in a ball on its stale mildewed mattress, metal coils stabbing her in the back, and cried for a week. The boulders came tumbling down. Miss Aloha Hula, the burning of the honu, walking out on her brothers and sisters, it all avalanched on top of her.

After a week she began to worry about other things. In Hilo, when you look for a job, you cast the net and waited for a fish to come to you. Sooner or later, something would turn up, or there would be a call, aunty so-and-so needed an extra set of hands. But if she reached

out to family in Maui, word would get back to Hilo of her where-
abouts. She told herself she wasn't trying to hide her pregnancy, she
just needed a little more time before Hulali found out, and she needed
to be the one to tell her. When she wasn't crying about that she was
crying about David, imagining where he might be, wondering if he'd
already been shipped off, imaging him in Vietnam, hurt or worse.
And through all the sobbing, the girl in the room next door left her
alone. Laka knew the girl could hear her, she certainly heard the girl
early every morning, creaking down the hall toward the communal
washroom to splash water on her face before slipping on her shoes
and disappearing. Laka assumed she had a job somewhere; from what
Laka could tell, all the girls did. One day soon she was going to have
to pull herself together and get a job to patch the holes in the bucket
of her savings for when the baby came, although she assumed David
would be back long before then. She didn't have a plan beyond that.
Her goal had been to escape the Big Island, to get away from Hulali
and her deadlock focus on land rights and cultural perpetuation, her
heavy presence, critical and demanding. There had been little thought
as to what she'd do once she got to wherever she was going. Arriving
hadn't been the point. Leaving had.

And then one day she woke up and realized her breasts didn't hurt.
She tried to recall the last time they had. Could have been a day or a
week. Time had stopped tracking.

She was hit by the sudden urge to pee. Peeking through a crack in
the door, she checked the hall before padding over to the bathroom
near the stairwell. The boardinghouse was usually empty at midday,
but she was in no state to be bumping into her neighbors.

In the stall, she checked her panties. No blood. She wasn't miscar-
rying. A wave of relief, then panic. She was going to have a baby alone

in a boardinghouse in Maui, where cockroaches skittered across the floor at night and the moon glowed yellow through a stained curtain.

Back in her room, she lifted her shirt. Her breasts filled her hands a little less than before. They were supposed to be getting bigger, she knew, not smaller. Other changes, she wasn't as sure. She'd stopped keeping soda crackers near her bed once the nausea had lifted, but after the first few months, that was normal. Her hunger hadn't returned, but she blamed that on how upset she was, how much she had to worry about. More concerning, the dreams that had come with the baby, distinguishable by a particular saturation of color, had stopped. She told herself those weren't necessarily a symptom of pregnancy. They could have just as easily been the lost spirit of her ʻaumakua in search of his shell.

And then came the absence, the palpable feeling of someone having left the room. Gone was the voracious fullness. Now when she closed her eyes she saw leftover balloons from a party long over, sinking to the ground, slowly losing air. She checked obsessively for blood. She didn't know what she wanted to happen, so she continued to stay in bed, ignoring the passing days, thinking that perhaps in this way they would not pass at all.

A few nights later, deep in sleep, the dark waves carried her away. The current pulled her in a direction she could not determine. The cold wet slapped her skin. Someone pulled the plug in the tub. The suction tugged her down. She resisted, fought and kicked to remain above the surface.

When she finally woke, blood was her sheets, the mattress, and the floor. Blood was the footprints left behind, the handprints on the wall. The ghost of the honu had come and taken her baby away. The cramping in her stomach was her body waving goodbye. She screamed, and that's when the girl all knuckles and knees, the `elepaio, crashed through the door.

THE CHIEFESS PALIULI HAD a house that rested on the wings of birds. It was thatched with royal yellow feathers. It was said that whenever there sounded a note from the `elepaio, it was time for Paliuli to come out.

LAKA'S `ELEPAIO WAS NAMED BEATRIZ.

The night Beatriz found her she said little, only hushing Laka softly whenever she tried to speak. When Laka started to shiver in fever, the girl with the strange green eyes that seemed to change color wiped her forehead with a washcloth and rubbed her fingers through Laka's hair until she fell asleep. She stayed with Laka that night, and the night after. When another wave of blood hemorrhaged out of her and soaked the sheets once again, Beatriz went to her room next door and brought back her own. When Laka's fever finally broke, Beatriz fed her bowls of hot chicken papaya soup and told her stories. Sometimes she told Laka stories of her family, of her Portuguese great-grandpa De Lima who had come from the island of Madeira to be luna at the sugar plantation that would eventually become the original HC&S sugar mill. He fell immediately in love with a woman he supposed was Hawaiian, asking her to marry him by the end of their first day together. It did not occur to him to confirm her ethnicity. Back then, Beatriz said, being Portuguese meant you were European, so when you got to Hawai`i you were offered an acre of land and a better contract than any locals would ever be offered. Not wanting to risk his land or contract, De Lima didn't mention his possibly Hawaiian wife. When they had a son, they registered him as Portuguese. De Lima's wife soon opened a small cafe that everybody swore served hands-down the best malasada and Portuguese bean soup on the entire island. By the time Beatriz's mom was born, the De Limas were considered as Portuguese as you could get.

Mostly, though, Beatriz told Laka older stories. Hawaiian stories, the kind Laka had grown up hearing, except these were rooted in Maui. In this way she began to understand that, while the Hawaiian Islands were connected like siblings, they were not identical. Each had a rhythm, a heartbeat, unique to itself.

Beatriz told her of the red waters of Wai`ānapanapa, of Princess Popalaea who caught the unwanted attention of Chief Kakae, who was not a great guy. He took Popalaea as his wife, but soon grew angry that she did not love him. Her friends helped Popalaea escape, taking her to hide in the lava cave of Wai`ānapanapa, which was shielded by a great pool of water, but which also betrayed them. Kakae found her by its reflections. He ordered his men to kill her, staining the cave red with her blood. Now, whenever the night marchers were out, the red opae gathered in the waters of Wai`ānapanapa and turned it red in remembrance of the slain princess.

Another of Beatriz's favorite stories was about an old blind woman who fished every night by the light of the moon at a pond on the other side of Hana, accompanied by her cousin, a mo`o. Of course Laka knew of mo`o, but she had only ever known them in the context of her island, of the shape-shifting, man-eating lizard Kikipua who stood in the way of Hi`iaka as she traveled to Kaua`i to rescue and retrieve her sister's lover, who was being held hostage in a cave by a band of mo`o. But the mo`o Beatriz described were different. Eventually the mo`o who escorted the old blind woman to the pond in Hana restored her eyesight.

Beatriz used stories to explain herself. Like the giant black lizard goddess Kiha-wahine whose spirit lived in a fishpond of Haneo`o. It was said that whenever there was foam on the pond, Kiha-wahine was there. A few days before Beatriz burst into Laka's room, Beatriz said she'd been at the Nahiku pond when the mo`o goddess Lani-wahine had appeared, a sure sign something terrible was on the horizon. Which is why, Beatriz explained, she'd been ready when Laka's scream came.

In Beatriz's stories there were always mo`o, sometimes as big and prominent as dragons, sometimes as small as a gecko sunbathing on a screen window, but always present. So much so that Laka started wondering if Beatriz was one. The Big Island was the island of Pele, not the mo`o women, but she'd had enough shape-shifting encounters with Hulali and her glimmers of `aumakua to believe it was more than possible. In spite of Beatriz's blazing green eyes and light skin, her Portuguese ancestors, Laka was starting to believe that Beatriz was the most Hawaiian person she had ever met.

Laka slowly regained her strength. But the blood still trickled from her womb, so Beatriz said it was time to take a trip.

THE BUS DRIVER GRUNTED, darts shooting out his eyes, mumbling to them to hurry up and get in. Beatriz winked at Laka and ignored him, keeping the door open so Laka could climb gingerly up the stairs and make her way down the aisle to a bench. Beatriz settled in next to her as the driver ground the bus into gear and let Laka rest her head on her shoulder as they made their way to Lahaina, tapping her on the thigh to wake her when they got to their destination.

They made their way down a rocky path toward the beach while Beatriz explained where they were going. The Hauola Stone was a healing pōhaku held by the ancients as sacred. Where Beatriz stopped, the shoreline was full of rocks, so at first Laka didn't see it. It wasn't until Beatriz instructed her to sit that she made it out. The Hauola was chair-shaped and half-immersed in the ocean. Beatriz guided her on until Laka was sitting fully in it, her back reclined and legs dangling in the water. Beatriz hitched up her pareo and knelt down to wash Laka's legs with the water surrounding the stone, dousing her upper thighs and lower back. She never stopped talking. Beatriz always had a story to tell, for which Laka was grateful. With Beatriz, she was never alone with her thoughts. Together they were washing away the last of the life created by her and David, from a time that felt forever ago, a time too painful to think about.

CHAPTER 6

1967

Laka learned to ignore the dull and perpetual empty that lived in the deep of her stomach. Her breasts shriveled down to size. Beatriz helped her get a job at the Hana Hotel, where she worked at the front desk. Beatriz had put in a good word for her with Oshiro, the boss, assuring him that Laka knew as much as she did about Maui and could give guests expert advice.

While Beatriz checked tourists into their rooms and helped plan their stay, Oshiro put Laka at the front door as a greeter. In spite of the implication of the title, Laka was encouraged to say as little as possible. Oshiro went on to say guests could *understand* Beatriz and would *connect* to her more, but what he really meant was that Laka's pidgin English was unrefined and guests would have trouble understanding her. Her duties included smiling and placing a lei around every visitor's neck, kissing them on the cheek as she did so. She was a photo opportunity. Ambience, Oshiro said, as if it were a compliment. He docked her first month's pay for the uniform she was required to wear, something she very well could have made herself had she been given the option, and insisted she wear heels like the other girls, given the visibility of her post. Whenever there was a lull in arrivals, she was asked to tidy up, to empty overflowing ashtrays and straighten the brochure displays.

The lobby was stuffy and the heels gave her blisters, but she clunked around and smiled, not wanting Beatriz to think she was ungrateful for all that her new friend had done for her.

Their days took on a steady routine. Now they both woke before dawn to shuffle down the hall to the shared bathroom and splash cold water on their faces before running for the bus. The county had recently expanded the Hana Road and everyone swore it made getting from Kahului to Hana a thousand times easier, but it still took over an hour to get from the boardinghouse to the hotel. The creaky old bus shuddered around narrow hairpin turns and across one-lane bridges all the way down Maui's deadliest coast, Beatriz sometimes nodding off but Laka sitting rigid and upright for every minute, determined to stay awake, sure they'd crash or plunge over the edge of the cliff the minute she stopped paying attention. It was in those times when thoughts of David crept in. Hana Road was so different from the smooth straight roads of Hilo, the cliffs so lush with blooming brush, the sparkling diamond white sand so dazzling it made her eyes hurt. Was he currently marching through the jungles of Vietnam? Was he even alive? By the time they reached Hana Bay, the plumeria trees and palm fronds that lined the entrance to the hotel swaying slightly as if waving hello, she was always ready to go to work to get out of her head. The bus let them off in the back, out of sight of the guest entrance, and from there everyone scattered: lifeguards to their stations, beach attendants to their towel racks, electricians to their fuse boxes, and Laka and Beatriz to the lobby.

Sundays were by far Laka's favorite day of the week, but what she loved most about workdays were their lunch breaks when they'd sneak off with the girls from housekeeping. Those girls were always giggling, comparing stories of the strange things they'd found under beds or the mysterious stains left behind. They laughed because most of what they all did was awful, their jobs thankless. To laugh was something they had the power to do.

Long before Laka showed up, Beatriz had told Oshiro that she was Catholic and couldn't work on Sundays. When she'd mentioned Laka, she'd said that they knew each other from church. It was a stretch, but Oshiro couldn't very well accuse them of lying, at least not to their faces. This meant that they had every Sunday off.

In a nod to the holy origins of their stolen time, it was Beatriz who first suggested they walk a portion of the trail that ran the length of Hana, through the grasses to Palapala Ho`omau Church overlooking the Kipahulu Point, where they prayed for all the things they didn't talk about. It quickly became their Sunday afternoon ritual. Laka held her breath as they passed the cemetery and exhaled only after they were standing fully on the red painted floor of the white church with its green hat and matching green pews inside.

In Hana, there were no winter blizzards or crisp bursting springs, but there was the season of full pews, the season when the famous pilot Charles Lindbergh and his wife and child, the one who hadn't been kidnapped and murdered, would move into their winter cottage in Maui to escape the noise of the world. When the famous man was there, the church crowd was polite, they took in his silence from a distance—when he was happy, they joined in, when he was sad, no one had to ask why. When positioned close enough, Laka stared at the back of his aging head. With her eye she drew on him a leather bomber cap, a flight jacket, a full head of hair. He never turned around or looked at her, a word was never traded, but she felt connected to him. They'd both lost a child. He was from another world, and yet his sadness was her own. His money, fame, and power had not protected him from loss. Although she couldn't help but think that if she or David had had any one of those things, he might not have felt compelled to go to war, her mother might not have worried so much that they'd lose their land, and maybe all that might have saved her baby. She watched the pilot's spotted hand grab hold of his seat to use as leverage to stand. He had all the things that would have saved her. Yet they hadn't saved him.

The pews emptied into the yard. In her mouth were the words that she was sorry, for him, for his child, that she too had woken up in that blood, but when he came close, she lost her nerve. Her eyes dropped to his feet and her words stayed in her mouth.

THE NEXT SUNDAY LAKA ASKED Beatriz if they could go somewhere besides the church. Beatriz said she had just the place, a different kind of holy.

The Seven Sacred Pools of Ohe`o Gulch were really more than that: up and up the gulch a series of waterfalls poured into one pool after another. The girls navigated the vines of thick jungle until they found the perfect pool, deep blue and clear with a waterfall all to themselves. Beatriz ripped off her clothes and jumped in. Laka was not far behind. They took turns floating on their backs, laughing as their breasts bobbed on the water's surface, pulling each other by the hands to make their hair fan out behind them, the water rushing to get out of their way.

LAKA COULDN'T PUT HER FINGER ON when exactly the change happened. Beatriz's uniform started fitting differently, just a little more snug around the waist. Beatriz said nothing so neither did Laka, but when her belly grew round enough to the point she was pinning the zipper of her skirt because it wouldn't go up all the way, Laka finally confronted her.

Beatriz sighed and made them tea, uncharacteristically quiet. Laka gulped hers with frustrated impatience and burned her tongue. She tapped her foot, waiting for Beatriz to tell her when and how she'd managed to get pregnant without Laka noticing. And where she was hiding her man. She assumed by then that she knew everything about Beatriz. Apparently not.

Instead of answering Laka's questions, Beatriz told her the story of Kamohoali`i, shark god and brother of Pele, Nāmaka, and Hi`iaka. He went often to swim in the waters of Waipi`o Valley, where he noticed a beautiful girl on the beach collecting seashells. The girl was a very good swimmer and spent much of her time in the water. Kamohoali`i watched and eventually fell in love with her. Since he could assume any shape he chose, he presented himself to her as a very handsome man. He summoned the waves. Just as she was about to be swept away, he saved her. In this way she became his. When she told him she was with child, he admitted to her why he only came to her at night. He was a shark, which meant she would have to care for the child without him.

EVENTUALLY LAKA RESIGNED HERSELF to the fact that Beatriz didn't want to talk about it. She focused on doing everything she could to help her friend. All the caring she'd once put into her brothers and sisters, she gathered up in a box and set at Beatriz's feet. Long hours at the hotel turned Beatriz's ankles into fat red stumps, so at the end of the day Laka soaked them in hot water and rubbed them. She let out the hems of Beatriz's uniform so it would fit over her swelling belly.

Sometimes Beatriz went back to telling her stories. Laka started hearing undercurrents of meaning in them and wondered what Beatriz was really saying. When they saw a pueo on a fence post, she thought about the owl god Pueonuiakea, the special protector who brought life back to wandering souls. Beatriz spoke of the baby as if she and Laka were the parents, about how Kamehameha I had considered himself created by two fathers. About the ancient system of hānai, when a woman cemented her bond to a childless friend by giving her one of her own. How, with a single-sentence proclamation, the baby became part of that new family, blood and guts and all. How irreversible and binding that was, how the child would die if the process was undone.

Whenever Laka got frustrated with Beatriz's continued refusal to talk in anything other than circles, she told herself it would come in time.

The only thing that came was the time.

GRAY IN THE FACE, Beatriz told Laka she wanted to go float at the Seven Sacred Pools. Her back hurt, and that was the only thing that would help. It didn't seem the greatest idea, but Laka took in Beatriz's eyes, her sudden heaviness of spirit, and prepared them to go. Together they made their way carefully up the gulch to their pond. Laka helped ease Beatriz in what Laka hoped was the same way Beatriz had once helped her onto the Hauola Stone.

At the edge of the water Beatriz went stiff. She grunted. The baby was coming. She dug her nails into Laka's shoulder. Her stomach clenched and relaxed, clenched and relaxed, a pulsing fist. Laka stroked her hair. Whatever was coming was coming. Beatriz's face exuded a solemn calm. Laka ran to the road for help.

It didn't take long for her to find someone willing to give them a ride to the hospital, but Beatriz refused to get in until both the driver and Laka promised there would be no hospital. Hospitals were for the sick and dying. A woman needed a safe place and other women around her to bring a life into the world, the way it had always been done, Before.

"Home," she growled through clenched teeth. The boardinghouse was not home for either of them but that's where Laka directed the car because there was nowhere else. They shuffled into the boarding-house, with its rice paper walls that were thin enough for all the other women of the house to hear.

WHEN IT WAS DONE those women returned to their rooms, leaving Laka to wipe the rag over Beatriz's forehead and smooth the hair from her face. They wrapped the baby in a sheet pulled from Laka's bed. Laka waited until both baby and Beatriz were asleep before slipping back into her room, where she curled into a ball on the bare mattress and let the tears fall until darkness finally came.

In the morning her body clock woke her automatically in time for the bus. She hurried to check on Beatriz and the baby before work, but the room next door had no Beatriz. Only a note and Laka's sheet and the bundle wrapped tenderly inside it.

CHAPTER 7

The truth hit Laka like cold water. A swimming sensation she took to be shock immediately replaced by the realization that she had been preparing for this outcome, had known it in her na`au from the beginning.

Amid the twisted sheets of Beatriz's unmade bed, the baby seemed to sense its uncertain place in the world. It waved tight furious fists, pleading with the air. Love me. Laka moved toward it, glancing at the note briefly. It was three words long, barely a sentence.

They locked eyes. Laka forgot to breathe. For a brief moment the room dropped away, the world and all its complications, nothing mattered, nothing existed except this child in front of her. Whatever happened the next day or the one after, Laka would worry about it then. There was no way to explain any of it, but she felt it with a certainty she'd never experienced. She belonged to that baby.

A small dent in the old worn mattress was the only trace of Beatriz left in the tiny room. Laka adjusted herself into the groove her friend's body had left behind. The baby calmed. When she rooted closer, a snarfle grunt escaped her. Laka knew what it wanted, what it sought, just as well as she knew what she couldn't give. Her nervousness kept her body stiff and unresponsive, awkward. She moved compulsively, reaching out as if to verify the tiny hands, every finger and every toe with their teeny tiny nails, every inch of miracle. The baby was unlike any she had seen before, this was nothing she had ever felt. She no longer wondered how her and David's baby might have looked. The baby in front of her was the only creation that could have ever been. Long and skinny, with skin so pale it was streaked with a faint blue. She was in awe.

She forced air into her shoulders, willing herself to exhale and relax her body. The baby pursed its lips, making desperate little sucking sounds. There was no bottle, no milk, nothing even for a stray mewing at the door. Laka lifted her shirt, feeling as if it was the baby who was taking charge, directing what happened from here on out.

She eyed the flat, brick-colored disk that was her areola, pinching her soft tapered mound of a nipple. It was supple, unsuspecting, still somewhat tender from her own pregnancy. She pinched it again, harder. When it began to pucker, she rubbed it on the baby's cheek. The baby responded immediately, latching on. Laka gasped. She'd watched this act countless times but was not prepared for the odd sensation of the suction, the discomfort of the pull. The baby sucked twice and then released. It whimpered. Laka ran her nipple again around the periphery of the baby's open mouth.

"Come on," she whispered. There was no milk, but she had nothing more to offer, her body just a pacifier, a disappointment, an apology. She whispered again.

"I will keep you safe. Blood of my blood, you are my child. My Hi`i."

By the following morning, both nipples were chapped and raw, distorted, unrecognizable. Laka rubbed them with coconut oil and bit down against the pain. The next time Hiʻi took one in her mouth, milk came down to greet her.

THE BOARDINGHOUSE WAS FOR unmarried, single women. It was not a nursery, not an orphanage. There were rules, no exceptions. She was given until the end of the week to find someplace else to live. She only had enough savings left for that long anyway.

A LITTLE OVER A WEEK AFTER the baby was born, the sad quiet man in the front pew of the church, Charles Lindbergh, the adopted son of Hana, died in his little cottage. Stars winked across Hana Bay, beckoning their beloved friend to join them. Laka was awake, worrying over where she would go and how she would get there, her brain scrambling for a plan. She heard the whisper of the famous pilot as he joined the eternities. She cried because she hadn't known him though his legacy made her feel close, she cried because he left behind a void she couldn't explain, and she cried because she was so exhausted she could barely breathe. The baby was a night creature. Moonshine made her coo, made her hungry and thirsty. Made her soil the cloth pinned to her bottom. Laka had no idea what she was doing, had no model for raising a child alone.

Sunrise found Laka still awake, staring out the window, watching the wind lift the edges of the curtain. The baby had finally drifted off, the white light of day signaling its time for rest. Black-feathered myna birds chirped and hopped from branch to branch on the tree outside, bright yellow beaks making them more than moving shadows. Their coloring reminded her slightly of her feathered Miss

Aloha Hula costume. Such a different, distant life, it was hard to reconcile with her reality now, the things that suddenly mattered, all that suddenly didn't. It was a clear day, clear enough to see all the way to the ends of the ocean. Laka considered the horizon, the touch of haze in her periphery, the Big Island. Hilo, its siren call. She shut the window and turned away. She did not know where to go, but she could not go there.

Her eyelids turned to lead. She tiptoed to the bed and crawled in, careful not to disturb the baby. The squeal of the mattress coils might as well have been the ringing of a gong.

An hour later, the screams turned hoarse, but still the baby bawled. She did not want to nurse, did not want to be rocked, did not want to be held or let alone, walked or not walked. Her face was swollen with frustrated fury. And suddenly Laka couldn't do it anymore. Her arms and legs turned to liquid. She sank to the floor and set the baby down. For a long while she cried alongside the infant. Her body shook as she got to her knees and pressed her forehead to the ground. The baby choked on a scream and kicked through her swaddle. Laka pressed her hands in prayer.

To the baby: "Please. Please tell me what to do."

To the ceiling: "Please. Please tell me what to do."

The ceiling was unmoved. A tiny foot caught her in the nose and tears sprang to her eyes. A mo`o crawled across a beam above her head and stopped. She asked it what it was staring at. Asked it if its name was Beatriz. Then asked herself if she had lost her mind.

There was no time to change or to do much more than pack a few things in a plastic shopping bag. When she heard the bus coming down the road, there was time only to clutch the baby to her and run. Her legs buckled. They were as tired as she was. But they made it on.

She'd never been to Ka'anapali, and Beatriz had told her little. The driver was unfamiliar. He did not smile as she boarded and did not bother waiting for her to find a seat before slamming on the gas pedal. She found comfort in his ambivalence.

Hi'i soiled her diaper before they got to their stop. Loose yellow kaka dripped onto Laka's shirt. She adjusted her grip on the baby so the other riders couldn't see. She asked a woman sitting across the aisle if she knew where Laka might find the De Lima family of Ka'anapali, a cafe that had the best malasada and Portuguese bean soup? The woman frowned. Plenty of places she could say had good malasada, although nowhere served bean soup as good as hers. And no, she was sorry, she knew everyone in Ka'anapali, but she'd never heard of the De Limas.

Laka's face fell. The woman told her not to lose heart, plenty of the old sugarcane families of Ka'anapali had moved to nearby Lahaina. Laka tried to recall if Beatriz had mentioned where exactly her family had opened their cafe. Her tired brain drew a blank.

LAHAINA WAS AN OVERWHELMING SWIRL of faces and traffic, buildings and business, honking horns—an entire place moving at swirling, liquid speed. She walked down one congested street after another, asking shop owners and hotel doormen if they knew the De Lima family, the one that owned a restaurant. When she hit a dead end, she started asking where she could find a malasada and a bowl of Portuguese bean soup. They all pointed her in different directions.

By the end of the day she was starving and needed a minute to get Hi'i changed before they took the long bus ride back to the boardinghouse. The baby rooted into her chest. At a small cafe she took a corner table near the door and ordered a bowl of fried rice, tucking the baby under her shirt to nurse while she waited for her food. She pulled Beatriz's note from her pocket.

Blood and all

She knew what it meant, that this child was now hers, but did she really believe it? This was not ancient Hawai`i. Hānai still existed, but its protocol—the single sentence voiced as the child was handed over to the new parent by its original ones, words that would forever after declare that that child was the child of that new parent in every way—did not seem as steadfast and binding in today's world. And, ignoring the legal complications she might have gotten herself into, did she truly believe Hi`i was now hers in every way? Was her belief that Beatriz was a mo`o who had given birth to a child meant for her, strong enough to survive in this world that said ancient Hawaiian customs and ways were nothing but the savage mythos of a people in need of salvation?

The rice when it came was dark brown, sticky with oyster sauce, flecked with Portuguese sausage bits and chopped green onions, exactly as her father used to make on a rare day in the kitchen. It smelled like Keaukaha in July, of Puhi Bay and Sundays. It felt like an intrusion. She was too exhausted to think about her father, didn't want anything reminding her of her mother or David or home. She started packing up to go, resigned. The waitress returned to fill her water glass and asked if Laka needed anything else. Did she happened to know a girl named Beatriz, from Ka`anapali? Light skin, ehu hair, freckles. The waitress shook her head. Plenty haole come here, the woman said. Dey all look alike.

Of all Beatriz had told her, one thing was clear. Laka was not to go looking for her, not meant to find her. If she had ever existed at all.

* * *

IT TAKES A VILLAGE.

Over the coming days, Hilo's siren call grew louder. They were there, waiting. She knew, she felt their impatience crawling over her skin. She cried almost as much as the baby. She cried so much she stopped being aware of it. Tears fell from her face without explanation. She now lived in a place beyond tired, where sleep did not exist. She pinched her skin and felt nothing. Hi`i needed a mom who was not deliriously tired. In Hilo, there was always someone around to help. No one suffered anything entirely alone.

UNDER THE WANING SHADE of a palm tree, she watched Hi`i sleep. From the bundled towel at Laka's side came a soft, steady snore. The spine of the tree dug into Laka's back. She adjusted her position the best she could without disturbing Hi`i's sleep. She was already failing as a mother, which stung her pride. After partially raising her brothers and sisters and spending most of her life surrounded by aunties and a mother with babies coming out her ears, she'd thought somehow that taking on the care of an infant would be second nature. So far it had been anything but, although she did sometimes wonder if perhaps that was a question of blood—if Hi`i had come from her opu, would she be better at caring for her? Or was it simply that she needed the village? The least she could do was suffer the discomfort of sitting in the dirt so as to not wake the child. They would be there a few more hours, until dark at least, and then she would do what had quickly become their routine: rummage for edible scraps in the bin outside the market and then walk in circles until it was late enough to go back to the boardinghouse undetected. For perhaps the hundredth time that hour, she fingered the velvet bag in her lap, touching the delicate shell strands inside with the tip of a finger, not daring to pull the necklace completely out into the open.

The last time she had worn it, she had been pregnant. Would she have miscarried if she had refused to put it on? At the time, she had not had the courage then to shame the family with thousands of people watching, had not had the courage to face Hulali's reaction even if it meant her baby's life. Had thought she could get away with it, just that once. As if the gods weren't watching. Her stomach soured. The miscarriage was her fault.

The few dollars in her pocket was the only money they had left. Since she had no one to take care of Hiʻi during her shifts, she'd had to give up her job at the hotel. Her savings were long gone. The Niʻi-hau shell lei was worth at least ten thousand dollars, probably much more. It was one of the few things she'd dared take with her when she left Hilo, but only because she'd feared what her mother might do if she left it behind, not because she'd ever considered it something of value she might need to use. If she sold it, they would have more than enough to get a place, to pay for the things they needed. Food, a place to live. Heck, selling it might even protect them from its power.

She got as far as the pawnshop door. With the honu shell destroyed, the lei was all that remained of the Naupaka moʻolelo. She desperately needed money to be able to take care of this baby. But in her pause Hiʻi had squirmed, uncomfortable. Laka understood. The baby was right. When that money was spent, that wasn't all that would be gone. The history, the memories of the queen wearing it, gifting it to her great-great-grandmother, the pride and grace of the kingdom it had come from, that would be gone as well. Ten thousand dollars was nothing compared to that. No amount could possibly match its value.

The baby calmed in agreement. Laka pulled the drawstring of the velvet purse closed and tried not to cry. Now what?

She rummaged in Hi`i's diaper bag until she found a pen and a crinkled piece of paper. She smoothed it against her thigh and steadied her pen. It was time.

As she wrote, she was careful not to let her tears drip onto the letter. She did not want the ink to run. She wanted to be clear. She sketched a picture of her daughter sleeping in a makeshift bassinet near a window. Hi`i Naupaka, she wrote, punctuated by the date and time of her birth, so Hilo could line up her birth with the stars, so they could begin to prepare for their homecoming.

The reply was nearly immediate, as if Hulali had been in the rafters all that time, readying to swoop. Back at the boardinghouse, Laka swallowed her panic and kissed the baby's feet, pressing them to her mouth. Her mother was already on her way.

CHURCH BELLS SHATTERED THE SILENCE of the morning. As Laka prepared for Hulali, the valley prepared for the famous pilot's funeral. Irons hissed; the air smelled of starch and freshly picked flowers.

Laka wiped the walls of her rented room in the boardinghouse with a mop to expend the anxiety surrounding Hulali's arrival, praying that they wouldn't get kicked out before she got there and that her landlord would show them mercy by leaving them alone for however long her mother planned to stay. The baby lay on the floor, kicking air.

Using a borrowed metal bucket, Laka soaked their threadbare sheets and the stained towels and rags she'd turned into diapers. She wrung them outside and left them on the balcony to dry. There was little more that could be done to improve her living quarters, but it was impossible to relax. She grabbed the baby and walked to the fruit stand on the corner. The sun was high, the smell of overripe bananas thick. She caught the merchant as he was closing up, about to make his way over to the memorial. For the last of her saved wages, he sold her everything on the verge of spoiled, what he would not have been able to sell the next day. A cloud of gnats followed her back to her room. She placed her fruit in a bowl on a small table near the window. Her eyes remained fixed on the table as she nursed the baby. The bowl of fruit had been meant to be comforting, to make the room feel more abundant, to show her mother they were not desperate, but it filled her instead with an unease she could not explain.

The crashing broomstick set off a ripple the moment it hit the floor. Laka jerked awake, upsetting the bed so much the baby bounced herself awake, letting out a long cry.

It could have been the wind.

She knew it wasn't. It was doom, its warning. She rushed to the fallen broom, sweeping the bad spirits out the door before righting it in its corner and hurrying back to the bed, where the baby gulped angrily at her breast.

"Easy," she whispered, marveling her hand over the soft down of Hi`i's head, the tiny caterpillar body swaddled in old sheet.

"My Hi`i."

Eyes like green marbles stared up at her, burrowing into her soul. Trusting her.

The door opened and the Hilo rain forest blew in. The baby trembled. Laka pressed her tight against her chest, pulling the blanket up around her head.

Hulali greeted Laka formally before looking pointedly at the bundle in her arms, motioning slightly to hold her. Laka made no move to hand the baby over.

"Wea da aftah-birt?"

Hulali's question threw Laka off balance. She had completely forgotten. "I . . . uh . . . it's not here. I mean, it's gone. Buried already."

Hulali's eyes flashed. "Buried! Wea you goin' bury da aftah-birt of one Naupaka baby, da firstborn no less, oddah den back home undah da tree wea everybody else buried? How goin' be connected to da `āina of our family? Tell me you saved da piko, at least."

Laka nodded. When the tiny nub of umbilical cord had hardened and fallen off, she'd saved it without knowing exactly when, if ever, she'd be able to bury it under the tree where all the afterbirths and piko of the Naupakas were. She couldn't very well have buried it in the dirt outside the boardinghouse. So she'd wrapped it in a cloth and tucked it away, yet another detail needing to be sorted.

Hulali crossed the room and tugged down the blanket. A protest rose from within Laka, her instincts chiming to life. She realized her mother was not as tall in this room, away from Hilo.

"Nobody had da baby dream," Hulali said, her voice husky, distant.

"Not every child come wit a dream, Ma."

"Every Naupaka baby does." Hulali paused. "Dis baby haole. Not your cowboy's."

It was not a question. There was no time to wonder how much Hulali knew about her and David, or if she had known somehow about Laka's pregnancy, not that it would surprise her if she had—her mother had a way of knowing things. It didn't matter now.

The baby stopped sucking, alert to the foreign voice in the room. She ejected the nipple from her mouth with her little pink tongue and turned her head. Big green eyes blinking at a stranger. Hulali put a hand on her chest and took a step back.

"Dis not a Naupaka baby."

Laka pulled the cocooned caterpillar tighter to her chest, the image of the burning honu shell flashing in her memory. Her hands curled into fists. "Hi`i is my daughter." Her voice was a hoarse whisper.

After a long silence, Hulali suggested they go for a walk.

Outside, the baby gurgled and waved her arms. Laka wanted her mother to turn around to see, but Hulali, as always, walked too quickly.

They crossed the glaring white sand of the shoreline and took the winding grassy trail toward the slopes of Haleakala. Hulali used her hat to swat mosquitoes along the way. A mongoose rustled in the bushes. Other than that, all was still. Hulali spoke in a long stream without changing her stride. "In ancient times," she began, "we walked on da Hoapili Trail, one of da last remaining sections of da King's Highway. Five hundred years ago dea was too much water in some places and not enough in others. Fishponds flooded on one side and wen go dry on da oddah. The king laid stone, connecting one pond to da next and den da next, so dat dea could be balance among dem. A field no can sustain itself if not connected to its source. Without da stones to connect dem, da ponds dry up and disappear."

She stopped to look over her shoulder, a glancing flicker to the baby draped across Laka's chest. Laka suddenly pitched forward as her foot caught on a root hiding in the dirt. Hulali shot through the air, steadying Laka with a firm grip. Her hand lingered. Laka adjusted the baby's carrier, pulling her arm away from her mother.

"We gotta make sure da stones of da trail stay pili. If all da stones stood alone, dea would be no trail, no connection. You da firstborn in a long line of firstborns. You a Naupaka. You critical in keeping da trail connected, yeah? Dis bebeh is somebody else's kuleana. You get yours. Tell da truth. Take dat child back to wherever it came from. Let it be where it belong. Den you come home, where *you* belong."

Laka considered telling her mother about Beatriz and her moʻo stories, about searching for her and her vanishing into thin air, about the feeling she'd had the moment she and Hiʻi first laid eyes on each other. Laka looked down at the warm cocoon strapped to her chest. Her mother had always openly believed in Hawaiʻi's supernatural elements, but did she believe it enough to override her belief in blood quantum laws?

Hulali tilted her head and squinted off into the distance as if she were having a conversation inside her own mind. She turned back to Laka and tried a different approach.

"You know, we Hawaiians was always differen' from haole in how we saw family. We always had hānai, da babies go to da gran'parens or to da frien' dat no can have bebeh. But Laka, if dis bebeh hānai, dis not da way. T'ings moa complicated now, yeah? Gotta have blood."

Any hope that Hulali would believe her evaporated instantly. She tightened her grip on the baby. "Dis child is mine."

By the time they returned, the chapel was empty, the memorial over. The famous pilot was dead and buried, and Hulali returned to Hilo alone.

"YOU PAY NOW!"

Mr. Kwok, the husband of the boardinghouse manager, banged his fist on the thin door. His feet were two shadows in the gap between the floor and where the door fell short.

"I know you inside!"

Laka whispered a silent apology to the baby for the hand she held firm across her tiny mouth, for the fingers pressing into the fat baby cheeks. They couldn't afford a whimper.

For once, baby girl was merciful. Eyes big as the moon, somehow knowing. The shadow under the door disappeared.

She had to go outside eventually. The fruit was long gone and the pile of soiled diapers was growing ripe. She missed work, the Hana Hotel with its pakalana blossom perfume and towels fluffed fresh in the dryers in the basement. She missed stealing hand lotion from the lobby ladies' room. Missed brushing her hair and not smelling of puke. Missed sleep. Mrs. Kwok was demanding double the rent. Two people means double occupancy, she said. She didn't have the money to pay rent for one, much less two.

Later, when the buses taking everyone to work were gone, she peeked her head into the hall. The doors of the other rooms were all closed. She grabbed the baby and tiptoed to the bathroom. Cushioning the dry bottom of the bathtub with a towel, she set the baby down and hurried back to the room for the mountain of urine- and shit-soaked diapers. She filled the basin with hot water and began to scrub.

Barely halfway through, she sensed someone join them.

"T'ink you so sneaky, yeah?"

Mrs. Kwok was the tiniest woman Laka had ever seen. When they'd first met, her thin legs had reminded Laka of the sandpiper birds that ran along the dunes. A petite black-and-white mutt yapped at her ankles. It growled at her feet and began barking at the bathtub. Laka positioned herself between them and the baby, holding her hands up in surrender.

"Aunty, tomorrow, I get da money but I gotta go pick it up today, I promise."

She used her soft voice, the one reserved for compliments and congratulations, for the receiving of praise. How long it had been since she'd used it. The last time was when she'd been crowned Miss Aloha Hula. How she wanted to laugh at that unbroken person she'd been, so proud and triumphant, troubled by problems that seemed so small now.

Mrs. Kwok squinted and shook a disapproving finger in Laka's face.

"I let you slide den all da girls going stop paying too. Den where I be? No. You pay now. My husband, he come with police."

She stomped a tiny slippered foot. Laka widened her hands, showing she had nothing, pleading, ready to say anything to buy them just a little more time.

"Please, Mrs. Kwok. I get da money. It's coming. I have a new job. I jus' have to go get my paycheck, okay? You goin' have it by tomorrow. I promise."

The Chinese woman considered her for a moment, then turned and moved abruptly toward the stairwell. The dog hesitated. She whistled for him, and called over her shoulder, "One hour. You get your stuff, you get out. Or I call police."

Laka had hit a dead end.

CHAPTER 8

1968

At the harbor, everyone was busy reading the newspaper. Poor widowed First Lady Jackie O. was spending some of her mourning time in Kaua`i and there were reports she would come to Maui next. The number of local boys killed in Vietnam that year was up to forty-two. Laka ignored the headlines and looked for the husband of one of the hotel cleaners she knew through Beatriz. He worked for Matson Containers and promised he could get her on a barge to Hilo, no problem.

The trip was uncomfortable, but uneventful. Laka made a seat out of her bag in the space between two house-sized steel shipping containers full of toilet paper and Spam. For as big as the barge was, it moved faster than Laka expected. The crescent bay of Hilo, the snow-capped Mauna Kea, and the green sea of Hamākua cane field appeared before she was ready.

Hilo. Laka was back, but something was different, off, as if everything had shifted an inch while she'd been in Maui. She tried to sink into the imprint she'd left behind, but either she or it had changed shape, she wasn't sure. Nothing and everything was the same.

Keaukaha, always and forever the place she felt most at home, now made her nervous. Would her siblings come to understand and forgive her for leaving them? As it was, she didn't know how to reach them without crashing into her mother. And would Hiʻi be accepted? Or would she be questioned, judged? Hiʻi had diaper rash and was cranky. Laka was uncertain of her abilities as a mother. She told herself that once she got a handle on the diaper rash, once Hiʻi started sleeping through the night, those worries would fade. Once Laka found her bearings, she'd be able to protect Hiʻi no matter what happened.

She bartered her way into a small room on the edge of a macadamia nut farm, waking while it was still dark to clean up after the men who harvested the trees at night. It didn't pay hardly at all and the room had rats that made her hover obsessively over Hiʻi even more than usual, but it put a roof over their heads and was work she could do before Hiʻi woke. But even without the burden of boardinghouse rent, she desperately needed money. To absorb the endless expenses a baby incurs, Hilo operated on a system of hand-me-downs and sharing. In separating herself, she'd separated herself from that too. She'd gone back to Hilo the town but was still resisting going back to Hilo the community. She crawled from one end of Front Street to the other, begging shopkeepers for work, promising to do any job they'd give her. It was no use. No one was going to hire a woman with a baby stuck to her tit. Her explanation, that the baby wouldn't eat from anyone else, fell on deaf ears. No one outside of Keaukaha recognized her as Miss Aloha Hula Laka Naupaka. She supposed she wasn't that person anymore anyway.

At the beach, a tourist asked her how much she billed per hour, mistaking her for a nanny, the white baby her charge. The men of Hilo recalibrated, sensing the disturbance in the finite ratio of men versus women on the island. They caught the scent of fresh bait. In those early days, Laka was too tired to notice. As if that made a difference.

Whoever her baby daddy was, he wasn't with her, and to Hilo boys, that was all that mattered.

WE CALLED TO HER in our dreams. We tugged her na`au, drew her like a magnet. We haunted her brain and barged into her thoughts. Keaukaha was an inevitability. She needed us as much as we needed her.

She was on her way back to the mac nut farm in a borrowed car after a trip to the market when, before she realized where she was going, she auto-pilot pulled into the parking lot of Richardson's, gathering all the babies around her as if they were medicine.

WE COULD HOLD A GRUDGE only so long. We tied our tongues, dogs on chains. Laka was home.

ON TUESDAYS AND THURSDAYS, hula nights, we left the babies to the twelve- and thirteen-year-olds. The hula halau staggered its practices, the girls of that age danced Mondays and Wednesdays. But even for those ninety minutes, as we forced our hips around and around for warm-up amis, as we hela'd side-to-side until sweat was dripping down our backs, Laka's babe wouldn't let her be. The squalling kid was tucked into a basket and set among the slippers outside the practice room. The closed doors and pounding ipu did little to drown out the screams coming from under the blankets in the basket. When the pitch rose high enough to shake the windows, Kumu stopped mid-chant. To learn a hula is to learn the choreography but also its accompanying poetry; there is no way to embody an element without first knowing what part of the element's story is being told—we needed to hear what Kumu was teaching in order to learn. The disapproving eyebrow in Laka's direction sent her into a dead run to the hall, pulling her shirt from the bound waistband of her muslin pa`u, freeing her breast as she ran.

Eventually, the former Miss Aloha Hula stopped coming to hula. We didn't need to ask why.

CHAPTER 9

1971

After George's funeral, Hulali moved to Oʻahu and Laka moved into the Keaukaha house with Hiʻi. It alleviated their money problems somewhat, but she remained on high alert, feeling like Hulali might try again to draw a line in the sand between her and Hiʻi. In those early days she hovered over Hiʻi as if she were a bird with a broken wing, but eventually, she exhaled. She got out the little cloth bundle filled with Hiʻi's piko that she'd been dragging around in her bag and finally took it to the backyard and buried it.

It was then, with her guard down, she finally said yes to Tony, the smooth-talking charmer who'd been asking her out for months. He wasn't the only guy who'd had his eye on her, but he was by far the most persistent. A peacock with his feathers on full display, it would have been funny if he wasn't driving everybody crazy, always talking about how beautiful she was, how he was going to be the one to catch her. He wasn't her type, with his tattoos and classic dark and handsome looks with a temper to match. He was different from David in nearly every way. But the more she said no, the more he persisted. It was his confidence that eventually softened her. By the time she relented, he'd placed her on a pedestal that made her remember the person she'd once been, feisty and rebellious. She'd returned from Maui feeling old and broken, her confidence that she knew what she was doing shattered. Tony's boyish charm was convincing enough to glue her shattered bits together again. What had been a one-sided pursuit quickly became a mutual infatuation.

Hi`i was four years old by then. She didn't need her mom as much. She went to preschool in the mornings and played at the beach in the afternoons. She slept through the night. If she was hungry, she pulled a banana off a stalk from the tree in the yard. When she wasn't working on the farm, Laka handled the newfound hours in her day the way a horse without a bit might, wandering aimlessly. She'd been so focused on learning the ropes of motherhood, Hi`i's needs guiding every minute of every day, that she'd forgotten how to be on her own, and now it felt uncomfortable.

The bar Tony took Laka to for their first date was dark and the best kind of seedy. A group of Japanese and Korean men swayed and spat into karaoke microphones, ignoring the dishes of kimchee and agedashi tofu the waitress piled on the table among the crowd of beer bottles. Put some food in your belly, the tattooed girl shouted. Soak up the alcohol. They sang off-key, ignoring the waitress. Tony grinned and asked Laka what she liked to do for fun, what kind of music she liked, what she did in her free time. The group's noise escalated, making it impossible to answer. Laka was grateful. What was fun, or free time? She didn't even know anymore. Overnight she'd gone from high school student training for Miss Aloha Hula to mom. She gave Tony another look. His eyes were full of laughter. Maybe he could teach her how to relax a little, to enjoy life before it passed her by. The waitress set a bowl of cabbage on the table between their drinks and mouthed an apology for the karaoke singers. Laka recognized her from high school. She was twenty pounds heavier and covered in tattoos that spread the length of her exposed shoulders and arms, but the angry sad pout was the same. Laka split her wooden chopsticks and picked at the cabbage, hoping the woman didn't figure out who she was. She didn't want a reunion, not right now. She was on her first grown-up date.

If the waitress did realize she was Laka Naupaka, she hid it well. She moved on to the next table, unimpressed and uninterested. Only deeper into the night, as the karaoke machine switched songs, Laka heard her name coming from a corner of the bar (Miss Aloha Hula runs away from home, disappears to Maui, and returns with a white baby—it was a story with enough juice in it to last years). The coconut phone, it was already ringing.

Laka called it a night.

MONTHS LATER, AS THEY LAY NAKED in his bed sharing a cigarette among the hapuʻu ferns in Mountain View, Tony asked her why they were still driving up mauka to spend time together when he spent half his time surfing and fishing in Keaukaha. It would make more sense to go to her place. She pulled at the twisted sheets.

"More quiet up hea."

He wasn't convinced. "Since when you care 'bout quiet? You shame be wit me?"

She barked out a laugh. "Dat so far from da truth it's funny. No, I not shame. You know, t'ings, dey complicated."

"You mean your kid? Da one you no like me meet? How come? You know I no mind you get one kid, but it's weird, like you trying for live two lives at da same time."

She stubbed the cigarette out in the ashtray on the floor and

released the smoke from her lungs in a long slow exhalation. She
watched the cloud rise and dissipate through the screen window. "Not
two lives," she said. "But my girl, she different. I not ready for answer
questions."

Tony mumbled under his breath. Questions were for people who
didn't know how to mind their own business, who liked to gossip. She
was going to have to trust that he was different.

And he was. The first time she brought him around her white-
skinned, green-eyed daughter, he was too stoned to raise an eyebrow.
It was just as well. Laka wasn't shopping for a father for Hi`i. Her
daughter didn't need anyone except her. It wasn't something she
would have ever admitted to him, but she found his ambivalence a
relief. She loved him for the way he made her feel like a woman. Not
the eldest daughter of Hulali Naupaka or a hula dancer or even a
mother. A woman. She felt herself around him, or the person she
was understanding herself to be. He was the first person since David who'd made her laugh. She needed more laughter. Tony was her
escape, her respite. For all these reasons but most especially for not
being concerned one way or another about the fair-skinned child she
called her own, Tony earned a place in her heart.

It was through Tony that she met Old Lady Tanaka. Their prop-
erties shared a stone retaining wall that ran directly down the middle
of a grove of avocado and mango trees. The relationship between Tony
and the old woman had developed over their crops—since the avocados were on one side and the mangoes were on the other, both were
always left with too much of one and not enough of the other. One
year, Tony left a box of surplus avocados on the wall between them.
The next day he found a box full of mangoes. They'd been happily
sharing produce ever since. When Laka told him that she needed a

job, he dragged her next door and turned her like a beauty pageant contestant.

"Your very own Miss Aloha Hula," he told his neighbor as she eyed Laka. "Da tourists going come like tsunami."

Since her return from Maui, Laka had told herself that the root of all her problems was her underemployment, but once she started working as a cashier at Old Lady Tanaka's store, the job didn't solve the things it was supposed to. She and her baby did not fall into Hilo's rhythm. She still woke up every day with the unsettling feeling that the world she was telling her daughter belonged to them would suddenly disappear, would prove itself untrue. Laka grew up in a place with no doors, open windows, and eyes everywhere. She'd felt claustrophobic at times, but looking back, she'd also felt safe, protected. Flaws and wrong choices were absorbed by the whole and accepted as part of the natural order of things. Life was one big roll with the punches. But Laka was beginning to realize things in Hilo were changing. The town itself was shifting shape, and she wasn't certain of her place within it anymore. Her possible wrong choices, her maybe mistakes, they were hers alone.

THE FIRST TIME TONY HIT HER was about six months after they got serious, which was just long enough for comfort to start setting in. Laka blamed the incident on circumstances—she'd pushed his buttons after he'd been drinking for hours and was already in a bad mood. She could hardly remember what the argument had been about, it had been that inconsequential. She'd made a comment about him not being productive, something along those lines. He'd warned her not to press him and she'd felt an irresistible urge to do exactly that, to see how far she could take his irritation. He was always telling her to chill, to stop being on edge all the time. Now who needed to chill?

The smack hadn't hurt, not really. The worst part of it was the presence of Hi`i, no longer a baby, whose big marble eyes turned to big sopping sponges anytime a pin dropped. Laka wondered if, at four, Hi`i's brain would start storing things.

"Toughen up," Laka said, and told her to get out, nudging her on her `ōkole.

Hi`i's eyes only widened and continued to watch, unblinking. Laka's irritation grew. Why couldn't the girl just play with her dolls and mind her own business? She was tired and a bit hungover and desperately needed a nap before her shift. But when she withdrew from the living room to the cool darkness of her bedroom, the girl followed and asked for lunch. Laka's vision went blurry. Before she could stop herself, she nudged Hi`i again, only this time the nudge was hard enough to knock the girl over. Laka stared at her child, waiting for her to cry or run away. Hi`i stayed on the floor where she'd fallen, splayed evidence of Laka's sharp edges. She told herself she was doing the best she could.

Every day the girl reminded her more and more of Beatriz. It wasn't just her skin or the way her hair flashed like fire in the sun, there were glimmers of her everywhere. Beatriz was there in the way Hi`i scrunched her nose when she tasted a food she didn't like. She was there in her chuckle and the way she turned everything into a story. She was there when Hi`i leaned up against Laka and fell asleep, reminding her of those long bus rides to the Hana Hotel. Over the years she'd grown more and more sure that Beatriz was a mo`o of the ponds who had gifted her back the child she had lost, but that did nothing to dispel the fear that she didn't know what she was doing with this

child so different from her, so seemingly fragile yet tenaciously resilient. At times the fear made her fierce and protective, ready to battle
the world to protect her child. Other times the fear made her so angry,
so frustrated with how much harder this had turned out to be, that
she lashed out at Hi`i. When she smoked with Tony sometimes the
record skipped and she forgot which chapter of her life she was currently in. Sometimes Laka pinched herself to keep from flying back
to Maui to find proof that Beatriz De Lima was a mo`o, to reassure
herself that they were safe. Other times she pinched herself to keep
from taking Hi`i somewhere far far away, where Beatriz would never
find them, in case she ever felt compelled to look. Always she worried
that her various missteps and flaws as a parent would be viewed as her
not being grateful or appreciative for this gift from the gods. A gift
given is a gift that can be taken back.

WHEN HI`I WAS FIVE (around the time we started thinking her limu
green eyes and ehu hair were going to stick), she brought a note home
from school, a reminder notice that her registration packet was incomplete, the birth certificate still missing. Laka crumpled the note
and sent Hi`i to her room. Hi`i was akamai. She was oblivious that
anything might be wrong, but she knew when she could push her
mom's buttons and when she shouldn't. She did as she was told.

The next day Laka walked Hi`i to her classroom door instead of
leaving her at the crosswalk as she usually did. Hi`i smiled proudly
and gave her mom a cheerful hug before slipping into her seat and
waving goodbye. Laka turned away from the classroom wishing she
could be as carefree as her child, as confident as Hi`i that the world
was going to let them be. At the school's front office, she noticed a

cousin, Momi, the daughter of Hulali's friend Pua, at the front desk, a phone strapped to her ear.

"Eh, cuz." She smiled when the phone call finally ended. She acted casual but hurried, as if she was late for work.

"Eh, Laka, how you?"

"Hi`i got one note yesterday that you no more her birth certificate, but I wen send in a copy dis summer."

Momi scratched her head. "Oh yeah, I t'ink I saw dat. You can bring one more copy?"

"No problem. Eh, but I gotta get to work, and maybe I t'ink I wen send her original to DHHL, you know, for homeland kine stuff, and da buggahs nevah send um back yet." Laka leaned on the counter as if exhausted. "Too much, yea, dis paperwork dey make us do every time."

Momi shuffled some papers and sighed audibly when the phone shrilled yet again. "You right about dat for sure. Eh, no worries about Hi`i's da kine. I'm sure it's around somewhere. I'll look laytahs. Sorry, I gotta get dis," she said, lifting the receiver and reattaching it to her ear. She rolled her eyes. "First-week craziness."

Laka gave her a thumbs-up and backed out the door as quickly as she could.

Every Wednesday from then on, Hi`i brought home another folder stuffed with paperwork full of questions for which Laka had no answer. Even if Hi`i was without a doubt a child born of a mo`o and therefore as Hawaiian as the rocks and valleys and soil of Hawai`i nei, that didn't make her Hawaiian by America's definition. But when Hi`i brought home the standard OHA questionnaire, the one that determined blood quantum lineage and any claims to Hawaiian scholarships, benefits, and, most critically, who could and would inherit the land they lived on, it was already filled in with pen.

"My teacher helped," she said when Laka asked her what made her check which boxes, the list of family that would prove Hawaiian blood.

"Teacher said no worries, we live Hawaiian Homes and everybody knows the Naupakas, everybody know we Hawaiian. Look, Ma, here, I wrote Tutu's name. Hulali."

Laka took the paper to the porch and lit a cigarette. She read through the list of questions on the OHA form. Two boxes, Native Hawaiian and Not. But what OHA was really asking was which one could they prove. Which one could be proved with documented evidence that would satisfy the United States of America?

The form allowed her daughter to be only one box or the other.

CHAPTER 10

1984

The older Hi`i got, the less Laka felt she could protect her, so she focused instead on toughening the girl up until the tears didn't come as quick. She wanted Hi`i to remain a happy kid, which she seemed to be, but she was also soft and sensitive. So she gave her daughter what she needed: a callused hide.

Because the job of children is to find all the things their parents hope they never find, and because Laka knew that if she let her daughter get too close to the fire that was Halau o Luahine, the halau she should have taken over from her mother, a volcano might erupt, Hi`i discovered hula. There was no talking her out of it.

Tony wondered about all Laka's pacing and nail biting. He rolled her a joint. "She Hawaiian, yeah? Not her fault she no look it. Kumu'll get over it," he said, taking a puff.

When Hi`i had come out of the halau that first day of practice alive and smiling, Laka was so relieved that her happiness spilled over. She couldn't quite say what exactly she'd been so afraid of, imagining Kumu punishing or shaming her daughter because she herself was supposed to be the one up there, leading the children, passing along the knowledge, and instead she'd quit, retiring her skirts with hardly a word, all that knowledge dormant in her bones when she should have been passing it to the next generation. Common sense told her that the woman to whom her mother had entrusted her halau would never do such a thing, but the feelings that had come with Hi`i's quest to dance for *this* halau had Laka upside down. She hadn't had an official first day of hula—what started as Hulali teaching her songs and basic moves in the carport of their home on weekends after chores were pau had just sort of snowballed into a practice schedule once others had come wanting to learn alongside her—but she remembered well the days of bleeding feet and tears, of her mother yelling, of her body resisting, and she wanted more than anything to keep her daughter as far from that world as possible. But then Hi`i's first day of hula was over and her daughter was smiling. Hi`i would not pay for the sins of her mother. Relief that day had turned her to jelly. They went to the plaza. To the Hello Kitty store. She would have sold a kidney to pay for anything Hi`i asked for, a souvenir for surviving.

But Hilo time marched in circles and wandered sideways. Anger crept into the cracks in the floors and slithered up her daughter's feet. Hi`i's eyes always watching, taking everything in. Green marbles, green sponges, now green flame, green lightning. Images crashed through Laka's mind as she slept, her daughter sitting in the cobwebbed rooms in her head, going through the archives, dusting off all Laka had worked so hard to bury. She climbed the stairs to push things farther toward the back, but then there came that unmistakable firm tenderness in her breasts, the fullness in her belly. In the years since Maui, she'd never once considered the chance she'd get pregnant again. Since the burning of the honu, Hulali's severing of her from her roots, and the pool of blood in her Hana boardinghouse room, Laka had assumed her womb, cut from the tree, would never bear a branch.

There was no rejoicing. The seed in her stomach was a bomb, it would destroy everything. There would be no way to hide anything then. There would only be more questions. She took refuge in her room, using illness and fatigue like shields. She wrote Beatriz letter after letter that she later destroyed. At night, she woke in a cold sweat, shaking. No blood, Tony said every time, swiping his hand across the white fitted sheet. He was overjoyed at the thought of bringing a baby into the world, but could not make sense of her fear. She did not explain her nightmares, could not put them into words.

When Hulali came from Oahu for that fateful Merrie Monarch, Hiʻiʻs first, the baby in her opu kicked, as if already ignoring her wishes, her attempts to keep their family together by keeping her mother as far away as possible. Laka did not know how to protect both her children from the coming clouds.

On top of it all, Hiʻi had been obsessed with the Miss Aloha Hula competition that year. Please God, no. By now she had resigned herself to Hiʻi dancing, but competing in MAH? That would be just asking for trouble.

She was every teenager, thinking her mother was not watching, that Laka was not putting two and two together. She braced herself for the day her daughter would announce her intention to follow in Laka's footsteps.

Then one day, Kumu called, wanting to know why Hiʻi had stopped going to practice. To Kumu, Laka acted unsurprised, as though she already knew. She told her daughter nothing when she came home from school that afternoon. It was for the best, Hiʻi leaving hula behind. Nothing good could come from it. The Naupakas were done with hula.

NOW TONY WAS IN PRISON, sending her into a semipermanent state of shock where nothing felt real. Hiʻi had still not admitted to Laka that she'd quit hula, leading Laka to wonder about the private life her daughter might be living. Hulali had moved in, complicating things. Malia, her mini me, was crawling and beginning to babble. Laka ached to spend time with her youngest child, to be alone with her the way she'd been with Hi`i. Which made her think about how far apart she and Hi`i had drifted, which made her heart ache even more. Too many winds were blowing on their door.

Malia. Her heart melted, then hardened with guilt at the possibility that she loved this one too much, or more, then melted again. No, she told herself. More was not possible. She loved them the same. Blood or no blood, the heart beat.

LAKA SIFTED THROUGH THE MEMORIES, trying to pinpoint when things had started to shift, when everything went south.

Her pregnancy was a giant blur of nausea and fear, except for Hi`i's trip to Waipi`o. That she remembered. Hi`i coming back early. The teacher calling her, explaining why. She'd been furious, ready to explode when Hi`i had walked through the door, but then the girl had come and it was as though she'd retreated completely into herself. They tiptoed around each other, what was done was done, and by the time Malia was born Hi`i seemed almost herself again. A smile, tortured and faint, visited Laka's lips. The horror of Tony on trial and the death of the boy lived side by side with the moment the midwife put Malia into Hi`i's arms, the ferocious love that had spread across the room, the quiet moments later with both her girls sleeping squeezed up next to her in bed, the Hilo rain pattering like walking sticks on the roof above their heads.

She would admit: when Hulali moved back in, it felt like she was sinking in quicksand to see her daughter pull away again, farther this time, but it had made everyday life easier.

THE WIND THAT FINALLY BLEW the door down was the haole girl, Jane. The one who used to make Hi`i so aggravated. We noticed the air shift, the tides change. Hi`i started leaving early to meet Jane before school, go to her house after school, and nearly always stayed long past dinner. They were always laughing around town, eating shave ice or going to the library to check out books about all the countries they were going to visit one day. We couldn't put our finger on exactly why, but it reminded us of those little earth tremors that happen before Pele erupts.

Laka and Hulali never discussed it, never turned their attention to the empty seat at the table. Malia made it easy to not pay too much attention to the divisions growing within their house, made it easy for Laka to tell herself this was just a storm that would pass eventually.

But eventually came and it was hard to say the last time Hi`i had spent any time in Keaukaha at all. Laka had never forced her to stay home, to eat dinner as a family a night or two a week. She had not left Malia with Hulali to spend a day with her eldest. She had not attempted to bridge the divide. She had used one daughter as the reason to not deal with the other. Not because she hadn't cared, or hadn't wanted to, but because she hadn't known how.

Jane came over alone one day in the middle of their school spring break, Hi`i nowhere in sight. She came dressed in a pink polo shirt with little buttons at the collar, a matching tennis skirt with pleats, and white sneakers. Teased bangs with a faint sparkle of blue eye shadow at the corners of her eyes. Not an outfit you'd see often in

Keaukaha, if ever. Girly with a dash of prep, Jane was not who Laka would ever picture being best friends with Hi`i. Facing Jane was like facing a chasm filled with all the things she didn't know about who her daughter had become while she hadn't been paying attention. She tried to pay attention now.

Sitting on the wooden bench on the porch with Jane, Laka felt an absurd urge to make this girl understand how much she loved her daughter, that she wasn't the mother she might seem. Instead, she held herself still and braced for whatever the girl had come to tell her. This storm was not going to blow over. It was time to face that.

Jane started their conversation by saying Hi`i didn't know she was there. She rushed through the rest, giving Laka the impression that the kid was nervous and uncertain but was trying to be a good friend to her daughter.

She told her Hi`i had joined and was now dancing for Jane's halau, and training to become that year's Miss Aloha Hula. Hi`i didn't want Laka to know, Jane said. She'd told Jane that they didn't have the money for halau dues, and they certainly didn't have the money competing would take, but she didn't want to make her mom feel bad, so it was better this way.

"But my dad was happy to pay for Hi`i's dancing and is more than happy to pay for whatever else she needs. Same like her college applications and stuff. I think it's dumb for her to not even try to get a scholarship for UCLA when my dad said he was sure she would get it if he helped."

It took all the willpower Laka had not to stop the girl right there and correct her. Laka had always managed to find the money for Hi`i's halau dues. And if Hi`i had bothered telling Laka that she was interested in going to college, she knew very well that Laka would have ponied up whatever money was needed for that! Here she was being presented as someone who couldn't provide for her daughter, but she hadn't been given the chance. But as her mind raced, the girl moved on.

"If my mom were alive, I know I'd want her around if I were competing at Merrie Monarch. I think Hi`i will regret not asking you to be there. She says you don't come to watch her practice because you don't like hula anymore. She'd never admit it, but all of this is a really big deal to her. You should see . . . you should see what she's chosen for the competition."

Jane wound a corner of her shirt around her finger, clearly distressed but determined to say what she'd come to say. Laka turned her head as if she needed to look somewhere, anywhere else, in order to process all of this new information.

"Your daughter is going to win. That's all I really wanted to say. Maybe you can come watch, even if she doesn't want you to. Just don't tell her I said anything, okay?"

After a beat Laka pulled herself together and tried to put the girl at ease, thanking her while showing her to the door. She watched from the porch as the girl walked down the street and turned a corner.

CHAPTER 11

D read blinded Laka, made her directionally challenged. She took left turns when she should have made right ones, missed exits and caught every red light. She honked in frustration at her own stupid driving. UCLA? Hi`i wanted to leave Hilo? When had she gone back to dancing? And what was all this about not having money? If Hi`i had shared any of this with her, Laka would have found the money. She always had. She slammed her palm on the horn again.

By the time Laka arrived at Hi`i's new halau, practice was well on its way. Music drifted across the parking lot from the large open windows of the studio. Her stomach turned as she trembled her way up the stairs into the building, her na`au blaring louder than a tsunami siren. She went down the hall only far enough to allow herself a view of inside the halau. She took a shaky breath and tried to calm down. There was no need for alarm. She didn't know anything for sure yet. Jane could be completely wrong. This could all be a huge misunderstanding. She told her na`au: suspicion is not intuition, it is not confirmation of anything.

The studio had floor-to-ceiling windows, pitched blond wood floors, and whirring black fans that kept the room cool as a Kamuela prairie. The bright and open aesthetic did not surprise her as much as the lightness did. The smiles, the open-beam ceiling, the tinkle of laughter in the hall, all lent itself to the feeling that this was a halau that hovered slightly above the ground. As the girls went through their drills, Laka was struck by what was most different about her daughter's new halau—it was Hiʻi herself. Gone was the distance, in its place a soft feather-like quality, as if her whole body were smiling.

The girls finished their drills and fell upon the water bottles leaning against the back wall. Instead of returning to their places, they tucked their skirts and sat. Only Hiʻi remained in the center of the room. The whispers fell silent as their kumu grabbed her ukulele. Laka looked on, curious. Jane had not told her about Hiʻi's ʻauana.

Hiʻi signaled to her kumu that she was ready. Her face was set with a determination Laka had never seen before. She lowered in perfect time, swayed with a force so powerful it took Laka by the throat and squeezed.

HIʻI'S MISS ALOHA HULA ʻAUANA:

She is a young woman who wants desperately for a child. Bereft, she travels from a distant island to the sacred maile groves of the goddess Laka, where she tells the goddess she will give anything to have a child. The goddess Laka asks for her heart, which the young woman gladly gives.

Hiʻi's body swayed heavily across the floor, emanating grief as her hands blazed a path through the maile groves. Her fingers clutched her chest to grab hold of the heart beating inside it before thrusting her hands upward without hesitation. Her hips moved in large sweeping amis as her body invited the seed of a child in.

Hi`i was dedicating her dance to her mother, to her Naupaka blood, to her heritage. The realization pierced Laka clean through to the other side. She sank into the corner of the hall, immobile, unable to breathe. Tears slid down her cheeks as she continued to watch. Hi`i motioned as if making a series of knots in a rope—a chain of the generations.

Dancing, her daughter went from beautiful to mystical. The reality that her daughter might actually compete in Merrie Monarch hit home. Her emotions scattered like a broken string of beads. The festival was televised. Would Beatriz be watching from wherever she was? Would the gods? And Hulali, would she publicly object to Hi`i dancing as a Naupaka? Laka went cold. The kid was a bucket with no bottom—the years of love she'd poured in did not add up to anything. With the new baby, the strain and stress of the trial, Tony in prison—Laka didn't blame her daughter for putting distance between herself and the chaos. Their link was weaker than it had ever been. If Hi`i knew the truth, Laka was sure she would lose her forever.

The foreboding she'd brought with her cooled, solidifying into a resolve. She would tell Hi`i nothing. She would not pull Hi`i from hula, nor forbid her from competing. She would accept her role and let the chips fall where they would.

WHEN HI`I CALLED OUT the beginning of the final verse, Laka closed her eyes. She could not bear to leave, but could watch no more. Laka let the lingering sound of the ukulele strumming its final chord fade before she turned to go, but no sooner had she opened her eyes than the sharp crack of an ipu sounded from inside the studio. Laka stayed where she was. Jane had not told her what Hi`i had chosen for the kahiko portion of the competition.

As Hi`i transitioned into her kahiko, her body replaced the soft fluidity of her `auana with a staidness that Laka had only ever observed in the most senior of dancers. Her arms, gentle and gliding moments before, now moved in stiff, resolute straight lines. Her hands, once inviting the observer into a story, now demanded attention with fists. Her feet, once playful and lithesome, now stomped and made themselves known. Her smile went serious. With one arm rigid against her chest and the other pointed with bold purpose ahead of her, she called out the beginning words of her dance's story and began.

No. Laka pressed her hands to her cheeks to try to cool them. What was happening inside the halau was impossible. Hi`i was dancing the Mo`olelo no Kuula.

This was the hula her great-grandmother had danced for King Kalākaua, the hula that had become a defining moment for the entire Naupaka family past, present, and future. This was the hula Hulali had wanted so much for Laka to dance when it had been her turn to compete for Miss Aloha Hula. She had refused, and her mother had never let it be used by anyone else. Yes, it was a gift to the Naupakas from the honu, an heirloom of a hula, theirs alone, but Hulali was still its keeper. She understood all that Hi`i dancing this dance symbolized. She understood why she wanted to dance it. But Laka could not let her.

BY THE FIRST CHORD of the second verse Laka was stumbling down the stairs, choking down her sobs, racing to get as far away as she could. She covered her ears so the chant wouldn't follow her. She peeled out of the parking lot. At the stoplight, she found herself unable to make the necessary turn that would lead her home, to Keaukaha, to the family property her daughter wouldn't inherit, the only home Laka had ever really known.

The orange gas light on her dashboard blinked on. She ignored it and kept going, minutes turning into miles, the road a blur. It wasn't until she hit dense rainforest thirty minutes later that she realized where she was headed. She rolled down her window at the guard booth entrance of Volcanoes National Park. The man working the booth slid his window open and held out his hand for her payment of the entrance fee. She shook her head.

"I came to pray," she said through her tears. He withdrew his hand, nodded, and raised the gate.

She left the car at the edge of Halema`uma`u Crater. The air at that elevation was biting, the drizzle cold. Her body shivered but she was too numb to notice. She paused in front of a steam vent, willing the sulfuric cloud to press itself through her. Once she was thoroughly damp, she hiked down the zigzag dirt path through the hapu`u ferns that led down, down into Pele's womb. The air went from damp to dry. The belly of Halema`uma`u had long been cool and flat, smooth black lava moonscape, but deep below the surface, Laka knew Pele's heart still beat, which was why park rangers had roped off a portion to keep visitors from straying off the path. With a quick look around, she went under the rope, got on her hands and knees, and began to crawl.

Smooth pahoehoe lava quickly turned into crusty aa, sharp as broken glass. Splintered shards bit into her knees as she made her way toward the soft center of the crater. Wind howled in her ears. Was she imagining that the ground was getting warmer, softer? At the center, Pele's piko, she bowed her head to the ground.

Laka had never had a plan. She'd only ever wanted to keep Hi`i safe, to shelter her from what she thought an unnecessary and potentially very hurtful questioning of Hi`i's place in the family. Those days were now over. Hi`i was her daughter, a gift from the mo`o. She'd believed that in Maui and she believed it now. Laka had always maintained that this meant Hi`i was a Naupaka. But seeing her dance that hula, Laka wanted to scream. Hi`i could have danced anything else and Laka would have fought for her. Why did she have to choose that one? She would give her daughter anything, but that was not hers to give. She had never agreed with Hulali about blood quantum being the determining factor of family, but this was more complicated than that. Hi`i needed the family's blessing for this to be pono. That meant Hulali. The only way her mother was ever going to give her blessing was if she accepted Hi`i fully and truly, and the only way she would ever do that would be if Laka told her the truth about Maui and Beatriz. She would have to trust that her mother believed in Hawai`i's supernatural forces enough to believe in this. But there was one huge thing she needed to do before she started worrying about how Hulali might react. She had to tell Hi`i.

LAKA FINALLY REALIZED what we had known always. There's no running away on an island. Soon enough, you end up where you started.

WHEN SHE RETURNED HOME hours later, no one asked her where she'd been, or why she was late, or why she smelled of rotten eggs.

She lingered for a moment on the porch, drinking in the familiar surroundings of Keaukaha one last time before she went inside, ready to face what needed facing. The mosquitoes danced. They chased the interrupters back to their hotel rooms and rented cars. The boys at the beach were readying the trucks for another beer run and pulling in the nets from the channel. The tide was coming in or going out. The coast was doing its daily shape-shifting. It was the time when the distance between things grew, the time when the truth of an ending could be ignored no longer.

Hi`i was bathing in the outside shower. The yard smelled of coconut conditioner and peppermint soap. Laka busied herself in the kitchen. She lingered in that final moment, when she could still with confidence call her daughter her daughter, when she might still come upon her and see love reflected.

"What's up, Ma?" Hi`i asked through the window.

Laka clutched that single word and let the others slide away. *Ma.* She pressed it like a flower into the flat pages of her memory, where it would be preserved, frozen in time, in case she never heard it again.

Then it was time for ho`oponopono, time to make things right. She pulled a shoebox from the top of the closet where Tony kept his hunting gear and rummaged until she found the note, tucked away like a bullet she'd hoped never to use.

HULALI COULD HEAR THE GIRL sobbing through the thin wall. She glanced toward Malia, who was sleeping on her stomach like a little ball on her futon bed, chunky toddler legs tucked under her. Hulali pulled the door to her room gently behind her before moving down the hall. Malia had a runny nose. She needed this sleep. This wasn't the time for the older one's antics.

She paused at Hi`i's closed bedroom door and took a deep breath before twisting the handle.

The room was a hurricane. Clothes in mounds on the floor half stuffed in trash bags, pictures and books in an overflowing garbage can, the poster of `Iolani Luahine ripped off the wall, an unmade bed with sheets torn away, the girl curled up in the middle of it all, a position sadly similar to the sweet babe one room away. Hi`i cringed at the sound of the door and swatted away the tears on her face as soon as she saw it was Hulali.

"You knew all dis time, didn't you?"

So Laka had finally come clean and admitted what Hulali had known from the beginning. She quickly recalibrated, tried to cover her surprise. Tunneled her way through the mess and sat at the edge of the bed, smoothing a corner of quilt to clear a seat for herself. Hi`i stiffened. Hulali grabbed a thin cotton shirt from the ground and handed it to her.

"Here. Blow your nose."

It wasn't the kid's fault that Laka had made a mess of everything. Wasn't the kid's fault she was who she was, whoever that was. It was the system to blame, the corrupt consequence of Hawai`i's history at work. Hulali could only hope that one day the girl would see that this was not personal. That this was just the way things were.

"You was a tiny little t'ing wen you was born," she began.

Hi`i shifted, accepting the shirt and wiping her face with it. She sniffed and cleared the hair out of her face. "You was dea wen I was born? How can, I t'ought wasn't she in Maui?"

Hulali patted Hi`i's leg and shook her head. "No, not right wen you was born, but not long aftah. My Laka, she was like one mama lion, growling if anyone got too close." She sighed.

Hiʻi pulled herself into a sitting position and leaned against the wall, bringing her legs with her. The space between her and Hulali widened. "Why you telling me dis now? Why you went along wit it?"

"Because wasn't my place. But she shoulda wen tell you a long time ago. She didn't tell me anyt'ing either. I knew, though. I no blame her for taking you in. It was neyah 'bout dat."

"Wat was it about, den?" The sobbing resumed. "I don't even care. I just wanna be alone."

Hulali felt sorry for her. It was Laka who was to blame. But what happened to the girl now wasn't her kuleana. Sometimes kuleana required sacrifice and perspective. She twisted the gold Hawaiian bracelet around her wrist in silence for a minute, then patted Hiʻi on the ankle.

"Gotta check on Malia. I'll be right back."

In her room, she gave herself a minute. Laka had finally come clean. Not to her. The insult stung, but there would be time to deal with that later. Hulali had nothing against hānai. Hawaiians had been raising children collectively for as long as she knew, and there was nothing wrong with letting a grandma or other family member raise a baby if it meant that baby was better off. It was a family decision. But Laka had hānaiʻed Hiʻi without consulting her, without telling her. She knew nothing about where Hiʻi had come from or the family that had given her up. Hulali felt a deep shame. She'd raised Laka to know her place in the family, especially their family, as well as the honor and burden that came with being the eldest. To Hulali, being a good Hawaiian had always meant kōkua when you can, but to never forget the forest for the trees. Can't help nobody else clean up their backyard if yours is a mess.

By the time she returned to Hiʻi's room, the girl had cried herself out. Her face was swollen from crying, her body depleted. She gazed at Hulali with an exhausted calm. Hulali waved her arm above her head to capture the room, the house, the air stagnant between them, the land outside, the faint sound of the surf pounding along the shore down the road.

"None of dis," she began, "is ours. We only da protectors. Our job is fo' keep t'ings going, to hold on and keep everyt'ing alive for tomorrow. Fo' da keiki. Hawaiians, we no can just mine our business and do wat we like or pretty soon Hawai`i just going be hotels and a playground. Already we da minorities hea. We get one responsibility, and dat's to da land. To our people and our ways. I nevah make da rules, but dey is wat dey is."

"Wat dat has to do wit me?"

"Has e'ryt'ing to do wit you. You say you wanna be alone? You graduating high school, den you is free, girl. Keaukaha not your kuleana. Go travel, see da world. You can be whoevah you like be." Hulali pulled an envelope from her pocket and handed it to Hi`i. "Laka get a responsibility hea, not you. Sometimes our kuleana is given to us, sometimes we gotta go fine 'em. Go fine yours. Dis is enuf fo' a plane ticket and to get you going. You need more, just let me know."

Through the thin wall came the sound of Malia crying. Hulali turned and stepped into the hall, leaving Hi`i with the unopened envelope. She heard the girl begin pulling clothes out of her closet, the wire hangers ting-ting-tinging together as they were left to dangle empty. Then she went to comfort her granddaughter, who didn't like waking up with no one beside her.

VERSE III

CHAPTER 1

1995

The Los Angeles freeway, that glorious impartial beast, was a blaring swirl of lights and metal and noise, a choreographed cacophony. Cars piled up in the rearview mirror, honking, angry. A Porsche flashed its lights. Hi`i waved for him to pass, then half-heartedly flipped him off when he streaked by. Where was he going that demanded such impatience, such inconsiderate rudeness? Didn't it occur to him that maybe some people were driving not to get anywhere, that some people might be in their cars simply because being on the road offered a feeling of normalcy, where traffic lights and stop signs went on with their business, no matter what happened? That some were on the road because that was the only place left where the world still made sense?

Drive. That's what Hi`i did now. How she passed the hours and survived the days. When she'd moved to LA, the freeway had terrified her, and since she'd only ever driven barefoot, every time she got behind the wheel she'd had to go through the rigamarole of shedding everything because she could not for the life of her drive with hardly more than a sock on her foot. She'd spent hours trying to find her way around using only side streets. She never would have guessed that, more than ten years later, it would be the only place she found relief.

As neighbors babysat her daughters, she drove aimlessly up the 405 and across the 10, lost in the sea of spotless sports cars and rusted work trucks, beaten-down minivans and sedans covered in bumper stickers. Everyone was equal on the freeway, everyone the same. Traffic didn't care how much your car cost or who was driving or where you were going, or if you had anywhere to go at all. Traffic didn't ask why your husband wasn't in the car with you, didn't tell you to chin up or offer awkward condolences at the news of his death.

Through her first year of LA life she'd marveled at the city's ambivalence, its anonymity. In Los Angeles you were either a Nobody or a Somebody, someone who worked in "The Industry" or someone who didn't, someone with too much money or someone with not enough. On campus where everyone was rushing from one place to another, it had been easy to disappear. She'd entered a strange world in which she was the stranger. Hilo struck her then as a fishbowl, where nothing went unobserved.

UCLA had a large Pacific Islander community that could have helped her assimilate, but she'd brushed it off. Refused to wear anything that even remotely resembled a Hawaiian print shirt or dress. Absolutely no pareos. Her daily outfits were bland and vague—jeans and a tank top in summer, jeans and a sweater in winter. She hadn't, though, anticipated the culture shock of everyday life or the sadness that gripped her at the grocery store, how the rows and rows of brands she didn't recognize would leave her feeling small and exposed. There was no section in the deli for poi and poke, and the rice she bought was sticky but still didn't taste anything at all like it did at home. Nothing did. To keep herself from hopping on a plane back to Hilo, she'd clung to a small silver charm in the shape of a he`e, her good-luck charm and the only sliver of Hawai`i she allowed herself. Dangling now from her key chain, it was the he`e that had fueled Hi`i's courage to take Hulali's money and buy a one-way ticket to California. For the octopus, survival came down to blending in with his environment, whatever that might be. Master of Illusion, Prince of the Kanaloa Kingdom, shape-shifter, magician—the he`e would cut off an arm if necessary. Alone, he`e was a painter, a living manifestation of a palette, a compilation of jars full of ink masquerading as cells, ready to blend, to survive simply out of his ability to disappear into the fold. Which is exactly what she had planned on doing—disappear into LA's folds and masquerade when necessary. And then she'd met Jacob.

IN THE SPRING OF HER FRESHMAN YEAR, she'd stopped by the UCLA Asia Pacific Center's Hawaiian Festival expecting to take a quick look around and return to her room to write the essay that was due the next day. But the smell of teriyaki chicken and the duo playing slack key on stage in the middle of the sunny quad convinced her to stay. Although her closet was now a carefully cultivated collection of closed-toe shoes and bland, monochromatic clothes that could have come from Anywhere, USA, it was comforting to suddenly be surrounded by the burst of aloha shirts and mu`umu`u, of rubber slippers and flowers tucked behind ears. She'd bought a lunch plate—white rice, kahlua pig and cabbage, mac salad—and found a spot on the lawn to eat and soak in the familiar sounds of home that she hadn't realized how much she missed until that moment. She made a conscious effort not to stare at the families spread out on picnic blankets around her but couldn't help wondering who they were and how they might be connected to Hawai`i. When the musicians finished their set the next group was welcomed on. Hi`i gathered her stuff to leave. But then the three little girls had filed out, plumeria pinned to their hair, matching skirts with bright yellow flowers. They started to dance, faces beaming. Two adults, obviously parents, knelt at the foot of the stage, video recorders following the girls' every step. The girls beamed. Hiʻi smiled so hard her cheeks began to hurt. Tears ran down her face. She felt sick and happy and homesick, so full and empty and lonely all at once that she didn't notice when someone plopped down beside her.

"You look like you are either extremely disappointed in that kahlua pig or just waiting for someone to invite you to the party."

He had no idea how close to the truth he was. She'd laughed until she cried. They hadn't been apart since.

Jacob was eleven years older, a part-time graduate student with an internship at the Jet Propulsion Laboratory in Pasadena. They'd been seeing each other for nearly two months when he took her to Ono's in Carson for the best Hawaiian food in the state. Up until then it had not occurred to her that Jacob might be Hawaiian, not a drop. He didn't look haole, but this was LA. There were a whole lot of things other than Hawaiian he could be. Plenty of non-Hawaiians went to Hawaiian festivals. Their dates had been filled with long drives to Malibu, his surfboard sticking out the window of the backseat, her doing homework in the sand while he surfed. Plenty of non-Hawaiians surfed. They hadn't yet gotten around to digging deep into each other's past; he'd asked where she was from and she'd answered vaguely, Hawaiʻi at large with no further details. To be fair she kept her questions about him to herself, even after he told her that he was a Hawaiian California boy, born and raised right there in LA with roots.

The restaurant was small but, judging from the pictures of smiling celebrities and faithful customers covering the walls, a beloved haunt. The manager was Jacob's cousin, his aunt ran the kitchen. A family production, Jacob said. They'd welcomed Hi`i with open arms and, at the family beach days and backyard barbeques that soon followed, asked her questions about her background that she found easy to avoid, shrugging when they prodded for details.

He'd only ever been to Kaua`i and O`ahu, so when he finally needled it out of her that she was from the Big Island, he begged her to take him there. By then she knew nearly everyone in his life, his parents, his friends, and cousins. He said he wanted to know hers. How to explain to him how impossible that would be given the silence between her and Laka, what had started as a cooling-off period but had, as time passed, cemented itself into something more permanent?

Jacob's family was a mix of Hawaiian, Japanese, and Swedish that had been in Torrance since a few years before WWII, Utah before that. (Our eyes couldn't see that far away. We could only assume that his family was a classic mainland Hawaiian family, which meant he was kanaka whether he had the tiniest drop or a bucketful of blood in him. The only time those quantums mattered was when the U.S. was trying to divide us, or when we was demanding something from it.)

His family loved all things Hawaii, HAWAII shirts and bumper stickers everywhere, but Hi`i found herself relieved to discover their Hawaiian connections were strongest within its California diaspora instead of the actual islands. Only once did someone ask her if she was related to Hulali Naupaka, the hula legend. She'd shrugged and said if she was, it was distant. She felt only slightly guilty. These were good people, warm and welcoming. She told herself she wasn't lying to them, not exactly. Being with them, being with Jacob, was like being home without the complications, and she'd wanted to keep it that way for as long as possible.

They'd gotten engaged her third year of school, and married

a month after graduation. It had been a small wedding, consisting only of Jacob's family and the surfing buddies he'd grown up with. A morning at the courthouse downtown and an afternoon reception at the Los Angeles Arboretum. Catered, of course, courtesy of Ono's. In the days before and too many after, Hi`i had picked up the phone to call Keaukaha only to hang up before the first ring because she didn't know what to say, didn't know if Laka would want to hear from her after so long.

Hi`i promised her husband she would take him to Hilo one day, would introduce him to her island and her family that lived there.

Which she had managed to put off for years. Years that had passed too quickly. Years that she would give anything to have back. Now it was too late to make good on that promise. Jacob was gone.

She glanced at the clock on the car dashboard and flicked on her blinker.

SHE MADE HER WAY through the winding curves of the Pasadena neighborhood where she and Jacob had bought their house after he was offered a salaried position at JPL. It still struck her as too picturesque to be real. She pulled into the driveway of their foam-green Craftsman cottage with its yellow trim around the windows (Jacob had painted those himself) and a glass mosaic embedded in the door (they'd found it when she was pregnant with Ruth and were scouring the Rose Bowl flea market for nursery decorations) and gave her car horn a light pop, as was their tradition. The front door cracked open and Ruth and Emma, five and two respectively, shot like cannons off the porch (the porch swing where they'd spent summer evenings drinking too much wine back when they were in eat-too-much-drink-too-much love, which had relaxed into "steak is not good for your cholesterol and get that ice cream out of the house I can't button my jeans" love, and then crosswords-and-muffins-on-Saturday-morning love, and then this, a vacuum love), across the overgrown lawn, and were at Hi`i's van door before she had a chance to open it. The girls hugged her knees with relief. This was new, this clinging, a result of Jacob leaving and not returning. It doubled the guilt she already felt for needing to go for these drives, for needing to be alone, for not having the capacity to take away her daughters' sadness and make everything better. Their neighbor Carol came out to the porch, wiping her hands on a dishrag.

"I fed them a snack. Emma wanted to save her grapes for her aunty."

Hi`i nodded. "Thanks."

There was no imagining how she could have gotten this far without her neighbors and Jacob's relatives. There hadn't been a single day since Jacob's diagnosis that someone hadn't popped over to drop off a casserole or pick up the kids to take them to a museum or the zoo.

"My pleasure." Carol waved off Hi`i's thanks and glanced at her wristwatch. "You all better get going, though, you don't want to get stuck in traffic."

The girls shouted and squealed.

"They're so excited, they've been marking the days off the calendar like it was Christmas."

Carol offered her a smile. They'd shown her the rows of days they'd x'd in purple crayon, counting down to the day with the palm tree on it, today.

The girls piled in the car and tried to buckle themselves in.

"Come on, Mommy," Emma begged. "Get Antee Maria."

"Aunty Malia," Hi`i corrected automatically. Emma had trouble with her L's.

Another round of squeals from the backseat.

Carol smiled warmly. "You must be so excited to see your sister."

Excited wasn't the word.

Carol waved as they backed out of the driveway. Hi`i headed toward the airport, praying for traffic, anything to slow things down. Malia would be landing within the hour. Hilo and Los Angeles, Hi`i's two worlds, were about to collide for the first time in eleven years. She wasn't ready.

JACOB AND HI`I HAD FOUGHT about it while on the way to the doctor's office for yet another round of tests. He was always so tired, so sick. There was no energy to push the girls on the swings or take them to the beach. He wanted a distraction for them, a respite from all the doctors' appointments and bottles of pills everywhere.

"You should take them to Hawai`i, take a break from all this. If I can't meet your family, at least they should."

Hi`i kept her eyes on the road. "Don't say that. The girls will meet them when you do. And you will. As soon as you get better, we're going. Really this time. I promise. But not until we figure out what's going on."

"I'll be fine. The doctors aren't even sure if there's anything really wrong. How about inviting them here? It would be fun, plus it would finally get my parents off my back."

Hi`i said she'd think about it.

Then they'd gone inside the medical building, holding hands in the monster glass elevator as it dinged past every floor, him squeezing her fingers to a beat he hummed under his breath. Hi`i grew more certain his doctors were overreacting with every elevator ding. They'd gotten the wrong guy. She and Jacob were young, healthy. He was barely thirty-six and in better shape than she was. Didn't smoke, didn't eat red meat (anymore, although she suspected he ordered burgers and milkshakes with the girls when they went out for their daddy dates). He jogged around Silver Lake Reservoir and still surfed whenever the waves were up. Jacob's version of partying was a second glass of wine.

The receptionist was gratingly nice. Hi`i was tempted to tell her to save it for the truly sick, which her husband was not. When their appointment was over they were going to get ice cream, screw the calories and cholesterol. From that day forward they were going to live life to the fullest. Go to church, volunteer at homeless shelters, never lose patience with the kids. They'd raise money for nonprofits and help lost dogs find new homes. They'd never take another day for granted. She'd stop complaining about Jacob's snoring, or about dirty dishes in the sink.

A nurse interrupted her spinning thoughts and called them into the doctor's inner office. They sank into the soft leather chairs. The doctor flipped through Jacob's chart. Frowned. Hi`i picked up where she'd left off, promises like prayers, if only they got through today with no bad news.

The doctor began with acronyms. A CAT scan, an MRI, to "grade" it. Hi`i didn't want to know what that meant.

"The grade determines the stage. How far it has spread," the doctor said.

Jacob sat in the same infuriating, accepting silence he had when she'd been pregnant and exhausted, when she'd cried and yelled and tried to pick fights and he'd wait with his hands folded, one thumb rubbing the top of the other. As the doctor continued, Hi`i fought the urge to jump from her chair, to block out the words that kept coming, to volley them back across the desk so they wouldn't touch Jacob. She plied the doctor with questions, she slid down logic's slopes seeking any possible explanation, anything to blame, to pinpoint exactly what she'd done wrong, why it was him and not her. Exocrine pancreatic cancer. Was it because she had insisted they eat more fiber?

No, the doctor said, she hadn't given him cancer through fiber.

(Looking back now, she was sure, yes, she had.)

No, it hadn't been all the organic, uncooked vegetables or the stacks of health books she'd never managed to get him to read.

(Yes, that too was to blame.)

She'd made him cancel a physical. Emma had been sick, she'd had a PTA meeting, it had seemed an easy enough thing to reschedule. But surely, if he'd gone instead, if they'd caught it earlier . . .

The doctor shook her head yet again. Pancreatic cancer is rarely detected in standard physical exams. That's what made it so deadly.

(But Jacob's situation was different. They would have caught it.)

Handouts on the table, covered in bulleted statistics.

THE ROLLER-COASTER HULA:

Up up up, survival rates were high for men in their mid-to-late thirties in general good health.

Down down down, there was no way to predict how he'd respond to treatment.

IA versus IB, 14% versus 12% for a five-year survival. Hi`i struggled to hold firm to the numbers, to find a loophole, an exit. Still the numbers came. The doctor rolled them off her fingers, memorized.

Stage IIA versus Stage IIB, 7% versus 5% survival rates. Stage II, a mere 3%; Stage IV, 1%.

Their life swirled down a drain of C's. Clinical trials and chemotherapy and cancer.

The Hawaiian alphabet didn't even have the letter C.

THEY'D BEEN SILENT AS they made their way out of the building and into the car. When they hit the freeway, Jacob asked her again to invite her family to visit them in California. There was no way to say no.

WHICH MEANT THAT AFTER the awkward and too-formal letter inviting the Naupakas for a visit she'd had to write again to say Jacob had died, much sooner than any of them had expected (as if she'd accepted that he ever would), before they'd had a chance to reply to her first letter, if they were going to reply at all. She'd meant it as a way to cancel out the first letter, the olive branch extension, the invitation to come meet her children, to see her life in California. They'd already had a memorial for him. Another time would probably be better, she'd wrote. But she'd known even as she pressed pen to paper that leaving her to her sadness wasn't the Hawaiian way. If one grieved, they all did.

What she couldn't have predicted was the condolence card that followed, Hulali's signature on the bottom. She was sending Malia, she said. For her spring break, to be a mother's helper. And that's how Hiʻi came to find herself inching through traffic at LAX, on her way to pick up a girl, her sister, whom she hadn't seen since she was a chubby toddler clinging to her grandmother's leg.

In the backseat, the girls chattered and giggled and made plans for what they were going to show Aunty Malia first, what games they were going to play, what they wanted to do with her, but now that they were circling the Arrivals terminal, the girls went quiet, staring out the window as if they knew who they were looking for. Hi`i wished she could tell them.

They parked and made their way to the luggage carousel, Ruth and Emma on either side of Hi`i, pulling her to go faster. Hi`i worried she might not recognize her. What if they walked right by her? LAX was a city within a city, and she was picking up a stranger.

Hi`i needn't have worried. There was no possibility of not recognizing her. The physical resemblance between Malia and Laka was a blow. There was the strong jaw, the almond-shaped eyes, the proud bearing she knew only too well. When she got within a few feet of the teenage, ponytailed version of the woman she'd known as her mother, the years that Hi`i had been gone from Hawai`i, time during which she'd become a wife and mother herself, slipped away. Malia was a baby, warm in her arms, holding tight to her finger. Sucking poi from her knuckle. Malia falling asleep on her chest, soft baby smells filling Hi`i's nostrils. She cried out, opened her arms, rushed forward. The girl stepped back, smiled cautiously. Hi`i stopped short and gave her an abbreviated hug and tried to ignore the stab of hopelessness.

What had she expected? A decade was a long time. Hilo had pressed forward too. She couldn't expect to pick up where she left off when and if she was ever ready to face it. Malia was no longer the toddler of her memories. She was a girl with sneakers covered in doodles made probably by friends Hi`i knew nothing about, a scab on her shin from who knows what, and a T-shirt with a team name for a sport that Hi`i would not have been able to guess.

Ruth and Emma looked toward their mom for confirmation and, getting a nod, raced to see who could get to their aunty first. Malia dropped to her knees and laughed as they tackled her. She whispered something into their ears and they burst out laughing. Hi`i savored the scene. She'd once blown raspberries onto this girl's belly. Kissed her feet and tickled the folds of fat around her neck. Now Malia declined Hi`i's offer to carry her bags, shouldering them herself to the car.

GETTING OUT OF LAX was a nightmare of blinkers and blaring horns. Hi`i welcomed the distraction. The girls begged Malia to squeeze between them in the backseat, which allowed Hi`i to sneak glances at her in the rearview mirror. Unlike the tense strangeness between them, Malia and her children were completely at ease sandwiched together.

Malia's bronze skin glowed with the sun she'd brought with her. Hints of Tony blended softly into Laka's dominant features, a branch clearly connected to a tree. A car sounded its horn. Hi`i jerked the wheel, swerving back into her lane. Her foot, shaky and erratic, stuttered between the brake and the gas pedals. Malia glanced up. Their eyes caught in the mirror. Malia looked away first.

FOR THE NEXT TWO DAYS, Ruth and Emma ran circles around Malia while Hi`i did everything to stay out of their way. Household chores had gone undone since Jacob died, so there was no lack of things needing attention. She started with the laundry but got through only a single load. One of Jacob's socks tumbled out of the dryer. She covered her mouth and ran into her bedroom before the girls could hear her crying. They were thrilled and distracted with Malia so, as complicated as it felt to have her there, it was also a relief. She wrapped herself around Jacob's pillow and gave way to her grief.

On the evening of Malia's third day, Hiʻi tried to pull herself together. While the girls kicked a soccer ball around the backyard, she washed her face and changed her clothes and pulled a frozen pizza from the freezer. Ruth and Emma cheered when she said they could eat outside.

By the time they were finished eating it was dark. The girls ran to get their flashlights. Malia chased them through the flower bushes along the back fence. It was a sweet moment, made of spun sugar, the kind that dissolved too quickly.

When they tired of playing tag, Malia and Hiʻi carried them into a bath, soaped them down, and fitted them into their pajamas. Emma, never one to leave a party early, started crying. She didn't want to go to bed until Aunty did. Hiʻi said they could go get their blankets and just this once stay up late and watch movies together on the couch. Emma claimed her spot on Malia's lap. Ruth went to their room for blankets and came out with a small photo book. Pictures of Daddy, she told Malia. Malia shifted Emma to make room for Ruth. Emma protested, said she wanted to see too. Ruth, ever the somber rule maker of the house, told her little sister that it was Aunty Malia who hadn't known Daddy, not Emma.

Hiʻi's heart dropped. She picked up a VHS tape and waved it in front of the girls.

"Who votes to watch this one?"

No one looked her way. Malia put an arm around Ruth's shoulders and said her lap was big enough that they could all see. Hiʻi rummaged furiously through the rows of videos in the cabinet, finally selecting one at random and shoving it into the player. She turned the volume up.

Ruth and Emma were asleep within minutes.

Hi`i lowered the volume and glanced at Malia. "How are you?"

The question came out so formal. Her years in California had erased her pidgin.

Malia kept her face directed at the television and shrugged. "Fine."

Malia gently nudged Emma off her lap and repositioned Ruth's head onto a pillow. Hi`i tried a few more prompts to get Malia to open up, but the more she tried, the more Malia retreated into herself. Eventually she stood and whispered, "Let's get them to bed."

Malia gave no acknowledgment that she'd heard Hi`i but after a moment pulled Emma into her arms and followed Hi`i down the hall. They folded the girls into their beds. Hi`i gently shut the door behind her. Malia moved immediately toward the living room and her make-shift bed. Hi`i reached for her arm to stop her. Malia flinched. Hi`i withdrew her hand. Thankfully Malia stayed rooted in place.

"Thank you. For coming. It . . . they've been through so much, they're so happy you're here. It means a lot."

Malia's face went rigid. She glared at Hi`i, eyes swimming in angry tears. Her hands curled into fists. "I'm hea fo' Mom and Tutu. Cuz dat's wat family does, yeah? Whatevah gotta get tru, we get tru togeddah, dat's da Hawaiian way, right? Oh wait, I forgot, not your style. You take off, handle by yo'self."

Hi`i held up her hands in surrender. "Malia, I'm sorry. You have every right to be angry. But please believe me that leaving had nothing to do with you."

"No, you listen to me." She stabbed at the air in front of Hi`i's face with her pointer finger. "I sorry yoa husband wen die. Really. But how

I can be sad about a guy I nevah wen meet? And how you can say dis no have not'ing fo' do wit me? Course it did. We family. You t'ink life jus wen on da same? Dat Mom was happy? You t'ink she was okay wen she heard you got married, wen she heard you was hapai? You even know about David, wat she did fo' him?"

Hi`i's defenses started to rise. She took a step back and crossed her arms. "You don't understand. You think she is entirely innocent in all this? Have you ever asked her why I left, or asked Tutu? Who's David?"

"Nevah mind, he not yoa business, I guess. And I no need ask why you left. No matter. You left. You my sistah, and you left. I will nevah forgive you."

WAS THERE A BIGGER WORD than *sorry*?

THAT NIGHT, HI`I INCHED toward Jacob's side of the mattress, the sheets cold. She used to like to press her body against his back when he slept. Clung to him as if he were a lifejacket.

Time, a soap bubble growing before her eyes, warped, expanded, collapsed inward. She felt herself losing control, the space she'd put between herself and Hilo slipping away.

CHAPTER 2

1984

A few months after Kainoa's brother's funeral, Hi`i took Jane up on her offer to hang out at her house. Mostly out of curiosity, but also because she'd fronted her allowance to pay Hi`i's dues to join the new halau and Hi`i was looking for a way to say thanks. Hi`i had gone to her first practice as Jane's guest and loved it, but there was no possibility of asking her mom for the money. Hi`i promised Jane she would pay her back. Jane told her not to worry about it, that sharing what get was the Hawaiian way, right? They still went to different schools, but now they saw each other at least twice a week at the halau. Up until the moment Jane invited her over, Hi`i hadn't really known how to act around her. If anyone had treated her the way she'd treated Jane over the years, that person never would have gotten so much as a nod from Hi`i, and yet here Jane was, lending her money and inviting her over after school.

It didn't take long for Hi`i to find out that wasn't the only thing strange about Jane. When they got to Jane's, Hi`i followed her through the front door and froze in the entryway. In front of her was an expansive living room full of natural light and big windows and wall-to-wall carpet the color of freshly whipped cream the kind you'd put on a pie, perfectly unblemished. And there was Jane, striding right over it with her shoes on. She hadn't even paused at the front mat to wipe them off.

Hi`i had never seen anything like it. And that was just the beginning.

Jane called her dad by his first name. Adam. Hi`i had never called an adult by their first name in her entire life. Adam insisted. She tried it out. It felt wrong. He invited her to stay for dinner and, instead of starting a pot of rice, Adam picked up the phone and ordered Chinese takeout, which they ate straight out of the cartons.

Compared to a home full of Hulali and Laka and the needs of the new baby and the weight of all the things not said, being with Jane and Adam felt easy. Hi`i started spending every free moment outside of school at their house, although she never got used to calling Adam by his name. It made the hair on the back of her neck stand up, like petting a cat tail to head. Adults came with titles—Miss, Mister, Uncle, Aunty— even inside her head. Even the homeless guy sleeping in a pavilion at Wailoa Park was Uncle. But Adam wasn't an uncle. He was a mister, a doctor, the kind of man people made appointments to see. He called the front room of their house the foyer and held his hands behind his back when he looked at things like framed art or Jane's homework. There were a few things here and there that hinted of Hawai`i—a series of framed woodblock prints on the wall in the study, rows of books about Hawaiian mythology and island history, a dusty set of `uli`ulis in a corner—but overall their house felt foreign. They made afternoon snacks of macaroni from the box or jelly sandwiches on white bread. Their cheese gleamed and came wrapped in individual plastic sheets.

AFTER LAKA TOLD HI`I about the circumstances of her birth, Hi`i's stays at Jane's had slippery-sloped their way to the point where she slept most nights at their house, after being given a carte blanche invitation to stay as long as she wanted (which Adam offered once he understood that Hi`i's mom had just had a baby, her grandma had just moved in, and things at their house were a bit chaotic. Hi`i told them that money was tight and Adam offered to pick up the tab of her halau dues, his gift to the growing family, something Hi`i wasn't exactly sure how to thank him for, even though money didn't seem a factor in their house. Adam said that, if hula was as important to Hi`i as it was to Jane, money shouldn't be a barrier. Hi`i couldn't imagine hula being as significant to Jane as it was to her, but she kept those thoughts to herself). She was still operating under the guise of extended sleepovers, never packing for more than a few days at a time, slipping in and out of the house when it was empty to grab a few things. If Laka noticed her dwindling closet, she didn't object. Hi`i always kept her eye out for a note from her mom, an entreaty to join them for dinner or something, but all she ever found was evidence Malia had started crawling, a toy on the ground, a blanket dragged down the hall. Since the day Hulali moved in Hi`i had gotten the sense that she put everyone on edge, and her absence made things easier. That maybe Hulali and Laka were relieved to have her gone.

The day of Laka's confession confirmed that ten times over. Normally, Hi`i would tell Jane something so big, but what was she supposed to say? How would someone even begin to explain what Laka had told her about who, or what, her birth mother was, and everything else that had happened in Maui? In a way, Leilani's old taunt was true.

That afternoon Hi`i walked in a daze through downtown, the revelations pulsing fresh in her ears and a folded check from Hulali burning a hole in her pocket. She was staring blankly into shop windows when she heard a shout from across the street. Jane.

Jane took one look at the backpack stuffed with clothes drooping off Hi`i's shoulder and grabbed her hand.

"Come on," she said gently as she directed them up the hill toward her house.

Hi`i was quiet. Jane chattered, nervous.

"You talked to your mom, huh? Are you mad? I wasn't trying to get you in trouble. You gotta believe me." Her voice dropped. "Today's my mom's birthday. Every year Adam gets out the old photo albums. I was looking at all those pictures, and then, I dunno, I started thinking of you and how you have your mom and how much I would want mine around if I was competing in Miss Aloha Hula. Sounds stupid now. I'm sorry. Please don't be mad."

Had Jane telling Laka about hula been the reason she'd finally told her the truth? Hi`i wasn't mad. Hula didn't matter. Nothing did anymore. She made a silent vow. She would never dance hula again. Not a single step.

When they got to the house, Hi`i finally spoke. "Can I see 'em?"

"See what?"

"The pictures," Hi`i went on. Of Jane's mom, the ones that had sent Jane to Laka.

"Sure," Jane said.

They found Adam in his study.

"I want to introduce Hi`i to Mom," Jane announced. Adam smiled.

Hi`i and Jane sat on the couch while Adam brought them a stack of heavy photo albums. They started from the top.

Black and white, a close-up of Jane minutes old, the smiling profile of her mom. Jane as she filled out, starting to sit, Jane bundled in a snow suit next to a snowman and a woman laughing.

"She's beautiful, yeah?" Jane ran her fingers over the woman's face.

"She was so nice. Everybody loved her. Always cooking, always laughing. She loved growing flowers. Look, here, this one. My birthday. She baked that cake herself."

Hiʻi peered at the photos, faded with age. Her mouth dropped open. "That's your mom? She, uh, she's not what I imagined. She doesn't look like you. I mean, you don't look like her."

Jane smiled. She caressed the edges of a cropped photo of her mom in a bathing suit sitting at what looked to be the edge of a campsite. The woman's bare shoulders and legs were the color of milk chocolate, her features remarkably familiar. Jane turned the page. The next photo was the same woman, this time caught mid-motion, knees bent, a hip extended to the side, hands out in front of her. She was wearing a bikini top and a pareo tied around her waist. Hiʻi looked questioningly at Jane.

"Jane's mom was Hawaiian," Adam explained. "Born on Oʻahu, but her parents were from the Big Island. They moved to Colorado when she was little, her dad got a job over there. She grew up on the mainland and spent most of her life there, but she talked about wanting to move back. I always said one day. When she died, well. Let's just say one day never comes if you don't let it."

Adam put his arm around Jane's shoulder and squeezed.

Hiʻi's cheeks burned with the memory of what she'd said to Jane on that very first day they'd met, at the old halau above the grocery store. Her stomach soured. Of the two of them, on paper, Jane was actually the Hawaiian.

That night after her shower, Hiʻi stared at her reflection in the bathroom mirror. A gecko scampered across the windowsill, holding still for a second before disappearing behind a cabinet. Hiʻi stared at the spot where it had paused, thinking of all Laka had said. Gecko as mo`o. Mo`o as legend, and now mo`o as what she'd come from. If it was true that Hi`i was a mo`o, she'd be able to shape-shift. But into what? She used to think Hawai`i was simple. You were either an outsider or an insider. Hawaiians looked a certain way that made it clear who they were and where they were from. She'd thought her haole-looking skin was a fluke, a mix-up of the stars. But if Jane was Hawaiian, that meant being Hawaiian wasn't just something you could point out in a crowd. And if it wasn't, then what was it? Who got to say?

IMPOSSIBLE QUESTIONS AND IMPOSSIBLE ANSWERS. Hi`i gave up looking for them and instead focused on finding a way out. She'd never left Hawai`i, but things looked easier elsewhere, far from the family. She still remembered all the places she and Jane had said they were going to go one day, and spent the final months of her senior year of high school taking all the advice and help Adam was willing to give, peppering him with questions on life in big cities and foreign countries, what people did, how things worked. She never told Jane about what Laka had told her about the mo`o, and their dreams began to drift. They'd once spent long nights staying up late, squeezed together on a twin mattress, ignoring the spare bed they'd brought into Jane's room for her, staring out the window at the stars dotting the sky, planning the adventures they'd have, hitchhiking through Spain, eating pasta in Italy, joining the Peace Corps, and backpacking through New Zealand. Making plans to take the world by storm, together. But as graduation drew closer, Jane stopped talking about passports and visas and started talking about what she wanted to do in Hilo after high school. She pushed away Adam's college pamphlets and scholarship applications. Hi`i gladly scooped them up.

***

AFTER HI`I MOVED TO LA, they kept in touch, but things were never the same. Hi`i was pregnant with Ruth when Jane wrote to say she was marrying Kainoa. Hi`i tried to picture her former crush and high school best friend together but couldn't. She sent them a card with an excuse as to why she couldn't fly over for the wedding. The space between their letters back and forth across the Pacific eventually got wider and wider, until there was nothing but ocean between them.

CHAPTER 3

1995

At the airport, as they were dropping her off, Malia handed Hi`i a newspaper clipping.

"Mom wanted me to give dis to you. She said maybe you'd wanna know wat's going on back home."

It was not the time or place to read it. Ruth had pulled her shirt over her head and was crying into it and Emma needed prying off Malia's leg, and they were parked in the loading zone. The girls begged her not to go. Hi`i wished Malia a safe trip back. They hugged, but it had the same awkward stiffness of the one they'd had when she arrived. No progress made.

BACK HOME, THE LAUGHTER and fullness were gone. The cold silent absence of Jacob swallowed them back up. Malia's blankets were folded in a stack at the corner of the couch. Emma and Ruth trudged into their room, Hi`i trudged to hers. She sat on the corner of her bed and picked up the little wooden box on her nightstand. Jacob. His family had put together a memorial for him at the beach. If they'd been in Hilo, the paddle-out would have included the scattering of his ashes. But his parents had wanted a place to be able to sit with him, to bring flowers and light candles, so they'd taken his ashes to the cemetery. Hi`i had asked for only a portion. A bit of him to take back to Hilo, to make good on her promise to introduce him to her home. She'd had every intention of doing it, but Malia's visit had laid out all the reasons not to. It was obvious that no one had bothered to share the full story of Hi`i's identity with Malia, and there was damage there that Hi`i wasn't sure could be repaired.

Thinking about Malia made her remember the paper in her pocket. Laka hadn't been the one to write, Hulali had. Hi`i had understood that to mean Laka was fine with their relationship being the way it was, even if Malia was furious about it. So why had Laka sent Malia to Hi`i with a piece of newspaper for her?

After scanning the article she took a shaky breath. Suddenly Malia's resentment felt like the least of her worries.

CHAPTER 4

1995

The letter to the editor in the *Hawaii Tribune-Herald*'s Sunday paper was a crack in the earth, the groan of compounded pressure releasing itself, opening into something unknown, a ground we could stand on no longer. The author had signed it as Anonymous, but in Hilo there was no such thing. Only one person could have written it.

Laka.

To enslave a people, the letter began, convince them of their inferiority. Take away their language, their musicality, and their history. Trivialize them. When discussing reparations, pat them on the head like children.

Which is, Anonymous asserted, exactly what Senator Akaka had done with his apology resolution and ultimately what Hulali Naupaka did by using her column in OHA's monthly newsletter to applaud his nice little thing for Native Hawaiians. Hulali Naupaka, the op-ed claimed, is walking around with wool over her eyes if she really believes any good would ever come of it. By definition, an apologist is someone who speaks in defense of something. Akaka's resolution was more than feel-good politicking—it was an out for Americans, a way for them to clear themselves of guilt and not be held accountable.

Hawaiians being recognized as a people was important, but had anything changed?

AUWE.

We folded the paper back into itself, but the words, they sank like seeds into our heads and would not go away. One hundred years too late, but better late than never, yeah?

I mua.

THE APOLOGY HULA:

Whereas, we lived in an organized, pono way.

Whereas, the U.S. used to do business with the Kingdom, recognizing full well its independence.

Whereas, on January 14, 1893 . . . the Minister of the United States helped Thurston and his cronies to overthrow the lawful Government of Hawai`i.

Whereas . . . when informed that the American military had landed on Honolulu's shores in support of the overthrow, Queen Lili`uokalani issued her yield to the United States of America. But only until the *Government of the United States shall, upon facts being presented to it, undo the action of its representatives and reinstate me in the authority which I claim as the Constitutional Sovereign of the Hawaiian Islands.*

AND RIGHT THERE, our eyes unglazed and our hearts snagged. The queen's message front and center in their grand Apology Bill. Again and again, the line never got old. So technical, so precise. Her wording was no accident. Within her final sentence, our case rested. Yielded her authority to the United States in the trust that—given a history of diplomatic relations and a shared belief in a Christian God—its justice system would help her get her kingdom back.

The bill continued.

WHEREAS, WITHOUT HELP FROM the U.S., the coup against the queen would have failed.

Whereas, the U.S. president described the actions of Thurston and his mob as acts of war. That the United States representatives who participated did so without authority. He then called for *the restoration of the Hawaiian monarchy.*

AND HERE IS THE PART where we grabbed the ruler, we the accidental activists, to pay attention to every deliberate *whereas* in that bill, to read line by line every deflection.

WHEREAS, WE NEVER GAVE UP our sovereignty or our lands to the United States.

Whereas, the health of the people is tied intrinsically to the land.

Whereas, we need our ancestral territory to pass down our culture, our language, our ways.

Whereas, this has destroyed us.

Now, therefore, Congress:

—apologizes for taking away our right to self-determination.

—is "committed" to acknowledging what a pilau thing was done so the U.S. and Hawai`i can shake hands and make up.

—says the President of the United States is sorry too.

YOU PAYING ATTENTION?

The indigenous Hawaiian people never directly relinquished their claims to their inherent sovereignty as a people or over their national lands to the United States.

Adopted by both houses of the United States Congress. Signed by Bill Clinton, president of the United States, on November 23, 1993.

So who was right, Laka or Hulali? Was this Progress? Or race-based, feel-good politicking, an admission of guilt? Should we cheer or mourn?

The smoking gun:

Our queen appealed to the United States government, to President Grover Cleveland, who had visited on diplomatic occasion, for assistance in evicting the chiisai chimpo who cockaroached Hawai`i and created a provisional government on the pretense of having the `ae, the go-ahead of the United States, which it never had.

As the overthrowers were overthrowing, the United States House of Representatives Foreign Relations Committee came to investigate. In their report, they "officially identified the United States' complicity in the lawless overthrow of the lawful, peaceful government of Hawaii." President Cleveland agreed. Sent his own envoy to kōkua. Started working to restore Lili`uokalani her kingdom and make things pono. Ordered Sanford Dole, president of the provisional government, to back the eff up. Dole, that cheeky buggah, told Cleveland what he could do with his order. Before Cleveland could smash that mosquito, the damn Americans voted in a new president.

Aloha `oe, aloha `oe. Farewell to you.

But they did come, they do care. It took one hundred years, but here we are, they're signing the apology. For all the people still insisting the United States got their mitts on Hawai`i legally, this set the record straight.

The horse's mouth:

"The logical consequence of this resolution would be independence," said Senator Slade Gorton.

So when they had the ceremony presenting the American resolution they called the Apology Bill, we was feeling good. Feeling empowered. Feeling like history was going to be righted. Now we had proof, now we had it in writing. Now we were an acknowledged people. Now we could lift our heads, talk about compensation, about reparation. Boom kanani!

IN THE LETTER TO THE EDITOR in the newspaper, Anonymous continued. Would this congressional act make DHHL award us land? The wait list was growing cobwebs. So many of us was on it for decades, living and dying, and no one was getting any land. Would this resolution that OHA and Ms. Naupaka was applauding put a stop to the abuse and corruption happening with trust lands? Would it give us all rights of nationhood extended to Native nations?

The United States Supreme Court answered.

The congressional resolution apologizing for the role of the United States in overthrowing the Hawaiian monarchy in 1893 does not affect the right of the state of Hawaii to sell public lands, nor to remove a tract of former crown land from the public trust and redevelop it. The "whereas" clauses have no operative effect.

HMMM.

Maybe we should have fought harder to point out that our kingdom was an internationally recognized nation-state. Maybe we should have made it clear it wasn't just "indigenous" Hawaiians who were victims of this illegal act. *All* Hawaiian nationals got fucked. Maybe this was the time to point out that it was the U.S. Congress that introduced those blood quantum requirements in the first place. But bumbai pau. We was so excited to have any recognition at all.

Ua mau ke ea o ka ʻāina i ka pono. The life of the land is perpetuated in righteousness.

Bulai. You apologized to Native Americans too. Look what that got them.

To be fair (why we even bothering?), we should have seen it coming. You called it the Apology Bill, not the We Did Wrong Now We Going Make It Right Bill.

Hulali Naupaka and Anonymous, they was both right, both wrong. The Apology hadn't made anything any less complicated. But that letter to the editor was a line in the sand.

CHAPTER 5

Emma forgot and asked when Daddy was coming home. She wanted him to tuck her into bed, not Mommy. Ruth told her Daddy was never ever coming home. Blind leading the blind.

Hi`i didn't know how to make them understand, she stayed away because she was protecting them from her grief. Jacob's family and the neighborhood network stepped in again, ferrying the girls through a nonstop agenda of playdates, after-school ice cream runs, and sleepovers. Hi`i sat in the window, watching people drive away with her children. Sometimes she found the strength to lift a hand in acknowledgment. Other times her eyes were already shut, heavy curtains that wanted to stay closed.

If life had a Pull in Case of Emergency lever, Hi`i would have pulled it.

ON GOOD DAYS, she reread the article blasting the Apology Bill and OHA's part in gushing over it. The letter challenged OHA head-on, saying OHA was a state agency and could not continue acting as if it were the sole representative of the Hawaiian people. In Hi`i's mind, Hulali and OHA were one and the same. Laka had sent this to her for a reason. She was Anonymous. She was sending Hi`i a message. Hulali didn't speak for everyone.

Hi`i shivered. Closed her eyes and tried to picture herself back home. Her promise to Jacob gathering dust on her side of the bedroom.

SPRING TURNED TO SUMMER, which turned to fall.

Ruth came home from school with a flyer announcing a multicultural festival at her school. An evening full of international foods and activities and performances done by the families themselves, to celebrate the diverse backgrounds of their student body. Ruth bounced on her toes as she described the details. She hadn't been this excited since Malia's visit. Her best friend's mom was going to do henna. Her teacher was Swiss, she was bringing a pot of melted cheese that you dunked things in. Then her energy faded.

"I wish Daddy and Aunty Malia were here so we could do Hawaii."

The flyer screamed. Guilt flooded in. Her daughters didn't know anything about her. Jacob's family couldn't teach them the full extent of their heritage, and neither could their father. But she could.

THAT NIGHT, HI`I SHAMPOOED HER HAIR. She couldn't remember how long it had been. The entire nine months Jacob had been gone? The cap of the shampoo bottle had been crusted closed for so long that she'd had to run it under hot water for a few minutes to get it open again. After her shower she went into the kitchen and opened the fridge. When was the last time the shelves had offered more than moldy yogurt or a puckered tomato? The next morning, she found the grocery store exactly where they'd left it. She bought one of everything, filling two entire carts. Later, she stood in the middle of the kitchen with the doors of the fridge and pantry wide open so she could stare at the shelves stocked full of canned beans and pasta and cereal, of milk and little tubes of flavored yogurt. The knobs of the stove had grown a grease-spattered film, so she wet a rag and scrubbed. Then she pulled out a phone book. It took three tries before she found a music store that had what she needed. The boy she'd spoken to over the phone had it waiting for her at the register by the time she swung by. In the car she fingered the thin cellophane wrapping of the cassette tape and decided to hold off on telling the girls anything, so as not to get their hopes up in case she couldn't pull off what she had in mind.

That night after the girls were tucked in bed, she inserted the cassette into the player and turned the volume so low it was as though memory itself was playing the music. But even so, her body immediately stood at attention, alerted by this deep familiar beat. Goose bumps rippled across her arms and down her legs as the words to the song appeared on her tongue, revealing that the entire database of Hilo knowledge stored within her subconscious was intact. Halfway through the first chorus, she fell to her knees and pressed her face into the carpet. A rush of tears seeped from her face, discoloring the threads beneath her. She was relieved when silence followed the final verse. Hilo faded from the living room. She remained prostrated on the floor.

"I'm sorry," she cried. She didn't know who she was saying sorry to. Jacob? Malia? Laka? Ruth and Emma? Herself?

A SQUARE TABLE WAS NOT MADE for three people. Hiʻi served the girls dinner on the round patio table in the garden instead, where there was no spotlight on empty chairs and vacant spaces. The sun bathed their faces with a delicate warm love. The days were growing longer now, the light lingered in the evenings. Dinner was quiet, but not particularly sad. Hi`i sensed they were recalibrating as a family. She repeated their outside garden dinners every night that week. By the weekend, Ruth and Emma were talking about things that had happened at school. Emma announced she'd drawn a picture of their family, a present for Mommy, and ran inside to get it.

In Emma's drawing, tall stick-figure Hi`i stood between stick-figure Ruth and stick-figure Emma. A scribble of grass ran in an uneven line under their invisible feet. A round circle with two eyes and an upside-down rainbow for a mouth hovered discombobulated in the air above.

Hi`i forced a smile.

"This masterpiece is going on the fridge," she said.

Emma beamed.

"I have news too," Hi`i said. "We're going to dance a hula at your festival, Ruthie."

The girls jumped out of their seats and ran circles in the yard, cheering until the stars came out.

That night, Hi`i dreamed of Jacob. He was a crayon circle and was talking to her, but she couldn't hear him. She shook her head, not understanding. Jacob mouthed the words again. This time she recognized them. They were the same four words he'd forced through his cracked colorless lips from that miserable hospice bed the nurse had brought into their home for his final days. His last words, barely loud enough to hear over the beeping machines that come with death.

Take the girls home.

* * *

THE NEXT EVENING SHE set Jacob on the coffee table in the living room and hit play on the cassette player. She tried to keep her body loose, to invite hula back in. When she broke a sweat she sat back on her heels. Taped along the walls were paintings the girls had made back when they'd spent weekends together gardening and doing art projects. There were pictures of rainbows and flowers, of the things that existed in the days before they knew the words *cancer* and *cemetery*. The pictures provided a rough timeline, one that stopped abruptly. Ruth and Emma had since been tasked with filling the blank spaces on their own, to color their lives without her guidance while she grieved.

She needed to make good on her promise to Jacob. Then maybe she could be a mother to their children, to give them the part of her that she hadn't been able to give him.

She exhaled and wiped her face with her shirt. Her knees cracked when she straightened them. As the tape rewound, she slipped off her shoes and pushed the coffee table flush against the wall. She pressed play and lowered into position, raising her arms to the level of her shoulders. But when the words came, she found herself unable to move. The gestures did not come easily, as the song had. She'd spent a decade erasing Hawai`i from her life, it seemed silly now to assume she'd dredge up the choreography without a fight.

A memory bubbled to the surface. The mirrored walls of her original halau rose up around her. The sweet humid air of Hilo thick in the room. The drip of rain on the tin roof. The rotating fan, making no difference. Kumu chanting, the words taking hold of Hi`i's body, moving her arms and legs almost without her consent. She rewound the tape again. This time when she hit play she closed her eyes and let herself sway into its rhythm. It seeped into her bones and dripped its way into her hips. It curled like fingers over her thighs, commanding them to flick, to turn, to twist. Her feet, her calves, her shoulders gasped awake.

Long into the night she danced, until her body throbbed and said *enough.*

CHAPTER 6

There was no way she could have done it all herself, but that was probably the point. If any of it had been for her, she never would have considered doing it in the first place.

Hi`i held on to the pot's handle as Ruth lined her footstool against the stove and mounted on tippy-toes to stir the vat of simmering coconut milk, holding firm to the long wooden spoon with the somber air of a cafeteria madam who'd been making haupia for two hundred her entire life. Of her daughters, Ruth had always been the more serious one. The justice seeker and rule maker, a classic eldest. But serious was not the same as somber. Since Jacob's death, Lady Justice had retreated into quiet reserve, as if her scales had tipped and left the whole world unbalanced. It was enough to break Hi`i's heart all over again. She rubbed her daughter's back and smiled down at her. When the milk started to bubble, Hi`i added a box of cornstarch and a heaping cup of sugar into the pot. She instructed Ruth to keep mixing slow and steady while she returned to the dining room table, where Emma was busy extracting stenciled flowers from multicolored construction paper with a set of clunky safety scissors.

Unlike her sister, losing her father had steered Emma in the opposite direction, from wild to wilder, a domestic animal let loose in a jungle. It was as though she was daring Jacob to come out from wherever he was hiding, to tell her to knock off all that screaming, jumping on the couches, and running around the yard with her panties on her head. Hi`i hadn't the heart to put that angst in a net and hold it in, so on usual days Emma fluttered like a spastic butterfly until bedtime, when she crashed into her pillow, hair uncombed and teeth unbrushed. But on this particular day she sat still as a cricket, tongue chomped to one side of her mouth in concentration as she cut paper flowers one after another.

By the time the haupia was setting in the fridge, they'd finished with the flowers and had moved on to portioning out lengths of yarn and plastic straws cut into inch-wide chunks. Hi`i helped Ruth and Emma make a lei each, crafting a needle with a strip of masking tape wound around a yarn tip, then threading it through the paper flower middles, using straw bits to space out the blossoms. When they finally finished that, the trio moved into the living room, where Hi`i stood her daughters on either side of her and began to dance, telling them to follow her lead.

THE WORN GLAZE OF the cafeteria floor tickled under her bare feet, giving her the feeling she'd slipped into an old favorite pair of shoes she'd forgotten she had. Currents of energy ran up her legs. She tried to remember the last time she'd walked around barefoot. What came was the vibration of the Merrie Monarch stage, the varnished smoothness of the halau floor, the thick black sands at Richardson's Beach Park—her feet carried their own memories of Hilo. It made her feel like the girl she'd been, the one she'd forgotten about. She felt so young that she experienced an odd sensation of the past and the present sandwiching itself, her young and older selves meeting for the first time.

On the afternoon of the Multicultural Festival, a team of parents and volunteers transformed the cafeteria into a makeshift, jumbled microcosm of the world's countries. Scanning the room she saw a Japanese father demonstrating how to fold origami paper cranes, a mother-daughter duo making Swiss fondue, a family at Thailand's table passing out little cups of pad thai, and a mom in a sparkling Indian sari applying henna to any child who promised to sit still for five minutes. Hi`i and the girls took shifts like colleagues, Hi`i manning their table of paper flower lei making while Ruth led Emma around the room, sampling curry from India and rice from Iran.

Hi`i carried the cookie sheets full of thimble-sized paper cups of haupia while the girls taped pictures of Hawai`i to the wall behind their booth and set up an easel for the display Hi`i had made, a brief elementary summary of Hawai`i's history, its flag, a picture of the queen, and the year the monarchy ended. Since other families were presenting the countries from where they or their ancestors had originated, she'd felt it more appropriate to present Hawai`i the kingdom, rather than Hawaii the fiftieth state. Only a parent or two bothered to read through the bullet points, preferring instead to tell Hi`i about the fantastic time they'd had during a trip there, how beautiful their hotel was. She smiled and nodded. One kid too many scrunched their noses at the haupia even after she told them it was pudding, but by the time the entertainment portion of the evening began, every neck in the room was banded with Emma's stenciled cuttings. Hi`i felt a bloom of pride. Squinting, it almost looked like May Day.

She reminded the girls to take off their shoes before they went on stage. The volunteer sound crew, a father and his garage band, tapped the microphones and waved them up. They slipped off their sandals and mounted the stage steps, Emma bounding, Ruth following warily behind. Hi`i gave her a soft nudge and placed herself between them. She took her mark, making sure to position herself a few inches in front so they could follow her.

She'd spent the weekend hunting through costume shops. The result was far from perfect, but good enough. There were no fresh flowers to tuck into Ruth or Emma's Hamākua honey-colored ringlets, no ti-leaf skirts around their little girl waists or shell kupe`e secured to their knobby ankles. But even in their T-shirts, hastily tied pareos, and leis made of paper flowers, the overall effect somehow worked. They were a team of dancers on a stage, about to tell a story to an audience ready and waiting for them.

There was no time to wonder if it was the wrong thing to do, if it had been too long. The music dripped like an IV into her bloodstream and took over. Her smile burst out the sides of her face with such force it made her cheeks ache. She stepped out of the way so the melody could take control. Ruth and Emma synched themselves to her as her hands caught air, as her hips swayed and shifted. They matched her move for move as best their age allowed.

The hukilau song was simple, a catchy song that children in Hilo learned in elementary schools about the ancient Hawaiian fishing practice of coming together as a group to cast a large net into the ocean and then pulling it back in to reap the rewards.

Oh, we're going . . . to a hukilau, where the laulau is the kau kau at the big luau. We throw our nets out into the sea, where all the `ama`ama come swimming to me.

The choreography was simple, the words in English and easy to remember, the gestures needed no interpretation. It was repetitive and rhythmic, after a verse or two, almost anyone could follow along if they wanted. Hotels had been teaching it to visitors for years. Hi`i was suddenly embarrassed that her children had not learned it until now, that this was the first and only thing she'd ever shared with them about who'd she'd been once upon a time, and that this Americanized ditty was what her children and their friends would now associate with hula. But it was the simplest dance she could think to teach them in such a short time, one that she could dance without thinking of Laka or Hulali, and there would be time to teach them more.

Besides, Ruth and Emma didn't know the difference between what they were dancing and what they weren't. They were standing at the front of the stage, holding hands, taking bows, looking back at her with hazel eyes sparkling with life, and that was all that mattered at the moment.

This was heaven, this was joy, this was a single heartbeat going thump. It was over too quickly.

THE GIRLS WENT TO BED with smiles on their faces and wilted paper flowers around their necks, singing the hukilau song until they fell asleep. Hi`i sat at the foot of their bunk bed rewinding the day. The walls no longer had enough photos. Their Silverstein-Seuss bookshelves felt suddenly bereft of pua`a and menehune. She opened the window but the air that entered was too thin. The fridge did not have the right smells. Everywhere she looked she found only space. The puzzle was suddenly missing too many pieces, obscuring the whole picture.

To the empty side of the bed:

What if the mosquitoes feast on their skin and eat them like zombies?

The empty side of the bed:
Take them.
To the empty side of the bed:
But what if there's no place for me there anymore?
The empty side of the bed had no answer.

CRISP MORNING LIGHT FILTERED through the trees and streamed through the windows. Hi`i woke facing Jacob's side of the bed. She opened her eyes, pulled his pillow over her face, and inhaled deep enough to pull the memory of him from its down feathers. A warm calm settled over her insides.

Yesterday she had danced a hula with her daughters. She could still feel its thrum throughout her body. She'd been Ruth's age when she'd first got it in her head that hula would be the defining force of her life, and then had spent a long time not allowing herself to think about hula at all. All it had taken was one night, one performance for everything to come rushing back—the energy and purpose it brought, the immediacy, the feeling of being connected to everything around her. Hula was a timeline, not a dead end. Recalling how she'd felt on that stage, she thought she understood now. Maybe hula had always been what would bring her family together, but maybe it had never been about Laka and Hulali. Maybe it was about Ruth and Emma. Wasn't that what Kumu had said all those years ago? The next generation. The fire goes out if the torch is not passed. Through hula it was possible to give her children what she didn't know how to give them otherwise. Home. A place to belong.

For the first time since Jacob's diagnosis, she woke energized. She swung her legs out of bed and made the girls pancakes. She and

Emma walked Ruth to school and, when Emma had a breakdown, she found herself able to wipe the girl's tears away. She held Emma steady, instead of crumbling right alongside her. When Emma cried out that night for her daddy, Hi`i didn't bury her head under her pillow. Now she pushed the covers away, grabbed her robe, and pulled it on as she moved swiftly down the hall and let herself into their room, fitting herself around her younger daughter and pressing her body against her, as if to physically absorb the pain.

She was learning how to be a mother again. Hula had given her that. It was hard to ignore the connection. She thought back to the letter in the newspaper that Laka had sent, her olive branch. Maybe now the time had come to learn again how to be a daughter. Time for the branches to turn on themselves, to fold down their tree trunks, to go back to their roots. Time for sorrow to let loose its grip, time to make amends, to say sorry, to let that word move them all forward. And if that was no longer possible, then at least she would be making good on the promise she'd made to her husband, for once offer him something more than an apology.

CHAPTER 7

1995

What good is an apology if they only going keep doing what they saying sorry for?

Airplanes vomit out the interrupters. Jumbo jets, record numbers.

In the backyard, we stop singing.

We put down our ukuleles.

We sniff the air. Dry sugarcane catches fire quick. Wind makes it grow.

THE NEWSPAPER HEADLINE HULA:

BUYMORE ANNOUNCES PLANS TO OPEN AN

OUTLET IN HILO.

A TWENTY-ACRE LAND PARCEL in Waiakea. Across the street from the plaza we'd said we didn't want because it was built on Hawaiian Homelands and we would have rather had the land, since we still living and dying on the waiting list, but they said that was it, just that one time, for our benefit.

Here we go again.

Okay, okay. Deep breaths. This time different. This time we get the Apology Bill. We not cut off at the knees. We had a friend in Bill Clinton (so did everybody else). We could finally walk around our house as if we owned it. We could walk around like we weren't ghosts haunting up a place. All we had to do was go to DHHL and OHA, tell them we didn't approve. That we didn't need more stores, we needed only to get off that waiting list.

DHHL and OHA said corporate leases increased their revenues so they could make more land ready, to bring water and roads and electricity to South Point.

We don't want South Point. We want Waiakea, we want Keaukaha. Hilo is our home.

Kanikapila turned into a community meeting. We needed to stop this, all the people flooding in, taking over. We needed someplace for ourselves. We needed a plan.

We couldn't go in with our eyes closed. Didn't take a genius to know who was the Goliath in this story. Ever since PKO snuck over to Kaho`olawe and lay down right in that red center of a U.S. military bullseye, we knew all too well how much it was going to take to get anything back—we'd had to blow ourselves up for an uninhabitable, bomb-incinerated island infested with wild goats, had to sneak over there in our boats and stand between them and their target practice, daring them to keep shooting. Keaukaha's Puhi Bay was prime beachfront real estate. Forget about it. America wasn't going to give that up without blinking. But by then we'd collected so many grievances they were spilling out of our pockets. We had to start throwing those pebbles at something or the weight of them was going to sink us straight to the bottom of the ocean.

All those years we been talking about it, now we had the apology on our side. If BuyMore could build, so could we. We was gonna build us a place to gather, to keep us out of the sun when there were no rains, to keep us dry when there were. Puhi Bay was the only beach the county hadn't peed on already, so that's where we were gonna go.

All the uncles had worked construction at some point or another—they knew their way around a toolbox. We passed the jar, pooled the money for the building materials. We surveyed the ground, laid out the plans. Then we got to work.

THE REALITY OF WHAT HI`I WAS DOING didn't hit her until the flight attendant handed her the Hawaii State Department of Agriculture Plants and Animals Declaration form. The form had never made sense to her; the Dept. of Ag. screened all bags leaving Hawai`i to make sure no one was taking fresh fruit or unapproved plants *out of* the island chain, yet there was no screening process to bring things *into* Hawai`i, whose ecosystem was decidedly more fragile than most, given its isolation, and all visitors were ever asked to do was fill out a silly form that would be easy enough to lie about if one really had their heart set on smuggling something in. But this time it wasn't the absurdity of the form that hit her. Now it struck her as intrusive, nearly confrontational. Every question on the form was full of layers she didn't know how to truly answer.

Question 1. I am a:
   a. Visitor to Hawaii
   b. Intended resident moving to Hawaii for at least one year
   c. Returning Hawaii resident

Question 2. Please mark the places you plan to visit:
   O`ahu  Maui  Moloka`i Lana`i  Kaua`i Kona Hilo

Question 3. Where will you stay?
   a. Hotel, condo, rental
   b. With friends or relatives

Question 4. The reason for this trip?
   a. Vacation
   b. Visiting friends or relatives
   c. Business
   d. Other

Her pen quivered. Was she a visitor? A returning resident? Was she really going to have the courage to get off the plane in Hilo? The reason for the trip? She didn't know the answer to any of the questions. They glared at her, waiting for her to tell them what she was doing, but she had no idea.

A SLIGHT HOPPING FROM foot to foot by Ruth and Emma tempered the swell of panic that greeted Hi`i at the gate of Hilo Airport. The clarity and certainty that she could pull off what she had planned had vanished, leaked out their plane's bubbled windows and plummeted into the dark waters somewhere over the Pacific Ocean. A week, she reminded herself. Long enough to find out what had prompted Laka's letter to the newspaper, give the girls a tour of Hilo, and fulfill her promise to Jacob. That's all she had to manage. If she could spend a little time with Malia, she'd consider that a bonus.

The luggage turnstile churned out bag after bag. The girls played tag and ran circles around their growing mountain of too much luggage, the snacks she'd bought in bulk, the towels and lotions, pillows and beach shoes and visors and toys, so much stuff it had caused the girls no small amount of wonder at their mysterious destination, this Hilo town.

The air was hot-shower-in-a-windowless-bathroom thick. The girls' faces turned pink and moist as soon as they stepped out of the terminal. The tips of their ponytails clung to their necks. Hi`i buckled them into the rental car and blasted the air-conditioning for the short drive to the Hilo Hawaiian Hotel on Banyan Drive, as close to Keaukaha as Hi`i dared go. The girls sat wide-eyed and silent in the backseat, staring out the window with wonder.

Her eyes burned. She was so tired, the floor of the lobby tilted under her feet, but when they got to their room thoughts batted around her head and kept her awake. She felt the suck of the vortex at the door, Keaukaha calling to her, the past eager to be appeased. She pulled out the wooden box in her suitcase and brought it into bed with her, to stay focused on why she had come.

HI`I KNEW HOW HILO worked. The coconut wireless must have rung all night.

They came the next day just as she anticipated, inevitable as the sun, in a caravan of dented rusted vehicles being eaten alive by the salty sea air. They wanted her children. They were not going to ask permission. She was glad for it. This meant they saw Ruth and Emma as part of the whole. As part of them.

They spilled into the lobby, filled the corridors strewn with bird-of-paradise flower arrangements. Tourists backed against the walls, held their cameras tight, traded nervous glances, unsure of what was happening and trying to gauge the danger—they'd heard the stories of the locals who might not be so ecstatic about their presence, they'd been warned not to step too heavily. Hiʻi wanted to laugh at the tourists' fear. Wanted to tell them yes. Be scared. Tiptoe.

Ruth and Emma were playing near the koi pond, feeding the fish crumbled bits of leftover French toast still dripping coconut syrup from breakfast, giggling as bulbous lips rose to the surface, bloop bloop bloop. The wave enveloped them; the fish were forgotten in an instant. Their eyes went wide as they were lifted by the current, stunned silent by the swarm's familiarity with them, as if this group had been hiding behind a giant curtain their entire lives, taking in every detail. Hiʻi recognized some faces, wizened, others who she remembered as keiki were now carrying their own keiki. Still others were hapai, bellies blooming. There were teenagers whose acne-spotted faces slightly resembled people Hiʻi used to know, and those she couldn't remember ever meeting, and yet the energy they exuded she remembered acutely. Round, thin, short, tall, pareos and surf shorts, rubber slippers, and chopsticks in their hair to hold their buns in place, the love with which they kissed her on the cheek, this had not changed.

This was good, this was necessary. This would have made Jacob happy. They would introduce her children to Hilo, to her Hawaiʻi, in a way she couldn't do alone. She expected nervousness, hesitation, the clingy uncertainty that had settled down upon her daughters the moment their father passed away, but was met instead with eager excitement and intuitive trust. Ruth and Emma inhaled Hilo as if these were their first gasps of sweet open air.

They grumbled and rolled their eyes (Emma hadn't quite mastered it, she mimicked her sister by shaking her head) and urged her to hurry as she applied pungent mosquito repellent and goopy mounds of sunscreen head to toe, fit their untested feet with rubbery water shoes, their thin little arms with inflatable water wings. By the time she fastened the chinstraps of their hats they were groaning, promising to keep everything on only after she threatened to make them stay behind if they didn't.

Her stomach fluttered as she scanned the lobby for Malia or Laka. There seemed a slim but real chance her sister would come, not for her but for her obvious love for Ruth and Emma. Laka seemed less likely, she had sent the newspaper article but no note, had not bothered even to sign Hulali's condolence card. To Hiʻi this meant one of two things: Laka had either not forgiven her for leaving or was relieved she had, with either being irreconcilable. But the lobby was empty of both mother and sister, and Hiʻi told herself this was for the best.

Without the girls, the clock splayed its legs and fell backward. She squirreled away in their hotel room, trying to sort out the girl she'd been from the woman she'd become, as if the separate parts of her were meeting for the first time. Then she took Jacob in his wooden box where she should have taken him years ago.

It felt a hundred years ago and yesterday to be there; places and smells and sounds that had been pushed to the back were now allowed to come forward. She explored the rim of Moku Ola, Coconut Island, kneeling every so often along the sandy borders. The beach was the same, but she'd lost possession of it. She'd forgotten how it moved without warning, swallowing the grooves of her footsteps. She wandered through the shaded paths of Nani Mau Garden and hiked the short distance from Rainbow Falls to Boiling Pots. She wandered across Bayfront, past the fish auction block and canoe clubs. Under the blue tarps of the Farmers Market she found all of her forgotten loves, ripe and ready for her. Yellow-green rainbow papayas, sharp spiked crowns of white pineapple, apple bananas in bunches, brown-yellow fingered hands waving, waiting to be called on. Avocados big as boulders, richer than butter. From the Filipino bakery she stole a plastic knife and spoon, at the beach she sliced a papaya in half and gutted out the goopy black seeds. She sawed into the pineapple and let the juices dribble down her arms, christening her home. Fishermen observed her from the bluff, sipping their beers, an eye on their lines.

Stuffed, she lay in the sand among the hollowed skeletons of crabs, the papaya skins and avocado rind baking in the heat of the hour. She smiled at Jacob in the wooden box and imagined what he might say if he saw her there, belly bulging, covered in sand, sticky as syrup. Probably that she had dragged him everywhere and nowhere.

Why hadn't she brought him here when he was alive? He'd been proud of his Hawaiian roots, his community in LA. He'd shared it all with her, and she'd shared nothing with him in return. Why had he had to die for her to finally do this? And now that they were there, a bit of her husband in her backpack, she was doing a grossly inadequate job of bringing Jacob home. There was one place Jacob would have wanted to see, and she wasn't ready to go there yet. She needed more time. So many things to figure out. How would she lay him to rest? Should she come up with some sort of ceremony? She'd been too busy battling demons to give it much thought before. She'd supposed it would all make itself clear once she landed in Hilo, but, if anything, things were more muddled.

Suddenly chilled, she left the beach and walked back to the hotel.

SHE TRIED TO DRUM UP THE COURAGE to call Jane, but every time she picked up the phone, she caught an image of herself, the girl who'd disappeared off to the mainland, never called and hardly wrote, who showed up out of the blue and wanted to pick up where they left off. Hi`i had been a jerk. There was no getting around that. She'd turned her back on Hawai`i and Jane. Had said she was too busy to come for Jane's wedding. Had pulled away from her long before that, if she were honest. At the time, it had felt like Jane's Hawaiian mother solidified Jane's place in this town in a way that Hi`i's uncertain origins never could, but Hi`i had only understood that years later, in California, and by then it had seemed easier to just let the friendship go. She'd severed so many other relationships, what was one more?

She tried to picture Kainoa, her schoolgirl crush. He'd been a good guy back then, no doubt he still was. Hi`i felt a twinge of jealousy and loathed herself for it. She wasn't jealous of Jane for marrying Kainoa—she treasured every second of the life she'd shared with Jacob, and the two children they'd created—but she envied that Jane and Kainoa had each other.

She slung a pareo around the length of her body, letting its silky cotton fall over her without needing to be a certain shape or size, to suck anything in. At the hotel pool, she fit her head into the deep bowl of a hat and watched behind dark movie star glasses as newlyweds rubbed each other with lotion and sought each other like missiles in the pool. The sparkle on the young girl's finger cast a rainbow prism over the rest of them. A retired couple tried to make conversation by asking her where she was visiting from. She turned over and pretended to sleep, just another tourist on vacation.

Dusk. The girls returned—Ruth, deliriously exhausted but giggly; Emma, with arms and legs a war zone of angry red eruptions. Hi`i wiped her chapped face as the girl mumbled in her sleep.

A plague on the mosquitoes. She would kill every last one. Didn't they know her children were off limits? Didn't they recognize them?

CHAPTER 8

She had returned, but only in body, and only in place. To us, she kept herself away, kept herself separate. So much like her maddah, she didn't even know. Hard head, that one.

Some families, they get that curse that goes in circles down the drain.

Laka fights with her mom, leaves, comes back. Hi`i fights with her mom, leaves, comes back. Different generations, same flight patterns.

Still. Hi`i didn't fight when we came for those keiki. Laka's youthful kalohe mischievousness had turned into a fierce fight for the kingdom, exactly like Hulali but from a different angle, so we had every reason to think there was hope for Hi`i yet.

We smelled up those girls with their little bird shoulders and nubbed pearls for teeth. They made the years fall out from under us, we was staring at their mother all over again. It was like feeding ducks at the park, they was shy and kept their distance until they saw the food in our open palms, saw we didn't take our hand away when they came close. Eddie would go, those two. Peeked out their little pink tongues to taste anything even though their mama never teach them nothing. After they ate we knew they was gonna be all good. They'd drunk the blood, ate the flesh.

The older one talked for them both. We asked her what she did in California, if she liked it. She said nails. We thought, nails like how we say when the waves are all washed out and unsurfable, wow she talking pidgin already! But no, she meant fingernails. She paints them different colors, puts glitter, makes Thumbelina-sized sunsets and flowers and fireworks. So Hollywood, so extra. We showed her the calluses on our feet. That was hard work, building those up.

Their mother always had soft nails, they gave if you pressed too hard, broke at the sight of a dish needed washing. Wow, they said. You know a lot about our mom. Better than she knows herself, we told them.

To show them what was what, we brought them to the loko i`a and sat them on the loko kuapā and asked them what they saw. Green, they said, staring into the fishpond. We put their feet in the water and asked them what they felt. Slimy, they said. Green muck mushed between their toes. Look, we said. The green on their feet wasn't like green everywhere else. Hawai`i green was magic same like Hawai`i was magic, farther from any other land than any other land in the world. Distance made it sacred. It wasn't the pond that needed protecting, it was the distance. If something else from somewhere else came into that pond it would eat up all that magic green and change the color and the fishpond would no longer be a loko i`a feeding us, it would just be a pond from anywhere, a sinkhole filled with water.

Akamai, those girls. They asked how the pond stayed a pond when there was a break in the wall separating it and the ocean. The ocean comes in, it brings the fish, it goes away and leaves them for us, we said. The ocean wasn't something else coming in. The ocean was part of the pond, the pond part of the ocean. Separate but connected.

Why?

Chicken why why, das why.

We were there when the coconut phone came ringing to tell us kaka was going down at Puhi Bay where the uncles were building the community center. We dropped what we were doing and headed over. There wasn't time to take those girls back to their mom, hiding in her hotel room as if Hilo was nothing but a lagoon full of sharks, circling at the foot of her door. Whatever was going to happen that day, we needed to be witness.

THE SALT HULA:

On the first day of the Puhi Bay standoff, it was one county car.

Put down those tools. Stop that building. No permanent structures allowed on the beach.

But this is our beach. Our land.

County says no can. Need permits.

Can. This not County. This Puhi Bay. Hawaiian Homes.

ON THE SECOND DAY, two county cars plus the sheriff.

Put down those tools. Stop that building.

Sheriff. Kala mai, but you not in charge here. This Hawaiian Homeland. We the Beneficiaries. Over there, across the street, we follow your rules. Here, you follow ours.

ON THE THIRD DAY, two county cars, the sheriff, and a DHHL commissioner.

Put down those tools. Stop that building.

Commissioner. Kala mai, but this is our gathering place. We need a roof, doors. For when the rains come, the tourists.

A permit? What kine permit? What you mean, wrong zone?

Speaking of zones. We been meaning to ask. That acreage over Waiakea side, zoned pasture lands. Papers saying you gave that land to BuyMore. How did that land get rezoned for corporate development? No one asked our permission. BuyMore never got a permit. How come we need one?

ON THE FOURTH DAY, two county cars, the sheriff, the DHHL commissioner, and a guest.

Put down those tools. Stop that building.

Near the skeleton of the community center's foundation, lumber was scattered throughout the grass, napping in the sun. The uncles kept their hammers in their hands. Sheriff kept his hand on his holster. County with badges pinned over their hearts.

HI`I'S GIRLS WAS QUIET as our caravan hauled ass down Beach Front to Puhi Bay. By the time we got there, cars were stacked as if it were a three-day weekend and the surf was up.

BuyMore nevah get permit. If BuyMore can build, we can build.

The guest stepped forward, introduced himself. A Hawaiianologist.

A Hawaiianologist! Wow, laulau. We never met one of those before. With a business card and everything. The caucasity!

You desecrating this `āina, Hawaiianologist says. What you're doing is kapu.

Eh look, Hawaiianologist knows Hawaiian words! Eh, Hawaiianologist. Turn this dollar into one hundred dollars. Like Jesus turned water into wine. Do that, and we stop right now.

Hawaiianologist pulled out a cloth pouch. Tucked his fingers inside and started to chant. Threw salt at our feet. He, a haole Hawaiianologist, chanting, throwing salt at our feet. Salt!

He knew what he was doing. We knew what message he was sending. We sprinkle salt to bless a space, to protect it from negative energy. This Hawaiianologist was telling us we was desecrating, that we was doing wrong by the land. That he was the protector.

No sooner had the first granule touched the earth than Laka exploded from the back of the crowd. She left her slippers right there on the road as if to hold her spot. We'd never seen her move so fast. Barefoot, soaring like the makani up the street to her house. She wasn't gone a minute, but somehow in that time she'd hemo'd her clothes, wrapped her body in a pareo, and let down her hair, billowing black clouds down her back. A younger Hulali, reincarnated. From her hands she threw her own salt, the salt of us all, and started to chant. Chicken skin all around.

The winds blew and the waves crashed against the rocks and the tide came up. Back and forth Laka and the Hawaiianologist chanted, throwing their salt. County looked to their badges for guidance. Sheriff took his hand off his holster. DHHL commissioner looked the other way.

The Hawaiianologist's pouch went empty.

We'll take this to court.

We not scared of you. Not anymore. Like we said—too many pebbles collecting in our pockets, and you taught us to read. We'll see you in court.

Consider this your warning: If we can't build at Puhi Bay, we sure as hell ain't letting you build no BuyMore.

THEY DROVE OFF ONE by one in their cars with their state-issued plates and windows rolled all the way up. The fire of Pele burning deep in her eyes, Laka chanted to the skies as she expelled them. Her voice went hoarse but she continued on. She shook us off as her chant broke out of itself and became a mottled cry—five generations' worth of impotence and indignation came pouring out. She was blind, enraged. She pointed to the cars coming down the road from outside: get out. She pointed to the tour ships headed toward the pier: get out. She pointed to the two little girls—in their rubber water shoes and inflatable water wings and sunhats obscuring their faces, standing out so clearly—in our midst: get out.

We tried to stop her but there was no stopping her.

She took a step toward them. They took a step back.

Wea dose kids' parents? Why tourists hea, what dey want? Dis not a luau show. Dis not for sale. Get out. Get out!

Crickets.

The girls froze. The older of the two stepped slightly in front of the younger one when she started to cry.

Laka, we think maybe better you . . .

Enough! Her scream made the water ripple.

Then Laka was gone and it was over; it was all over and it was only just beginning.

VERSE IV

CHAPTER 1

1994

The little bell fixed to the storefront chimed. Laka glanced at the clock on the wall and pushed aside the pair of Mango Cafe bentos she'd been doctoring, adding extra furikake on the rice of one and removing the steamed egg from the other.

The skies outside were howling. The young man dripped on the doormat. His shirt was soaked through and his wet black hair was plastered to his forehead. If it weren't for the hardened defiance etched on his face, he'd look to Laka like a child. A damp rolled wad of cash filled his fist. He approached the counter and held it out to her.

"Silver only," she said, shaking her head.

He nodded, crumpling the American money and stuffing it into the back pocket of his faded jeans. She asked him where he was from and who was his family. He introduced himself the island way.

"Name's Frankie Boy. From Honolulu," he said, naming a Hawaiian family that played a prominent role in the kingdom's activity in the O`ahu districts. "My uncles sent me. You know, to see if can help. Dey know your mom."

Laka guessed he was in his mid-twenties. She quickly did the math. Hi`i would be turning twenty-six soon. Laka examined the features of the young man as if through him she would be able to see how her daughter had grown into a woman. She took in the laugh lines around his eyes, the barely-there sprout of silver hair at his temple. Would Hi`i have silver combing through that `ehu red someday, would gray show in hers the way it did in Laka's crow black? In the years since Laka had seen her, how had she changed? She shook herself out of her cobwebs and showed Frankie Boy where he could exchange his money. He nodded and pulled the collar of his shirt over his head in a makeshift raincoat, crouching like a sprinter to race across the street to where she had directed him.

Thunder rumbled through the dark clouds blanketing downtown. Laka held up a hand and spoke out loud to the empty shop.

"Enuf already with da blessings," she said. It had been raining nonstop for what felt like a year.

While she waited for Frankie Boy to return she fixed plastic lids to each of the bentos and secured them with a rubber band. She ignored the clock, enough guilt setting in without its constant henpecking. She couldn't lock up knowing someone was on their way in. Exposing the occupation of the Hawaiian nation and the complicit and continued violations of international humanitarian law, keeping the public informed about the kingdom's efforts to organize, and resurrecting the constitution of the queen were all important elements of her work, but growing their numbers was the most critical. (Unlike the convictions of her mother, who saw the Hawaiian kingdom as dead and gone, still preaching that the only chance Hawaiians had to survive was to carve out protections within U.S. law and state agencies.) She looked around at the printouts of the 1907 and 1949 Geneva Conventions, part of the kingdom's strategic plan to get its citizenry informed and active in their civic duties. She should be rejoicing that this young man had flown all this way to join them, not worrying about her lunch getting cold.

Frankie Boy was back in a matter of minutes, a fresh pelt of rain on his shoulders. He handed her a bag of silver and she in turn handed him a rag to dry off. She led him through a labyrinth of boxed legal files and case studies toward the corner of the shop-turned-headquarters that she'd designated the photo booth.

"You get da papers?" she asked.

He produced a thin folder from under his shirt. To protect it from rain, he'd wrapped it in a plastic grocery bag. She slid the file out of the bag and flipped through the forms inside. She did not ask why he wasn't naturalizing in one of the Oʻahu district offices. She had enough of those discussions—who counted as a Hawaiian, who got to say what was good for Hawaiʻi, sovereignty versus kingdom—with her mother. If people came in wanting to give up their American citizenship and declare allegiance to the reestablished Hawaiian kingdom, it was her policy to ask only the questions that were her business. *Why* wasn't one of them.

She took his picture and stapled it to his paperwork for his passport and ID card and continued on with the protocol, running through the pamphlet she'd created to help newly naturalized citizens.

"Memorize dese t'ings here or keep dis in your pocket till you get it," she said, tapping a finger on the top two bullet points. "Dese your rights as a citizen of da kingdom. Understanding dat, and ours as a nation, critical in surviving undah occupation. If someone give hard time 'bout any of dis, call dis numbah."

She tapped the paper again. He nodded reverently and carefully fitted the pamphlet into his wallet before grabbing a flyer from the top of a stack. The flyer had all the information about that evening's meeting.

"See you tonight?"

He nodded and stood, kissing her on the cheek in respect before disappearing into the rain.

As soon as the door clicked closed she went into high gear, stuffing the cooling bentos into her straw bag and making her way out the back. A few short leaps over puddles to her car and she was finally on her way.

Crossing town in a rush under that much water was like trying to sprint across the bottom of the ocean. Cars forded across stoplights followed by great fans of water. At this rate it would take another half hour to get to Prince Kuhio Plaza, and she was already almost an hour late for her standing lunch date with David.

DAVID. LAKA HAD HIM TO THANK for guiding her toward what she now considered her life's purpose.

The year Malia was born had been a perfect storm. Tony got into the crash, Hulali moved in, and Hiʻi drifted away. It had taken every ounce of energy just to keep her head above water through the trial. She'd watched most of it on TV because of the baby, which added to the feeling that everything playing out was happening to someone else. She got to the point where she watched television more than she did anything else. Which was how she found David.

She'd heard about Sand Island before it showed up in the news, of course. When her brother Kekoa came back from Vietnam he moved to Honolulu because he said there was more work there than in Hilo.

But the war messed with his head, lived inside him. He drank too much, went from boat to boat to work and eventually got kicked off every one.

Kekoa wasn't the only one struggling. Plenty of guys were losing work, and the work that did exist offered less and less pay. Honolulu rent was doubling every year. It seemed like everyone in O`ahu was moving into their cars. Kekoa started hanging out around Sand Island, which at that point was just a dredged landfill in Honolulu Harbor that nobody cared about. The Honolulu airport was right across the lagoon, the constant noise of airplanes taking off and landing, so no one was going to build anything there. Dump trucks brought trash every day and the air was sour from the sewage treatment plant nearby, but there was a little shack where the guys could drink and play music without anyone bothering. Soon enough, more and more people were coming down, entire families in the cars they lived out of. Kekoa had a breakdown and ended up at the VA hospital, but Sand Island kept growing.

(IT WAS PART OF MOKAUEA, an area that had once been fishponds and lagoons that had fed the entire west side of O`ahu. We remembered the lessons of our kūpuna. We dropped net, picked limu, dove for lobster. With the ocean providing more than enough food, we used scraps from the dump to build shelters so we could move out of our cars. We started cleaning up the grounds, making nice. Our shelters grew into houses. That's when the state took notice and issued eviction papers. By then there was more than four hundred of us living there. We was proud of what we'd made, Sand Island now a symbol of the health and happiness waiting if we went back to the ways of land

and sea. So we said no way, we wasn't going anywhere. The cameras really started rolling after that.)

THIS WAS ALL HAPPENING while there was still fresh glass on the road from Tony's crash. Whenever she wasn't following the coverage of Tony's trial on TV, Laka watched as reporters stood at the entrance of Sand Island to record what was happening. She recognized some of the faces. She caught sight of David among them. A ghost. She thought at first she was mistaken. She pressed her face so close to the screen the image blurred, but she needed to be sure it was him. The state moved in with enforcement agents, barking dogs, bulldozers. An agent put a steel chain attached to a bulldozer around one of the houses and used a bullhorn to order the people out of the house. From where the camera stood, it had a clear view of three people holding on to the house posts, refusing to move. One of them was David. Older, thicker, but definitely David. The agent waved his hand. The bulldozer moved, pulling the house and shattering it into pieces. The footage switched to another camera, a different angle. Laka jumped, startling Malia awake. From the new camera angle, it was impossible to see what had happened, to make sure David was okay. The news replayed the same footage over and over. That night, Sand Island was nothing but rubble, Honolulu city lights shimmering in the distance.

David was arrested and taken to court. Because Laka was already in daily contact with Tony's lawyer, it was easy to get the name of a lawyer in Honolulu who might be willing to help.

In the year that followed, Laka flew to Oʻahu to see David as much as possible. Or at least what was left of David. Back at home on the Big Island, Hi`i had moved out with barely a goodbye, Tony was serving his time, and Hulali had retired from OHA and taken the lead on raising Malia, so helping David was a welcome focus. She learned from others how he'd changed his mind about the military, done a bunch of drugs to flunk the physical exam, and gone underground. When he'd come back up, David was only half there. The guys from Sand Island assured her he'd been clean for years; taking care of the lagoon had been a big part of his recovery, but it hadn't been enough to undo the damage to his brain. Scrambled eggs, they said. When she'd seen him for the first time since Merrie Monarch all those years ago, he had only offered a polite smile, the kind you offer a distant relative. The David she'd once known and loved was gone. It made her heart hurt. But in the following days, she observed his routines, the quiet yet determined way he went about things, and was certain she saw an occasional flash of the passionate stubborn boy she'd fallen in love with, the boy she considered to be Hi`i's father in a way, the father of the spirit that eventually became Hi`i. He was no longer someone she could imagine spending her life with as her lover or partner. But that did not mean the love was lost. It had just changed color, to something tender and compassionate and longer-lasting. In Laka's eyes, David was now family.

Laka argued that the state of Hawaii and the United States of America had no jurisdiction over David, and therefore David had not "obstructed government operations." David's legal team agreed. They decided that, instead of going to court to defend his actions, they would go to court to prove that the court itself had no say in the matter.

Ultimately, the case never went to trial. Laka decided right then that she wasn't leaving David to fend for himself in O`ahu. There wasn't another Sand Island for him to go to. She called Tony in prison and told him she was bringing David home. She built a small ohana for him in the back. She'd prepared a whole speech about second chances in case Tony put up a fight about Laka bringing home her ex-boyfriend, but being behind bars had taken all of Tony's fight out of him. He agreed easily, supporting her decision, once she explained the drug use, the brain damage, the broken man he had become.

Sand Island had doubled Laka's conviction that they needed to push harder to get the kingdom back. Her mother meant well, but Hulali's insistence in working with the state and trusting it to do the right thing was leading the people of Hawai`i in the wrong direction.

LAKA SPLASHED THROUGH THE PUDDLES of Prince Kuhio Plaza. When she got to the shop, she called out David's name. He wasn't at the front desk, he never was, but calling out as if she didn't know where he was was part of their routine. She knew exactly where he would be and what he would be doing, but it was an inside joke between them that he found extremely funny some days (and ignored completely on others, but since there was no telling which it was going to be, she did it every time).

Aloha Spirit was so unrecognizable from its early days under the ownership of Mrs. Tanaka that most people hardly remembered the epicenter for all things cheap and fake that it had once been. Every item lining the shelves was now sourced exclusively from local artists and merchants. MADE IN HAWAII was on every label. She smiled when she thought of her cantankerous former boss and her peculiar ways. She'd pooh-poohed Laka's ideas for years, but in the end, Mrs. Tanaka had turned out to be one of Laka's biggest supporters, selling her the shop when she was ready to retire, coming around for years after to make sure Laka was "doing things right."

Laka made a beeline for the storeroom, ignoring the cubbies stuffed with boxes of informational pamphlets and flyers to events long past, letting the sloshing sound of the printing press lead her to David. She put a hand on his shoulder. He barely registered her arrival.

"Sorry I late. Good business today?" she said, clearing off a space on the table for them to eat.

He stayed focused on the press. She smiled.

"You know it going keep printing even if you stop watching. Come kau kau, da rice getting hard. Ten bucks you nevah eat breakfast."

He didn't eat unless a meal was waved in front of him, a task that usually fell to her. Hence the guilt at being late. Even if he was oblivious to time, she certainly wasn't. She pulled apart her wooden chopsticks and gave them a quick rub to smooth the splinters before digging in.

It had taken a while for David to register that he wouldn't be returning to Sand Island, although for her, the addition of him to their household felt so natural and complete that it quickly became impossible to imagine going back to how it had been before. He hadn't come close to filling the gap Hi`i had left behind, but he'd lightened the tension between her and Hulali, which, after all these years living under the same roof, had gone from explosive to resigned, from shouting to eye rolls, the same conversation in circles on repeat. They'd somehow managed to raise Malia, even if the consequence of their bickering was that the girl had absolutely no interest in conversations about Hawaiian identity. She cared about soccer and little else. But she'd grown up with a parent in prison for manslaughter, and no one would dispute the fact that Hulali had helped Malia through the un-comfortable transition when her father returned home. For that Laka gave her credit. Malia had taken cues from her tutu to provide a road map for how to feel about torn and tortured family, which mostly meant focusing on things like homework and housework and sports, practical and unsentimental.

When Tony was released, Malia wanted nothing to do with him. She ran to the beach and stayed in the water until dark and pretended not to hear him when he spoke to her at dinner. Hulali insisted that he was her blood, her father regardless, and therefore should be treated with respect. Malia had to let Tony in. It wasn't perfect, there was still the occasional tensing of the shoulders, a noticeable cringe in Malia's body if Tony got too close, and there was the time he tried to reprimand her and she laughingly told him to eff off, that she wasn't going to let an ex-con tell her what to do, but every year they spent together—Tony and Laka, David, Hulali, and Malia—felt a little bet-ter than the last. The biggest elephant that remained in the room, of course, was Hi`i's absence, but Malia had been too young to remember Hi`i in the house, or so Laka thought, and for that Laka was grateful. She was acutely aware of the empty chair at the table.

The printer spat out its final sheet and the room fell silent. Laka waved David's bento under his nose to catch his attention. By then she was done eating. She scanned the freshly printed flyers for typos, then lifted the stack off the tray and wedged it into a large cardboard box. When the box was full, she pressed the lid closed and pushed it over toward three others.

"Help me load dis in da car when you pau, okay? I gotta get dea early."

By the time she and David loaded all the boxes into the car, it was nearly two in the afternoon. She sent David back to the shop. It was true, she had to get going, but she reversed out of her spot and drove to the far side of the parking lot, where she could see both the Prince Kuhio Plaza and the large overgrown plot of land on the other side of the street. The weeds were thick with scattered heaps of broken bottles and cigarette butts. She imagined a new subdivision there, a farm and a few houses. If Hulali was right, DHHL was going to give this land back to the people who had been on the waiting list for Hawaiian Homelands for decades. It was about time.

On her side of the street, the shops within Prince Kuhio Plaza glowed bright with unnatural neon light. She remembered the day she'd taken Hi`i to the Sanrio Hello Kitty store to celebrate her first hula lesson. She'd been worried Hi`i would pick out something beyond what she could afford. More than anything, she wished she could go back to that time, when she'd thought she knew what she was doing.

She scoffed to herself. There was still never enough money.

Tony worked full-time at Ali`i Ice delivering frozen ice blocks to hotels and bags of crushed ice to gas stations and convenience stores around the island, and still made time to be fully involved with her kingdom work, which was probably why their relationship had found new life after he was released. If anything, working on behalf of the reinstated kingdom had been a godsend for him. He'd been so racked with guilt over the life he'd cut short that for a while it seemed he'd hold on to the pain forever, finding solace only in self-condemnation. By then Laka's involvement in the Sand Island fight had led her to the kingdom. The rest was history. For Tony, it had been a way to stay focused on something besides the daughter who wasn't quite welcoming of his sudden presence, his hugs, his after-school questions about her day. For Laka, kingdom work quickly became more than a job, more than simply lending a hand. It had become a mission, a way of life. Politics hadn't been a focus for either of them before, but Laka and Tony found themselves equally committed to the cause. Hawaiʻi had suffered a deep historical injustice, a flagrant violation of international law that was now a wound too long infected. The kingdom was not a damsel in distress. No one was coming to rescue it. If they, as individuals and as a group, turned a blind eye, waiting and hoping the wrong would right itself, the injustices would only continue. Unlike her mother, Laka felt this was a burden shared by all the peoples of Hawaiʻi, not just people with a certain blood quantum.

CHAPTER 2

1995

The sky was growing dim. Dammit. Laka was going to be late for the Keaukaha Neighborhood Association meeting. Since retirement Hulali had spent most of her time with her various mo`opuna or on the sidelines of Malia's soccer games (Laka and Hulali had agreed long ago that Malia's soccer schedule was the universe's way of keeping peace, since Malia put up with Laka not attending her games as long as her tutu was there), but she hadn't missed a community association meeting since moving back from O`ahu, and tonight Laka and Hulali needed to show a united front. Laka often suspected that Hulali used Malia's sports commitments as a way to make herself unavailable for speaking engagements and further usher Laka into a leadership role (they didn't see eye to eye, but Hulali was sure Laka would come around eventually). Instead of accepting the role she'd been groomed for as kumu of Hulali's hula halau, Laka was relieving Hulali of a schedule crammed with neighborhood meetings and political events, leaving the matriarch of the Naupaka family free to cheer on her granddaughter and spend the rest of her time giving cultural demonstrations at the university and working on a collection of essays about Hawaiian mythology. But this meeting needed both of them. The newly signed Apology Resolution had given them momentum, Hulali insisted, and now they needed to come together as a community to agree on how best to capitalize on it. Laka disagreed, but kept her thoughts to herself. Her mother was getting older. Attending the meeting and keeping her mouth shut was an olive branch.

When she got to the house she ran inside. Hulali would be waiting for her, ready to go. The lights were off. She called for Malia and then remembered she was having pizza with her soccer team. She called for Hulali. The county board meeting was down the road at the school cafeteria. Hulali had probably walked or gotten a ride with a neighbor. Wanting to make sure before she drove off, Laka went into Hulali's office. Her lamp was on, her desk a pile of papers. Hulali took great pride in the column she wrote every month in the OHA newsletter (when she left OHA she said retirement wasn't a mute button, she was going to stay involved), and she always wrote multiple drafts before letting the column go to print. It was something that Laka had come to ignore, a mirror image of how Hulali dealt with Laka's kingdom work. Laka took a peek at her latest draft as she reached over to turn off the light. She regretted it immediately.

Her mother's praise of the Apology Resolution was offering unnecessary applause for an apology that was ultimately America weaseling its way out of being held accountable for anything. Reading the column, Laka felt her blood begin to boil. She set the notepad down. That's when she noticed the letter, handwritten, on paper she didn't recognize but with a name on the envelope that she very much did. She fell into the chair. The clock ticked, but she was frozen.

* * *

WHEN HULALI CAME HOME, Laka erupted.

"Wen dis came? How long you was planning to wait before you showed me?"

Hulali calmly put down her purse and unpinned her hair from its bun. "Aiyah, calm down. Jus' came. Was addressed to all us, I nevah look who was from. Was goin' give 'em to you, I just forgot."

Laka stood, shook the letter in Hulali's face. "Forgot? I no believe you. All dese years not a word. She finally reach out, inviting us back into her life, and you forgot?"

"Wat's a few days after so many years? If you wanted back into her life so bad, how come you nevah reach out? Wasn't a mystery wea she was."

"I was tryin' fo' respect her decision. No can force someone into a life dey no want. I had to find my way back to Keaukaha on my own, remembah? She wanted to leave. I had to let her."

"Remembah dat. No need jump as soon as she say jump. She needed to go find her kuleana, you needed to take care yours, yeah?"

Kuleana. It was no accident that the word meant right and responsibility and privilege. The day Laka had first laid eyes on Hiʻi, she'd thought she'd understood hers. Now she had Malia and David and the kingdom to dedicate her life to. But if her mother was right, why did it still feel like there was a big gaping hole in her heart? All these years, she had kept what happened in Maui a secret thinking she was protecting Hiʻi. What good had it done? The worst had already happened. She locked eyes with Hulali and motioned for her to sit down. It was time to tell her what she didn't know about Maui.

The story spilled from Laka as if it were afraid it was going to be stopped. Hulali was silent for a time, her face revealing nothing. When she finally broke the silence, her voice was smooth as deep waters.

"How come dis da first time I hearing any of dis?"

"Cuz it wouldn't have mattered," Laka answered, armor on, swords drawn. "She no more one birt certificate to prove blood quantum, and dat's all dat's important to you."

In the dim light it was impossible to read Hulali's face. Laka waited for a response, but none came. Hulali rose, said the day had been long, and that she was going to bed.

LAKA WENT BACK TO the desk. To her mother's OHA column. To what had always come first. The state. The state that told them who was family, the state that put parameters on how they defined themselves. Laka was done with it. Hulali couldn't speak for all of them, not anymore. She would write her own letter, put it in the newspaper for everyone in Hilo to read. Enough was enough.

To enslave a people, convince them . . .

CHAPTER 3

We met in the gaps between black rain clouds.

Down at Richardson's Beach, it was the final hour for the lifeguards in their red shorts to stand guard in their towers. Weary men in rubber boots and coveralls grabbed their hoses and sprayed the last of the day's fish blood and guts from Suisan's decks. At dusk in Hilo, all that was left were footprints and lingering odors, smudges where the interrupters stick their noses against the glass to get a good look at our life. The buses finally cleared out.

To the interrupters, Hilo is a rented room. A wreckage of piña colada paper umbrellas, empty water bottles, and sunscreen are left in their wake. We are forced to be the housekeepers of this land our home, to clean up the messes of others. It was almost time for the meeting that night, but we couldn't leave Richardson's until we cleaned trash from the bushes, gathered abandoned boogie boards and forgotten fins, a punctured snorkel half buried in the sand, a pink shovel floating facedown in a tide pool. Only then we could go, kau kau and bocha fast kine before heading over.

DHHL had done us dirty. Promised a plan to increase their revenue for water lines and electricity and roads that would get us on our land quicker. They didn't mention the part about giving away our land to do it. The lease with BuyMore was worth millions. DHHL said it was money for operating costs. They were handing out leases to American corporations to pay themselves for the job they weren't doing, which was getting us off the wait list. As for BuyMore, they hadn't asked how we'd feel about that. They'd made the call for us, and they'd called it wrong.

WE'D SWALLOWED THE BALONEY BEFORE, that commercial concessions like these were the cost of living in paradise. Gotta give a little, they say. Where had that gotten us? Hotels paid us unlivable wages, if they hired us at all. An American businessman owned Lana`i outright. The Robinson family owned Ni`ihau and enough of Kaua`i to call that one theirs too.

Islands on an auction block.

`A`ole pilikia, they say. No make trouble. Live aloha.

Now we coming together in aloha. Coming together to say enough was enough. We was gonna get pono again.

For the county board meeting that Laka was supposed to attend, we marked our calendars and called all the Beneficiaries, the Wait Listers, the Homesteaders. We needed everyone to testify. We told the county (who said these types of decisions had nothing to do with them) that we were coming. When we invited the city council, they issued a statement in advance, saying the issue wasn't within their jurisdiction. They warned us not to bother (DHHL makes its own decisions, they said, but when we contacted DHHL to ask them how they could rezone the land for BuyMore but not rezone for us, they said zoning was an issue to take up with the city council and the county). They were trying to get us to chase our tails, but for once, we were onto them. We pressed. So they said they'd come, they'd listen to what we had to say. On this night, we would not be indecisive or divided. Laka had helped organize, asked us to meet ahead of time, to work out our differences (or at least put them on the back burner), and plan our move forward. We'd unite. On this night, Hawai`i for sale would end.

We set out on foot. It rained heavily all day, sheets and sheets. The sky was exhausted. Puddles lingered, the ground was swollen and full. The student body of Keaukaha Elementary had cleared out hours before yet the presence of the children remained, a menehune-sized thumbprint over every inch of slide, jungle gym, and swing. The yard echoed with their laughter. Midnight oil burned in classrooms, teachers grading papers and wiping down chalkboards. The cafeteria was locked, as expected. The janitor heard the whistle, he jangled over, Hawaiian John Wayne with his giant lasso key.

Within minutes the cafeteria was wide awake, fluorescent bulbs cracking, metal chairs clanging as they were set in place. We tested and retested the mic and speakers. With the right sound system, maybe we would be heard. It was that microphone that could lead us toward a new constitution, reestablish our monarchy, fix all the wrongs. We turned up the volume—tonight we had a voice and there would be ears to hear, someone would finally be listening. But we forgot our initial objective and started arguing with one another. And then it was time.

The councilman's office had been vague about his attendance. We set a chair on the stage anyway, a hot seat.

We poured in through the doors. The scuffed lacquered floors groaned under us giants, the wood used to mini-people. Metal chair feet squealed like piglets escaping the pigpen. Rules of the meeting were reviewed: Testimonies and presentations on the agenda did not have time limits. Statements from the public did. There would be no shouting; save the questions for the end. We would be civilized.

The council arrived, one by one they leaky-faucet dripped onto the stage. The ringleader cleared his throat into the mic. The air switched on, went electric. He wore a short-sleeved aloha shirt, button open at his collarbone. His I'm One of You uniform. The small riser lifted off the ground away from us, backpedaling until it was a million miles away. He greeted us from above. As if he'd organized this coming together of the community, as if he'd asked us to gather to hear our concerns.

He performed a condensed version of his campaign stump speech, including the "I'm raising my kids here too" bits. His commitment to fighting big corporate development. Rattled off his statistics. Unemployment rate 8.3 percent, as if we didn't live and breathe that number every day. This would mean jobs, opportunities, economic revitalization.

Hot potato, the mic moved down the row.

The wind shifted. Councilwoman in her flower-print sheath. Good cop, bad cop.

This is an undeveloped, underutilized piece of land, she said. Not zoned for housing, for anything that would help Hilo. (What did she know? She was from Honolulu, had gone to private school, owned two houses.) This would bring in money, this would benefit everyone. (Who was she talking about, who was she talking to?) Thousands of employment opportunities. (It was like BuyMore was paying her a dollar a word.) The council would work to make sure any agreements would include a stipulation that Native Hawaiians got preference when applying, she promised. Hilo people would get first crack at the jobs. (DHHL chiming in from the back: And the money! The lease payments! Money for infrastructure! Affordable housing for Hawaiians sooner!)

We created a line, questions burning holes through our tongues.

When was this decided, who decided, who has that say? Who is accountable? And why did this meeting not happen *before* they awarded that lease, why didn't anyone ask us? How can they think they know better than us what is good for us, what we need?

Why are so many lots vacant when more than half of us here have a claim to land we cannot use?

Hot potato, hot potato, no one on stage wanted the mic. Ringleader sighed, used his "I'm talking to children" voice.

We'd done our research. We had real questions. We thought this was the beginning. But as the meeting wound down, we knew. We put two and two together. It didn't look good. It was only later, down at Puhi Bay toward the bottom of the first beer, after we closed the lights and locked the doors, that we realized they hadn't come to hear us. They'd been sent to waste our time, to keep us distracted. We'd been played.

The dragon we'd needed to slay wasn't in that cafeteria. If we'd looked up, we would have seen it, in the clouds, scaled wings coming closer, fangs dripping, eyes a black bottomless hunger.

CHAPTER 4

Laka and Tony had attended the monthly county board meetings for all of 1994, studying. They knew they needed to come prepared. Time allotted for public comment during these meetings was limited. To face a beast as big as BuyMore, community testimony would need to be sharp as spears. Communication between the kingdom sister groups throughout the islands increased into a steady, daily rhythm. Laka, Tony, and David blanketed Hilo with flyers inviting the public to come and speak up. The stakes had never been higher.

When it came to all things kingdom, indignation normally fueled Laka like caffeine. But there was something about this fight that filled her veins with lead and kept her up at night. BuyMore had an army of lawyers and a bottomless vault of money. It would bankrupt local business, turn Hilo inside out. This was a battle against the full might of American capitalism—a fight they'd been fighting for decades, a century, with little to show for it. Her nightmares told her she was setting her community up to be steamrolled.

Worse, the factions were not united. They all agreed on what they were fighting against, but not about what they were fighting for. Hawai`i was being pulled in different directions, a tug of war in which they'd all end up the loser.

Hulali had drummed up the Homesteaders. Within that group were the Wait Listers and the Beneficiaries. The Wait Listers were people on the waiting list, decades of waiting, struggling to make ends meet, their only hope for a better life being a plot of land to call their own. Until then, all they had was a spot in line and a qualifying blood quantum. The Beneficiaries were those who'd jumped through the same hoops as the Wait Listers and got their land eventually. For those who ran in Hulali's circles, the general consensus was that Hawaiians needed to get what they could, survive and accept the system as it was, work from within to get ahead and make a better life for their kids.

For her part, Laka had focused her efforts on the kingdom. These were people with varying degrees of opinion that Hawai`i needed to rise up within itself and demand the kingdom be reinstated. Playing by the rules and accepting the system was exactly what they'd been doing, and all they had to show for it was the tread marks on their backs.

And then the meeting happened. Laka and Hulali were both no-shows. Until the column came out, we had no idea why.

A WEEK LATER, we met at Puhi Bay for a post-meeting meeting. Laka brought sour poi bread still warm from the oven as a sorry for leaving us hanging at the meeting with the county. She asked for a debrief. Leilani, now a teacher at a charter school that taught exclusively in Hawaiian, reported that nearly all her students' families had shown up to testify but had been told there was not enough time for any of them. Once again, we had been given no chance to speak.

A scuffle broke out in the shadows. Tony, dressed for once in a collar shirt to mark the formality of the occasion, got into it with a guy who'd been on the wait list for eighteen years. He'd inherited his place on the wait list, the guy shouted. His mom had been on for seven before that. Meanwhile, he was scraping pennies to make rent. DHHL was corrupt, he said. Needed cleaning out. Tony scoffed. Said the guy was focusing on the wrong crime. It wasn't the people working for DHHL, it was DHHL working for America. The United States shouldn't have control over Hawai`i. Queen Lili`uokalani had entrusted her kingdom to the United States with the stipulation that Hawai`i could become a part of it IF AND ONLY IF the United States followed its own rules and took the matter to Congress. And since Congress hadn't wanted to be called out for being colonizers, they never passed a treaty to annex the kingdom.

Tony climbed onto the picnic table. Shouted into the darkness: The annexation treaty that would have made Hawai`i part of the United States didn't exist. The U.S. Congress had conveniently ignored the part of history where the kingdom was stolen by a group of individuals. They'd chosen to treat the matter as a domestic issue. Simply an American territory being voted into statehood. Tony bent slightly to stick his finger in Wait List Guy's face. Said his next words slow and loud as if talking to a keiki. No annexation meant, according to international law, the kingdom was and always had been intact. If the guy wanted his land, there was no need to wait for a fake state to give it to him. In Tony's eyes, it was already his for the taking.

Wait List Guy put his beer on the table. Told Tony that the only reason Tony was saying any of that was because Tony didn't have enough Hawaiian blood to qualify for land himself. Laka stepped toward Tony, pulled him down from his soapbox just as Hulali showed up. She was straight from a soccer game but in a mu`umu`u nonetheless, Malia in tow still wearing her uniform. Hulali motioned for Laka to stand at her side. Laka left Tony and in two large steps was shoulder to shoulder with Hulali, understanding immediately what her mother was trying to do. She reached out for Malia and pulled her close. The only way they were going to win was by standing together. Hulali knocked her hand on the table and called for everyone's attention.

"Enuff. We gotta refocus. Getting back to da `āina, getting back to pono, dat's da point, yeah? Nobody get job, food at da store too expensive and no good anyways, making us sick, and our keiki not learning what dey need to 'bout dis place. We keep fighting wit each oddah, dat not going change."

Hulali paused and looked at Laka. "Wat I saying is we gotta pull togeda. BuyMore, eh. Dat store not going make us pono, but dat `āina dey like built it on can. Dat's why we gotta stop it. And da only way we going do dat is if we focus on wat we get in common, yeah? Not wat we don't."

Laka nodded. She understood. Since her letter had appeared in Sunday's paper, she and Hulali had circled the ring. Now her mother was finally ready to address it, in typical Hulali fashion. Chiding her for writing to the newspaper but also, to Laka's surprise, conceding a point. She began to sing, her voice deep and clear. After the first line, we joined our voices, raised them up to the night.

All Hawaiʻi, stand together. It is now and forever
Raise our voices, hold our banners high
We shall stand, as a nation
To guide the destinies of our generation
To sing and praise the glories of our land

TO OUR TEARS THAT FOLLOWED, Hulali spoke.

"Ua mau ke ea o ka ʻāina i ka pono!"

The life of the land is perpetuated in righteousness. The life of the land is perpetuated in righteousness!

A plane flew overhead.

350

CHAPTER 5

Hi`i pressed the fingers of one hand to her temples, using the other to refold the newspaper and tuck it facedown under her room service at the Hilo Hawaiian Hotel. Laka's article was months old, but the outcry about BuyMore was only growing louder. BuyMore was not backing down. She was horrified. BuyMore in Hilo? The newspaper called it yet another example of Hawaiian Homelands up for grabs to the highest bidder. Hi`i tried to imagine how small shops like Aloha Spirit would stay in business with a superstore in town. A shark in a fishpond.

It made her want to get outside and join the fight. There was power in numbers, that's what she'd always been taught. She flipped the newspaper open again and stared at the front page, the blown-up pictures of protest signs taped to windows of homes and businesses throughout Hilo.

HAWAIIAN LAND BELONGS TO HAWAIIANS

HAWAIIAN BLOOD = SOVEREIGNTY

HAOLES GO HOME!

Hawaiian blood. She'd never seen her birth certificate, if she even had one. Had Hulali seen this coming? Was their home in Keaukaha what she'd been referring to when she'd said Laka's kuleana was there, but Hiʻi's wasn't? Because she was family only if a birth certificate said she was? But if that were true, why had Hulali reached out, why had she sent Malia?

She ached for Hilo. Ached for Jacob. Ached for what they had both given her at different times of her life. The feeling of being home, of belonging to something.

She held Jacob in his box. Considered taking him to Keaukaha. Maybe it was time.

A rumble of running feet in the hall stopped at her door. Ruth and Emma. Her two biggest accomplishments, her greatest source of joy and purpose. She cleared the rain clouds from her face. She opened the door ready for their smiles, ready to be delighted with happy stories of what they'd seen and done during this initial taste of what it meant to be a Hilo kid.

Instead, their story hit her like a paddle. She didn't want to believe it, but the evidence was there in the cheeks streaked with tears, faces red and blotchy. With Emma sobbing in her lap and Ruth buried in her blankets, Hiʻi asked to be told again what happened. But no matter how many times the story was relayed, she could not understand. Laka had called out her children. In front of the entire Puhi Bay, she had told them to leave, that they didn't belong there.

It was unbelievable. Impossible. She did not take into consideration that Laka had never met her granddaughters, that she might not have known who they were. Laka had insisted Hiʻi was her child, fully and completely. If that were the case, wouldn't some part of her have recognized them as kin? Laka's insistence that Hiʻi was her child had driven a wedge between the Naupakas. Even as Hiʻi struggled for years to believe the full extent of her mo`o origins, she'd always believed Laka about that. Had Laka changed so much that she no longer believed it? Enough to call Hi`i's children outsiders? It made no sense.

Unless.

Hi`i's eyes fell on the newspaper, the posters. Maybe her mother believed in blood quantums after all. Maybe the time had passed when Laka considered herself Hi`i's mother.

SHE WAS ON THE PHONE faster than a mongoose crosses the street.

She called the travel agent. They needed to change the date of their tickets back to California, needed to leave immediately. But there was only one flight out of Hilo a day, and they'd missed it. Tomorrow evening was the soonest possible. Hi`i booked it.

SHE KEPT THE GIRLS within the boundaries of the hotel for the remainder of the evening. The night was plagued with uneasy sleep and bad dreams. In the morning, she called the front desk and ordered pancakes (banana for Emma, buttermilk with coconut syrup for Ruth), and got dressed. When the food came, she set them up in front of the TV and put on *The Lion King*. They'd seen it a dozen times, but their eyes locked on to the screen the minute it started. By the time the movie was over, she promised, she'd be back and they would go to the pool. In the meantime, they could stay in their pajamas and eat all the syrup they wanted. They were under no circumstances to open the door or answer the phone while she was away. Then she rested her hand on Jacob.

I'm sorry. I can't bring you there.

She could not fulfill her promise to him.

SHE DIDN'T CALL TO SAY she was coming. Laka didn't deserve that kind of consideration. No, Hiʻi was going to give her mother a piece of her mind once and for all, and she wasn't going to bother giving her advance notice. Hiʻi's stomach tightened as she inched closer to the epicenter of her childhood. She took a left off Banyan Drive and turned into Keaukaha. It was immediately clear that something was wrong. There was nothing unusual about it being quiet at this hour, it was too early for kids to be on the rails jumping into Ice Ponds, but there was something different about this emptiness. There were no cars, no road signs, nothing open, as if the place had been vacuumed of its people.

Hiʻi wouldn't be deterred. She was no longer a confused kid. She was a woman now, a mother. She was heading back to California, but this time she would leave on her own terms. She put her foot on the gas.

She saw them as she neared Keaukaha Market. There'd been no sirens at dawn, no electric shock buzz from the radio, and yet here was an endless stream of cars piled nose to tail, the entire homestead trying to leave all at once via a one-lane road. Keaukaha was emptying itself with a solemnity usually reserved for tsunami warnings.

She didn't recognize anyone in the cars. They watched in silence as she passed, giving her a look that said she was going the wrong way. She couldn't fathom why. The waters were calm. The sky was clear. No tsunami siren. None of the usual red flags that warned of impending doom were sounding, and yet there was a charged electricity in the air. Hiʻi pressed on.

There were KEEP OUT signs nailed to the coconut trees at Puhi Bay and orange cones blocking the parking spaces. Chicken skin ran across her arms and up her neck.

She turned off the main road that skirted the beaches of Keaukaha and ventured into the neighborhood. If Hawaii had tumbleweeds, they would have been somersaulting down the street. Her old stomping ground had never been so empty. No one outside with a weed eater, no uncle sinking in a plastic chair, no kid running around in the grass, no bare-chested boys assessing the surf. And there in the middle of this new ghost town, the Naupaka house, dark and empty. The front door was closed. In all her life, she'd never seen the front door closed. They'd only ever used the screen door. She idled in the driveway for a moment before killing the engine. She'd come too far to stay outside.

She ascended the porch steps and approached the door with growing uncertainty. She'd mentally prepared for a number of hypothetical scenarios, but this hadn't been one of them. She reached for the doorknob and stopped herself. Knocked softly, then again harder.

"Hello?"

Nothing. Even the dogs in the back were gone. Where was everyone? What was going on? She tried the door. It swung open as if it had felt uncomfortable being closed.

Dishes were piled in the sink. The rice pot was still warm. Wherever they'd gone, they hadn't taken their time in leaving. On the side table were stacks of flyers printed on letterhead with the seal of the reinstated kingdom, calls for community meetings with dates past. She moved through the empty house, running her hand along the walls and peering through the doorways into spaces she thought she'd never see again. Into her old room, which looked remarkably unchanged since she'd left it. Down to the crooked picture frames on the walls, everything was hauntingly the same. She'd traveled through a time portal into her childhood, where only memories lived. She paused at a collage of Malia's soccer team and various pictures of her on the field. Even after seeing her in LA, it was difficult to connect the chubby toddler Hi`i remembered with the fiery young woman smiling in the photos. In one, she was sandwiched between two of her teammates, the three laughing with arms draped around each other's shoulders. Her heart tugged. There were pictures of Hi`i on the wall too. Malia hadn't grown up with her absence. She'd grown up with her ghost.

There was nothing to do but wait for them to come back. She turned on the television. Maybe it could offer an explanation for Keaukaha's sudden evacuation. Didn't take long to find it.

The reporter, a Japanese hapa woman who looked uncomfortably out of place in her dress and heels, was standing in a pit of tall weeds that Hi`i recognized in an instant. The large undeveloped plot of land positioned between the airport and Prince Kuhio Plaza. The camera panned the scene. From the looks of it, an entire artery of Hawaii had spilled onto the field. A sea of coolers, wide-brimmed hats, small pop-ups—if not for the somber faces and protest signs waving above their heads, it could have been a festival.

The camera zoomed. Police cruisers, a van with bars on the windows. Dogs, police in riot gear, batons in hand. Dragging people from the field into the van. Screams, shouts from every direction. Hulali, lifted by her elbows. Then Laka, heels digging tracks in the grass as they pulled her from the crowd. Malia followed close behind, shouting through tears, pleading with the officers to stop.

Hi`i's throat caught. The picture on the wall, that was her. No matter what it said on paper, this was her home. She didn't own it, but it owned her. Hilo, same.

The police slid the van door closed. The faces of Laka and Hulali disappeared inside. The camera followed as the vehicle left the field. A knife in her gut. She had to do something to help.

SHE HADN'T BEEN IN THE HOUSE long, but by the time she slammed out the screen door, the road was miraculously clear. Hi`i raced out of Keaukaha unhindered, tires squealing as she wheeled a curb turning into Banyan Drive for the girls. She'd already left them far longer than she'd planned.

"Ruth! Emma!"

SHE BURST THROUGH THE DOOR, not seeing them at first, a brief moment of panic, but there they were, in a blanket fort between the beds. She hurried them into sundresses and bundled them into the car. She still had to pack if they were going to make their flight that night, but she would worry about that later. They needed to go.

CHAPTER 6

Tony called them the Hens. Always pecking at each other. After Hulali's call for unity at Puhi Bay, he was comforted by the thought of Laka and Hulali backing down for once, banding together. But they'd barely slipped off their slippers at the front door before the clucking resumed.

Laka told Hulali she was relieved that they were finally on the same page. Hulali raised a thin eyebrow. Said they'd always been on the same page, Laka had just been reading it from a different direction.

Laka stopped unloading the cooler of food they'd brought to the beach.

"Wat da hell you mean by dat?"

A gecko crawled across the kitchen windowsill. Hulali pointed. "I no moa all da answers. But da oldah I get, da moa I see we gotta adjust, expand our t'inking, focus on da nex' generations, teach dem how fo' take care da `āina and connect with da akua."

Laka followed the direction of her finger. Tears sprang into her eyes. She pinched the bridge of her nose. "A little late fo' your change of heart, Ma. Wat you saying, you finally believe me about Hi`i? Damage is done."

"I saying maybe I not da one who need to believe. I da one who wrote da girl, who convinced Malia to go. You was all gung ho after she invite us but den you do a one-eighty when her husband die. How can, dat kine? Somebody die, we no leave dem fo' cry by demselves. Dat's not how we do. You know dat."

"She tole us not fo' come! She nevah introduce him, nevah invite us to da wedding. I gotta hear 'bout my mo`opuna tru da coconut phone. She send an invitation, den take it back. I only evah tried fo' love her da way she asked fo' be loved."

Hulali shook her head sadly. She'd never regretted giving Hi`i what she considered an encouraging nudge to leave. Laka's newfound dedication to Hawaiian politics was proof—with Hi`i around, Laka had been withdrawn and a little too focused on the girl, in Hulali's opinion. She would have continued holding them all back, and for what? Hi`i moving to California had been for the best. But at the end of the day, Hi`i was keiki o ka `āina. Maybe not a Naupaka in the ways Hulali had once needed her to be, but family nonetheless. "Honey girl," she said as Laka dumped the remains of the cooler in the trash and turned it upside down in the sink to dry, "you was always so quick to jump headfirst into da watah. Sometimes dat good. But sometimes you gotta stop and read da ocean first."

THE DAY FINALLY ARRIVED. The showdown. Everyone, from every side, coming together to stop the tide. Laka couldn't sleep. She tiptoed to the porch and sat until dawn, listening to the surf in the distance, the chirping grass, the occasional croak of a frog, praying it wasn't the song of the inevitable, of history making its rounds.

When the moon linked elbows with the sun, Laka gathered her pareo around her shoulders and went inside to gather her family.

DAVID HAD SPENT THE NIGHT in his ohana making signs. He stopped only when the roosters belted out their mele.

`A`OLE BUYMORE

SUPPORT SMALL BUSINESS

KEEP HILO LOCAL

HAWAI`I IS NOT FOR SALE

"Maika`i!" Laka said when she saw the messages. David blushed. Tony gave him a high five. They loaded David's signs into the trunk and piled into the car.

"Eh, wait for me!" Hulali called from the front porch, rummaging through the shelves for her slippers. Tony raised his eyebrows at Laka. Laka shrugged her shoulders.

"I guess we all going in one car," she said.

David cleared a seat for Hulali in the back. Tony revved the engine and popped the horn. Malia came running down the steps and squeezed in.

"Okay, full load. Family field trip!" Tony laughed.

They jittered with nervous energy. Laka stole a look at everyone in the car, wondering if there would ever be a time when she didn't see the empty space, the missing person.

David's stomach groaned. They laughed. Hulali handed out musubi, one for everyone. "Eat. Going be one long day."

Laka nibbled her salted rice as they fell into the line of cars inching their way out of Keaukaha. She'd never seen so many cars at once. Tony whistled. "You t'ink dey all headed same place as us?"

"No way," Laka whispered. "Must be one accident."

But the backlog of cars did not ease as they came to the end of their neighborhood, nor did it clear when they turned left toward the airport. No ambulance siren broke through the air, no flashing lights. The cars did not drift or ripple but instead held steady and firm, an unwavering solid mass.

The field was a sea of purpose, simmering with nervous excitement.

This was what they needed. No more political impotence, no more festering wounds buried under bandages. She wasn't the one to say which words were the right ones, which wrong. They were voiceless no more, and hopefully never would be again.

When they arrived, Laka, David, and Hulali immediately set about organizing the troops, setting up shades and chairs for the eldest among them while their kids passed out bottled water and snacks to keep energy high as they marched and chanted and raised their signs to the passing cars. Malia helped Leilani keep an eye on the keiki from her charter school who'd come with their families. Power in numbers.

The newspapers and television cameras showed up a few minutes after the police. The flash of the cameras caught three generations of Naupaka women—the elder two notorious for their disagreements when it came to Hawaiian politics, the youngest for her disinterest in the subject. Two folded into the back of police vehicles, handcuffs glinting in the sun, one left behind, but all there for the same reason.

The message was loud and clear: what they were fighting against was bigger than any fight between them.

CHAPTER 7

Laka refused to post bail. Doing so would have been an admission of guilt, an acceptance that she'd done something wrong. How can you trespass on land that belongs to you?

The police were quiet as they stuffed them in. *Sorry, Aunty*, they said under their breath as they led Hulali and Laka by metal cuffs to their cell. No one made eye contact. She understood, felt sorry for them. This was not their fault, everyone was paying a price. In their cell, Hulali began to sing. The concrete cell block echoed with the sound of the others from the field being brought in.

Laka turned toward the wall, steeled herself. When she finally faced her neighbors and friends, the community who had listened to her, who'd followed her into the dragon's mouth, she reminded them that they'd been prepared for this, that they had solid legal counsel well aware of everything that was happening. They knew their rights, knew this was simply an attempt to intimidate them. An officer stole down the hallway and asked if there was anything he could do. They'd gone to high school together. He tapped his wedding ring nervously against the steel bar. She could see on his tired face the request, the plea to please not make him choose between the state and the people, between his job and her nation. She thanked him and said she was fine.

And she was, until someone turned on the television in the room where the police officers did their paperwork and put the volume up loud enough for the entire jail to hear. Maybe someone thought she'd want to know.

BuyMore's permits had been approved. After nearly a year of fighting, they'd lost.

The news hit her in waves. How could it be true? It felt surreal, impossible. This kind of corruption had been going on forever, but wasn't it supposed to go differently once they joined together as a unified lahui? Did they not have any power, any say in their lands, even as that?

Their voices had fallen on deaf ears. All their meetings, their organizing, the people who had flown in, donated money. For what? Laka looked around at the faces of the people she'd put behind bars—her eighty-year-old neighbor, her mother—and felt the sharp stab of her failure. Her spirit felt like a falling leaf. Their broken hearts were her fault. She'd convinced everyone they had a chance.

AS THE NEWS SPREAD, shoulders, so newly inflated, crumpled. Hope floated out the window and was carried off by the wind. Someone kicked a bench, punched a wall. The cell filled with silent angry tears. Laka felt sick to her stomach. All this, for what.

And then she heard it. The voice. One she hadn't heard in over a decade. Her body prickled, on alert. She glanced around to see if anyone else in the crowded cell had noticed the sound coming from the door at the end of the hall. Maybe this was proof that reality had paused, that something had finally heard their pain, disrupted the planets and rearranged the order of things.

From the outer room, above the drone of the news reports coming from the television, the voice again. A police officer responded. In Laka's ears, drums.

Her mind raced wild up the tight cell block walls. The cold concrete blocks changed shape, images of Hiʻi looking up at her the first time she had held her in her arms. Hiʻi as she took her first wobbly steps in the sand. Hiʻi, her daughter, blood of her blood. The drums in Laka's ears beat louder.

Thump. Not enough. Thump. You did not try hard enough. Thump.

Guilty as charged. For all she had done, for all she hadn't. She'd convinced herself not to go to California in the wake of her daughter's widowhood because she'd been terrified of saying the wrong thing, of being welcomed with a closed door. Sending the article hadn't been enough, not even close. None of it was enough. She'd been fighting for the kingdom, but hadn't put any fight toward getting her daughter back. They'd told her she was back and she'd waited stubbornly for Hiʻi to make the first move, knowing she wouldn't. Why, why did she resist? What had she been trying to prove? The walls closed in, air siphoning out of her lungs. A sharp cramping in her naʻau. She stumbled to the bars of her cage, clung to them with fluttering moth fingers. She pressed her face to the cold metal and tried to calm her mind. Still, the voice down the hall persisted.

It was slightly different then she remembered. Years had given it a confidence and husky authority it hadn't had. The anger within the voice as it argued with the police officer was familiar, but had grown bristles and distance, had whittled itself down to a sharp edge that could make fresh wounds out of old scars.

The dull tap of shoes on linoleum grew louder. Keys rattled like a saber.

When Hulali and Laka were called forward, the group parted, releasing them from its folds. When Hulali didn't move, making a point to remain with the group, Laka hesitated. This would put an immediate distance between her and the people who were there because she'd asked them to stand with her, to trust her to lead them. She should be the last to be set free. She had more to pay for. But for Laka to turn away from that voice was not an option. She'd made that mistake once, paid that price.

She looked at Hulali before following the guard. Hulali nodded slightly. It didn't matter whether Laka stayed or went. Both were the wrong thing, there was no right way.

Nearly twelve years. An eternity and yet no time at all.

HI`I WAS THINNER THAN SHE REMEMBERED, her entire body a tensed muscle. Laka strained to see more of her; she felt suddenly parched, thirsty for the sight of her daughter. The years lost between them had been bearable only because she'd convinced herself that her silence was what Hi`i had wanted, so it had been the only thing she could give her. But now that she was here. Now that she was here. A burly officer stood between them, explaining the conditions of her bail.

Hi`i was focused on a pair of little girls at her side, arms winged over them as if shielding them from a hailstorm only she could see. Laka caught a glimpse of a profile, chubby fair cheeks that looked slightly familiar but she couldn't quite put her finger on why. By the time the officer finally allowed her to pass, the room was empty. She ran in the direction they had gone.

She caught up to them in the parking lot. The woman her daughter had become was reaching into the backseat of a rental car, buckling the harness of a child's safety seat. Laka saw only the child who had once needed her, who'd screamed whenever she strayed too far away. Hi`i stiffened visibly when Laka put a hand on her arm. She shut the door before turning to face her. They kissed. It was stiff and slightly awkward, but it was a start.

"Are you okay? I wanted to help. I'm . . . I'm sorry I wasn't there at the field. I didn't know."

Laka's smile was sad, defeated. "We lost. We tried, and we lost. But you. You're here."

It was both statement and question.

"No. I mean yes, but something came up. I have to leave tonight."

"Tonight! What? Already? But my mo`opuna. I haven't met them, you haven't come . . ."

Laka took a step forward, Hi`i a step back. The distance between them maintained. Hi`i planted firmly between Laka and the rental car. Fire suddenly in her eyes, a flash of Pele, molten red lava. "Actually, you have. Take a look through that window. You don't recognize them? I'll give you a minute."

Laka studied the little heads in the backseat, bobbing in their belts to try to see what was happening outside. A vision of the burning honu shell, dying another death. Its second, its third.

"Puhi Bay. Now you remember?"

Realization dawned slowly on Laka's face. She felt light-headed. Covered her mouth in horror. Shook her head. She didn't know, hadn't known. Something had come over her, she barely remembered a thing. The two little girls at Puhi Bay, they were all hats and sunglasses and floaties. There was no way she could have known.

Hi`i folded her arms across her chest and examined Laka as if she wasn't sure she believed her. The possibility that Laka would not have recognized Ruth and Emma had never crossed her mind. That was on her for never bringing them back until now. But she obviously had valid reasons for keeping them away. She reached for the handle of her car door and tossed Laka a parting shot. "I guess you weren't. They look haole, not Naupakas for sure. Blood and birth certificates, right? That's what matters to everybody here. You know, I was actually beginning to believe your story about the mo`o. Why did you keep me if you weren't going to fight for me, protect me? Never mind, forget it. I came to help, to bail you out, and I did. Now we're going."

Her daughter's words were an icy wind racing across the snow-capped peaks of Mauna Kea. She felt an old anger rising. How much Laka had done for the woman-child seething in front of her, how much she'd loved and sacrificed for her, all the times she'd fought for her and defended her. Her cheeks flushed with the heat of her rage. "You t'ink I was sitting in dere waiting to be saved? You been on da continent too long. You no understand not'ing. I nevah said blood or birt certificates da only t'ing dat matter, I nevah said dey mattah at all. Don't go assigning dat to me. My fault I no recognize my grandbabies? How I was supposed to if you nevah bring dem home, introduce dem to da ohana? No one tol' you go. You did dat on your own. And now you come all Miss Righteous? You like me apologize to you for your hard times? Look around. No one having one picnic ovah hea. You like help Hilo, good, we need it. But if you came fo' pity, just get on dat airplane and go back to wherever you now call home."

The words rained down from the dry sky. It took her back to when Hi`i was a child, when she'd lose her temper. Hi`i—always the one who brought out the best and worst in her.

The car door opened and the older one peeked her head out.

"Ruth, get back in the car. I'll be right there."

Ruth. A single syllable that stampeded across Laka's body, a sound brought together by two feet in plastic jelly sandals, two knobby knees, a cotton dress with periwinkle stripes. A button nose freckled with pixie dust, deep eyes full of sadness. A Hawaiian princess. She stared at Laka with trepidation. Laka racked her brain for something familiar, to try to imagine this girl at Puhi Bay—surely she would have known her own grandchild? She truly could not remember having seen this child before. She felt a shiver of uncertainty.

"Mommy," the girl said softly. "Emma has to go potty."

It took everything Laka had to not follow Hi`i when she swept the girls out of the car and ushered them back into the building. The youngest allowed herself to be dragged by the hand while staring over her shoulder, examining Laka with a wariness that made her want to beg them to stay.

Mother. The most haunted, haunting word. A blade sharp enough to slice out your heart.

The burning honu. Laka knew now. She had become her mother.

CHAPTER 8

By the time Emma was done in the bathroom, a crowd had gathered in the lobby, many familiar faces. Hi`i pushed forward toward the exit. Within the mass she thought she saw a flash of blond. She slowed, following the head with her eyes until she was sure. Jane. A little aged, hair now a bit shorter, skin looking well sun-baked, a professional-looking green shirtdress revealing a slightly thicker frame, but undoubtedly her. She considered leaving before Jane noticed her. She waved her hand and called out before she could talk herself out of it. In spite of her lack of effort to stay in touch, she missed her friend.

"Jane!"

Jane smiled when she got close enough to talk without shouting. "Eh, Hi`i. Heard you was in town. These your babies?"

"Hi," she stammered. "Um, girls, meet Aunty Jane. Sorry. For, well. I been meaning to call. It's been one thing after another. You know how it is."

Jane's smile tightened. "Yeah, sure, I know how it is." Jane looked over Hi`i's shoulder and waved at someone behind her. "I didn't know you were involved in all this."

"You been gone a long time. Gotta help if can, right?"

Emma squirmed to be free. Hi`i tightened her grip on the little hand.
"How's your dad?"

Jane's attention shifted. "You know Adam, always keeping himself
busy. Look, Hi`i, I gotta go. But if you're sticking around, give me a
call, okay? Me and Kainoa would love to see you."

When they kissed goodbye, their cheeks hardly touched. In the
parking lot, Laka had vanished.

HI`I MANAGED TO HOLD IT TOGETHER for the drive across town to the
hotel, the long slow ride up the elevator, the walk down the windowless corridor to their room, the clicking of the television and turning
up the volume and telling Ruth and Emma that she was going to take
a shower and then they needed to pack for their flight and ignoring
the questions in their big eyes watching her. She locked the bathroom
door and turned both the sink and the bathtub faucet to full capacity.
Only then, muffled by the sound of water, did she curl up on the floor
and let the tears come.

She'd wiped out. Waves had tumbled her across the ocean floor,
across sharp coral reef. She was broken and bruised, and she had no
one to blame but herself. A he`e she was not. Shape-shifter, magi-
cian, who had she been kidding? No mo`o either. She was only what
she was, whatever that was. Hilo was her home, had always been her
home, would always be her home. But there is no crossing a bridge
after it's burned to the ground, and she'd burned every one. Failed her
husband, her children, her sister, her mother. Her friend. Grief ripped
through her body.

A knock at the door.

"Mommy?"

Ruth. Hi`i gathered what she could of her voice, steadied its shake. "Mommy will be right there, baby."

Washed her face. Turned off the water. Packed their things. Jacob in his box. Silenced the television, walked the long windowless corridor, let the elevator take them down, put their suitcases in the trunk, and drove away.

AND DROVE AND DROVE AND DROVE. To the airport, and then away from it. Across the Hamākua Coast, down the three horseshoes and back. To Volcano, to Pele. The girls fell asleep, slumped against each other in the backseat. Mamalahoa Highway to Punalu`u. In Na`alehu she spotted the tiny sign that she didn't realize she'd been heading toward until she saw it. She followed the sign off the thoroughfare and bumped down a rough lava road until she saw it. South Point. The southernmost tip of the United States. The road got rockier and the rental struggled, so she slowed to a stop and rolled down all the windows. They were still a ways from the cliffs but she had a clear view of where they fell away, the rough choppy gray waters spreading out indefinitely. The sound of the wind and the waves were the only things to hear. This was one of the few places left that remained sacred and unspoiled, the land too raw and fresh water too scarce for a housing development or golf course. The mana of the `āina seeped into the car, palpable and undeniable. The girls continued to sleep, Ruth lifting her head and fluttering her eyes for a moment before settling again. Hi`i stared at her daughters from the rearview mirror before turning her attention back to their surroundings. She felt a stirring. She had had to drive more than a quarter of the entire island, two hours without stopping, to get to this place free of tourists and airplanes and the noise of America. To get to this place where she could feel her island. Her island. The words echoed in her heart. She shook her head.

Laka shouldn't have singled out Emma and Ruth, but didn't she have good reason to be angry? Hundreds and thousands of reasons, actually? Generations of anger and frustration, political impotence. It lived dormant in Laka, inherited from Hulali inherited from Ulu, avalanching its way through history, fed with every eviction notice, every promise broken. Maybe what was necessary wasn't protecting her children from that anger, wasn't getting on a plane and leaving it behind. Hulali had told her to find her kuleana. Maybe her kuleana was to face the source of that anger, to understand it so as to understand how to fight not with one another but together against that continued threat of extinction, to learn how to keep things alive so Emma and Ruth might have the Hawai`i she had had as a child. Maybe that was the only way their children might too.

She started the car and went back the way she'd come.

NO ONE WAS HUNGRY, but they made dinner anyway. To not eat was to be defeated. This was not, could not be, the end. They picked at their rice, their shoyu chicken. At the sound of a car crunching down the driveway, Laka told Malia to see who it was this time of night.

Malia called from the porch. "Mom, you'd bettah come out hea."

Laka's eyes adjusted to the dark. It took her a moment to recognize the car. She stepped off the porch. Hi`i met her halfway, holding up a small, delicately carved container. "I'd like you to meet my husband," she said. It would not fix everything, but it was a good place to start.

* * *

THEY MADE THEIR WAY in the dark. Hulali and Laka walked on either side of Hiʻi, who carried Jacob in his box. Malia stayed behind, Ruth and Emma clinging to her even in their sleep.

At Puhi Bay, they crossed the lawn toward the towering wall of palms, the sentinels. Stepped carefully over the jagged tide pools to where the open water began. Hiʻi pressed noses with Hulali first, then Laka. Shared breath. They put Jacob in the water.

Simple was not the same as easy. Simple was elemental. The sun and the moon and the stars. Impenetrable.

CHAPTER 9

1996

Throughout the hearing, we maintained that we were not at Puhi Bay illegally. It was our land. We, the Beneficiaries. DHHL, the people whose job description it was to care for us, was sitting on the other side of the aisle against us instead. The way it's always been.

BLUE TARP HULA:

> JUDGE: What's the problem?
>
> DHHL: They building without a permit.
>
> JUDGE: This is your land?
>
> DHHL: Yes.
>
> WE: Uh, Judge?
>
> JUDGE: Yes?
>
> WE: If DHHL has the deed, the title to that land, we will
>   stop building our structure, our gathering place.
>
> JUDGE: It's settled, then.
>
> DHHL: Uh, judge? Little complication there. We don't have
>   the deed, not exactly.

JUDGE: No decision until I see that deed.

DHHL: They erected a structure there already. They need to take it down.

WE: Temporary structure. Tarp only.

JUDGE: The tarp stays until I see the deed.

THE TARP STAYS.

Temporary maybe, but it was going to stay until we could put up something else.

We caravanned to Puhi Bay, honking our horns all the way. A victory was a victory.

We tore down the tape, the KEEP OUT signs. Tossed the orange cones aside. Brought out the ukuleles. Long into the night the G-C chord melody went on, louder and louder. We sang the songs of the good old days, or maybe the days that were right now. Songs of what would always be, and what would never be again. When the airplanes roared overhead, we roared back.

FOR AS LONG AS ANYONE COULD REMEMBER, Prince Kuhio Plaza sat surrounded by plots of unbroken land, a fishling in a tide pool, defenseless as worms in a bucket. On the day construction broke ground across the street, we gathered at the plaza, unsure where to go from there. Jackhammers sent shivers through the earth.

According to the flyer in the mailbox, the 9,000-square-foot superstore would open in a month. It boasted more than 25,000 products, bargain prices. It would even sell groceries. There would be no need to shop anywhere else. Of the 204 open positions, only a handful of top managerial spots hadn't come prefilled by "experienced executives" shipped in from elsewhere. For the remainder, an ad was placed in the Classified section of the *Hawaii Tribune-Herald*. The ad included a phone number to call to request a spot in line. The strategy was the suggestion of Hilo's labor office, which had already received 1,900 applications. In the box that asked for desired position, most checked Any and All.

Orange cones blocked every entrance of the newly paved lot. Tents and metal chairs were divided into orderly sections across the expansive lot to accommodate the 2,500 who called in advance and made appointments. The tents were labeled to expedite the two-day-long interview event: Registration, Paperwork, Preliminary Interviews, Second Rounds, References, and so on.

We had our pride, but also kids to feed. Our history, but also bills to pay. We'd fought, we'd tried, and we were not ever going to stop. We'd lost the battle, but there was still so much to fight for.

On the morning of the first rounds, the executives who had flown in to conduct the interviews sipped their coffee and made their way to their tables. Shortly before nine o'clock, we pushed forward, knocking over the cones, ignoring the chairs, needing to be the one they chose, the one they called. It was hurry up and wait, then wait and hurry up. The orange cones spat us out on the other end of the parking lot. There was nothing more to do except what we always did and hope the phone rang. We ran errands, we grabbed a bag of papayas from the market on the way home, hung laundry, fed the babies, took them to the beach.

In Hilo, we are the ʻāina. Its mist is our breath, its rain our tears, its waters our blood.

Our veins run deep, our song louder than their noise. Roots too deep to extract. That's the thing about hula. Burn your books, rewrite your history, build walls, plant flags. Hula is written within the swirls of our feet. It's our umbilical cord, our pulse. Our battle cry, our death rattle, our moment of conception. The chants are archived in the stars. Hula is the heat rising from within our volcanoes. It is the pull of the tides, the beat of the surf against our cliffs. It is our hair, our teeth, our bones. Our DNA.

You can steal a kingdom, but the kingdom will never belong to you.

WE WERE THERE WHEN Hi`i cheered from the sidelines at Malia's game, Malia acting like it was no big deal but eyes shining like polished wood. We were there when Laka presented Hi`i with the old Ni`ihau shells. Hi`i, suitcases unpacked. She picked ti for lei and cooked rice, said Jane, Kainoa, and Adam were on their way. Family dinner.

HULALI AND KUMU AGREED that it was time for a new keiki class. We showed up for open enrollment, pushed the new keiki forward. Ruth and Emma, we showed them how to tie the skirts around their waists. Under the tarp at Puhi Bay, we told them of their mother, their grandmother, and all the Naupakas before them.

At Richardson's, they screeched like banshees, racing across the hot sand toward the water, Laka at their heels. At the edge of the glistening womb, she held them still.

HE INOA NO HILO!

AUTHOR'S NOTE

In spite of the title, this book is not meant to serve as a hula reference manual, nor is my interpretation and explanation of its practice and origins the only one. Hula remains a sacred discipline—one that continues to evolve and change shape within the expert hands of its dedicated kumu and haumāna—and I am neither an authority on, nor a teacher of, this art form. The inner workings of the fictionalized halau founded by Hulali Naupaka, including any songs, chants, choreography, protocols, and rituals described in these pages, are a product of my imagination. If you are interested in learning more about hula and its history, I encourage you to look to sources such as the Edith Kanaka'ole Foundation. Other resources can be found on my website: www.jasminiolani.com

I grew up in Hilo at a time when the air crackled with a growing movement that continues to shape Hawai'i's politics and expand our understanding of the history of Hawaiian land and sovereignty. I am indebted to a number of scholars, cultural leaders, kūpuna, activists, and historians who continue to work tirelessly to write books and teach courses that offer a version of Hawaiian history and cultural practice that counters the texts and misinformation that emerged from its colonization. I relied heavily on these resources to fill in the gaps of my understanding regarding my home so I could write about it with the respect and honor it deserves.

This book started as a tribute to my hometown, a simple story of a complicated family. But history is our context. Because it informs who we are, how we think, and what we value, there was no way to adequately capture the struggles and motivating forces of the Naupaka women without also including the history that molded them, the kūpuna who preserved the ancient knowledge of the islands, and the communities who have and continue to fight for Hawai`i's preservation and future. There is no way to adequately tell a story set in Hawai`i without Hawai`i itself playing a role.

This novel is a work of fiction, and the characters and dialogue portrayed in it are the product of my imagination. While the major historical events depicted within the story are based in truth, I have in some cases condensed or simplified them, and this book should not be read as history. Similarly, while many of the organizations portrayed here have counterparts in fact, my characterizations of them are fictional, with my research and experience serving as a jumping-off point.

My research relied on a variety of sources, including stories gifted to me by my personal kūpuna, family, and community. In some instances, memories of those times were augmented by what has been recorded about them. The overall sentiments presented by the various community groups and the characters within were enriched by existing essays, articles, and reports from those periods. *Pacific Business News*, the *Honolulu Star-Bulletin*, and the *Hilo Tribune-Herald*, along with records from the Hawai`i Employment Services Division, aided my memory of the Walmart development protests. For details of the occupation of the Hawaiian Kingdom, the results of the 1978 State of Hawaii Constitutional Convention, the creation of OHA and the PKO, and the history and challenges of the Department of Hawaiian Home Lands, I sought guidance from Hawaii State Archives, `Iolani Palace archived materials, Kamehameha Schools, University of Hawai`i at Mānoa, HawaiianKingdom.org, ulukau.org, protectkahoolaweohana.org, the Department of Hawaiian Home Lands, and many others, including those on the list that follows below.

One final note: The decision to not include a glossary was deliberate. What prevailed in the end was the desire to avoid othering the story as much as possible—no italics, no footnotes—to preserve as much as possible the experience of hearing this story from one of my aunties as they would tell it from a seat in their living room, a story for Hilo as much as it is a story about Hilo. Because *Hula* captures a time when the language and punctuation were inconsistent at best, I tried to stay true to my muddled memories of that time, and some may notice that not everything is spelled as it is today—since then we have seen a steady shift toward acknowledgment and inclusion, reflected in the increasing usage of the Hawaiian diacritical marks `okina and kahakō. For any meanings I have failed to make clear within the text, a glossary and other materials can be found on my website. As many Hawaiian words have layered meanings, wehewehe.org is an invaluable resource for `ōlelo Hawai`i.

"Public Policy of Land and Homesteading in Hawai`i," Ulla Hasager and Marion Kelly, *Social Process in Hawai'i*, 40 (2001)

Return to Kahiki: Native Hawaiians in Oceania, Kealani Cook (Cambridge University Press, 2018)

"Breach of Trust? Native Hawaiian Homelands," a summary of the proceedings of a public forum sponsored by the Hawaii Advisory Committee to the United States Commission on Civil Rights, October 1980

Lovely Hula Hands, Frontlines of Revolutionary Struggle, Haunani Kay-Trask (Paper first presented at Law & Society Conference in Berkeley in 2008)

From a Native Daughter: Colonialism and Sovereignty in Hawaii, Haunani Kay-Trask (Latitude 20, 1999)

A Nation Rising: Hawaiian Movements for Life, Land, and Sovereignty (Narrating Native Histories), Noelani Goodyear-Kaopua and Ikaika Hussey (Duke University Press, 2014)

Dismembering Lahui: A History of the Hawaiian Nation to 1887, Jonathan Osorio (University of Hawai`i Press, 2002)

Holo Mai Pele: An Educator's Guide, Edith Kanaka`ole Foundation, Halau o Kekuhi

Aloha Betrayed: Native Hawaiian Resistance to American Colonialism, Noenoe K. Silva (Duke University Press, 2004)

Hawaiian Blood: Colonialism and the Politics of Sovereignty and Indigeneity, J. Kehaulani Kauanui (Duke University Press, 2008)

Paradoxes of Hawaiian Sovereignty: Land, Sea, and the Colonial Politics of State Nationalism, J. Kehaulani Kauanui (Duke University Press, 2018)

The Great Vanishing Act: Blood Quantum and the Future of Native Nations, edited by Kathleen Ratteree and Norbert Hill, Jr. (Fulcrum Publishing, 2017)

Blood Will Tell: Native Americans and Assimilation Policy, Kathering Ellinghaus (University of Nebraska Press, 2017)

Articles on Writers from Hawaii, including Liliʻuokalani, Lois Lowry, Fletcher Knebel, Robert Kiyosaki, Tara Bray Smith, Lois-Ann Yamanaka, Haunani Kay-Trask, Kiana Davenport, W. S. Merwin, Allan Beekman, and Leon Edel (Hephaestus Books, 2011)

Speaking of Indigenous Politics: Conversations with Activists, Scholars, and Tribal Leaders, J. Kehaulani Kauanui and Robert Warrior (University of Minnesota Press, 2018)

Decolonizing Native Histories: Collaboration, Knowledge, and Language in the Americas, Florencia E. Mallon (Duke University Press, 2011)

ACKNOWLEDGMENTS

I never could have imagined the years and obstacles this book would encounter, nor the incredible village it would build. This book would not exist without the unwavering dedication of my brilliant agent, friend, and all around gem of a human, Sarah Bowlin. It is no exaggeration to say that the day we met changed my life.

Enormous eternal thanks to Daniella Wexler, who trusted and loved this story from day one and never wavered from protecting what needed protecting and for asking all the right questions. You are a true champion. Many thanks also to the team at HarperVia for helping make this vision a reality.

I grew up in Hilo at a time when the only thing taught in our schools about Hawai`i was the date it became the fiftieth state. I am enormously grateful to the many who continue to work tirelessly to make sure that time is behind us. This story would not have been possible without those who challenged the narrative told by conquerors and colonizers, who blazed trails to preserve the `ike and history of Hawai`i in book form so someone like me could find it: Queen Lili`uokalani, King Kalākaua, Mary Pukui, Lilikalā Kame`eleihiwa, Kealani Cook, Noelani Goodyear-Ka`ōpua, Ikaika

Hussey, Erin Kahunawaika`ala Wright, Samuel P. King, Randall W. Roth, Jonathan Kamakawaiwo`ole Osorio, George Cooper, Gavan Daws, Nathaniel B. Emerson, Stephanie Nohelani Teves, Ronald Williams Jr., Noenoe Silva, and the many I have neglected to name here who fight for a better Hawai`i every single day.

I am filled with appreciation for the legendary Pua Kanaka`ole Kanahele and Nalani Kanaka`ole, sisters who are an integral part of Hilo's DNA, from which I and many others have benefitted. To Kumu Kekuhi Keali`ikanakaole Kanahele, who planted seeds that took root. To Halau o Kekuhi and the Edith Kanaka`ole Foundation for working every day to protect ancient Hawaii perspectives and ways of life from the dangers of extinction. Culture and language live only when they are not put on a shelf and left to gather dust.

For the mo`olelo: Karin Ortiz, Taupōuri Tangarō, Pat Kahawaiolaa.

To all who offered encouragement and support when I needed it most: Jennifer Silva Redmond and the Southern California Writers Conference crew, Myriam Gurba, Liz Prato, Cheryl Strayed, Lan Samantha Chang, Jennifer Basye Sander, Elaine Gale, Annie Lareau, Jeff Hamilton.

Hedgebrook and its radical hospitality allowed the mystical space and time needed for this to be born, complete with a cabin in a woods where ancients feel free to rise up and speak. Valerie Steiker gave it early love and enthusiasm. Rebekah Jett offered encouragment and invaluable insight.

For the time you gave answering my unanswerable questions: J. Kēhaulani Kauanui and Esther Kia`āina.

For the faith, love, and everything else: Dan and Anne Hakes, Brian Hakes, Tom Anthony, Paula Anthony, Karla Sibayan, Warren

ACKNOWLEDGMENTS

Anderson, Sasa Lee, Kari Kaloi, Leslie Rosehill, Stephanie Hamilton, Aly Sharp. For the slaps: Iliahi Anthony.

To my partner in crime Laura Lynne Powell: I thank my lucky stars that you are always game to find out what awaits around the next curve on the path.

To Steve Napolitano, who believed in this book (and me) way before I ever did.

To Ting and Katrina: you mean the world to me. To Mila and Riana: you are my inspiration and driving force, not to mention the best things that have ever happened to my life. You both gave up a lot for this book to be a reality. I hope it makes you proud.

To Grandma O and the generations before her: I am because of you. The courage and stamina needed to pull this off was drawn from an invaluable inheritance passed to me from a fierce, unapologetic matrilineal line that only a place like Hawai`i could produce. Without roots, the tree falls over.

And finally, to Hilo. The land of the kanilehua rain, the waters to which I belong. This is my ho`okupu.

Here ends Jasmin `Iolani Hakes's
Hula.

The first edition of the book was printed and
bound at Lakeside Book Company
in Harrisonburg, Virginia, April 2023.

A NOTE ON THE TYPE

The text of this novel was set in Adobe Caslon Pro, a reliable, popular typeface, a version of the font used to print the first edition of the US Constitution. Adobe Caslon Pro belongs to the Caslon family of serif fonts created in the eighteenth century by Englishman William Caslon, a punch cutter of high renown. Caslon fonts can be identified by a capital *A* with a scooped-out apex, a capital *C* with two full serifs, and a swashed lowercase *v* and *w* in the italic. In 1990, designer Carol Twombly created Adobe Caslon, a modernization suited to the demands of digital design and printing.

HARPERVIA

An imprint dedicated to publishing international voices,
offering readers a chance to encounter other lives and other
points of view via the language of the imagination.